Praise for *A*

"*A Mosaic of Wings* is a beautifully rendered historical novel of depth and emotion. I hope you find it and its heroine as captivating as I have. I'm predicting this is the first of many for this emerging fiction talent."

—Jerry B. Jenkins, novelist, biographer, and founder of the Jerry Jenkins Writers Guild

"Nora Shipley isn't your average historical romance heroine. She is an entomologist—a corset-wearing, nineteenth-century graduate of Cornell University who is fascinated by bugs. This unique premise had me eager to dig into *A Mosaic of Wings*. Painful mistakes, romance, adventure, courage, and an endearing hero kept me engaged and turning those pages until the very satisfying end. An excellent first novel by Kimberly Duffy."

—Tessa Afshar, award-winning author of *Daughter of Rome*

"Grab a cup of masala tea and journey to exotic India in the company of two unforgettable characters who learn that love isn't always what it seems and choices have consequences beyond their wildest dreams. *A Mosaic of Wings* inspires, educates, and entertains. This is one debut novel you won't want to miss!"

—Laura Frantz, Christy Award–winning author of *An Uncommon Woman*

"This vivid, vibrant tale is a powerful journey that will challenge the reader's heart, mind, and soul."

—Kristi Ann Hunter, RITA Award–winning author of *A Pursuit of Home*

A Mosaic of Wings

KIMBERLY DUFFY

BETHANYHOUSE
a division of Baker Publishing Group
Minneapolis, Minnesota

Published by Bethany House Publishers
11400 Hampshire Avenue South
Bloomington, Minnesota 55438
www.bethanyhouse.com

Bethany House Publishers is a division of
Baker Publishing Group, Grand Rapids, Michigan

Printed in the United States of America

Library of Congress Cataloging-in-Publication Data
Names: Duffy, Kimberly, author.
Title: A mosaic of wings : a novel / Kimberly Duffy.
Description: Bloomington, Minnesota : Bethany House Publishers, [2020]
Identifiers: LCCN 2019050996 | ISBN 9780764235634 (trade paperback) |
    ISBN 9780764236259 (cloth) | ISBN 9781493425198 (ebook)
Subjects: GSAFD: Love stories.
Classification: LCC PS3604.U3783 M67 2020 | DDC 813/.6—dc23
LC record available at https://lccn.loc.gov/2019050996

This is a work of historical reconstruction; the appearances of certain historical figures are therefore inevitable. All other characters, however, are products
of the author's imagination, and any resemblance to actual persons, living or
dead, is coincidental.

Cover design by Jennifer Parker

Author is represented by the Books & Such Literary Agency.

20 21 22 23 24 25 26   7 6 5 4 3 2 1

To the Creator of all things.
You heard a little girl's dream
and wove a story greater than anything she imagined.

And to Grainne, my aspiring entomologist.
I love how much you love creation.
You make me see the world in a different way.

Part One

ITHACA, NEW YORK

May 1885

Chapter One

Nora Shipley's ears buzzed as though a thousand bees were trapped inside her head. Her back stiffened against the dining chair. She forced her grip on the May issue of *The Journal of Eastern Flora and Fauna* to relax, smoothing the creases at the corner of the page with her thumb.

Nora placed the journal on the table and gazed at her stepfather, Lucius Ward. Society deemed the house Nora grew up in his. But it wasn't really. Her father, Alexander Shipley, had bought this house when he secured his teaching job at Cornell University. It would always be her father's house, yet Lucius sat in her father's chair across the dining table from her, calmly eating his eggs, not realizing she barely contained an angry swarm behind her pinched lips.

Lucius wiped his mouth with a napkin. "Well, Nora, what do you think of our latest printing?"

Nora took a bite of toast to avoid answering. She flipped the periodical open to the most offensive spot, page sixteen. The advertisement, titled in a ridiculous and fanciful font, called for submissions from those willing to pay to have their articles published. As she chewed her toast into nonexistence, she silently read the destruction of her father's well-respected nature journal.

Finally, she swallowed and looked up. "Have you turned the journal into a commission publisher?"

Lucius's eyes darted to Nora's mother, who sat at the end of the table. Lydia Ward made a small sound in her throat, then placed her attention firmly on her teacup.

Putting his fork down, Lucius coughed. "I had no choice. It was no longer self-supporting."

Nora raised a brow. "Really? It did fine under my father's control."

Red infused Lucius's face. Nora couldn't tell if it was from embarrassment or anger—he looked the same with both emotions. "You forget I was his partner. We started the journal together."

Nora remained silent. She glanced at her mother, who motioned for their housemaid, Alice, to refill her cup. Mother always drank tea when she was upset.

Nora turned her attention back to the periodical and flipped through, slapping it down on the table when she found the offending article. Jabbing at the title, she lifted her eyes from the page. "Is this what you will be publishing from now on? Articles from hobbyists, rife with inaccuracies?" Nora could hardly hear her words, muffled as they were by the furious sound of the bees trapped inside her head. "As a biologist, why would you be willing to promote bad science? It's misleading. And more than that, it mocks the exceptional reputation this magazine has earned."

Lucius sighed and scrubbed his thick fingers over his jowls. "I can't pour more of my own money into it. If it doesn't generate income, it will become defunct. I know you don't want that. Neither of us do."

Nora reached for the napkin beside her plate and twisted it between her fingers. She shook her head. "But you knew the author was wrong. Why didn't you edit the article? This isn't the same academic journal you ran with Father."

Lucius had taught biology at Cornell University for twenty years, until he was abruptly released the winter before. A bright man, he dabbled in all facets of natural science—entomology, botany, chemistry—and knew the difference between solid research and vain posturing. What would their subscribers think when they read this month's issue? They couldn't possibly take it seriously.

Lucius waved his hand at the journal beside her plate. "These writers, they're so fragile. Correct them, and they pull their work and commission."

Nora shot to her feet, and the bees forced themselves out. "You'll turn my father's legacy into a laughingstock. I do not want to publish a journal that compromises his intent."

Lucius clambered from his chair and placed his knuckles on the table. He leaned forward, and Nora saw the flecks of mahogany flame against his brown eyes. Even though he spoke in a low tone, she didn't miss the warning in his voice. "It's a good thing, then, that this isn't your periodical. Nor is it, any longer, your father's."

His words stung, and Nora pressed the napkin to her middle.

"Alice," Mother called, her voice trembling, "please help me to my room. I believe I'm tired."

"You've upset your mother." Lucius placed a beefy hand beneath Lydia's arm. "Let me help you, my dear."

Mother stood, then swayed.

Nora's anger fled at the sight of her mother's white face and quivering lips. "I'm sorry, Mother."

Mother gave her a little smile, took Alice's arm, and left the room on silent steps.

Lucius sat and picked up his fork. "You're always sorry, Nora, but you speak without thought. It's not entirely your fault. Your father did you no favors in leaving you that inheritance without stipulation. A young woman would do better to marry than pursue a degree she will never be able to use."

Nora listened to Lucius prattle. She'd heard it before. Four years earlier, when he'd married her mother, Lucius had tried to convince Nora it would be wasteful for her to pursue a college degree. It galled him that Nora had ignored his advice and spent the inheritance her father left her on attending Cornell. In two weeks she'd have her bachelor of entomology. With determined application, Nora had been able to complete her degree in three years. Her money was gone, but what she had used it for would always be accessible in the form of an education.

"Your father should have known better, letting you believe you could—"

Nora blinked. "My father was a man of integrity and intellect."

Lucius slurped at his cup. When he set it down, tea sloshed over the rim and spread in a circle on the snowy white tablecloth. "Yes. He was also idealistic. Too idealistic, if you ask me. You need to marry, Nora. There's nothing admirable about becoming a spinster, especially when you're an only child. Your mother wants grandchildren." His voice turned almost plaintive, and he leaned toward her. "Let me introduce you to my friend. Mr. Primrose is successful and intelligent."

Nora groaned. "I've already told you I'm not interested in marrying right now. If you'll excuse me, I have a meeting with Professor Comstock in an hour, and I must prepare."

She swept from the room, her skirts swishing around her ankles. She couldn't listen to another word. Lucius was unbearable, and she was glad there were men in the world like her father and John Comstock. Men who viewed a woman's intellect on par with a man's. Men who believed God had made women in His image, not as a pale imitation of Adam.

Nora climbed the steps to the second floor and stopped to peer into her mother's bedroom. Through the dotted Swiss curtains of the canopied bed, she saw Mother reclining atop a pile of pillows, her hand against her head.

"Are you well, Mother?"

"Yes, quite, darling. I'm just going to rest awhile." By the time her words made it to Nora, they were a whisper.

Nora blew her mother a kiss and followed the hallway to her own room, where she gathered her hat, cloak, and the box containing the *Scutelleridae*—commonly known as the jewel bug—she'd received yesterday. It did look like a little jewel. It was almost as pretty as the Lalique cicada brooch her father had given her on her thirteenth birthday. The insect would send her mother into a swoon, but Professor Comstock was sure to admire it.

Just before Nora reached Cornell's White Hall, it began to rain. A sudden, heavy spring shower that drenched her head in moments. She groaned and ran the rest of the way, ducking beneath the door and into the corridor. She pulled off the tiny hat that had done nothing to protect her from the rain, and smoothed the curls twisting from their pins and beginning their corkscrewed ascent from her head. Of all the ridiculous things God could have given her, her wild hair topped them. Why she couldn't have shiny, well-behaved locks, she didn't know.

There was nothing for it. She'd just look like a sheep the rest of the day.

The entomology laboratory occupied the north end of the second floor, and Nora did her best to tuck as many frizzy curls back into their pins as she could while she climbed the stairs. The moment she stepped through the door of the lab, though, her irritation over her hair and the morning's stress slipped from her shoulders like a butterfly shaking free from its cocoon. Nora never brought her burdens into the lab. Crowded with long wooden tables, shelves of books, and stacks of nets, the room seemed almost sacrosanct, and she didn't want to disturb its peace. It was home. Even more so than the house she'd lived in all her life. That hadn't been home since her mother had married Lucius.

Professor Comstock sat on the edge of his chair, peering into the eyepiece of a brass microscope. Nora set her box on the table and settled onto the stool beside him. He either didn't hear her or chose not to acknowledge her, because he continued to study his slide, making clicking noises with his tongue and murmuring.

"Professor," Nora said.

He held up a finger.

Nora grinned. She well understood the excitement of discovery. When Cornell first received the microscopes, Nora had spent hours studying the world she'd previously been unable to see. Pulling away to attend to the mundane was always difficult.

Professor Comstock sat up straight and shook his head. "Look and tell me what you see."

She pulled the microscope toward her and bent over it. Expecting the brilliant scales of a butterfly's wing or the spiky hairs of an ant's mandible, she was perplexed by the translucent orbs clinging to what looked like a tortoise shell comb. "Pollen? Are you studying botany now?"

"Only as it relates to apiculture. The pollen is clinging to the legs of a honeybee. It's fascinating. I'm beginning a new class next year. If you pursue your master's, you will take it."

"I've used my entire inheritance to obtain my bachelor's degree, but I'll attend your lectures." Nora thought she'd spoken well, with no trace of tremor in her voice.

He patted her hand. "Perhaps Lucius will . . ." He grimaced.

She laughed without humor. "We both know that's unlikely. Especially after Cornell released him from his job the way they did."

The professor sighed. "That's the second time the university has done that—let someone go by announcing it in the paper. And at Christmas! So unprofessional." He shook his head for a moment, then rapped the table with his knuckles, as though trying to wake himself up. "Tell me what you've brought today."

Nora pushed the cardboard box toward him and leaned

forward, the anticipation delicious. When her father died, she thought she'd have no one to share her love of insects with. She'd have to suppress her joy when she discovered an orb-weaver's web or a centipede crawled into her upturned palm. But Professor Comstock and his wife, Anna, filled that empty place. They hadn't yet had children, and they'd watched Nora grow up. She'd joined them and her father when they tromped through the gorges. Her little hands could reach into the crevices behind wet rocks to pull out the insects hiding within. Nora wasn't sure how she could have managed the last six years without them.

Professor Comstock flipped open the box, and a delighted grin pushed his thick mustache northward.

She craned her neck to see into the box and recapture the moment she first saw the mounted insect. "What do you think?"

With gentle movements, he pulled it out and set it on the table. "He's beautiful. Where did he come from?"

Nora scooted her stool nearer and stared at the bug secured by brass pins. She liked the romantic-sounding name of jewel bug, but it was also known as a metallic shield bug, and that was more appropriate. An iridescent green and red scutellum shielded its abdomen and wings, and it looked like it wore armor—a miniature soldier waiting for battle orders.

"My father's old friend, Mrs. Martín, lives in the Philippines with her husband, who is a Spanish diplomat. She's an amateur entomologist and often sent insects to my father, but she stopped after his death. I wrote to her months ago and told her I'd still love any she thought might add to my collection, and this is the first I've received. Isn't it incredible?"

Professor Comstock nodded. He lifted the insect and peered between it and the card. Satisfied, he set it back down. "It will make a nice addition. I do wish we could get a look beneath its wings. . . ." He glanced around as though searching for his scalpel.

Nora slipped the bug back into the box, imagining him slicing into it, bug parts flying as he figured out all he could about the internal workings of her magnificent little soldier.

He caught her surreptitious movement and smiled. "I promise to leave him in one piece." As he gazed at the bug, a faraway look clouded his eyes. "Wouldn't it be something, studying insects like this in Asia?" He turned to her, one brow raised in question. "Nora, I've just had a wonderful thought. A British colleague is in India, collecting butterflies for a book commissioned by the Crown. He's had the worst luck with illness—his assistants are dropping like flies." He gave her a wry smile. "He's asked if I can recommend anyone to join him. What about you?"

A short laugh escaped her throat as Nora imagined herself clad in linen and traipsing through the jungle with an umbrella net, capturing golden butterflies the size of her hand. She blinked away the unlikely dream. "I couldn't possibly." She was content to live and study in Ithaca. And to save the journal from Lucius's terrible management. "Did you know Lucius turned my father's journal into a commission publication?"

The professor's expression turned thoughtful. "I'd heard. It's a shame. It was such a beautiful publication."

"Now line space will be sold to the most willing buyer—anyone with a smattering of knowledge and a desire to be published." She couldn't keep the disgust from her voice. It dripped from her lips like honey, thick and cloying.

He tapped his finger against his chin. "Maybe Lucius needed the money after his dismissal. Commission publications can generate a decent income."

Nora shook her head. "That's what he said, but why? Mother's inheritance will last years."

Professor Comstock ducked, but not before Nora saw dismay in his narrowed eyes.

"What is it?"

"It's nothing. Just speculation and rumors." He patted her hand. "Even if Lucius does ruin the journal, you have other talents. You'd be a wonderful researcher. And India beckons. Imagine the insects you could collect there."

"If Lucius insists I meet this Mr. Primrose he's always going on about, I might have to go to India just to escape." She swiveled toward the table and rested her chin in her hand. "No, I mostly want the journal. It's all I have left of my father. I'm not ready to let it go, and I think he'd be proud of me if I saved it. Helped keep it alive."

"You made him proud the first time you caught a *Lampyridae*. He was thrilled when you mounted your first *coccinellid*. You inherited his passion for nature and insects, and he loved that."

Nora heard his words and recognized the truth in them. But a child's interest in lightning bugs and ladybird beetles wasn't going to save her father's legacy. His journal could be around for decades, and people would know her father's name and work. Even in death, he could claim recognition. And she would do anything to make that happen.

A light rap sounded at the door, and the tapping of heels against the wood floor followed. Anna Comstock entered the room, her stride efficient and her expression serene. Nora stood and smiled at her mentor, glad to put her attention on something other than the web of thoughts spinning in her mind. "Anna! I didn't think I'd see you until our session on Thursday."

Anna smiled, full of warmth and quiet joy. "I'm glad you refuse to admit you've surpassed your teacher's skill and still want art lessons."

Nora laughed. "That will never be true. And I wouldn't admit it anyway."

"Excellent. After my wood-engraving class, I'll have something new to share with you. The teacher need only be one step ahead of the student." Anna turned to her husband. "President White wants to see you in his office."

"Of course," he said. "Nora, if you have some time, would you mind mounting a few of my *Apis mellifera*? They're already prepared." He motioned toward the long table in the middle of the room, and Nora saw a trio of kill jars, a fuzzy yellow-and-black honeybee in each one.

She nodded, and when they left, she closed her eyes, inhaling the musty scent of books, solvents, and memories. The sun spilling through the bank of windows warmed her face, and for a moment, here in this place she loved, things didn't seem as awful as they had that morning.

If only she could spend the rest of her life in the laboratory.

Chapter Two

Nora gathered tools from the large, glass-fronted cabinet at the far end of the lab, then grabbed a stack of cork mounting boards on her way back to the table. A moment after she settled into her chair, just as she'd lifted one of the bees with a pair of small tweezers, the door slammed open.

With a yelp, she dropped the insect. It bounced before settling into a gouge created long ago by a student bored with a lecture.

"So sorry, Nora." Rose Keller rushed across the room in a rustle of skirts. "I didn't mean to enter so loudly. My mother would be horrified. But that door is just so heavy."

"It's fine. I was only surprised." She nodded at the bee lying on its side.

Rose scooped it into her hand. "How lovely. I just adore honeybees."

Nora used the tweezers to pluck the insect from Rose's cupped palm. She placed it on the mounting board, careful to display it in a way that showed off its fuzzy thorax and the spread of its wings.

"Let Nora finish her work, Rose," Bitsy Templeton said, gliding across the room without a sound. Her words were draped in a cultured English accent and spoken in an even tone, so different from Rose's rapid and breathless speech.

Pulling a pin from the box beside the board, Nora worked it just left of center of the honeybee's middle. She finished the next two in the same manner while Bitsy watched from across the table, her wide mouth relaxed and a placid expression in her blue eyes. Rose inched ever closer as Nora worked, shiny blond curls framing her sweet face, and just as she seemed about to tip over, Nora straightened and put a hand to her lower back.

"All done."

Rose sank onto the stool beside Nora and sighed, as though holding her words in had proved too difficult a task. "We were hoping to find you here. Bitsy wondered if we should walk to your house, but I reminded her that it was Tuesday, and why would you be at home when Professor Comstock is in his lab, doing whatever he does? I know you prefer to spend your time helping him."

"Indeed. Where else would I want to be? Does that make me *peculiar*?"

The girls laughed. They'd heard other students whispering about them as they climbed the ranks in their classes, made honors, and out-tested their classmates. Someone began calling them Peculiar, Percipient, and Phenomenon. Nora knew the names were probably meant as an insult, and she didn't know who was who, but she rather liked them. They fit.

"You're right, though. This has become my second home."

Bitsy gave Nora a shrewd look. "Because you love being here, or because you hate being at home?"

Rose covered her mouth with her fingers. "Bitsy! What an awful thing to say."

Bitsy raised a brow, but the movement did little to break her stoic expression. "It's not awful if it's true."

Rose's fingers tapped their way across the table until they met Nora's. "You don't have to answer Bitsy's question."

"Don't be so dull, Rose. Interesting things lie in what people *don't* want to say."

Nora looked between the two of them and shook her head. She couldn't have made two such disparate friends if she'd set out to. She imagined most things seemed dull to Bitsy, with her staggering intellect and capacity to remember anything she'd read or heard. Rose was smart in a different way. Her mind worked like a hummingbird, always flitting to the next thing. Rapidly absorbing her lessons, she retained only that which interested her—mainly in the subject of zoology.

"I don't mind answering," Nora said. Bitsy inclined her head, a self-satisfied smirk curving her beautiful lips. Even Rose sat up straighter and looked more interested. "I prefer the laboratory because everything I love is here." She spread her arms wide, encompassing the tables and insect display and scientific tools of their trade. "My insects, my teachers, my friends, the opportunity to learn and discover. . . . But more than that, I feel my father here. Hovering over me, guiding me, teaching me. And he's no longer at home."

They grew quiet; even their breathing slowed.

Then Rose, never comfortable with prolonged silences, jumped to her feet. "Enough of this. If you're done with your bees, Nora, I suggest we go for a row on the inlet. The rain has stopped, and the day is perfect for it."

Nora sent a longing glance at the now-mounted bees. She'd rather spend the afternoon with her insects.

Rose bounced on her soles before grabbing the front of her floral-sprigged skirt and darting toward the door. Nora bit the inside of her cheek to stem a laugh. Rose's enthusiasm couldn't be contained, and Nora knew she wouldn't be allowed to hide in the lab. No matter how much peace she found there.

The little white rowboat smelled of fish, but the sun sent dappled light through the tall oak trees, creating flickering patterns on the water of the Cayuga Inlet.

Nora's breathing slowed to match the whispering breeze. Bitsy steered the boat around a pebbly beach, and Nora ducked beneath the branches of a Juneberry tree. As they slipped forward, she reached up and snapped a twig from a branch. "This was a perfect suggestion, Rose. I needed to get out and enjoy myself."

Bitsy wiped her forehead with the back of her hand and shoved the oars into the water. "Why don't you take a turn rowing, Nora? My arms are about to fall off."

"Do stop complaining. You're ruining the quiet," Rose called over Nora's head from where she sat in the bow.

A damselfly flew nearby, and out of habit, Nora reached for it, waiting to see if it would land on her finger. It had only happened once, when she had been about eight. Her father had told her damselflies represented change, and when one visited, you should expect a shift in perspective. The damselfly's wings beat the air, and the light movement brushed her hand. She held her breath. Hoping.

She needed a change in perspective. She needed a change, period. The animosity at home sent her outside so often, she sometimes wondered if she should burrow into a hollow tree and make a den like a fox. She didn't think her mother would miss her. Lucius would help her dig.

The insect's luminous cobalt body trembled and darted away. Nora sighed, dropping her hand to the peeling wooden seat. She fiddled with the twig before tossing it into the water. "If you pull off, we can rest, and then I'll row back home."

Nora's comment renewed Bitsy's vigor, and she put muscle into her rowing, causing the boat to shoot forward. It soon floated into shallower water, and Bitsy shoved the oar deep into the rocky bank, leveraging it until they pulled onto the narrow beach, pebbles scraping the hull. She climbed out and shook her elegant striped skirt. Nora and Rose joined her on shore.

Nora snapped open the blanket she'd grabbed from the bottom of the boat and laid it on a grassy knoll just past the beach. She sat down, tucking her feet beneath her, and stared at the water lapping the shore. The little rowboat creaked and moaned as tiny waves bounced it. A hint of rain hung in the air, and she wondered if she'd shut her bedroom window. The last time she'd forgotten when it stormed, Lucius had lost his temper, threatening to sell her collection and use the proceeds to replace the ruined curtains.

Bitsy settled beside her. "What are you so distracted by?"

Rose sank to the ground and pulled a chocolate bar from her skirt pocket. She peeled back the gold foil and snapped the bar into three pieces to share.

"My stepfather has turned *The Journal of Eastern Flora and Fauna* into a commission publisher." Nora nibbled the corner of the chocolate, giving the girls time to digest her news. They'd understand how serious—how awful—it was.

"Oh no," Rose said, her words skipping past a groan. "That's not right."

Bitsy touched Nora's shoulder. "Didn't you expect him to hand it over to you after graduation?"

Nora nodded and swallowed a bite of chocolate, hoping to dislodge the lump in her throat. "I assumed . . . Lucius always complained about the work involved. The writing, editing, gathering, hiring of artists, paying the printer, mailing them out. It never made much money—our readership doesn't exceed a thousand—and it is a lot of work. I figured I could just take over when I finished school this term."

"I'm so sorry," Rose said. She tucked the rest of her chocolate into Nora's hand, as though confections could soothe the defeat eating at Nora's peace.

Nora took a bite, knowing Rose only wanted to make her

feel better. She didn't think anything could make the situation right. The chocolate stuck to the roof of her mouth, and she flopped backward onto the ground.

"We could dress as businessmen and buy it," Rose said with a giggle. "Doesn't that sound glamorous? 'Hello, I'm Rose Keller, editor of *The Journal of Eastern Flora and Fauna.*'" She stuck out her hand, and Bitsy shook it.

"How would we buy it? You spend all the money your parents send you on chocolate and ice cream sodas." Nora wrinkled her nose and squinted up at the sky. "I've used nearly all of my inheritance on school, and Bitsy has nothing except what her aunt gives her."

"That sounds so somber," Bitsy said. "But I do believe Rose could buy all of Ithaca if she stopped eating chocolate."

A cloud in the shape of a butterfly scuttled across the sun. Nora turned toward a bent silver maple shading the inlet, its thick tangle of branches arching over the water in a graceful pose. She pushed herself onto her elbows. "It wouldn't matter. Lucius doesn't believe women should work. Especially me. He keeps harping on making a match with his dreary business acquaintance."

Bitsy made a growling sound. "He's so conventional. Why your father started the journal with him is beyond me."

"I'd like to know why your mother married him." Rose sighed.

"In Lucius's words, 'You needed a father, Nora. Your mother knows a strong male figure is important to the raising of children.' Not that he's ever been a father to me. He could never be that." Nora's chest clenched. He'd tried once or twice, too soon after her father died. She hadn't wanted him to pretend to love her then. And when she was ready, their relationship had already soured. "Anyway, Mother said he was different when Father was alive. We all were, I guess." She jumped to her feet, tugged the blanket from beneath Rose and Bitsy, and wadded it into a ball. "I'm ready to go. Enough of this depressing talk."

"As long as you're rowing," Bitsy said.

Nora stomped over the rocks, the blanket smooshed beneath her arm. A black-and-orange blur stopped her. She followed the monarch's ascent as it fluttered toward the silver maple, disappearing behind the trunk. "They're early this year."

Bitsy came up beside her. "Who is?"

"The monarchs."

Nora shoved the blanket at Bitsy, then backtracked and rounded the tree. At the base of its trunk, roots shot out and clung to the shoreline, which pitched steeply over the water. She peered up through the lacy blanket of spring buds, and her breath caught at the sight of hundreds of monarch butterflies resting along the length of the trunk. She skirted back around the tree and held her finger to her lips. Rose and Bitsy stopped their approach and looked at each other with bewilderment until Nora drew the back of her skirt between her legs and tied it to the front in a tight knot.

"What are you doing?" Rose screeched. "You look like a harem girl."

"Shush, Rose. I need to get up in that tree."

Nora positioned herself on the opposite side of the tree as the butterflies and considered her climb. She already had a monarch in her collection, but she didn't want to pass up this opportunity. It would be magical. Her hands began to tingle at the prospect. She lifted her foot to the lowest tree limb, hooked her boot heel over it, and with a suppressed huff, lifted herself into the tree. She paused and gazed up the trunk, making sure she hadn't startled the butterflies. Satisfied they hadn't noticed her, she climbed to another branch.

"I don't think this is a great idea," Rose called.

Nora glared down at her. Bitsy, her hand shading her eyes, said, "Just let her do it, Rose. You know she won't be dissuaded."

Nora climbed until she thought she'd reached the height where the monarchs had gathered. Then she inched forward, pressed her body against the tree, and swung her foot to the next branch over. With her feet firmly planted on two different branches, she piano-keyed her fingers around the trunk until she could shift her weight fully to the second branch. She ignored Rose's gasps punctuating the silence and repeated the process until she stood only inches from the kaleidoscope of butterflies.

She wished she had her sketchbook. Instead, she committed the visual to memory, their brilliant segmented wings reminding her that her father often said nature displayed the artistry of God. She couldn't disagree. She didn't think any museum held a more beautiful display of creativity. Every insect she studied, every bug she duplicated in watercolor and pencil, pointed her toward a God who loved beauty. And she loved being outside admiring it.

If you take over the journal, you'll spend too much time at a desk.

Nora ignored the thought and reached to brush her fingertip across one silken wing. Her father's dream was worth the sacrifice.

"Nora!" Rose's shout pierced the silence. "Get down here before you kill yourself!"

As a group, the butterflies lifted from the tree. They surrounded Nora in a cloud, tickling her ears and scalp with their fluttering wings. She laughed, then quickly closed her mouth when she felt them brush her lips, as soft as Chantilly lace. She steadied herself on the branch and slowly, with gentle movements, lifted her arms above her head. The monarchs crisscrossed around her in a sunrise-hued blanket. Then they lifted into the sky and flew northward.

For a moment, Nora didn't move. Her arms still raised, she listened to herself breathe and followed the flight of the butterflies as they disappeared from view.

"Did you see that?" she called to Bitsy and Rose.

"Incredible," Bitsy answered, shielding her eyes and looking up at her.

Rose wrung her hands. "Please, now, won't you come down? There's someone coming."

Nora looked past the tree and saw a rowboat making a lazy path toward them. She sighed and began her climb down. When she reached the halfway point, someone called out to them. Nora strained to see over a tree branch obscuring her view. Standing on her toes, she just made out the little boat and a man's straw hat.

She didn't know how it happened. She'd been climbing trees since she could walk, but for the first time in her life, she found herself slipping off the branch that snugged her against the trunk. She flipped over, scraping her cheek against the rough bark. With only enough time to recognize Rose's shriek, she dropped through the air.

Chapter Three

ora landed in a heap, bottom in the water, one leg stretching from her still-knotted skirt onto the muddy earth.

Rose splashed through the water toward her. "Oh, dear. Are you all right?"

"She's fine," Bitsy called from the shore. "She didn't fall that far."

Rose put her hands beneath Nora's arms and, with a grunt, tried to lift her.

"Goodness, Rose. Let go of me. I'll be fine if you give me a moment to collect myself." Nora pressed her hands into the soft earth beneath the water and pushed herself to her feet, sending pain through her right ankle. When she groaned and sank back down, Rose attempted to hoist her by the elbow, releasing her only when Nora smacked her hand away.

"I don't think I can make it." Nora clutched her foot in her lap.

"Bitsy, come help me lift her," Rose shouted.

Bitsy pointed at something behind them. "Why don't you ask him?"

When Nora turned, she saw her classmate Owen Epps sitting in the rowboat, the oar resting over his lap. He pushed his hat back with his forefinger. "Need some help, Phenomenon?"

Nora wished the water would rise and cover her. Owen Epps was the last person she wanted help from. They'd spent the last three years locked in academic competition. Out of the twenty students in the entomology program, Nora and Owen were the top performers. But where Nora focused on studying, Owen's good grades seemed to be part and parcel of his charmed life. She'd never seen him express any real seriousness toward his education.

She looked at him, lounging in his boat with his jaunty straw hat, and clenched her jaw. "No, I don't."

"How'd you end up in the water?"

"I fell out of the tree."

He gave her a crooked smile. "What were you doing in the tree?"

"Climbing it." She attempted to stand again, but the pain stopped her before she could straighten her knees. "To get a better look at the monarchs. The entire tree was crowded with them."

"They're early this year," Owen said, watching her from beneath his shaggy blond brows.

"Yes, I know." She sighed. She wasn't going to be able to make it out of the water by herself. She sucked in a deep breath and exhaled her pride. "I need help, Owen."

He grinned, sprang from the boat, and pulled it aground, splashing toward her a moment later to scoop her against his chest. She held her arms rigid, trying not to touch him any more than necessary.

"Relax, Nora." He laughed into her hair. "I won't hurt you."

"I seem to have managed that on my own."

Reaching the shore, he asked Rose to shake out the blanket, and then he set Nora down on it.

"You might want to . . ." His glance skittered to her bottom half then away toward the water.

Looking down, Nora saw her stockinged legs, the knot in her

skirt settled on top of her knees like a lump of coal. "Not one word about it, Owen Epps." After she yanked at the knot and rearranged her skirts, she tugged her boot laces loose, sighing when the pressure against her ankle eased.

"Do you need to see a doctor?" Bitsy asked.

Nora flexed her foot and then stuck her hand down the side of her boot. She prodded the area above her ankle, feeling mild tenderness and some swelling. "I think it's just sprained. I'll rest here a few moments, and then we can head home."

"Your face is a mess." Bitsy patted her own smooth cheeks.

Nora ran her fingers from her cheekbone to her jawline. She definitely had some abrasions, but when she looked at her hand, there was no blood. She couldn't think how she'd explain her injuries to her mother, though, who thought Nora had stopped climbing trees once she donned long skirts.

She looked up at Owen, blinking against the sunlight that shaded his face and cast a glow over the tousled hair that escaped from underneath his hat. "Thank you for your help."

"Am I being dismissed?"

"Oh no." Rose grabbed his arm. "Nora is so grateful. Here . . . sit. Sit." She tugged him to the blanket and sat across from them once he'd been settled.

"You may as well join our little party, Bitsy." Nora scooted to give Bitsy room and bumped into Owen. She cleared her throat and forced a tight smile.

Bitsy arranged herself on the blanket and lifted her long, tapered fingers to her lips. It was a look Nora knew signified scheming. Bitsy may have been descended from British gentry, but that didn't preclude her from being manipulative.

"I believe it would be best if you took Nora back to town, Owen," Bitsy said. "I'm sure you row your boat much more quickly than we do. And then you can help her home."

Nora's cheeks flushed. "I'm sure we'll manage just—"

"I'd be happy to help." Owen grinned at Nora. "I'll be your valiant knight."

Bitsy's self-satisfied smile set Nora on edge.

"I don't need a knight," she snapped. When Owen drew back and blinked slowly, regret poured through her, cold and heavy.

Bitsy shook her head and pursed her lips, then turned away and picked at a patch of clover.

Rose glanced at Nora, the dimple in her chin deepening, before she turned to Owen. "Were you at the party, Owen?"

Owen tore his attention from Nora, offering her a reprieve from his judgment and censure, and smiled at Rose. "No. Delta Upsilon helped plan it, but I was sick that night. Did you have fun?"

Nora had noticed he hadn't been there. Even behind a mask, she would recognize him—he stood half a foot taller than the other men in her class. More than a foot taller than she herself.

Rose nodded and blushed, turning a pretty shade that matched her name. "The girls and I decided to make our masks match our majors. I was an elephant, Bitsy a crane—isn't that perfect for her? They're so elegant—and Nora—"

"Don't tell me. Let me guess." Owen turned toward Nora. "You were a *Blattellidae*."

Rose frowned in confusion. "No. She was a butterfly. Why would she be a . . ." She shot Nora a look of regret. "Oh."

Nora ground her teeth. She hated cockroaches, and Owen knew it. He'd laughed, along with everyone else in the room, her freshman year when she'd jumped onto her chair and tried to shake one from her skirt.

Ignoring the pain slicing through her ankle, she shifted, turning her back on Owen.

"Come on, Nora. I'm just teasing. I'm sure you made a lovely butterfly." His fingers grazed her shoulder. "I'm sorry. I didn't realize you were still upset about that. It happened over two years ago."

Nora twisted her head to look at him. "You humiliated me in front of the entire class. In front of Professor Comstock."

"I didn't humiliate you. You were the one jumping around

like a Mexican hat dancer. All because of an insect. You *study* insects and handle them every day." He waggled his overly expressive eyebrows, and Nora itched to smack down the cowlick standing at attention over his crown. "What was I supposed to do? The entire class was laughing."

Nora clambered to her feet, gingerly testing her weight. Her ankle twinged, but she could stand. "I think I'm ready to return."

With a sigh, Owen stood and let Rose take his arm. He led her to the boat, then returned for Bitsy and helped her over the rocky ground. When they reached the water, he whispered something in Bitsy's ear. She patted his arm and climbed in behind Rose, who'd managed to avoid rowing back to town. Owen pushed them into the water.

Before he could return for her, Nora started toward the second boat with an awkward hop-step.

"Let me help you," he said, coming beside her.

"I'm fine."

"Don't be angry with me. I was only teasing you."

"I'm not angry." She stepped away from him, yelping when her ankle gave out beneath her heavy step.

He bit his lower lip, concern wrinkling his brow, and her heart softened. He hadn't truly instigated the laughter that day.

She sighed and took his proffered arm. "I'm the only female entomology major. You have no idea how hard I worked to prove myself in that class, and in one moment of absurdity, I destroyed what it took a year to build. No one took me seriously after that. There were complaints of hysteria-prone women in the sciences, and I had to start all over again, proving I deserved to be there. That I was a serious scientist."

"You *are* a serious scientist. I don't think anyone could say otherwise. You've gotten top marks in every class."

"But I still have to work twice as hard for the respect you're just given."

Owen was silent as he helped her into the boat, his hand

tightening on her arm when she gasped at the pain shooting across her ankle. He pushed the boat into deeper water, pebbles scraping the bottom as they slid into the inlet. Then he sat on the opposite bench, facing her. "I didn't think about all of that. I won't bring it up again."

She sent furtive glances at him as he guided their boat from shore.

He caught her look and smiled, his straight teeth gleaming. "Forgive me?"

She nodded. Rose thought Owen was charming. The entire female student body thought Owen was charming. Nora had never really seen it before, but for a moment just now, he seemed almost thoughtful. There was something rather . . . attractive about it. She shook the thought free and waved as they overtook Rose and Bitsy. Rose waved back with her typical enthusiasm, and Bitsy snapped at her to stop shaking the boat.

"Do you want to come back to school and get your master's?" Owen asked.

Nora squinted up at the sky to avoid looking at him and his perfect teeth. "I can't afford it."

As the sun scuttled behind a cloud, she shifted beneath her wet serge skirt. She wanted nothing more than to change into dry clothes and pull out her sketchbook. If she could hold on to the memory of the butterfly-covered tree, she could maybe do the scene justice. It had been glorious. Worth the tumble and embarrassment.

"My father is a trustee." Owen didn't elaborate, and she wondered if that should mean something to her.

"Yes?"

He put some force into steering the boat around a muddy bank, and his muscles shifted beneath his rolled-up shirtsleeves. Nora had to agree with Rose that Owen was good-looking. What a shame such an attractive specimen housed someone with so little motivation, other than to best her in class. She knew he was naturally bright and rarely studied. He didn't take life seriously, but what could one expect from someone raised in the lap of luxury who had never experienced trial?

Owen rested the oars over his lap, and the boat meandered forward. "My father told me that one of the trustees has established a scholarship for graduating entomology students. To continue their education."

His words drew Nora's attention. "A scholarship?"

"Maybe it will be awarded to you, Percipient." He stuck the oars back in the water and grinned. "Then again, maybe they'll offer it to me."

She frowned. "Why would you need a scholarship? Your father owns the largest publishing house in New York."

He leaned into the oars and grunted. The boat lurched and then skimmed over the water toward the dock. "My father is convinced entomology is a waste of time. He wants me either to go to law school or to join him at the company. He's already said he won't pay for me to continue my education if I"—he deepened his voice and modulated his tone—"'insist on pursuing this fool path.'" He smirked. "Those were his exact words. In my father's opinion, law and publishing are the only two viable career options. I'm lucky he paid for these four years."

"Why *did* you choose entomology? Does someone in your family study it?"

He shook his head. "No. My older brothers—I have four—all either followed my father into business or pursued law. One's in politics. My father begrudgingly gave me the option of pursuing a science if I didn't want to go into law. I think he was hoping I'd choose medicine." His face took on the expression of a child dipping braids in ink. "He was utterly baffled when I told him I wanted to study entomology. But entomology is interesting enough. And it's not as difficult as other sciences."

Nora considered Mr. Epps and his opinion on insect study. Owen's father was immeasurably successful. He'd accomplished more in his lifetime than anyone she knew. He had to be a determined man. A hard worker. So unlike his son. What would it be like, being a man used to success and having a child who took everything for granted? A child who showed no more thought for his future than a honeybee did. Actually, a honeybee showed more consideration than Owen Epps. At least the bee worked hard and prepared.

She primly folded her hands in her lap. "While I disagree with your father's opinion on entomology, I think *your* pursuit of it may, indeed, be a fool's path. You don't seem to care one bit for the science, other than the fact that it isn't terribly difficult—a sentiment I wholeheartedly challenge—and you derive joy from confounding your parent and his desire for your life."

The boat bounced against the dock, jarring Nora from her seat. She planted her weight against her feet, and pain shot through her injured ankle. A gasp whistled between her teeth. "You could have warned me we were close to docking."

"I was so caught up in your assessment of me, I didn't even notice. And you were looking right at it, Nora. You must have been distracted too." Owen grinned at her before balancing on steady legs until the rocking stopped. He looped a rope over the post, jumped onto the dock, and held out his hand, which she ignored.

She stood on legs not quite as seaworthy as his, her ankle throbbing in rebellion. She managed to climb over the side of the boat, but she tripped over her wet skirt as she clambered onto the dock, landing on her knees.

"Let me help—"

Her hand shot up, silencing Owen, and she stood. Her face grew warm beneath his gaze, and the scratches on her cheek pulled at her tender skin as she clenched her jaw.

A shout reached them from the water, and Rose and Bitsy's boat came into view. Rose waved. "Hello!"

Nora waggled her fingers at her friends, pulled her skirts away from her legs, and limped down the boardwalk toward the road.

Owen jogged after her. "Let me help you home."

"I'll wait for my friends. Don't put yourself out."

"You're probably half right about me anyway."

She halted. "I'm rarely only half right." She squinted up at him. "Have you ever wondered why you spend so much time teasing me, Owen? It's tiring."

He rolled his lips together, but she still saw the beginnings of a smile, and she couldn't ignore his snort.

"Why do you want to pursue your master's anyway?" she asked. "It doesn't sound like you love entomology. Why not do as your father asked and join him in business?"

Owen shoved his hands deep inside his pants pockets and bowed his head. Surprised by his sudden soberness, Nora felt her breath hitch. Had she hurt his feelings? Her stepfather often told her she spoke with too much boldness. Without enough thought and care.

She blinked twice when Owen raised his head and his smile tipped to one side. "I'm not ready to work yet. Another two years of taking it easy, and then maybe I'll let my father talk me into law school."

Inside her damp shoes, Nora curled her toes, and her nails dug into the soft skin of her palms. She kept her expression calm, however. Placid. He was teasing again. He had to be. Owen thought the scholarship was his because life came easy to him, but if she could obtain her master's degree, she'd be able to secure a teaching position. Maybe even at Cornell, though they hadn't yet hired a female professor.

She could be the first. And then she'd be following her father's path. As a teacher and as someone who published the best entomology journal in the country. That would almost make up for the loss Cornell and the scientific community sustained when he died.

Owen bent toward her, and his caterpillar brows met over the center of his nose. Two golden *Halysidota harrisii* kissing each other. "What are you thinking in that busy mind of yours?"

That your brows look like sycamore tussock moth caterpillars behaving a little too friendly for public viewing. "That you shouldn't become too attached to the idea of that scholarship. I believe my grades are better than yours."

Owen straightened and held his thumb and pointer finger an inch apart. "Just a bit. Plus, the scholarship isn't only based on grades. They're looking for someone who completes a summer research project and gives a great lecture before the end of next year." He grabbed the lapels of his jacket and rocked onto his heels. "I just happen to be an excellent public speaker. And Professor Comstock has offered me the opportunity to work with a team in India. I'm considering it."

Nora reared back and stared at him. "But he offered me that project."

Owen shrugged. "And you said no."

"I might change my mind!" She'd have to reevaluate her hasty rejection if Owen was going. How could she compete with India?

Rose and Bitsy guided their boat to the dock and tied it off. They were at Nora's side in a moment, and she hooked her arms through theirs.

"They'll see me home," she said. "I believe I can walk without your help, Owen."

He tipped his hat. "Ladies." He smiled at Nora. "May the best man win." Tucking his hands back into his pockets, he sauntered away, whistling a jaunty tune.

"Or the best woman," Nora called after him.

Definitely the best woman.

Chapter Four

Nora ran a dustrag over the gleaming surface of her walnut insect cabinet. Alice did most of the cleaning, but Nora insisted on polishing the cabinet herself. Her father had ordered it from England when Nora was ten. Only a third of the thirty drawers had been filled when he died.

Mother had been glad to send the cabinet to Nora's room. With no interest in insects—she preferred they stay outside, dead and alive—she wanted it out of her parlor. Nora had filled another five drawers since then and imagined her father watching her from heaven with approval.

She pulled out each drawer in turn and wiped the glass tops of the display cases, reciting the orders as the rag passed over the insects within. *Lepidoptera, Odonata, Hemiptera, Coleoptera, Embioptera.*

Nora's mother loved to look through thick books with pictures of animals from around the world. Elephants, camels, and kangaroos. But when compared to the insect world, mammals showed so little variation. So little color and uniqueness. Nora thought nothing could be as lovely as the wings of a Luna moth. Nothing as fascinating to watch as a simple garden spider spinning.

She wondered if she could find one in the garden. Every year their lovely webs filled the cherry tree beside the gate. She'd caught a chill the day before, after falling in the water, but a glance out the window told her the sun shone over Mother's sprouting garden.

Nora's fingers itched for her pencils. She gathered her supplies and headed outside. Her mother was often bedridden, too weak and ill to do much, but she always had time for her flowers. Even if it meant hiring a boy to weed and plant, Mother made sure her garden was tidy and charming. In the summer, Nora loved to walk down the pebbled paths, running her fingers over the heliotrope and begonias. A rose-covered pergola offered escape from the sun and was the perfect place to watch butterflies and honeybees enjoy the lavender. It was too early in the season for most flowers, but the cherry tree had begun to send out shoots, and she might be able to find a spider in its unfurling buds. But she'd check the spring bulbs first.

When she got outside, Nora crouched just below the parlor window, where the golden heads of the daffodils bobbed to the tricolored cottage maid tulips. She set her sketchbook and pencils in the grass and poked her nose beneath a cluster of flowers. Spreading her hands between the stems, she peered into the shadowed space under the leaves, hoping for a glimpse of the black-and-yellow spiders.

With a sigh she sat back on her heels. No luck.

She set her pad in her lap. At least she could sketch the flowers before moving on to the cherry tree. It might take her mind off what Lucius planned to do to the journal.

For a few moments it worked. She lost herself in the form of a particularly jolly daffodil, the frilled rim framing its cup making it look like an old woman in a bonnet. Caught up in shadowing its petals, she startled when she heard her name.

"I don't want to lose her too, Lucius. Please." Fear strangled Mother's words.

"You wouldn't be losing her, my dear. But I believe Nora would do well with a change of scenery. Staying with my sister on Long Island may be just the thing for her."

Nora gripped her pencil. He wanted to send her away?

Lucius continued, "Martha could use the company. I'm sure she's been lonely since her husband took ill. She can hardly leave the house, and now that Nora is nearly done with school, it would give her something to do. Martha would be such a good example for Nora. She's well-respected in society and an excellent wife. Also, Mr. Primrose has family in the area, and he's planning to take a trip home in the next few weeks. Imagine if they made a match, darling. I'm sure Nora would warm to him if she gave him half a chance."

Nora stifled a groan. Again with Mr. Primrose. She had no desire to meet him and even less to "make a match" with someone of her stepfather's choosing.

"Lucius," Mother said, "I'm not well, and she's such a joy to me. What would I do without her?"

Nora leaned forward, tilting her ear closer to the window. As much as Lucius despised her, he'd only ever treated her mother with love and concern.

There was a squeaking, as though someone had shifted on the settee. "It would only be for a year or so. I don't think my sister's husband will survive much longer."

Long enough to let you destroy the journal.

Though, in his defense, he more than likely didn't see it that way. Nora didn't think he purposely wanted to ruin the journal. But that would be the end result anyway, and she couldn't let that happen. She wouldn't let that happen.

And she wouldn't let him send her to his sister—whom Nora had only met twice before—on Long Island. Not when there was a possibility of winning a scholarship and continuing her education. She needed to do a research project over the summer. Possibly in India.

She stood, hugging her sketchbook and pencils to her chest. When her head crested the window, her mother gasped.

"Nora! Whatever are you doing out there?"

"I was drawing the flowers, Mother, and I heard your conversation. My intention wasn't to eavesdrop."

Lucius looked up from his seat beside Mother on the rosewood sofa, and Nora could see his doubt. "Why don't you come in here, and we can discuss this?"

She shook her head. "I don't think that's necessary. I'm not going to Long Island."

His nostrils flared, and her mother seemed to deflate. Nora didn't want to argue with him and upset her mother, but she also wasn't going to allow him to dictate her future and ruin her plans.

"My sister needs help," Lucius said.

"I think you should visit her. Take Mother. The change in scenery would be good for both of you."

His jaw clenched when she parroted his own words back to him.

She stepped closer to the window, careful not to crush the flowers, and gripped the sash with her free hand. "I have plans here, Lucius."

"What plans would those be?"

Nora took a deep breath. "I intend to return to Cornell to obtain my master's."

"How will you do that?" Lucius asked. "You have no money left."

Mother touched his hand, and Nora didn't miss how it settled him down. She wondered if her mother knew how much she affected him. Nora couldn't understand how none of her own reasoning ever made a dent in her stepfather's twisted logic, but her mother's soft touch instantly calmed him.

"Lucius," Mother said, "I'd be more than willing to pay for Nora's schooling. Alex would have approved."

His head whipped around. "You will not use your inheritance to pay for that. Not at Cornell, especially. I won't have you waste your money."

"It's hardly a waste." Mother offered Nora a wavering smile. "Nora is brilliant, and I want to see her succeed."

Warmth filled Nora's belly. Sometimes she wondered if her mother's love for her had diminished when she married Lucius. She appreciated her mother's willingness to support her, though she'd never ask her to pay for school. It was obvious Lucius didn't agree with his wife from the way he licked his lips and tapped his foot in a nervous staccato. In fact, he almost looked afraid.

"I won't need your money, Mother," Nora said, keeping her eyes on Lucius. "I plan to obtain a scholarship. As valedictorian, and with the possibility of an exciting research opportunity, there's a good chance I'll be considered."

Lucius stood and crossed the room. He wasn't a tall man, but his broad shoulders were imposing, and even Nora could admit he had presence. She forced herself not to shrink from him but instead kept her gaze steady.

"Let's make a deal," he said in a low voice. Too low for her mother to hear. "I won't say another word about you going to my sister's if you are awarded the scholarship. You can continue living here and attend school."

Nora narrowed her eyes. "But if I don't get it, you want me to go to Long Island, is that it?"

"Without complaint."

She looked at her mother, who watched them with fearful eyes, then back at her stepfather. His eyes glittered, and she knew he thought she would lose this bet.

But Nora never lost anything. Except her father. She wouldn't allow herself to lose again. And if she raised the stakes . . . "Okay. On one condition: when I graduate with my master's, you turn the journal over to me."

He gave a brittle laugh. "Why would I do that?"

"Because I love it, and you don't."

Lucius studied her, his dark eyes partially hidden beneath heavy lids. Nora clutched her hands into fists around her sketchbook. "I'll think about it. But either way, I want you to consider Mr. Primrose's attention. For your mother's sake."

She swallowed but didn't argue. She wouldn't risk him changing his mind. "I want your answer before graduation." She stepped away from the window. "No more talk about me going to Long Island, and the journal will be mine once I receive my master's."

"*If* you get the scholarship, Nora. *If* you graduate with a master's." The look in his eyes told her he didn't think she would. "And *if* I agree to your terms."

~~~

Nora picked her way through the waist-high grasses and overgrown brush. She could already hear the water of Cascadilla Creek crashing over the falls. The sound drew her forward and drowned out the conversation she'd had with Lucius earlier that day, which had bounced around her head like a grasshopper and left her with a dull ache at the base of her neck.

When she reached the creek, she dropped her rucksack and settled onto a sandstone outcropping, her legs dangling over the silty water.

She'd grown up coming to Cascadilla Falls. Had taken some of her first steps at the edge of the water, her father holding her fingers and tugging her back when she became too curious. Even after twenty-one years of visiting, she never grew tired of its beauty. Hemmed in by high shale walls, with the sound of the water cascading down the stepped rocks, the falls could have been miles from civilization. In actuality, it took ten minutes to walk there from Cornell University, and they offered Nora a place to disappear for a while.

Recent heavy rains had swollen the water tripping down the

gorge. Very much like the afternoon six years ago when she and her father had explored the area above where she sat now, looking for insects. The day he died, the falls had crashed over the rocks and made the stream that flowed past her as wide as a river.

Nora shook her head, releasing the morose thoughts. She dug through her bag and found a pillbox, then stood. She arched her back in a stretch as she crossed the uneven ground toward a thicket of densely packed shrubs.

She always found peace in the study of insects. Peace, joy, and hope. All those good things derived from creatures most people considered pests.

After a five-minute search, she found something worth watching. A black speckled Calligrapha beetle eating a chickweed leaf. She scooped it into the pillbox, snapped a leaf from its stem, and returned to sit beside her bag near the water. Crossing her legs, she spread her skirts over her knees, making a shelf.

"Here you go, little one." She spilled the beetle onto the leaf she'd placed on her lap. It scuttled around while Nora sat still so she didn't startle it into flight. Finding the leaf, it settled on top of it.

Satisfied it wouldn't fly away, she held her magnifying glass over it. It wasn't the most fascinating or exotic thing to watch, but something about its lumbering movements and waving antennae soothed her. Centered her.

"You have no thought beyond your next bite, friend." She smiled at her silliness, but it felt good to talk to someone, if only an insect. "You don't worry about your education, your family, your future . . ." She sobered. "Your past."

She rubbed at the sudden ache crawling up the back of her neck. At least she could massage away that pain.

"My father died here," she whispered, though there was no one around. No one but the beetles and trees and rocks to witness her confession. The rocks had already seen her father's death, though. Had been complicit in it.

She laid the magnifier over her captive, trapping it between her skirt and the glass, and then gazed at the falls. She could point out, even now, exactly where it happened. Where his body released its spirit.

The trees and grass rustled behind her, alerting her to someone's approach.

Looking over her shoulder, she caught a glimpse of a straw boater hat, and her stomach shot to her throat. She did not want to talk to *him* right now. Owen appeared anyway, heedless of her desires, carrying a thick book and a ratty blanket.

He stopped when he noticed her. "Oh."

"I can leave," she said and grabbed her rucksack.

He stepped forward. "No. Don't do that. There's enough room for both of us." He tucked his book under his arm and snapped the blanket open. It settled to the ground in a dingy, holey heap. He cast Nora a sheepish smile. "That didn't work out as I planned."

"Most things don't."

"Do you want to share my blanket?" he asked.

She raised a brow. "I'm not sure it's much cleaner than the ground."

"You're probably right. I've been using it since I started at the university—at least once or twice a week—when I visit different falls and gorges. I don't know that I've ever had it washed."

Nora eyed a crusty brown stain marring the edge of the blanket. She shuddered, then refocused on Owen. He chewed on his lip, and she saw the invitation for what it was—a peace offering. Setting aside her reservations over the stain's origins, she shifted onto the blanket.

"What do you do when you visit?" she asked.

He held up his book—*Twenty Thousand Leagues Under the Sea*—and said, "I read, mostly. Sometimes I think. But mostly I read because too much thinking is dull."

"I didn't take you for much of a reader."

"I love fiction. Adventure books of all sorts. *The Three Musketeers, Moby Dick, The Last of the Mohicans.* My father thinks they're a waste of time, much like entomology, but if I'm destined to live life safely behind the confines of a desk, I'd at least like to experience adventure vicariously."

Nora scooped the beetle onto her fingertip and poked at the sky. It lifted from her finger and sought its freedom in clumsy flight. "Is that what you want? Adventure?"

"I want to travel and discover new things. I want to experience everything this world has to offer."

"That sounds exhausting."

He laughed, and she was surprised to discover she enjoyed the sound of it. "I went to Europe before college, and it was . . . uninspired."

"Europe is uninspired? You sound jaded. And spoiled."

He nodded. "Oh, the museums and sights are all right. The food is wonderful. But everything was so orderly and . . . it's hard to explain." He held up his hands, palms facing each other. "It's like I was in this box, and everything was the way it was supposed to be. But I know outside that box"—he clenched his fists and quickly opened them, puffing air from between his lips—"the world is wild and unexpected. And I want to see it all."

The way he explained it, Nora could almost see herself traveling the world, living outside society's box.

But wasn't she already? A woman in a man's field. Maybe Ithaca wasn't the jungles of South America or the Arabian Desert, but it was uncharted territory. She could still be a pioneer.

"Your version of the future sounds risky," she said.

He leaned toward her, and she scooted back, his presence a bit too big, crowded on the blanket with her. Everything about Owen—his height, mannerisms, and dreams—was too big for her comfort.

The scent of licorice drifted toward her as he spoke. "What do you want?"

He looked so earnest—like a little boy—that Nora bit the inside of her cheek to keep from smiling. When the urge passed, she answered. "I want to get my master's, maybe become a professor, take control of my father's scientific journal."

"Your father's journal?"

"My stepfather, his partner, now runs it. But he's changing it."

"You don't like change?"

"Not this type. He's turning *The Journal of Eastern Flora and Fauna* into a commission publisher." She shuddered and wondered if she would ever get used to saying that. She hoped she didn't have to.

Owen stilled. "Your father was Alexander Shipley."

She blinked. "I thought that would have been obvious."

"I just never connected you with him. I met him when I accompanied my father on a visit to the university about seven years ago. But I didn't meet you until I started attending, so I didn't think . . ." His eyes widened, and he looked at the falls, though Nora could tell he tried not to.

"Yes, this is where he died." She picked up the novel from beside him and flipped through the pages. The words bled together. Owen touched her wrist, and she dropped the book, her eyes darting to his face.

"I'm sorry," he said.

She could tell he was. He didn't look embarrassed or uneasy. He didn't say the expected yet unhelpful platitudes most people relied on when they found out her father had died. *He's in a better place.* Yes, but he was there without her. *You won't feel this way forever.* Six years later, and it felt like forever. *At least your mother was able to remarry and give you another father.* Lucius would never be her father.

Owen didn't say any of those things, and she was grateful. He remained silent, letting her guide the conversation. She guided it in a different direction.

"So I guess your father doesn't support your dream of traveling the world and experiencing *real life.*"

"Not at all. Not that I've told him about it. He wouldn't understand."

"Can you do it without your father's approval?"

"I couldn't finance it. Not until I work for a few years, and then I'll be too far in to leave. Stuck in a fourth-floor office, reviewing contracts and meeting with lawyers and printers."

"You want to stay out of publishing, and I want to get in."

"You wouldn't want to if you had to shelve all of your dreams to follow those of someone else. Publishing isn't my dream. Law isn't my dream. My father thinks it doesn't matter, but I'm almost sure I'll shrivel into a husk if I have to do what he does every day for forty years." Owen glanced at her. "You think I'm exaggerating."

She shook her head, but she did think he was exaggerating. The life he faced didn't seem so bad.

"You don't know my father," he continued. "He's not supportive of anyone's desires but his own. When he wants something, he goes after it, even if what he wants ends up hurting someone else. And he works constantly. All day long. Every day. I hardly saw him growing up. I'm not made like that. God doesn't mean for me to do what my father does. I know it. I just don't know how I'm going to do what I am made for."

Nora couldn't hold back a sigh. "Owen, not many people have the opportunity to pursue their dreams. Life doesn't work that way. And to be honest, your life isn't that awful. Even if you have to sit behind a desk and do something you don't passionately love, at least you have the comfort of a career."

He picked up a jagged piece of shale and wedged his fingernail between the layers. The top layer chipped off, and he rubbed it between his fingers, grinding it into a smear of gray. Finally he spoke, still not looking at her. "I don't believe that."

"You believe most people have the opportunity and wherewithal to travel around the globe and live a grand adventure?"

"I don't believe most people want that anyway. But I do. Doesn't that mean something?"

She shook her head, unable to reconcile the brilliant university student who nearly beat her grades with this idealistic, irrational man. "It means you have dreams and desires bigger than society's allowance. You're not the only one."

He rose up onto his knees and grabbed her hands. Startled, she looked down at his fingers grasping hers, spreading disintegrated slate all over her skin. She hadn't held a man's hand since right before her father fell into the falls.

"It's not just an idle dream, Nora. I almost believe I'm *called* to it. I asked my father when I was fifteen if I could go to seminary and do mission work. He refused. But I still feel this . . . ache inside of me, telling me to go."

His voice grew louder as he spoke, ringing out so that Nora could almost imagine him traipsing down seashell-lined paths, calling out to the lost. Her pulse leapt, and she became acutely aware of his thumbs resting atop her knuckles.

She cleared her throat and extricated her hands from his. "Why are you telling me this?"

He sank back onto his heels, and his hands danced in his lap, as though it hurt him to remain still. "I don't want you to think I'm some loafer without any direction or motivation."

His words sent a wave of remorse through her. She *had* thought that. "It doesn't really matter, does it? Graduation is in a few days, and we won't see each other again. Who cares what I think of you?"

His hands paused their jig. "I care. I want you to think well of me."

For three years they'd skirted friendship, too focused on competition. Now he wanted her to like him? "Why?"

His lips tipped into a slight smile. A secretive smile. "Because, Peculiar, I think well of you."

Chapter Five

Even though Lucius had taken ownership of the library, Nora still thought of it as her father's room. Everything about it, from the long banks of windows—which her father had insisted on, though they weren't the style—now hidden behind fussy brocade and lace draperies, to the wood-paneled walls and tiled fireplace, reminded her of him.

She rarely entered it—the memories the room evoked were too painful—but she found herself unwilling to wait another moment without Lucius's word that he'd turn the journal over to her. She'd given him a week. That was plenty of time.

She rapped at the door, entering at Lucius's impatient, "Come in. Come in."

He set down his newspaper when she crossed the threshold and began tapping his fingertips against the polished surface of the desk. She nearly reconsidered her mission but raised her chin and strode across the room, the clicking of her heels giving way when she reached the plush carpet. Well, what used to be a plush carpet. Nora noticed its fraying edge and worn patches as she crossed it.

When she reached the desk, she pushed all thoughts of carpet and curtains from her mind and clenched her fists at her sides.

"Yes?" Lucius said after she stared at him for a moment.

"I wanted to talk with you about the journal."

He heaved a long-suffering sigh. "I haven't decided yet if I agree to your terms."

"I'd like you to know how much this means to me."

His fingers stopped their rat-a-tat on the desk, and he rested one hand on top of the other.

"The journal reminds me of my father. I'm his daughter in every way, and I believe I can keep it from folding while staying true to its origins as a publication that has garnered the respect of scientists and naturalists."

Nora had always thought Lucius a cold man, and his eyes seemed to reflect his frigidity, but at the mention of her father, the chill thawed and the tight corners of his lips softened. "It reminds me of him, as well, and I want to honor him with it. I know that's hard for you to believe, but he was my closest friend." His chair creaked beneath his weight when he leaned back against it. "But do you really think you will be able to run a periodical? You have no idea how much work is involved. You are only a young girl. And despite your headstrong ways, I do know what's best. Marriage and motherhood never made any woman unhappy."

Her spine stiffened, and a vise gripped her head. She rubbed her temples, trying to ease the weight of resentment that took residence beneath her scalp.

His voice dipped lower and became velvety. "Will your husband want you spending your time running a periodical? What about when you have children?"

Nora's knees weakened. "I will gladly live my life without the joy of family if it means I can honor my father's memory and pursue the work he set out to accomplish. He meant it to be a place where rigorous scientific work could be shared. You're changing it, and I don't understand why. Why would you do that to his memory?"

Lucius stared past her, his eyes going toward the open door, which framed the stairs leading to the bedrooms. "I've done everything I can to take care of your father's family. I've loved your mother and tried to guide you, though you make that challenging. I've maintained his home and supported his dream of making the journal successful. I've been around longer than you, and I know how the world works. It's not easy for a woman to make it in a man's world. Why won't you take my advice?"

She swallowed and backed up a step. Away from his vulnerability, which left her feeling as though the world had tilted on its axis. Away from his demands that she bow to expectation and deny her dream. "I don't want to go to Long Island after graduation. I want to get this scholarship and continue my education. I want the journal."

His eyes darted toward her, and she felt like an insect, trapped beneath his critical gaze. "Your mother isn't strong. She wants to see you wed and taken care of."

Nora clasped her hands behind her back, hiding the nervous picking of her cuticles. She avoided his gaze, which seemed to pierce her exterior like a mounting pin. After her father's death, Mother's health had taken a downward turn that she'd never recovered from. And no amount of Nora's love or attention could fix that. Nora could shield her mother from worry and ugliness, but, in truth, Nora knew she was culpable.

She shook off the traitorous thoughts. "I need an answer, Lucius. If I'm offered the scholarship, will you give me the journal? I agree to your terms. I will not fuss if I have to go to Long Island. And I'm willing to *meet* Mr. Primrose. Invite him to my graduation dinner. I'm trying to meet you halfway."

Lucius stared at her for a moment before giving a tight nod. "Fine. I don't want it said that I wasn't fair to you. I still think it would be a mistake for you to have the journal, but if you prove yourself by obtaining an advanced degree, then I guess I'll have no reason not to give it to you." He turned his attention to the ledger lying open on his desk.

Dismissed, Nora backed from the room, knowing she had to do everything in her power to make sure she was offered the scholarship. Even if that meant joining Professor Comstock's friend in India. Because losing the journal didn't just mean going to Long Island. It meant losing the only way she could make everything up to her father.

~

Nora preferred pencil to watercolor. She liked the precise control it allowed her, creating thick or thin lines, shading, feathering, outlining. Watercolors bled and often disobeyed dictates, but Anna Comstock told Nora she should practice using the medium since she so often neglected it.

Nora swirled her brush over the moistened magenta cake and traced the green wings of the Luna moth she was working on.

Anna lifted her head from her canvas and inspected Nora's. "Nicely done. I know watercolors aren't your favorite, but you work so well with them."

Nora stepped back from her work, glancing from the mounted moth on the table between them to her painting. "It's tolerable."

Anna laughed. "You're too hard on yourself. After only a few years of instruction, you've surpassed my ability. I'm not sure why we continue to meet. I can't teach you anything else."

"Because I value our friendship and enjoy your company. Painting or drawing with you in your garden gives me great joy."

Although Anna was only a decade older, she bestowed a maternal smile on Nora. "I'll have Katie bring us some refreshment. It must be nearing three." She disappeared into the house through the back door, and Nora closed her paint box.

When Anna returned, they settled into a pair of wicker chairs nestled beneath the maple tree at the corner of the garden. Katie, the Comstocks' Irish maid, tripped across the yard, carrying a tray. She set it on the iron table between them, poured steaming cups of tea, then, with a clumsy curtsy, skipped away.

Anna shook her head and gave a little sigh. "She's an odd girl, but she has such a lively outlook."

"I'd love to bottle some of her joy and release it at home. Maybe it would drive away some of the tension."

Anna clucked her tongue in sympathy. "I'm sorry. Lucius is a difficult man."

"Very unlike Father. Our house was a place of happiness when he was alive. I miss him, but perhaps I miss that most. He made life pleasurable and interesting."

"You mustn't allow the atmosphere of your home to decide how you respond to life. That will make you miserable. You may already know that Mr. Comstock's childhood was anything but comfortable and joyous. He decided long ago that he, not his circumstances, would be master of his own happiness."

Nora lifted her teacup and sipped. It was true—she did occasionally surrender to melancholy. When she compared her life now to before her father's passing, she couldn't help but notice the broad contrast. If—when—she was awarded the scholarship, maybe she'd move onto campus. She could stay with Rose and Bitsy at Sage Hall. Rose had another year of school, and Bitsy planned to obtain her master's degree, thanks to her aunt's largesse.

Nora set down her cup and plucked a cherry from the dish on the tray. She enjoyed its tart sweetness as she considered living among the one hundred female students in Sage Hall. It would be a drastic measure, leaving her home to live only a few blocks away. She wasn't sure she could convince her mother it was a good idea. What reason could she give?

She shook her head. She couldn't avoid conflict if she were to be master of her own happiness, as Professor Comstock had done. She'd just tell her mother it was what she wanted. That would have to be enough.

Satisfied, Nora smiled at Anna, who fiddled with her hair, tucking a lock of it behind her ear. It kept falling forward, though. "I'm growing it out," Anna said.

"I see. It looks nice." Anna had kept her hair in a short bob after losing it during an illness a few years earlier. "Why aren't you keeping it short anymore?"

Anna's eyes crinkled at the corners. "Mr. Comstock suggested one of us should have long hair. Either him or me. I thought growing out my hair would be a much less painful process than if he grew out his." She fingered the ends and released a wistful sigh. "I do like it short. It's so easy to care for. But long hair is a sacrifice I'm willing to make for Mr. Comstock. He asks for so little."

"You don't think short hair is too masculine?"

"Of course not." Anna's face twisted into a scowl. "Believing our hair makes us feminine is absurd. Just like believing an interest in nature makes us masculine. Mr. Comstock would say all people—women included—are created in the image of God, and our interest in nature, the living world around us, is divine."

"Do you think so?"

Anna gave a firm nod. "Your father thought so too. Why, he encouraged your love of insects, didn't he?"

"He did." Nora couldn't remember a time he wasn't taking her on expeditions through the gorges and woods, intent on allowing her the discovery of all the interesting families of insects at work—spinning, flying, weaving, mating, growing, changing. When they stumbled upon some flying or creeping creature, Nora would grow quiet as she watched it. Her father would stand beside her, anticipation setting his hands twisting and waving—much the way Owen's did, now that she thought of it.

Anna reached across the table and cupped Nora's cheek. "You are who you are for a reason. You can ignore it, but that would be no way to chase happiness, would it?"

Nora leaned into Anna's touch. "I believe I'd be very unhappy, indeed, if I neglected my work. Or worried overmuch about my hair." She blinked, then sat up straight against the cool seat. Her words mimicked Owen's. She had censured him when he spoke of his desire to travel and explore, but she knew that if she ignored her aspirations, she'd be just as unhappy as he would be working for his father's publishing company or a law firm. She pressed her hand against the center of her chest where a small lump had formed. She should apologize to him.

"Are you all right?" Concern colored Anna's words.

"Yes. I just recalled something I need to do at graduation this afternoon." Nora took another sip of tea, then stood. "Will you be there?"

Anna followed Nora back to their easels. "Of course. I'm looking forward to hearing your speech—Cornell's first female valedictorian. I'm proud of you."

Nora smiled before turning to study the Luna moth on the table. It was a lovely green, the color of limes. "It's a shame we have to kill them."

Anna glanced at the moth. "Sometimes one dream needs to die before another can be realized. He wouldn't have lived much longer anyway, and his death benefits science more than anything else he could have done."

Just as Nora lifted her brush from the easel, the back gate smacked open. "Miss Nora!"

Nora whirled and saw Alice running across the yard, her white apron strings flying behind her. Nora's heart slammed into her ribs. She dropped her brush and paints and flew to Alice, who met her, huffing out wheezing breaths.

"Miss Nora, your mother had a terrible spell. She fell down the stairs, and Mr. Ward couldn't wake her. The doctor's been sent for, but you must come home."

⁓

Nora dashed into the house, grabbed fistfuls of her skirt, and took the stairs two at a time.

Lucius paced outside her mother's bedroom door. He stopped when he saw her, scrubbed his hands through his salt-and-pepper hair, and sighed. "I couldn't stop her fall, Nora. I heard her cry out, then saw her tumble, but I didn't make it in time. I tried. I swear."

Nora pressed her back against the wall, horrified by the tears in his eyes. They signified a much worse situation than she'd expected.

"The doctor is with her now," Lucius said. He lifted his hand toward the door, then dropped it. "She was so pale."

A tremble began in Nora's legs, spreading up her body until she shook like a spider web caught in a hurricane. She made her way to the oak chair outside her mother's room and sank into it. She avoided looking at Lucius, whose frenzied pacing made her think the worst.

A moment later, Dr. Johnson slipped from the room, sporting a black medical bag and a grim expression. Nora jumped to her feet, and both she and Lucius converged on him.

"She will be fine, I believe," the doctor said, "with adequate rest. She cracked a rib in the fall, but she's lucky that was all. More disturbing is the reason she fell."

Nora held her breath captive, trapping it between her chest and throat. Willing it to stay put until the doctor told her something that would set it free in an exhale of relief.

"She's been weak since she lost the baby after Nora, but the fainting spells have increased. They alarm me. Her blood pressure is low, her heart rate fast." Dr. Johnson shook his head. "She's not a healthy woman. I want her abed for a week at least. Feed her lots of rich broths, puddings, and fresh milk. And, above all, keep her calm. Don't allow her to become stressed."

Nora and Lucius nodded in unison. "I'll see you out," Lucius told the doctor. "Nora, please go sit with your mother."

When they descended the stairs, Nora crept into her mother's dark room and perched on the edge of her bed where she slept, her long lashes resting on pale cheeks. Nora brushed wispy hair from her mother's brow. She looked so small. Nora realized with a start that she'd stopped looking up at her mother years ago, before her father had died. Her mother *was* small. And frail. She'd always been sickly. So unlike Nora.

Lydia's lids fluttered, and she blinked before focusing on Nora. "Oh, darling."

"Mother, are you feeling all right?"

She smiled. "I'm better now that you're here."

Nora slipped to the floor and rested her head on her mother's chest. "I'm so sorry I wasn't here."

"What could you have done? Lucius wasn't even able to help me. It happened so quickly." Her hand grazed Nora's shoulder before resting back on the bed. "I'm glad you're home, though. I do so rely on you."

Nora's stomach clenched, all thoughts of moving into Sage Hall extinguished at her mother's words. What had she been thinking? She couldn't leave her mother with only Lucius to care for her. And India! What a ridiculous notion. She'd just have to make do with the research trip to Illinois Professor Comstock would be leading this summer. Perhaps Owen wouldn't be able to go to India either.

The clock downstairs struck the hour, reminding Nora that she had to get ready for graduation. She stood to go to her room to prepare for the moment she'd been working toward for three years. The moment that made all the demeaning insults and patronizing comments worth it. The moment she'd dreamed of with her father as they trekked over Ithaca's hills.

The moment she would never get back.

But her mother gave Nora's hand a weak squeeze, and a sigh of contentment whispered from her lips. "Must you leave so soon? I love when you're near."

Nora sank back onto the cushions and raised her free hand to her throat, careful to conceal the movement from her mother. A lump had settled there, and she eased it free with her fingers. She couldn't miss her graduation.

She couldn't leave.

"I'll stay," she whispered. "As long as you need me to."

Owen, as salutatorian, would have to give the address while Nora sat in a dark bedroom, trapped beneath her mother's fine-boned hand.

A delivery boy stood on the front step, a box in his outstretched hands. "Got a package at the post office for you, miss."

Nora glanced in the mirror and tucked a lock of hair back into her chignon, then reached for her reticule, which hung from the hall tree. She dug through it, locating a penny, and exchanged it for her package. Seeing the return address, she squealed and sat on the front porch swing.

Before she could pull at the jute string holding the box closed, Owen ambled up the walk, his hands shoved deep within his pockets.

"Professor Comstock sent me to see if you want to come to a picnic with the class."

Nora's stomach growled, and she realized she hadn't eaten today. She'd skipped breakfast in favor of reading to her mother, who still, nearly a week later, remained confined to her bed. But Lucius sat with her now, and Nora hadn't left the house since her mother's fall. Nesting birds chirped in the oak tree at the corner of the yard, and the sun, though high and bright, shone through a blanket of white clouds. It was a lovely day for a picnic, and she needed to get away from the house for a while.

"I'd love to." Excitement about her delivery made her feel generous, and she patted the seat beside her. "Sit with me a moment and see what Mrs. Martín sent me. She is a respected entomologist and an expert on *Lepidoptera*, specifically moths. She's been working on a catalogue of *Tortricidae* for over a decade, and she occasionally sends me a specimen she believes I'll find interesting." She opened the box, finding a folded note and a smaller box tucked inside. She opened the note and read,

"'Dearest Nora, this is the *Amata huebneri,* or the wasp moth. It is a Batesian mimic I've only found a few times. I have never seen the larva.'"

Nora glanced at Owen and mirrored his broad smile. She pulled the smaller box into her lap and set the other near her feet. With gentle movements, she pried off the top and pulled the tissue-thin paper away. "Oh!"

Nestled inside sat a moth that more resembled a child's fanciful drawing than an actual creature. Fuzzy dark blue and orange stripes marched down its abdomen, and its black wings were peppered with white spots.

Owen poked at it. "Incredible. I'll never cease to be amazed by the variety in the insect world."

"On that we agree." She closed the box and stood. "I'll let my mother know I'm leaving."

When she rejoined him a few minutes later, Owen led the way off the porch.

"Where are we headed?" she asked. She paused at the gate, securing a serviceable hat to her head with a pin. Owen offered to take her shawl, which he draped over his arm.

"Professor Comstock's. They've taken the liberty of hosting the entomology graduating class. No one has seen you in a week. And you missed graduation."

"My mother took ill. I've been staying close to her."

"I'm sorry. Will she be all right?"

"She's never been strong, but she's been having dizzy spells lately. This time she took a tumble down the stairs. She'll recover, but I'm not sure if this is going to progress. . . ." Nora didn't like the direction her confession had taken. She couldn't lose her mother, the only person left in her small family. "Will you be returning home soon?"

To Owen's credit, he allowed her to change the topic. "Next week, unless I decide to go to India." He smirked. "I'll be back, though, to give my lecture, and I'm sure I'll end up staying . . . after they offer me the scholarship."

She laughed. "It's unlikely you'll need to stay. But we'll all miss you."

"If I don't come back, I'll miss Ithaca. I've enjoyed living here."

"Thinking about giving up your vagabond ways and settling here?" She meant to tease him, but his expression turned serious, a sight she wasn't used to.

"If I ever have the chance to travel and I grow tired of it, I would consider settling here. I love Ithaca. The waterfalls and gorges. The constant growing and flexing. The people."

Nora understood his sentiment. She hadn't traveled much, but she imagined there weren't many places like her hometown. Everything she could possibly want perched on the edge of the Finger Lakes. Ever since Professor Comstock had brought up the possibility of research in India, though, she'd begun to imagine the insects she could study in their natural habitat. Sliding mounted or dissected pieces beneath a microscope surely couldn't compare to in-person observation.

She huffed. Ridiculous. She couldn't leave her mother. And fanciful daydreams didn't make a thing practical. Or even possible.

"Here we are." Owen opened the Comstocks' gate and allowed her to precede him around the house to the backyard.

Scattered around the lawn, twenty students sat on blankets in groups. Professor Comstock held court in a wicker chair while Anna and Katie passed out glasses of lemonade.

"Our valedictorian has arrived!"

Professor Comstock waved Nora over, and the knot of students at his feet opened to welcome her. She settled on the blanket, and when Owen sat beside her, she scooted over a few inches. He seemed to have no concept of personal space. She didn't think he took up more room than necessary on purpose, but it made her uncomfortable, all the same.

"We're talking about our plans now that school is over," Thomas Nichols said. "I've secured a position with a textbook company in Boston. I heard you're both trying for the scholarship."

Curtis Wiggs, who sat beside him, nudged Thomas in the ribs and guffawed.

Professor Comstock scowled at them. "I believe you're placing bets on who receives it."

"It's only a bit of sport, Professor. No harm done." A silly grin tugged at Thomas's thin lips when he looked at her. "Odds are on you, Nora."

Owen snorted beside her, and she ignored him, pleased they considered her the top choice. Wouldn't that irritate Lucius.

Thomas continued to gaze at her until Professor Comstock coughed, breaking whatever spell had captivated him. Thomas looked at Owen. "We all know it's going to be one of you two."

"If I don't come back, I guess I'm going to law school. That's my father's plan for me," Owen said. He didn't mention anything about travel or adventure.

"*When* the scholarship is mine," Nora said, "I plan to obtain my master's, then maybe go into teaching. I might even teach at Cornell."

"Do you think they'll hire a female teacher, Professor?" Thomas asked.

"One day. Cornell has been inclusive since its beginning. I imagine it will happen sooner than later." The professor regarded Nora, his forehead puckered and his heavy mustache drooping low beneath his frown. "I'm not sure if you should be the one to break that barrier, though, my dear girl."

Nora's mouth fell open. Heat climbed her neck when she realized the entire group had grown quiet and was sending furtive glances in her direction. Owen shifted beside her, closing the gap between them, and his fingers brushed her hand. She withdrew, drawing in tightly. How could Professor Comstock be so unkind? He'd been a reliable source of encouragement and affirmation since her father's death.

His gaze softened. "Don't be upset. I only meant that I don't believe teaching to be a good fit for your skills."

"But my father was a teacher."

"And an excellent one. But you . . . I believe you will shine elsewhere."

She swallowed against the lump in her throat. "Where?"

"You need time, Nora. And space. Time to explore and discover and study. Space to think, draw, and create. Teaching would stifle your natural gifts."

Nora drew her brows together and shook her head. He made her sound like Owen!

When Anna approached and pointed out the table laden with a spread of sandwiches, pickles, fruit, and cakes, Nora leapt to her feet, eager to escape the awkward discussion. The pitying looks of the others. Owen's too-close and physical sympathy. As she filled a plate with food she knew she wouldn't be able to eat, she kept her head tucked, not wanting to meet anyone's eyes.

Settling in the bower of a weeping willow, she picked at her food, hardly tasting anything. Too soon, the branches parted, and Owen joined her.

She pursed her lips and stiffened when he sat on the ground beside her.

"You look so sour, Nora. I'm sure he didn't mean anything by it. I think you'd be excellent at anything you chose to do."

"It's okay that I'm upset. You don't have to fix it." She set her plate on the ground and sighed.

He nodded. They looked at each other, and Nora wondered if she should ask him to leave. She wanted to be alone with her disappointment and hurt.

He must have seen it on her face, because he stood. "I guess I'll go."

Before he could, though, Professor Comstock stepped through the branches. Nora stifled a groan. How could she process her thoughts surrounded by chatty men?

"I'm glad you're both"—Professor Comstock looked around the hideaway, delight apparent in his toothy grin—"in here. This is very nice. I've never been under this tree."

Nora pressed a hand to her head while the men discussed

the merits of what was supposed to be her quiet refuge from them. Finally they noticed her and grew quiet.

Professor Comstock cleared his throat. "Yes, well, what I wanted to say, Nora, is that I hate to see you isolate your talent to our fair—but tiny—city. I expect you to do great things in our field, and I don't believe you can do them stuck here."

"Isn't becoming the first female professor at Cornell a great enough thing?" Nora asked.

He nodded. "I suppose, but there are greater things waiting for you. Do you recall discussing the possibility of India?"

"I don't recall discussing the *possibility* of it." A cheer went up from the students gathered outside their tree, shouts of "Ice cream!" drawing Owen's attention for a moment. Nora stood and brushed off her skirt. "I considered it, but after Mother fell, I realized I'm needed at home. With her."

Professor Comstock rubbed his hands together. "Frederic has lost most of his team to dysentery. He's desperate for help, and he's exhausted his pool of entomologists willing to go. He needs to rely on students, and he trusts my judgment. This is a once-in-a-lifetime opportunity for both of you." He bounced on the balls of his feet and clapped his hands. "You couldn't do any better. Just think, in a month you could be collecting your own exotic insects to send back to me."

Her refuge beneath the tree had grown too tight, bursting with the professor's excitement and plans. Nora crept toward the swaying curtain of leafy branches. "I plan to join your short trip to Illinois next month with the seniors. It will be enough. And I'd only have to be away from Mother for a couple weeks."

Professor Comstock shook his head. "Imagine the opportunity. You'd be in India, working with an experienced field researcher. You might even have the opportunity to discover a new species. What do you think that will do for your chances of being offered the scholarship? The position is only six months long, Nora, but he needs you right away." Using his arm, he swept the drooping branches aside. "Think about it." He left.

Owen looked from Nora to where Professor Comstock had disappeared and back to Nora again. His eyes glinted, and a slow grin spread across his face. "I don't have to think about it," he said. "I'm going."

Nora couldn't help but feel he had just issued a challenge.

Chapter Six

Rose and Bitsy sat, heads together, at the wrought-iron table beneath the arbor in Nora's backyard. They made a pretty picture—Rose with her blond hair piled into curls beneath a jaunty feathered hat, and Bitsy, not as conventionally pretty as Rose, but with a magnetism that drew people to her. As Nora moved closer, they pulled apart and stared at her with wide eyes. Rose's even looked wet.

"Whatever is the matter?" Nora asked, rushing to her friend's side. She tugged a stool around toward Rose, sat down, and took her friend's hand. "Why are you both here? Has something happened?"

"Oh, Nora!" Rose cried. "Owen told us about India. Are you leaving?"

"Let her explain before you jump to conclusions." Bitsy arched a brow, then turned to Nora. "India! Just imagine. I had an uncle who was in India with the military. He married an Indian woman, and they had half a dozen children. My family never recovered." Her sardonic smile told Nora that she was rather proud of her family member's scandalous behavior.

"I can hardly go to India," Nora said. "Not with Mother's illness."

"Your mother has Lucius." Bitsy tipped her head. "She's not your responsibility."

Rose gasped. "That's so heartless. Of course Nora feels responsible for her mother. She would never be so selfish."

"Oh, come now." Bitsy twirled the pearls circling her wrist. "You must sacrifice your own desires and allow Nora to follow her path."

Rose pouted. "It's not selfish to want Nora to remain in Ithaca, safe and surrounded by loved ones." She withdrew her hand from Nora's and clasped hers together at her chest. "I promise, Nora, I just want you to be safe. I'm not being selfish."

"Of course not," Nora said. She shot a warning look at Bitsy, who only shrugged a delicate shoulder. "Besides, I'm *not* going to India."

"Owen is going," Bitsy said with a twist of her expressive lips.

Owen had made that clear right after Professor Comstock reminded them about the opportunity. He'd rather travel than work for his father over the summer. It fit with his hoped-for adventures. He probably dreamt in Hindi. Or Mandarin or Polish or Russian. Nora felt certain he dreamt of vibrant birds resting in banana trees and sari-clad women smelling of sandalwood. Her face burned.

"Why should it matter if Owen goes?" she asked.

Bitsy shifted her weight toward the front of her chair and leaned against the backrest, one arm draped over it in affected indifference. "I'm sure it won't matter at all to the trustees when they are ready to choose a scholarship recipient." She tilted her head. "How will it look when they see Owen went to India . . . and you pursued economic entomology in Illinois's cornfields?"

Nora stared at her. Was that what Bitsy really thought? That the scholarship could rest on who had the most exciting summer? No, not that. But they would, as Professor Comstock said, look at who had invested the most time and energy in proving their dedication to the science.

Nora buried her head in her hands, and Rose patted her back. "It'll be okay," Rose said. "You don't *have* to get your master's. Why, you could get married!"

Bitsy chuckled. "For Nora, that's not the promise of utopia it is for you. Besides, she's married to her insects. And nothing would satisfy her greater than thwarting Lucius's plans for a good match."

Nora crossed her arms and narrowed her eyes. "It has nothing to do with Lucius. I just can't think of anything better than insects to commit myself to."

And she would prove it to the scholarship committee, with or without a trip to India.

On her way out the door the next day, Nora peeked into her mother's room. Lydia lounged on the floral chaise near the window, a walnut lap desk perched atop her skirt. Sunlight spilled over her, and Nora thought she looked almost healthy.

"Mother, I'm heading over to the laboratory. Do you need anything?"

"I'm quite well. See that Alice comes up before you leave. I need to plan the menu for your dinner." Her expression became animated, and she clapped her hands together. "Oh, Nora, Lucius told me you've conceded to allow Mr. Primrose to join us. I'm so glad. Lucius is positive you'll like him."

Nora swallowed a groan. She'd forgotten about the dinner and Mr. Primrose. She wouldn't dream of asking to cancel the party in honor of her graduation—Mother might grow stronger with the joy of planning it—but she couldn't think of anything she'd rather do less than make polite conversation with her stepfather's friends and pretend to be satisfied with the thought of settling down and marrying.

"I will let Alice know." Nora did as her mother asked and then set off for the school.

When she reached the cemetery, she pushed open the rusting gate and picked her way across the grass. She grimaced as she skirted a newly dug grave, the dirt packed down in a mound. Guilt pricked her conscience. She hated that the quickest route from town to school cut through the graveyard, but it was what all the students did. She avoided looking in the direction of her father's Gothic headstone, increasing her pace as she passed the gravel path that led to it. She never visited his grave. She couldn't. Couldn't imagine him, so full of vigor and life, moldering in a casket beneath the ground.

Head down lest she accidentally see the headstone, she hurried toward the road and bumped into someone standing just outside the gate. "I'm so sorry."

Owen turned and blinked down at her with a crooked grin that turned shy. "Fancy running into you. Or rather, you running into me?"

Nora glanced back at the graveyard and considered running for real. Hiding behind one of the stones. Climbing the oak tree and disappearing within its branches. Of course, she'd probably fall out.

When she looked back at him, his smile had slipped, and she saw exhaustion in the tightness around his eyes and the deep crevice between his brows. His normally parted and pomaded hair fell forward into his face as though he hadn't taken the time to properly see to his morning toilette. With a flick of his wrist, he swept back his incorrigible cowlick, then stuck his hands into the pockets of his gray plaid trousers.

"I'm going to see Professor Comstock," he said, a foreign gravity in his tone.

"Why?"

"I need to discuss the position in India with him. I'd like more details. I spoke with my father yesterday." He wagged his brows, but the gesture seemed false. "He's not pleased." A carriage rolled by, and Owen guided her to the side of the street, away from the churning dust and spray of pebbles. "I want to catch him before he leaves for lunch. Walk with me."

He took long strides, and Nora trotted after him. A block later she was puffing heavy breaths.

He glanced at her and slowed. "I'm sorry," he said. "I'm excited to tell Professor Comstock my plans."

"What did your father say when you told him your intention to go to India?"

Owen stared ahead, his jaw working. "He said he would not finance it, which doesn't matter, as I imagine I'll be fine on my stipend. And, of course, I won't have to cover travel expenses. Then he told me he expected I would fail, and when I did, to come home so he could put me to work before I head off to law school in the fall." He gave her a sad smile. "Maybe if I hadn't been shown up by a female, I could have become valedictorian and won his approval."

Nora stepped nearer to him, closing the gap. They weren't so different after all. She touched his arm and offered him a small smile, a peace offering. "I know how impossible it is to win someone's approval when their mind is closed to it. Even being top of your class wouldn't help."

Owen stopped at the foot of the steps when they reached White Hall. "Thanks for walking with me."

She preceded him up the stairs and into the building. "I'm actually headed toward the lab too."

He jogged after her. "Have you made a decision about India?"

Nora nodded.

"I hope you've decided to join."

"Really?"

"Of course. You're the smartest student at Cornell. Talented and adventurous."

She looked away, her face flushed. Owen, with his love of travel and interest in novel experiences, thought she was adventurous? She knew he meant it as the highest compliment. He offered his elbow as they climbed to the third floor, and her heart tripped when she tucked her hand into his arm.

Professor Comstock wasn't in the laboratory, but they found him in his cluttered office next door. With his legs stretched out, feet resting on his desk, the professor slept in his chair. His arms dangled from his sides, and he snuffled, causing his head to loll off the headrest.

Owen chuckled. This wasn't the first time Professor Comstock had fallen asleep while working. Nora ignored the urge to stay in the doorway, her fingers trembling atop Owen's coat sleeve. Remain in the glow of his praise and presence.

You're being absurd.

She dropped her hand from Owen's arm, shook it as though trying to release the memory of his warmth imprinted on her palm, and picked her way over crates and towers of books. She jostled the professor's shoulder. "Professor."

He startled awake and blinked owlishly. The fog in his gaze parted, and he gave her a slow smile. "Nora. What a delight."

Owen stepped into view. "We've come to talk with you about India."

Professor Comstock swept his legs from the table. "Excellent. Come, have a seat. Tell me what you've decided."

They cleared stacks of paper from the green upholstered club chairs and sat.

"I'm going to take you up on the offer. I have no doubts," Owen said in a rush. He leaned back against the chair, and Nora thought he looked relieved.

The delight in Professor Comstock's eyes was unmistakable. "Wonderful choice, Owen. This is an opportunity not many your age have. I expect you'll learn and grow while there." He turned to Nora, expectation written all over his face.

She hated to disappoint him. "I'm sorry, but I must decline. I can't leave my mother."

Professor Comstock crossed his foot over his knee and pressed his mouth against his steepled hands. "Are you sure? There likely won't be another opportunity like this one."

She fiddled with her cicada pin. Tension ran up the back of her neck—a wave of pain that crested the top of her head and forced her eyes closed. She knew not going might mean losing any chance of being offered the scholarship, especially when Owen was going. And losing the scholarship meant losing the journal. But her mother's pale face and Dr. Johnson's worried expression forced her back straight. She couldn't allow the fear of missing out to dissuade her from her duty. She'd just have to figure out a different way to ensure she topped Owen's summer.

She opened her eyes. "My mother is my first priority."

"She's married. She's your stepfather's first priority," Owen said, sounding so much like Bitsy that Nora wouldn't be surprised if they'd discussed it.

"I also don't care to traipse across the world. I have no desire to escape home. I'm happy here. I don't need adventure to fill my life with meaning."

She'd only wanted to convince herself—try to forget the daydreams she'd been having of wearing white linen, pushing through dark forests and studying some ancient, undiscovered insect. But Owen drew back as though he'd been slapped, and Nora saw the hurt in his eyes.

Professor Comstock's mellow voice filled the silence, drawing attention away from her hastily spoken words. "Nora, I've known you a long time."

"Since I was a child."

"In all of that time, I've never known you to be anything but an adventurer. Always seeking out another thrill. Maybe not a *physical* thrill, but knowledge. You've always been insatiably hungry for knowledge. You thrill at the discovery. For you to act the homebody comes across as inauthentic."

And I learned my lesson a long time ago, Professor. Sometimes the quest for knowledge could be just as dangerous as risky behavior.

The professor shook his head. "I agree with Owen. Don't let your dedication to your mother keep you from pursuing your own path. She is a married woman and, as such, is Lucius's responsibility. You have a rare gift. It would be a shame to bury it."

Owen stood and shook the professor's hand. "Thank you for offering me this chance, sir."

Nora watched as he left the room with stiff steps, his back straight. He stopped at the door and offered them a wooden smile before disappearing.

"That was in poor form." Professor Comstock's voice held compassion even though his words battered her conscience.

Nora couldn't meet his gaze. How embarrassing that he'd witnessed her thoughtlessness. His opinion of her meant the world to her, more than anyone's, except maybe Anna's.

"Owen was only trying to help you see past your ill-placed sacrifice. He meant no harm."

"I know." Her whisper barely escaped her lips. "I will apologize."

He regarded her with a sad expression, his eyes drooping along with his mustache. "I won't send a telegram until Monday. I can't wait too long because my associate hopes to receive help by the beginning of July. If you don't tell me otherwise, I will ask another student to take your place."

She nodded and left the office, feeling his gaze on her as she walked away. As she passed the laboratory, she saw Owen standing at the insect cabinet, a few drawers pulled out.

She stopped. "Owen?"

He turned and leaned against the cabinet, his feet crossed at the ankles, his arms across his chest. If she hadn't seen his wounded expression after she insulted him, she would assume his stance channeled anger or arrogance. But now she knew better, and she wondered how many times her impulsive words had caused him to look like that. How many times she ascribed character flaws to him that weren't really his.

She skirted the tables and drew close to him. So close she could see the circle of cognac rimming his pupils, bleeding into the blue pierced with silver. She'd never noticed how interesting his eyes were. She turned from him and ran her fingers along the drawers of the cabinet. There. She pulled the drawer open to reveal a collection of South American butterflies resting inside glass cases.

"Look," she said, waving him closer.

He peered over her shoulder, giving her another glimpse of his extraordinary eyes. She pointed to the blue morpho. *Morpho achilles*. "Your eyes, in *Nymphalidae* form."

He smiled at her, the silver in his irises shining and streaking like silverfish.

"I'm sorry," she said.

"I forgive you, Percipient." He looked like he was about to say something else, but he wavered, his face drawn into a mask of indecision.

"I won't insult you again, Owen. Please tell me what you're thinking."

When he bit his lower lip, she wondered how a man, all angles and planes, could have such a soft mouth. He grasped her elbows. Had any other person as tall and commanding as Owen done the same thing, she would have been afraid. Intimidated. But Owen made the gesture seem almost protective.

And he looked so earnest. "I hope you consider how this trip could impact your career. If you go to India and make a discovery, it could guarantee you the scholarship. Maybe even attention from the scientific community."

Nora laughed. "What type of discovery?"

"I don't know, but you could make one. You . . . you could be the next Amelia Phelps. Be elected fellow to the American Association for the Advancement of Science. Lecture, teach, discover, write. There are so many incredible female scientists who have shaped our field over the last century. You belong with them."

The fervency in his voice set off a spark in her belly she knew could be fanned into something that might burn her. Or it could set ablaze a new course.

"I'm just telling you," he said, bending so close that she could see the silverfish swimming, "that this could be the thing that makes all of your dreams come together. Don't allow another's expectations to hinder you."

He squeezed her arms, then released her and trotted from the room as though pursued by the passion in his words.

Nora blinked at the empty space he'd filled, then looked back at the blue morpho. Go to India? Leave everything familiar for the unknown. For the sticky heat of the tropics. For the possibility of scientific discovery.

The blue morpho's wings shimmered in the sunlight piercing through the window, and Nora wondered what Owen's eyes would look like beneath an Indian moon.

Chapter Seven

"Oh, darling, you look beautiful!"

Nora took her mother's outstretched hands and allowed herself to be twirled. Lydia's eyes were bright, and her cheeks were pink for the first time since her fall. Nora didn't have the heart to tell her mother that she hated the dress made for the graduation dinner. She looked like a tiered wedding cake, dripping with ribbons and lace flounces.

She lifted her gloved hand to her cheek and ran one finger over the ridge of healing scabs. Every smile and frown caused her skin to pull, and she had avoided looking in the mirror while Alice arranged her hair. Nora did have some vanity. But this dress . . . Nora took comfort in knowing only her stepfather's and mother's friends would be present at dinner. Invitations hadn't been extended to Nora's friends, and for this reason alone, she was grateful. Mother had invited John and Anna Comstock, but Nora knew they would pay little heed to her gown.

"I'm so pleased that Mr. Primrose is joining us tonight, darling."

"Don't get your hopes up, Mother. I'm not interested in marriage right now."

Mother pinched her lips together, a mulish expression that didn't bode well for Nora's chance of a low-key evening. "Lucius only has your best interest in mind, and you can't remain single forever. Your beauty would be wasted on spinsterhood. Mr. Primrose is well-respected, successful, and handsome."

Nora took another glance in the mirror. Beauty? What did beauty have to do with anything? "I'd rather my mind not be wasted on marriage to a man I have no interest in marrying."

Mother patted Nora's arm. "Maybe you will be interested once you meet him. Give him a chance."

Nora huffed. The last person she'd choose as a possible spouse was someone Lucius thought suitable. But there was no reason to take that out on her mother. She smoothed her expression before offering her arm to her mother. "I will engage him in conversation."

Mother smiled brightly, looking almost healthy, and Nora thought, as they made their way to the parlor where guests awaited them, that she'd almost be willing to allow Mr. Primrose to court her if it meant her mother got better.

Nora engaged in small talk with the guests, something she didn't hold in any fondness, until dinner. Lucius approached her, an attractive man about fifteen years older than her by his side.

"Nora, I'd like to introduce you to Carlton Primrose. He owns the printers that publish our humble journal."

Nora held out her hand, which he bowed over, and took in his straight nose, the slight graying at his temples, and the deep-set eyes that sparked with intelligence and interest. Mother had gotten a couple of things correct. He *was* handsome. And successful. His business provided nearly all the printing in Ithaca and the surrounding areas. And in a college town, there was a lot of printing to be done.

She let Mr. Primrose lead her into the dining room, where they sat across from Professor Comstock and his wife. By the time the hired staff had set the first course before them—a vibrant roasted beet soup drizzled with cultured cream—Nora found herself drawn into a conversation regarding photogravure, a new photograph printing method.

"I believe, one day," Mr. Primrose said with a self-important air that needled her, "magazine illustrations will become a thing of the past."

Nora laughed. "Surely photographs cannot capture the details a skilled artist can, though."

Mr. Primrose snuck a wink at Professor Comstock. Nora slid her spoon into her soup and brought it to her lips, waiting for an answer she hoped wouldn't diminish her opinion of him.

"It may astound you, young woman, but things rarely stay the same." He patted her hand, and when it remained there a moment too long, Nora pulled away. "Don't spend a moment worrying on it, Miss Shipley. Just know that, though illustrators aren't facing an immediate redundancy of their work, technology is leaping forward exponentially."

She patted her lips with her napkin. "Very unlike society's expectations of women, which appear to be inching backward."

Anna gave a light cough, but Nora kept her attention fixed on Mr. Primrose. He tugged at his ear, and a wrinkle appeared between his brows. Then his expression cleared, and he laughed. "Tell me you're not one of those 'new women' Henry James writes about."

"You know about James?" she asked.

"I'm a printer. I see all manner of alarming notions."

"What's alarming about a woman taking control of her own life and doing something more than marrying and having children?"

"Do you not want to marry and have children?"

"I do. But I don't see why one precludes the other. My father, the best parent in the world, was successful in both his career and personal life."

Mr. Primrose sat back while a server took his bowl. He didn't take his eyes off Nora, and they held a calculating gleam she didn't care for. "I understand this dinner is in honor of your graduation."

"Yes."

"And you're valedictorian."

"I am."

"Tell me, do you believe you earned that honor?"

"Yes. I worked very hard to obtain my degree, and my scores reflect that." She allowed a server to place a plate before her. She eyed the trout blanketed in mousseline sauce, wondering why her mother would put something on her dinner party menu that Nora held in such distaste. Then she glanced at Mr. Primrose and knew it was because Lucius preferred trout. Everything, from menus to company, revolved around Lucius's wants. So different from her father, who constantly sacrificed his own well-being for Nora's happiness.

"Mr. Primrose," Anna said from across the table. She nibbled at the fish speared onto her fork, waiting for him to turn his attention toward her. "What are you insinuating? Cornell University isn't in the habit of handing out undeserved accolades."

"Do you think it fair that a woman is given something that would, in all actuality, be of better use to a man? What will you do with the honor of being valedictorian, Miss Shipley? With your degree in general? Don't you feel you are stealing what could make a man's career in order to, what, stroke your own vanity? Women cannot be good wives and mothers *and* work. It's not possible."

Nora met Anna's eyes, and they had an entire, silent conversation, debating the merit of putting this oafish man in his place. Anna lost.

Nora turned back to her would-be suitor. "It's amusing that Lucius thought I'd entertain the idea of aligning myself with someone who displays such a disparate ideology. You're quite modern with your views on photography and business. But that interesting trait is tempered by your myopic view of society in general and women in particular. Cornell University—and the printing business, evidently—have marched forward with time, but you have been left behind. You suppose the university is placating me, but I've worked just as hard as any other student, maybe harder."

Mr. Primrose gave a brittle laugh. "Or maybe your brain is an anomaly. Perhaps you have lost every trace of feminine virtue."

The dozen people around the table had grown quiet, and every head swiveled in their direction. Heat rose to Nora's face, and the flush made her head spin. "That's a possibility. But I think it more likely you've forgotten what it means to be a gentleman. You're successful in business, it's true, but you profit off the printing of other people's ideas. Your income stems from their creativity and intellect. And that threatens you, doesn't it? Because you're incapable of an original thought. You're an insignificant man. One who will never deserve the hand of any woman, because all of them are more worthy than you."

"Nora!" her mother said on a breath of shock. "That's enough."

Nora glanced around the table. Lucius's neck had mottled, and he clenched his fork with white-tipped fingers. Mr. Primrose stared at her with his mouth open and redness infusing his face, as though her insult had been a physical slap.

The dining room, which only moments ago had been filled with the scent of celebratory food, the sound of clinking glass and china, the presence of friends wishing her well, had now turned into a mausoleum—quiet, the air growing thin and smelling of regret.

The curls piled atop Nora's head and dripping down her neck offered nothing but exposure. She couldn't hide from the shocked expressions on her guests' faces, the censure in Lucius's eyes, the disappointment in her mother's.

"This is what happens when a woman is overly educated. It gives her all kinds of odd notions." Lucius's booming words filled the silence, and he shook his head, his expression twisted into a parody of compassion. Nora saw the heat flash in his eyes, though.

Her face burned. Her mother turned sad eyes toward her, her hands fluttering above the table like the wings of an injured butterfly before settling at her waist. Something else peeked from behind the veil of disappointment, though. Anger? A cold fist gripped Nora's throat. She couldn't remember another time her mother had been angry with her. Perplexed, yes. Even frustrated. But this . . . this rigidity in the gentle slope of her jaw . . . it spoke of something more than embarrassment at a breach of manners.

Nora scraped back her chair and stood. "Please excuse me. I'm feeling unwell."

She darted from the dining room as fast as her unwieldy skirts allowed. In the hall she met one of the hired servers, who carried a large tray heavy with platters of chicken Lyonnaise. Nora pushed past him in her rush to the stairs, ignoring his shout as the tray fell and sent poultry, sautéed onions, and china crashing to the tiled floor.

Through her bedroom window, Nora saw the last guests leave. The buggy's wheels crunched across their gravel drive, and she watched until the light from the lamps wavered, then disappeared.

She dropped the curtain and sank onto her bed. She'd done it again. And she didn't even know why. Yes, Mr. Primrose had been boorish, but she had encountered similar people many times before and hadn't felt the need to put them in their places.

She pulled a satin pillow into her arms and hugged it to her chest. Maybe it had been misplaced anger toward Lucius and his plan for the journal, but she had hurt her mother and offended a guest celebrating her in the process. Mr. Primrose's behavior had been deplorable, but so had hers. Lucius had every right to be angry. And so did her mother, even though that had been surprising.

She set the pillow aside when she heard heavy footsteps in

the hall. They paused outside her room before Lucius entered without knocking, her mother trailing behind him.

"You have no idea what you've done." His quiet voice held back the rage Nora could see in his eyes.

"I'm sorry. I didn't think—"

He sliced his hand through the air. "No, I don't suppose you did. Which is ironic, given your little speech."

Nora sank against her bedframe, and the turned spindles bit into her back. "I will see him tomorrow and apologize."

"Yes, you will," Lucius said, "but that may not be enough."

"Enough for what?"

He looked at her mother, whose face had turned pasty. She crossed the room and sat beside Nora. "Your stepfather was hoping Mr. Primrose would offer him credit. That he would continue to print the journal for us at a substantially reduced rate until we began turning a profit again. Mr. Primrose was offended, Nora."

Nora saw Mr. Primrose's red face. The way he sat, frozen to his seat, grasping his lapels as though they alone would redeem his wounded pride. "How long has the journal been in trouble?"

Lucius tugged at his cravat, loosening it. Nora wished she could pull the ridiculous lace from her throat. Maybe then she could breathe again. "That doesn't matter," he said.

"Of course it does." She jumped to her feet. "You've dragged my father's magazine into the mud. You've turned it into a rag not worthy of the paper it's printed on. And now you're telling me you don't even have the resources to continue printing it?"

Lydia tugged at Nora's sleeve, her trembling fingers tangling in the ribbons at Nora's elbows. Nora jerked away. "Mr. Primrose had been considering you as a prospective wife, Nora. He's seen you and thinks you're beautiful. He so wants to marry, and Lucius had been speaking about you for a long time. That would have solved everything. It could have meant more than an extension of credit. It could have meant a forgiveness of debt."

A vein in Lucius's neck throbbed. "I had it in hand. You, with your need to prove yourself, have caused our current dilemma.

Your bitterness at not being allowed to behave like a man has possibly destroyed everything. You are merely deflecting your mistakes."

"My father would have never allowed this to happen." Nora dropped her eyes to the knotted fringe edging the rug, unable to meet her stepfather's gaze. She'd been so wrong. Had succumbed to her wounded pride. But Lucius, with his poor management and arrogance, had brought them to this place. "And I'd never agree to marry a man who doesn't believe in me, no matter what he offered you."

Lucius crossed the room, the tips of his fashionable, two-toned shoes coming into view. She focused on the buffed leather, even as his words lobbed stones at her conscience. "You have spent years comparing me unfavorably to your father. Do not do so again. I am tired of defending myself against a dead man who so obviously failed at parenting."

Nora's mother choked back a cry, and Nora looked up to see her pressing a fist to her mouth. But Lydia said nothing, and Nora saw every tear dripping down her cheek as a silent betrayal of her father's memory.

"The only thing my father failed at was trusting and be-friending you. If he could see what you've done to his work, his family . . ." Nora shook her head. "You couldn't have been half the father he was. Just like you're not half the scientist. And if my mother is honest, you aren't half the husband either."

Lucius released a guttural cry, and spittle flung across Nora's face. She jerked her head away and stumbled back a step, her legs hitting her bed. Lucius turned and kicked her insect cabinet, setting the glass plates wobbling. After he stormed from the room, Nora and her mother stared at each other.

"He's never been this angry." Lydia curled into a ball atop Nora's bed, making her silk-draped figure as small as possible. "Why must you say such things? He really tries. He's not a terrible husband, and he's had no experience in parenting. You can't expect him to fill your father's shoes."

Nora sank down beside her and patted her back. "Don't be too upset. He'll calm down."

Lydia lifted a tear-stained face and shook her head. "I think you've pushed him too far. He knows he can never please you. Why have you never been able to give him a chance?"

Nora ignored her mother's cynicism and questions. Lucius didn't care a whit about her opinion, just as Nora didn't care about his. But her mind whirred with ways to make everything right. She hated that her ill-timed words may have caused harm to the journal. She'd apologize to Mr. Primrose, of course, but once that task was accomplished, she'd find a job. If she received the scholarship, she'd work through school and use every penny to save the journal. Maybe she could talk Lucius into turning it over to her now, before he destroyed it past redemption.

Alice appeared in the doorway, wringing her hands.

"What is it?"

"Miss, I'm afraid Mr. Ward has—" she darted a glance behind her, then moved in closer—"lost his mind."

"Why do you say that?"

Before Alice could answer, Lucius pushed in behind her and, without looking at anyone, pulled open Nora's insect cabinet drawers and removed four cases. He stacked them in his arms, then left.

Nora leapt off her bed. "What are you doing?"

Lucius didn't answer. His footsteps thumped down the back stairs. Nora dashed after him, and as she exited the kitchen doorway into the backyard, she could see flames licking the sky. Her stomach dropped as Lucius threw the first case into the bonfire.

"No!" Her cry reverberated across the yard and was caught up in the flames. She ran toward him, but Lucius ignored her as he tossed the cases onto the burning logs. Glass shattered, sending off popping sparks as it expanded in the heat. A groan slid past Nora's slack lips as light bounced off the metallic blue and green wings of a dozen beetles. Her *Calosoma scrutator* slid from its base as the pin melted.

Her first mounting.

Her father stood behind her, his arms, thick with muscle and blond hair, wrapped around her shoulders as he helped arrange the beetle's legs just so.

"You must pin it slightly off-center, Nora. That's how to keep an insect completely intact."

She nodded and slid the pin through its thorax as he kissed the top of her head.

Every insect, most bound to memories of her father, burned. Her life's work, her father's life's work, turning to ash.

Nora shrieked and reached for the corner of a case, but the fire crackled and sent out a spray of sparks that nibbled her forearm.

Lucius, his chin showing hardened determination, turned and walked back toward the house. Nora tore across the yard, and she didn't look back as she overtook him. She pushed past Alice, who stood in the kitchen with her hands covering her mouth, and raced up the stairs.

She slammed her bedroom door shut and twisted the lock. "He can't do this." Tears clogged her throat. How could he? He knew she saw her father's collection as her legacy, a thick cord that linked her to him forever.

Lucius slammed against her door. "Alice!" His shout boomed across the house, and Nora heard Alice join him. "The key."

"But, Mr. Ward—"

"The key if you want to keep your job."

Nora gasped and sat in front of the door. She pressed her back against it, her feet braced against the cabinet. The lock clicked, and despite her straining muscles and the desperation making her legs tense, Lucius slid her forward enough that he could enter the room.

"Please, don't. I'm so sorry, Lucius. No more." She threw her arms over the cabinet, pressing her face into its gleaming, lemon-scented top. *Please, God, don't let him.*

But God paid no attention. Lucius flung her away, gathered another four cases, and disappeared.

Nora sank to the floor, tears dripping from her nose into her lap. Her mother, ineffective in most things and completely useless in this, buried her head beneath Nora's pillow, her slender shoulders shaking.

After Lucius had gathered her entire collection and destroyed everything she held dear, Nora made her way outside. The clear sky canopied their yard in stars, and Lucius stood before the dying flames, his hands clasped behind his back.

She crept through the soft spring grass. It tickled her ankles through her stockings. Such a mundane thing to notice. The charred remains of her cabinet poked from the embers, pointing toward the heavens that housed a God who'd ignored her pleas.

Beside the fire, a *Bombus bimaculatus* lay prone in the ash and dirt. Nora sank to her knees and scooped it into her palm, running her thumb over its prickly fur.

"Little Bumble Bea, come gather with me."

"Papa, my name is Nora."

"Your middle name is Beatrice, after your grandmother, and she loved walks in the woods. Let's go find something to honor her by."

Nora closed her fingers around the bee and pressed her hand to her cheek. *This is all that's left, Papa.*

Her words clawed past the pain and emptiness swirling in her chest. "I will never forgive you."

In a voice so soft it would be mistaken for tenderness coming from another man, Lucius said, "I will not be compared to your father again." Then he left her alone.

Nora watched as the dwindling fire licked at the remains of her beautiful collection and said nothing until her mother joined her on the ground. Lydia choked on a cry and touched Nora's arm, brushing against the burns that throbbed almost as painfully as her heart.

Nora pulled away and lifted her chin. "Mother, I'm going to India."

Part Two

KODAIKANAL, INDIA

July 1885

Chapter Eight

The oxen's rumps swayed as they pulled the two-wheeled cart, which the driver had called a *mattu vandi* when he met them at the guesthouse in Madras. Above his head, Nora watched the dirt road wind into a copse of pine trees. All around them the hills dipped and lifted, disappearing into the hazy blue horizon toward the Nilgiri Mountains in the distance.

Nora raised off the floor a little. She could just spot the large lake thickly fringed by trees. Like jewels strung across a bangle, red-roofed houses crisscrossed the roads leading to and through the Kodaikanal hill station.

The oxen lowed, and the driver clicked his tongue. When the wheel hit a rock, the cart jostled, and Nora tumbled backward. One of the porters following their conveyance, carrying trunks above his wiry body, shouted at her, and her face filled with heat.

"You're going to fall from this cart like you did from the tree on the inlet if you don't settle into your seat." Owen pulled his cap from his face and lifted his head.

"I thought you were asleep." How he could sleep through the amazing sights and sounds and smells, Nora didn't know. But he'd spent the majority of the three weeks they'd sailed on the steamship from London to Madras snoozing.

"How can I sleep when you insist on throwing yourself from the cart every time we round a corner?"

She dug her elbow into his rib cage. "Sit up and look. It's incredible."

He scooted away from her but straightened in his seat. His gaze arced from right to left, and he nodded with approval. "It's amazing. Kodaikanal is a beautiful place. And the weather is an improvement over Madras."

Nora nodded. She'd never experienced heat like Madras. The moment she had stepped off the ship, a thin layer of gray sweat sprang from her exposed skin. Her wool traveling suit had turned into a wet blanket threatening to suffocate her, and she couldn't get out of the city fast enough. The farther into the hills they traveled, the more lovely the weather became, though. She didn't blame the American missionaries and British officials for moving their residences to Kodaikanal. It was even more beautiful than Ithaca, and maybe lovelier than paradise.

They passed just beneath a pear tree, small black and orange birds flitting among its branches. The driver shouted, and the oxen stopped. Standing, he waved at the three porters behind them, and they shuffled toward him. After a rapid exchange in Tamil, the porters hustled onto a narrow road disappearing into the Bombay Shola—the woods on the eastern side of Kodaikanal Lake.

The driver looked at Nora and Owen. "I send ahead. They fast." He sat, and they set off again, following the porters at a more leisurely pace.

Berries hung heavy from the myrtle trees growing along the road, which had turned into a path the farther they followed it. The trees shaded them, casting shadows over the packed dirt and blanketing everything in a hush that whispered ancient stories. Overripe fruit scented the air with spicy incense, and Nora clasped her hands in her lap, compelled to prayer.

A flash of iridescent rose caught her eye. Grabbing the poles supporting the fringed shade of the cart, she hoisted herself to her feet. "Stop!"

The driver smacked at the oxen with a whip, and when she vaulted out of the cart and darted toward a tree, he yelled after her and waved his whip as though wanting to smack her, as well.

"Nora, what are you doing?" Owen called. He huffed and followed her.

"Look at that." She stood a foot from the tree, watching the progress made by a flower chafer beetle. "I've never seen one with cephalic horns in person. Only in illustrations." She reached a finger toward it and stroked its pitted thorax.

Owen watched her with a smile. "I'm sure we'll see many more interesting things while we're here. Come on. Our driver is growing impatient."

She looked back at the driver, who glared at them from beneath the white cloth wrapped around his head. With a final glance at the insect, she followed Owen to the cart and allowed him to lift her into it. "Do you think I should collect it?"

"I'm sure they're endemic to this area. You'll have another chance." Owen's voice sounded tired, which Nora couldn't fathom, given how much he'd slept on the journey. "Besides, I'm hungry, and I want to meet the team."

As the sun dropped behind the hills, they rolled into a neat camp on the edge of the shola. A ring of white tents circled a clearing, a rough cabin holding court in the center. Four men clustered outside a tent. The porters crouched beside a fire, where an old Indian woman rubbed sand into the bottom of a pan. Nora saw her trunks stacked near the tent closest to the cabin.

A slim man sporting a feathery mustache and dark circles beneath his eyes separated from the group and sauntered toward them, flicking a cigarette. Owen clambered from the cart and held a hand toward her, which she clutched as she climbed out.

"I'm Frederic Alford, lead researcher. You must be the two sent by Professor Comstock." His mustache twitched along with his left eye.

Owen introduced himself, and then Mr. Alford looked at Nora.

"Nora Shipley," she said, releasing Owen's hand.

A curse slipped through Mr. Alford's clenched teeth. "I asked John to send me his two most promising students. He assured me he would."

"And he did," Owen said.

Mr. Alford stared at Nora and sucked at his cigarette. "What will I do with you? The only woman in camp is Pallavi, and she hardly makes an acceptable chaperone. She goes home at night."

The woman near the fire looked up at the sound of her name. She used her sari to wipe at the corners of her eyes, then turned her attention back to the pan she was cleaning.

Nora ran her hand over the wisps of hair puffing around her temples, pushing them down and bidding them to obedience. "I don't need a chaperone. I'm a scientist, and my sex is irrelevant." She drew herself to full height, which did little for her confidence.

"Of course you need a chaperone. You are an unmarried woman under my care. How John thought this was a good idea is beyond me. I always thought him to be a pragmatic fellow, but this bit of foolishness shows otherwise." Mr. Alford put his hands on his hips and scowled at her. She met his gaze and refused to break eye contact. She had done nothing wrong, and she wouldn't be bullied by a British man with outdated notions.

"Nora will be an asset to the team," Owen said. "And I'm sure Pallavi will be a suitable chaperone."

"I don't need a chaperone." Nora pierced Owen with a sharp look. How would anyone take her seriously if she was trailed about by the cook?

Mr. Alford spun away. "Come eat some dinner."

He stalked toward the khaki-clad men who sat on camp

stools, scooping bits of sauced rice from tin bowls with their fingers, and muttered words Nora couldn't hear. Owen and Nora followed him, and one of the men offered her his seat. She sat in it, grateful for the chance to get off her shaking legs.

Another man nudged a bowl of water nearer to her with his foot. Nora dipped her fingers into it and let the cool water remove the journey's dirt and grime. She wiped her hands on the scrap of fabric Mr. Alford tossed to her.

Pallavi offered her a bowl of something that smelled heavily of spices. Eager to prove her mettle, Nora tried to use her fingers like the men, scooping bits of rice and sauce into her mouth. Most of it fell back to the dish before she managed to get it into her mouth, but she smiled at Pallavi anyway. "Delicious."

Owen settled cross-legged beside her and dug into his dinner, having no problem with the lack of utensils. Soon the other men went back to their meals, no longer staring at her with curiosity.

She'd eaten only a few bites, not nearly enough to quell the hunger biting her belly, before Mr. Alford motioned to the man who'd given up his seat for Nora. "Leonard, you may as well tell them how our days are run. I can't very well send her back home. There are three rules governing life here—do your work; if you're going more than half a mile from camp, take someone with you; and don't cause any problems." He smacked a palm against his neck. "Blast these mosquitoes. Blast dysentery. Blast it all." He threw his dish to the ground, glared at her, then stalked into the weeds rimming camp, his feet stirring up dust and his curses stirring up anxiety.

The food in Nora's mouth turned as thick as glue, and she forced it down her throat.

"Ignore him." Leonard unfolded himself from the ground and took Mr. Alford's camp chair. "He's only discouraged that so many on our team have succumbed to illness."

"And my arrival last month didn't help matters." The young-est man, a boy, really, shrugged. He had a wide pleasant face made pink by the fire, and a shock of blond hair. "My welcome was no warmer than yours, Miss Shipley." He grinned at her. "I was raised in India, and we summered in Kodaikanal. I was an obvious choice to join the team."

The third man, sitting outside their circle, snorted. He puffed on his pipe and rubbed at his scruffy mustache. "You are no more obvious a choice to join us than Miss Shipley, you upstart pup. You being here has everything to do with the fact that your father is close to that gibface leading the missionary alliance in town."

The younger man shrugged, and his grin grew in width. "Come now, old man, you're only jealous you had to work hard your entire life for the advantages I have just for knowing the right people."

"Let's not give a poor first impression. I am Leonard Taylor." Leonard pointed to the pale young man with the infectious smile. "This is William Abbott, and the one over there is Jeffrey Steed. He's always puffing on that pipe. If it bothers you, tell him, and he'll put it out."

"I'll do no such thing. It's medically necessary for my asthma." Mr. Steed took a deep draw.

Mr. Taylor shook his head. "We each have our own tents. Make yourself comfortable, for it's the only private space you'll have. Mr. Alford currently has us searching for a *Papilio buddha*."

"A Malabar banded peacock. I never dreamed I'd see one in person." Nora glanced at Owen, and he smiled. "Professor Comstock will want to hear our observations."

"Be sure to wear appropriate clothing tomorrow," Mr. Abbott said.

Nora raised an eyebrow and looked down her nose at him. "I always wear appropriate clothing."

Owen coughed to hide a laugh, and Mr. Abbott went red. "I only meant that the sun is bright. You'll need to wear a wide-brimmed hat and something comfortable for hiking and climbing."

Mr. Taylor slapped his hands against his knees. "It's been a long day, and you must be tired from your travels. We usually relax a little before turning in. Pallavi serves breakfast at"—he looked over at where she sat, scouring a pot beneath a tree— "well, whenever she feels like it." He stood and looked down at Nora. "I don't care what sex you are as long as you are able to withstand disease and carry a rucksack. I, for one, am glad to have both of you on our team."

Nora's tent held only a cot and her two trunks. Near the flap, which could be opened and pinned up or released to close the tent in darkness, she had wrangled a slab of wood over two upturned crates, creating a sort of desk that sported her microscope, jars, boxes of pins, and other accoutrements.

She flipped onto her back and tapped her feet against the cot's frame. Even though she'd turned in right after dinner, sleep hadn't come. Owen, no doubt, had nodded off while chatting with the men around the fire. She'd been lying in bed for an hour, but the unfamiliar night sounds wouldn't allow her to rest. Monkeys chattering, parrots squawking, a cicada of some type joining with its family in an otherworldly chorus.

The men sat outside her tent, discussing the day's work in elegant British accents. Mr. Alford's voice set her on edge.

Nora stiffened at the sound of footsteps at her tent flap. "Nora," Owen whispered.

"One moment." She stood and grabbed her calico wrapper from the end of the cot. Donning it, she quickly did up the buttons and settled back down. "Come in."

Owen ducked beneath the flap, then pinned it up so that the doorway framed the men, the dancing fire casting shadows on their faces. Mr. Steed peered into her tent, squinting to see through the inky blackness of the night separating them. Nora ignored him.

Owen grabbed the upturned bucket she had set beneath her

desk to use as a stool and dragged it toward the cot. He set an oil lamp on the floor beside him before sitting.

She tucked her legs to the side. "Is it okay that you're in here? It's highly unusual."

"Everything about this is unusual, Peculiar," he said as amusement bloomed across his face. "I think we'll have to relax convention here. While the other men are just outside your tent, in full view, I believe it should be acceptable. I wanted to see how you're doing. You were so quiet at dinner, and then you disappeared."

"I don't believe my presence is agreeable."

He folded his fingers and rested his chin atop them. "You'll win them over. They won't be able to ignore your brilliance as soon as they see you in the field. Just give it time."

"Prove myself."

He nodded. "You will."

She raked her hands over her scalp, disrupting the braid she'd woven earlier. Prove herself. Again. Over and over, in every part of her life, forever and ever, she'd have to prove herself. The thought sometimes seemed daunting. Would there ever be a time when she wouldn't have to prove herself? When her accomplishments would be validation enough? "I wonder if Mary Davis Treat had to prove herself to Darwin when they began corresponding. Or when she had insect species named after her. It seems very unfair that I have to prove myself when dozens of women before me already have."

Owen crossed his legs and wiggled his foot. He bit his lower lip, studying her in the flickering light of the lamp. "It is unfair. But it's unfair that I don't have a father who supports my endeavors, and it's unfair that the men who worked with the team previously had weak constitutions and became ill, and it's unfair that Pallavi is spending her dotage scrubbing pots for foreigners instead of napping beneath a banana tree." He shrugged. "We all have handicaps we have to overcome."

Nora took a deep breath of honey- and cumin-scented air

and looked at him. Really looked at him, past the handsome face and expensive clothing and cavalier charm. She'd come to realize over the past weeks that he wore his don't-care attitude as a measure of protection. Because occasionally he said something so profound that it couldn't possibly have passed through Owen Epps's lips.

"You aren't as apathetic as you would have us believe," she said.

"Sometimes people see what they want, never looking deeper than the masks we all wear."

"What mask do I wear? A *Blattellidae*?" She held her index fingers over her head, wiggling them like antennae.

Owen leaned toward her, and she was grateful for the dim light that hid the color filling her face at his nearness. A very masculine scent drifted across the small space between them and brushed her nose. She dropped her hands to her lap and licked her lips, her throat going dry when the action drew his attention.

What was this? She'd never responded to Owen in such a way. She didn't want to now. *It's the exhaustion of travel. Being in an exotic country. The strangeness of him sitting so near me.* She cleared her throat and scooted toward the fabric wall, not quite believing her arguments.

"I saw through your mask a long time ago, Nora. You pretend you don't care. That your blood is ice in your veins, and you have no room for anything in your life but insects and education. But I see." His voice dipped. "I see you."

For a moment Nora felt exposed, as though she'd forgotten to don her wrapper. As though she stood before Owen, vulnerable and unclothed. She didn't want him to see her. Didn't want him to notice there was anything more to her than insects and education.

Raucous laughter erupted from the men outside, and one of them cursed.

Owen tossed a glance over his shoulder. "Gentlemen."

With a few sighs and huffs, they settled down, but Nora could sense some antagonism still. She shook her head. "I don't believe this is going to end well."

"Don't give it another thought. Do your work. Discover something interesting." He chucked her beneath the chin. "Keep that mask up for a while longer. Until the day when you feel safe enough to take it off."

Chapter Nine

A chattering monkey woke Nora early. With bleary eyes and an exhausted body, she dressed and spent a few moments jotting a letter to her mother.

I've arrived. India is beautiful.

Knowing she could better explain the sights with paint than with pen, she gave up and picked her way across the camp toward the fire, where Pallavi held out a tin mug.

"Masala tea," Pallavi said.

Nora took the cup and sipped at the fragrant drink. "It's delicious. Thank you."

She'd never enjoyed coffee, but this spicy, sweet tea seemed a good way to start the morning.

Pallavi grinned. "It is good for your health."

Nora smiled. "Your English is very good."

"My father worked for a British colonel in Trinomalee, where I'm from. My brother's employer asked him to move to Kodaikanal nine years ago. I have no husband, so I came too."

Nora had heard the porters speaking in a tangle of Tamil—the words sounding like poetry—so different from the Romance languages she was familiar with. She'd never had a natural propensity for languages, and she wondered how someone navigated between Tamil and English.

She left Pallavi to her chores and approached the ramshackle cabin—the only permanent structure in camp. Wooden walls rose to about five and a half feet. An open timber frame supported a thatched roof. Pushing aside the canvas flap that served as a door, she peeked inside.

Three long tables formed a *U* around the perimeter of the building. They were cluttered with microscopes, nets, boxes of scalpels and pins, stacks of pillboxes and glass jars, and corklined setting boards. A slim table pushed against the far wall sported a dozen books and myriad art supplies—paints, pencils, vials, canvases, and brushes.

Early morning sunlight filtered through the gaps between the roof and the walls, sending dust motes twirling. Someone stepped around her.

"The insects waiting to be catalogued and illustrated are in boxes beneath the far table," Mr. Alford said.

Nora took a sip of her tea, eyeing him over the mug's rim. He didn't look as tired today, the circles beneath his eyes having faded overnight. He still appeared to be put out by her, though. He tapped his teeth with a fingernail and studied her like a schoolgirl would a spider found in her bed.

She turned from him and surveyed the room. "It's quite dark in here. How do you see to study?"

"We normally bring the tables and supplies outside. That will work until the monsoon season comes. When it does, our research will be dependent on the rains. We were supposed to have finished by now, but everyone kept getting sick. Hopefully you Americans will prove hardier than us Brits."

A metal racket sounded outside, and he grimaced. "That's Pallavi telling us it's time for breakfast."

Nora followed him from the cabin, and they joined the rest

of the team at the fire. Pallavi stopped beating a dinged-up pot with a stick and handed out tin plates piled with sauced lentils, a green chutney, and soft rice cakes.

Nora settled into a camp chair and attempted to eat her meal, the cakes breaking and plopping through her fingers onto the plate. Her stomach growled, and she wondered if she'd ever manage to eat her fill while in India. She accepted a tin cup filled with some sort of tangy-smelly preparation, thankful at least she wouldn't have to eat *that* with her fingers. One sip, though, and she wished she'd kept to the rice and beans. She forced the drink down her throat. "What is this?" she asked Pallavi.

"*Moru.* Salted yogurt. It's good for you."

Nora sniffed the drink, wrinkled her nose, and as soon as Pallavi turned her back, shoved it beneath her chair.

Owen sat beside her and offered a bright-eyed good-morning.

"Are there any forks?" she asked Mr. Alford, who held his plate aloft and deftly scooped his food into his mouth with his fingers.

He shook his head. "This is a research camp, not a fancy parlor."

Nora huffed. "I'd have packed one if I thought utensils would be in short supply," she said under her breath.

Owen chuckled. He expertly balled up a portion of the rice cake with the lentils, tipped it into his fingers, and pushed it into his mouth. "It's quite good." He must have seen the despair in her expression, because he set his plate down and wrapped his hand around hers. "Let me show you how. It's simple once you get the hang of it."

She allowed him to guide her fingers and, with his help, managed to eat the majority of her meal. He offered her his napkin, which she used to wipe her fingers, then lifted his plate and ate the rest of his own breakfast.

Mr. Abbott, wearing a wide-brimmed hat that shaded his face, settled into a chair beside her. "Did you sleep well?"

"I did, once the heat lifted."

He nodded, his freckled face turning sober. "It has been hotter than normal this year in Kodaikanal. But this is nothing. The air isn't as heavy here in the hills. You should try Madras in May. It's like breathing through wet wool. And call me William, please."

After she extended the invitation in kind, he cast a nervous glance at her hat—a simple straw boater. "Is that all you've brought with you? Have you a parasol? The sun is beastly."

"I believe this is sufficient."

"William is terrified of burning, aren't you, pup?" Mr. Steed ambled over to them, his hands shoved into his pockets. He didn't look as surly as he had the night before. He tapped the brim of his own hat—a narrow one that would do little to protect his skin. "I, on the other hand, have my Italian mother to thank for skin that only becomes golden. And I look dashed handsome."

Mr. Alford tossed his plate into a bucket of water near the fire. "All right. Let's get going. I'd like to see if we can capture our elusive butterfly."

Mr. Steed ambled off, his voice lifted in an opera that showcased a more-than-passable tenor. She stared after him, having trouble reconciling the beauty of it with his difficult personality.

William leaned toward her. "He's been taking medicine again for his asthma."

"It makes him sing opera?"

"It makes him happy. And we all prefer him happy."

Nora shook her head, then looked at Mr. Alford, wondering what job he'd assign her on their walk. Owen already carried a heavy canvas bag, and Mr. Steed was lifting another one over his shoulder.

Mr. Alford caught her gaze. "Miss Shipley, I told you about the butterflies beneath the table in the cabin. Please begin with those. Watercolor, I think." He waved at William. "Pull the table and art supplies out so she can work in the sun."

Nora looked from him to William, who had jumped from his seat at the command and darted into the cabin.

"Is Nora not coming with us?" Owen stole the question from

Nora's mouth, which she appreciated because it seemed the words had stuck in her throat.

Mr. Alford motioned to a spot when William appeared, carrying the rickety table in front of him. "We are behind on our illustrations."

Mr. Taylor and Mr. Steed stacked half a dozen cardboard boxes beside the table. Nora lifted the lid of the first and found three vibrantly hued butterflies resting in cotton.

"There must be at least a dozen specimens." She looked at Mr. Alford, but he gazed off toward the woods.

"Yes. I hope you work quickly." He gave her a sharp look. "Professor Comstock assured me one of you is a skilled artist. I assume it's you."

"It is."

He approached her. "We've been commissioned by the Crown. I hope you can do these butterflies justice. This book is to be the very best quality."

"I'm sure you will be pleased with my renderings." She crossed her arms. "Will I be able to join your expeditions once I've caught up?"

His attention had been snagged by William, who clutched a pair of butterfly nets. "Don't forget the kill jars this time."

William hustled back into the cabin, emerging a moment later with a sack tossed over his shoulder.

Owen joined Nora and Mr. Alford. "Is it safe for Nora to be here alone?"

The leader of their group sighed. "Pallavi will stay in camp. I believe she does laundry today. Nora, you may join her at the stream if you feel unsafe alone."

She blinked. "Do the laundry?"

He threw up his hands. "Or not. Just get those illustrations done." He stomped off, yelling at William not to break the jars during their hike.

Nora looked at Owen and shook her head. "It seems I've crossed the world so I can do your laundry."

"And illustrate, which is something you're particularly skilled at." He rubbed the back of his neck. "I can stay with you. I don't feel right leaving you here alone."

"I'm sure I'll be fine. Let's not give Mr. Alford any more reason to believe I'm a burden. I will do my drawings." She settled into the chair at the table and arranged her brushes, paints, and jars. She'd illustrate the butterflies.

But she hoped Mr. Alford would see her worth soon. She hadn't come this far just to paint pretty pictures.

When the men walked back into camp late that afternoon, Nora was just putting the finishing touches on her fourth butterfly. She spread the canvases over the table so the sun could dry them.

Mr. Alford approached to assess her work. Nora hoped he liked them. She hated herself for caring, but maybe if she could impress him with her illustrations, he'd be more apt to allow her to do some actual work.

He nodded once. "I think I'd rather see the *Aphnaeus elima* done with pencil. You could better illustrate the markings on the wings. You can do it tomorrow."

Nora gathered the specimen she'd been working on and placed it back in the box. She forced her tone to be even, not wanting to seem too desperate. "Did you discover anything exciting today?"

He gave her a distracted look. "Nothing you'd be interested in."

Nora clenched her teeth. How would he know what she was interested in? "Given my degree in entomology, I'm sure I'd be interested in anything you found."

He blinked, then twirled the end of his mustache with exacting care. He looked down at her, and Nora wished she were taller. It would be much easier to feel equal to a man if she were.

"Your mind is equal to any man's."

Her father's words, spoken so many years ago, stiffened her spine.

"*Don't allow convention to limit you. Know who you are.*"

"*Who am I, Papa?*" Her ten-year-old voice had sounded breathless. She often sounded like that, speaking to her father. She hung on his every word.

"*You are Nora Beatrice Shipley. My daughter. A child of God. And you will never allow someone to dismiss you because their mind is too small to understand that we are all more than our parts.*"

Nora didn't soften her stance. She didn't offer Mr. Alford relief from the awkwardness. She didn't flirt with him or stroke his ego. She held herself erect, secure in the knowledge that she was Nora Beatrice Shipley and deserved his respect. He might not realize it. He might not be willing to give it. But she wouldn't settle for anything less than what her father had demanded for her.

He broke eye contact first. "Yes, well . . ." And then he wandered away.

Owen approached, scratching his head and offering a wry smile. "Mr. Alford was hoping to spot the *Papilio buddha*. He believes it's the most beautiful butterfly native to the Western Ghats and wants to spend time observing its habits, but we never did see one."

"What did you do, then?" She was hungry for information. If she couldn't be with the team in the field, she could at least have a description of their work.

He shrugged. "Nothing much. We hiked to all the spots they normally visit, spent some time exploring a waterfall that turned up some interesting caterpillars." He dug through his rucksack and pulled out a couple of jars. Inside, a jumble of spiky pupae rolled around the leaves scattering the container's floor. "I'm going to raise them and see what they turn up. None of the men were familiar with them. Other than these, Mr. Steed found a flying lizard we studied for a bit, but that's it. It was a lot of waiting. And talking. I discovered Mr. Steed and Mr. Alford taught together at Oxford. They don't seem particularly close, though." He held up a jar and squinted into it.

Nora took it from him and shook it gently, causing one of the pupa to uncurl. "Let me know if you need any help. I've raised butterflies since I was a child." She didn't wait for an answer, just shoved the jar back into his hands and went back to her pens and paints on the table.

Mr. Alford avoided Nora for the rest of that night as the group ate rice and lentils and drank cups of warm buffalo milk. He chatted with the men around the fire after the moon had risen and hung heavy in a sky as black as India ink. Nora, near the men but so far away, tilted her head and watched the progress of a shooting star. She inhaled deeply, her jasmine-tinged breath perfuming the resentment making its home within her.

"What are you doing?" Owen asked, leaning over the arm of his chair, his head inches from her face.

She looked at him. The moon's light set off the silver darting across his irises. "Stargazing."

He assumed her position, face upturned and a small smile twitching his lips. She reluctantly turned back toward the sky. She preferred watching the moon reflect in his eyes.

~⁓~

The next morning, while Nora sipped her fragrant masala tea, William dragged the table and art supplies from the cabin again. She blew across her mug and watched as Mr. Alford stacked the insect boxes.

"I believe you have about six drawings left." He didn't look at her, instead focusing on lining the brushes up so that their tips made an even row across the table. "We will probably have another specimen or two for you today."

"And when I finish?" Nora wrapped both her hands around her mug.

"Finish with what?"

"With the illustrations, Mr. Alford. When I finish, will I be welcome to join you on your expeditions?"

Pallavi began to sing, her voice tripping so high, Nora could almost see the vibrations rippling her tea.

Mr. Alford's eye twitched. "That infernal noise. Pallavi. Pallavi!"

Pallavi winked at Nora, turned her back on them, and continued to sing. Mr. Steed stumbled from his tent singing some Italian opera in a falsetto that made Mr. Alford clench his jaw. Pallavi paused, but for only a moment. Then her raspy soprano joined Mr. Steed as she hummed along.

Mr. Alford stuck a finger in his ear and wiggled it around. "Just finish the illustrations, please." He handed Pallavi a few coins, then looked back at Nora. "Why don't you go with Pallavi to the market this morning? You might find it interesting."

The men left camp, Mr. Alford's complaints drifting toward her as they tramped into the woods. Nora crossed her arms and glared at the tree line they'd disappeared into. Pallavi joined her, staring into the forest, then looking at Nora, one brow raised in question.

"Top of my class, Pallavi, and he wants me to pick out ripe mangos."

Pallavi shrugged. "I will help you." She squeezed her hand into a fist and held it to her nose. Pumping her hand and sniffing at it, she said, "It must be soft and smell like flowers."

A laugh bubbled up inside Nora. "At least I'll return home having discovered *something*."

After Nora had finished redrawing the *Aphnaeus elima* in pencil, she jammed her hat onto her head, slung her bag across her shoulder, and watched Pallavi bend at the waist to lift a basket. The skin around her midsection rippled and folded upon itself, and as Pallavi lifted the basket to her head, her biceps bunched. She was a couple of decades older than Nora's mother, but her body was made of sturdier stuff.

A flap of wings drew Nora's attention skyward, where a great hornbill soared ten feet above her head. It landed halfway up a tree, its tail feathers looking like a Chinese fan, and shoved its beak into a narrow slit carved into the trunk. Nora took a mental picture of it to tell Bitsy about when she returned home.

Pallavi passed Nora, her hips swaying with gentle rhythm, the basket held steady atop her head. Nora pulled her attention from the male bird feeding its nesting mate and followed her from camp.

Pallavi's sandals slapped against her cracked heels as she stomped along the path. Nora's eyes flitted from tree to bush to flower like hummingbirds. There was too much to see. Too many things worth noticing. She'd never experienced color so vibrant. The heavy scents of earth and decay and water carried her toward Kodaikanal. She pressed her hand to her chest as she inhaled and allowed herself to release her worries.

A flash of red against green caught her attention. As Nora hurried toward the bush, she pulled a kill jar from her sack. "Look at it! Oh, it's gorgeous."

Pallavi, ten feet ahead, set her basket down and watched with interest as Nora scooped the *Buprestidae* into the jar. She held it up to her eyes, watching as it scuttled around until the cyanide did its job. She grinned at Pallavi.

Pallavi shook her head and threw her hands in the air. "Why do you kill them?"

Nora frowned at the jewel beetle. "So I can study them."

"Why?"

She approached Pallavi. "I . . . because I'm interested in them. In learning about them."

"Why can't you learn about them when they're alive?"

Nora stood taller than Pallavi—a rarity—and she looked down her nose at her. "You wouldn't understand."

Pallavi sniffed and tucked her sari tighter around her waist. "*You* don't understand. The insects don't live for your sake. They have their own purpose."

"Yes, but don't you believe we should understand that purpose?" Nora waved her hand. "It doesn't matter."

It didn't. Pallavi was uneducated. Not a scientist. She made meals and did laundry and went to the market. She sang warbling songs to her idols and wore a length of cloth instead of proper clothing.

Pallavi smiled at her, but in her deep-set eyes, Nora saw something that told her Pallavi understood more than Nora gave her credit for. Nora saw herself reflected—arrogant, dismissive, and proud—and her face went hot.

She was Mr. Alford! Even worse, she was Lucius.

Ice flooded her veins, and she wrapped her goose-fleshed arms around herself. *How easy it is to see splinters through the forest.*

She tucked her jar into her rucksack and grabbed Pallavi's arm. "Let me tell you why I study them. Why it's important."

She spent the remainder of their walk trying to convince Pallavi of the importance of economic entomology, of pest control, of the possibility that insects held medical cures. But she knew she was trying to convince herself that she had an open mind and didn't judge people superficially.

By the time they reached Kodaikanal and the market, Pallavi held her hands over her ears. "Shush, shush. I understand."

Nora grinned, then allowed Pallavi to lead her from one stall to the next, arguing with fruit sellers, sniffing and then discarding bananas and onions, and piling bags of lentils and rice into the basket.

The market, teeming with people, stood in stark contrast to the woods they'd just walked through. Nora found she couldn't discuss the finer points of choosing cucumbers with Pallavi because her voice got lost amid the hawking and arguing. She couldn't admire the baskets of lentils and buckets of passion fruit because everywhere she looked, color assaulted her—from the vibrant saris to golden bangles and rings.

They ducked beneath a canopy, and Nora found herself facing a dizzying array of spices mounded in silver bowls on a red cloth. They dazzled the senses. Filled the air with a heady aroma and her eyes with a profusion of color rivaling insect wings.

Pallavi pinched a powdered bit of something bright red and rubbed it between her fingers. She touched the tip of her tongue to it. Her mouth drooped, and her eyes flashed. *"Ni oru dhrogi."*

The merchant, sitting cross-legged at the head of his rainbow of masalas, curries, and seeds, shook his head. A vehement argument poured from between his lips, and his words tangled and wrestled with Pallavi's.

It was all too stimulating. Too much.

Nora pulled away and edged toward the lake, which sparkled and winked at her, calling her to its shore. Calling her from the exotic and overwhelming market to something that reminded her of Ithaca.

She picked her way over the uneven ground, skirting piles of cow manure and hopping birds. Rose would love to be here, watching animals in their natural habitat instead of trapped behind bars in a zoo. When Nora reached the lake, she closed her eyes. For a moment she heard and smelled and tasted home—in the lapping water at her feet, the breeze rustling through the evergreen trees, the scent of water.

A keening pierced the peace, and the cry formed itself into a name. "Lukose!"

Nora's spirit absorbed the grief in that word. She'd experienced that sort of wrenching sadness when her father died. She knew the sound of hopelessness.

On wobbling legs, she skirted the water and looked around, trying to locate the source of all that pain.

She found it in the shape of a woman wearing a black crepe gown and sitting at the edge of the lake, her legs tucked beneath her. Her small face was upturned and her pinched lips colorless. Dark, shiny waves of hair fell from the knot at the back of her head and over her shoulders. Everything about her spoke of shadows and clouds. She worried a small painted tin boat between her long, tapered fingers.

"Lukose." The word caught on a sob.

Seeing the pain etched on the woman's lovely face, Nora allowed herself to reimagine her father lying on the shore of Cascadilla Creek, his white face glistening in the sunlight. She sniffed.

The woman started, her head whirling and her eyes growing wide.

"I'm sorry," Nora said. "I didn't mean to interrupt."

The woman curled in on herself, her chest caving toward her back. She drew her knees up and pressed the little boat against her cheek. "He's dead. Typhoid fever."

Nora approached and sat near her. She could see tears making tracks down the woman's cheeks and the vacant look in her eyes. "Who?"

The woman began to wail, the sound squeezing Nora's heart. She gripped Nora's upper arms, the child's toy biting through her sleeve and into her flesh.

"It's okay," Nora said, pulling the woman into her arms. "It's okay."

It didn't matter who had died. Nora understood this. She knew what the woman needed, and even though she didn't consider herself a consoling sort of person, she was a person. And being alone made grief even more unbearable.

By the time the woman's weeping had calmed, Nora's bodice was soaked through with tears and sweat. The sun burned upon their heads, and she almost wished for the parasol William had suggested. Glancing back toward the market, she realized Pallavi had probably left and gone back to camp.

The woman's crying had turned to sniffles, and she spoke with a lyrical accent. "I'm Swathi Davies."

Nora pulled back. "I'm Nora Shipley."

"My son died of typhoid fever a month ago. He was eight."

"I'm so sorry."

Mrs. Davies nodded. "I was too sick to attend his funeral. My husband bundled me up and brought me here once the doctor said I would survive it." Her eyes skittered toward Nora's. "I didn't want to survive it."

Nora, so confident in her intelligence, had no words to give. What had people said to her when her father died? What had brought comfort? She couldn't remember. She had buried herself in her bed, and when people offered solace, her mind had her at the waterfall, watching her father tumble to his death. "I understand."

"He was my only child. I'll never have another." Mrs. Davies sighed, the sound coming from a thousand miles away. "We lived in Madurai his entire life. He never saw anything else, but he always wanted to. And now we're here. Without him."

"How did you end up in Kodaikanal?" Most of the city was made up of American missionaries and British military. There was only a smattering of local people.

"My husband is Eurasian, his father a British general who secured him a position with the Greater British Missionary Alliance. After Lukose died and I wasn't able to regain my strength, the alliance sent us here to convalesce. My husband is working with the director. It's supposed to be a great blessing, but I want to go home." She looked at Nora, her lips twisted into a grimace. "I want to be where my son's memory lives."

Clouds gathered overhead, and a few fat raindrops fell. Nora stood and lifted Mrs. Davies with her. "Let me take you home. Can you show me the way?"

"Across the mountain, before death." Mrs. Davies dropped her head and allowed Nora to shelter her beneath her arm. "But I'll show you where I'm living."

Nora strained to see Pallavi when they passed the market, but most of the merchants were packing up, and she knew Pallavi had left her. Mrs. Davies led her down neat streets to a one-story bungalow fronted by a long verandah.

As they climbed the stairs, a man rushed out the door and caught Mrs. Davies's arms. "Where have you been, darling? I was so worried."

"I went to the lake." She sounded so tired that Nora thought she might drop onto the tiled floor the moment they entered the house.

"The lake?" The man met Nora's eyes over his wife's head. He led them into a small parlor, where Mrs. Davies sank onto a settee, resting her head against the backrest. Nora, aware of her mud- and grass-stained skirt, stood beside her.

"Nora, this is my husband, Charan Davies." Mrs. Davies's words dropped from her lips like stones. She still clutched Lukose's boat, her fingers smoothing over it as though it were a rosary. After a moment, her fingers stilled, and her head nodded forward, lashes fluttering before dropping closed. Her shallow breaths caused her chest to rise and fall in sleep.

"Thank you for seeing her home," Mr. Davies said. He motioned for Nora to follow him back toward the front door. "I'm sorry for her behavior. She hasn't recovered from the death of our son, and she's still weak from illness."

"She told me."

He nodded once. He was a handsome man, hazel eyes contrasting against bronze skin, but strain had carved deep lines on either side of his mouth. He ran his hand over his face, and Nora didn't miss the way it trembled. "We've lost our child, and I may still lose my wife. If not to this disease, then to melancholy." He smiled, but it didn't reach past his lips. "Thank you again for helping her."

When he opened the door for her, they saw the rain tumbling from the sky like a waterfall.

He looked at her. "Would you like to wait it out?"

Nora shook her head. She didn't want to worry Owen or give Mr. Alford any ammunition. "No, I must go."

She slipped from the house and hurried down the walk, eager to get away from the overwhelming grief and regret that covered Mr. and Mrs. Davies and blanketed their home.

Chapter Ten

Determined to finish her assigned illustrations before the end of the day, Nora had woken when she heard Pallavi rattle into camp, dressed quickly, and pulled the table into place before the sun had fully risen. It had rained through the night, and the heat hadn't yet burned the moisture from the ground, so she settled one of the Jamakkalam rugs from her tent under her feet. It was coarse beneath her toes, and the orange and red stripes brought a smile to her lips when she remembered how Pallavi had shoved the rugs into her arms the night before when Nora finally made it back to camp, two hours after the cook. The rain had slowed her down, and she'd taken refuge beneath a tree for the better part of an hour.

"You got lost?" Pallavi had asked. The men crowded behind her, fear and anger flashing in their eyes.

"Where were you?" Owen's cheeks went taut, and a tremor underscored his words. "We were just about to leave and search for you."

Nora hadn't wanted to betray Mrs. Davies's story, so she busied herself untying the string around the rolled-up rug and then watched as it unfurled. It was narrow but long enough to offer some comfort when she got off her cot in the morning. Something to soften the canvas floor and brighten her tent's drab interior.

She assured the men she was fine, told Pallavi she was too tired to eat, and marched into her tent, dragging the rug behind her. As she stripped off her sweat-soaked clothing and wiped a damp, tepid cloth across her heat-prickled skin, she listened to them argue about her.

"She needs to stay put. I don't have time to go out and search for her." Mr. Alford didn't even try to mask his anger or hide his words.

"If you insist on keeping her trapped in camp, she will find ways to get out and explore on her own." Nora wanted to be angry at the confidence in Owen's voice. He didn't know her that well, after all, and it seemed presumptuous of him to speak on her behalf.

But it was true.

Their voices dropped then, and she fell onto the cot, her arm flung off the side and her fingers trailing over the rug's knobby weave. She'd fallen asleep to the sound of their heated whispers.

Nora lifted a brush from the table and wiped her thumb across the splatter of orange ink marring the wood. She wanted to finish illustrating the specimens. Wanted to prove she was capable of hard work. If that meant she forwent rest, so be it.

She wiped the bristles on a square of linen lying on her lap and dipped them into the cake of orange watercolor. Leaning over her work, she carefully drew the tip of the brush through the *Aphnaeus schistacea*'s cream wing.

Pallavi shuffled over and glanced at her painting. With a shake of her head, she moved toward the fire, where *sambar* was boiling over the flames. She stuck her finger in the pot and brought it to her mouth before pouring and pinching and shaking an assortment of spices into the stew. Leaning near, she wafted the steam toward her nose and inhaled with a whistle.

Satisfied, she drew back and pushed a flat, circular griddle over the flames.

"What are you making?" Nora asked. So far, breakfast had been *sambar*—a stew made with lentils, vegetables, and tamarind— along with rice.

"*Dosai*." The word tripped over Pallavi's tongue, and Nora tried it out while the cook disappeared into the cabin. A moment later, she reappeared and took slow steps toward Nora's workstation, carrying a dented metal bowl covered with a light cloth. She jerked her chin toward Nora's canvas, and when Nora moved it, she set down her bowl. "*Dosai*," she said again, pulling off the cloth.

Nora leaned over the bowl and sniffed the foamy, sour-scented batter. "Pancakes?"

Pallavi made a tsking sound and pulled the bowl back to her belly. "Come. Help."

Nora looked at the last two butterflies needing to be illustrated— two small *Hesperiidae*. Skippers weren't her favorite—most didn't have interesting markings and were a dull shade of brown—so she'd saved them for last, knowing she could paint both on one canvas in less than an hour. She could have them done before Mr. Alford awoke, leaving him with no excuse to abandon her at camp. But Pallavi stood above her, clutching the bowl and watching her with narrow eyes, as though daring Nora to ignore her invitation.

"All right." Nora stood and followed Pallavi to the smoking pan.

Setting the bowl on the ground, Pallavi lifted a jar of ghee and poured a bit in the center of the griddle. With rapid strokes, she rubbed the oil onto the hot surface. Taking a wide ladle from the box of utensils at her feet, she dipped it into the batter and spread it in a thin circle in the pan. After a minute, she turned it with her fingers, then motioned to the stack of metal plates in a nearby basket. Nora retrieved one.

With a few flicks of her fingers, Pallavi folded the pastry into quarters and set it on the plate. She dipped a spoon into the *sambar* and poured it beside the *dosa*. She pulled waxed canvas off a small jar of tomato chutney and dropped a dollop onto Nora's plate, then motioned for Nora to eat.

Nora still hadn't gotten used to using her fingers as a fork, but she managed to tear off a bit of the steaming bread and scoop up a good portion of the lentils and chutney. The spicy-tangy flavors burst on contact with her tongue.

"It's delicious." She ate and watched Pallavi expertly make a small pile of *dosai*. After her last bite, she said, "Can I try?"

Pallavi sent her a startled glance, but she handed over the ladle. Nora dipped it into the batter, tipping a bit out when Pallavi grunted and pushed against her hand. When Pallavi jiggled her head, Nora poured batter onto the griddle and tried to spread it, only succeeding in making a mess.

Pallavi's fingers curled around Nora's wrist, and she guided Nora's movements so that the batter began to look somewhat the way it should.

"Flip," Pallavi said.

Nora pinched the crispy edges and flipped it, burning herself in the process. She popped the tip of her index finger into her mouth. Pallavi pulled Nora's finger free and gently cupped Nora's hand in the palm of her own, twisting the injured finger one way and the other as a small blister formed. Nora hissed when Pallavi poked at it with her nail.

Muttering a string of Tamil, the cook dug through the basket of utensils at her feet and emerged with a jar. "Honey." Using a clean spoon, she pulled out a dab and gently spread it over Nora's burn, then patted the top of Nora's hand.

For a brief moment, Pallavi's fingers, dry and papery, stood in stark contrast to Nora's. One dark and wrinkled, the other fair and smooth. And for an even briefer moment, Nora felt a connection to the Indian woman. Her mother had never cared for Nora after an injury. Had never taken a moment to tend to a scrape or burn or wound. It had always been the other way around—a backward way—the daughter caring for the parent.

The attention felt nice.

Footsteps approached. "Can you please try to keep yourself safe?" Owen said.

Nora ignored him and withdrew her hand from Pallavi's. She ladled out more batter and made another circle, this time without help. "Get yourself a plate. I'm making you breakfast."

Owen snorted. "Are you becoming domestic?"

She scowled and pressed a fist into her hip, but before she could open her mouth, he nodded toward the griddle, where the edges of her *dosa* had begun to burn. She flipped it, spreading the burn on the tip of her finger to the pad. But she wouldn't let him notice. She gritted her teeth and pressed her thumb against the pain, spreading the honey.

After she plated Owen's breakfast, she handed the ladle back to Pallavi and waited with more curiosity than she cared to admit. He shoved a large bite into his mouth and watched her while he chewed. Then swallowed. Then ate some more.

When he finished his meal without saying a word, Nora rolled her eyes and went back to her table. She settled in, pulled the last two butterflies closer, and jumped when he drew near and whispered in her ear.

"It was delicious, of course. You do everything well."

A smug smile curled her lips.

"We're going to search for the *Papilio buddha* again when it cools off this evening. Want to come?"

Her smile drooped, and she turned toward him. "Really?"

For a moment, he stared at her, and she stared back. They'd both taken to a simpler mode of dress. The Indian sun was too harsh, the rain too capricious, to insist on all the layers of current Western fashion. Maybe if they lounged around airy bungalows in town, being fanned by servants, they'd be willing to subject themselves to proper attire. She wondered if she'd chosen too relaxed an outfit in wearing only a simple linen skirt and an unadorned challis blouse, and she fingered the bit of lace at her throat, pushing the top button she'd undone as she worked it back through its hole.

Owen blinked, took a step back, and nodded. "You have my gift of persuasion to thank for that."

Attire forgotten, she crossed her arms. "I'm not thanking you for convincing him to allow me to do something he should have allowed me to do from the very beginning."

He shrugged. "I don't need your thanks. I'm pretty proud of myself. Do you want to put your work away and see if we can find anything interesting that lives outside the order of *Lepidoptera*?"

Nora glanced at her little brown skippers and bit her lower lip. She needed to finish these. Her focus on this trip was butterflies. But India held a wealth of interesting insects, and she didn't want to miss the opportunity to find some to add to her collection. She especially didn't want Owen finding them without her.

Without a word, she packed up her supplies and specimens. Owen helped her load everything back into the cabin, and they grabbed their rucksacks on the way out of camp just as the sun was burning the moisture from the grass and trees.

"Where should we go?" Nora asked as they trudged through foot-tall grasses. Seeds wove a delicate pattern into the fibers of her skirt, much like the ones that graced the saris the women in this exotic place wore. She picked one off and bit into it, the fresh taste washing away breakfast's heavy spices.

Beside her, Owen shrugged his rucksack onto his other shoulder and put a steadying hand on her arm. He let it rest there, offering her a firm place to lean against when the ground curved upward, moving them closer and closer to the blue-tinged hills of the Western Ghats.

"There's a stretch of shola on the other side of this hill I want to explore. Let's head there."

The hike took long enough that the soles of Nora's feet began to burn inside her snug boots, and her calves screamed for respite. She stumbled, and Owen's broad hand cradled her lower back as she righted herself.

"Almost to the crest," he said. "Look."

Her gaze following the direction of his pointed finger, Nora saw nothing but wide swaths of bare ground peeking out from sunburned grass. But then, as though a mirage had come to life, half a dozen animals roughly the size of a mountain goat but sporting curved horns appeared, their sturdy brown bodies blending into the backdrop of dirt and stone.

Nora stopped shuffling her feet forward and stood still, not wanting to startle them as they grazed. "What are they?"

"We saw them the other day. William called them *varaiaadu*. It means precipice goat, but it's not really a goat. I believe it's a kind of tahr. He said there used to be large herds all over these mountains, but hunting has diminished their numbers. I'm not sure they'll recover."

The creatures moved with a grace peculiar for animals so solidly built. A chill swept Nora, icing her blood and prickling against her spine. The Western Ghats held an astounding diversity of flora and fauna. There were certainly undiscovered species of both making their home in the grasslands, hills, and sholas. How many had disappeared before a scientist had ever noticed their unfurling petals, creeping bodies, or stretching legs? Would the *varaiaadu* become extinct and be lost to future study?

She shifted her bag and sat on the ground, heedless of the biting rocks. Flipping open the rucksack's flap, she pulled out her sketchbook and pencils and set about capturing the tahr with firm strokes.

"What are you doing?" Owen asked, settling beside her.

His interruption should have irritated her, but she felt nothing except the satisfied reassurance of being in the presence of another human being. Companionship with a person who understood the fragile themes exposed by nature.

"Rose has spent years working with the animals at the Cin-

cinnati Zoological Gardens. She is particularly interested in their conservation efforts. I think she'd appreciate learning about this animal before the ability to understand it is lost." She finished the drawing and began jotting down notes on the edges of the page about its size, movements, and interactions with others in its herd.

Owen shifted closer, sparking that missing irritation, and she scooted a few inches away. "I wonder how many insect species have faded into history without making an imprint on humanity's consciousness," he said.

Nora snapped her face toward him and recovered the distance she'd created only a moment earlier. "I was just thinking the same thing."

His smile softened, and he was no longer the flirtatious man who prodded and joked, but a scientist of deep thoughts and even more lovely words. "If you're done, maybe we can discover a species before it's too late."

She grinned, shoved her supplies into her bag, and leapt to her feet as easily as the tahrs did when her movement startled them. The animals' legs pumped, and they soon disappeared over the hill's ridge, their pounding hooves an echo of what used to be.

She shook off her maudlin thoughts and traipsed with renewed energy over the crest of the hill and down to where the shola took over and ensconced them within its embrace.

"I already love the shola," she said, her voice dropping to a whisper. "There's a peace here I have never felt before. It feels like a sanctuary hidden deep in the country of a thousand idols. A place where God's fingerprints point to His plan." Her face burned as the words slipped out, branding her as sentimental.

But Owen didn't tease. He didn't use her words to prove the silliness of women or unsuitability of her gender in a man's field. He took her elbow, his warm fingers slipping across her skin, and said, "I agree."

She smiled up at him, not sure why she had ever hated him

in the first place. Sticky threads kissed her cheek, and she froze. "Stop! I don't want to destroy whatever it is I've run into."

Owen's eyes took in the web encasing her face, spending more time in examination than seemed necessary. "It's not damaged. You only disconnected a few strands. Here." He pinched at the bits of silk and rubbed them free of his fingers.

As soon as Nora knew she wouldn't ruin one of nature's most beautiful displays, she took in the web strung between two mahogany trees. About five feet in diameter, it shone like spun gold in the light filtering through the upper story of the shola. "It's a *Nephila pilipes*." She poked a pinky toward the hub, which radiated outward from the top center of the web. The sticky capture strands filled the lower part of the web, but the spider had wrapped and moved five insects into a cache above the hub. The golden orb weaver rested near her cache, observing her viscous kingdom. "Do you have one in your collection?"

"I don't," Owen said, "but feel free to make it yours. I think a spider with this level of dimorphism should become the prize of an equally strong female."

A laugh bubbled up in Nora's throat, one she couldn't capture, and it spilled out with enough force to sway the spider web, sending the golden orb weaver south toward where Nora's laugh had vibrated the silk threads. Half a dozen tiny males, ten times smaller than the female, scuttled around with nervous energy. "Pull out my large kill jar, Owen. Quickly."

He shuffled through her bag and handed it to her. Twisting off the lid, she clamped it between her teeth, reached for the female spider, and pinched around its opisthosoma. Its gold and black jointed legs stiffened before wrapping fully around Nora's wrist. One of the largest spiders in the world, it would make an impressive addition to any collection, especially one that had been decimated.

Before it could bite her, she shoved it into the jar and jammed the lid back on. Holding it up between their faces, Nora grinned at Owen. "Beautiful, isn't she?"

Owen peered into the jar. "Do you suppose you're the only woman on the planet who thinks that?"

Nora shrugged. "Possibly."

"Does it bother you, being unlike anyone else?"

"Should it? What's the alternative? Being afraid of creatures like this?" She flicked her nail against the glass and shook her head. "I wouldn't want to be anything but who I am."

Owen grinned, a crooked one that did odd things to her belly. "I wouldn't want you to be anything else either."

Early that evening, after Nora and Owen had returned from their exploration, Mr. Alford formally invited Nora to join them for the outing. He thought they'd be more likely to find a *Papilio buddha* after the worst of the day's heat had dissipated, so they set off after a light dinner, each of them carrying a rucksack over their shoulders and a few of the men bearing lanterns for the return trip.

"Of course, gather anything you think might be useful, but I mainly want to find the Malabar banded peacock. I had one in my collection before leaving for India, but it wasn't mounted properly and degraded." Mr. Alford led them deep into the forest, and soon the towering pines blotted out the sun and a carpet of needles muffled their steps. A light drizzle misted the air, and he groaned. "Let's fan out. We'll be more likely to find the butterfly that way. Hopefully the rain doesn't begin in earnest. Call out every few minutes to keep track of the rest of the group. I don't want to have to search for anyone. Plus, the noise will frighten away any animals."

He stomped in the opposite direction as Nora, muttering about bad luck and the quickly approaching monsoon.

Nora disappeared around the bend in the path, eyes peeled for the *Papilio buddha*'s bright green and aqua markings. Every few moments, a male voice called out "Here!" but she hardly registered the shouts. It wouldn't hurt to be the one to find the butterfly Mr. Alford most wanted. She knew how much a prized insect could soften the heart. She swiveled her head in every direction, paying particular attention to the fruit trees the butterfly loved to feed on, and pushed even deeper into the forest.

The air was heavy and moist, cloying as it threaded sticky tendrils around her exposed skin. She strained to see through the fog that filled the woods with clouds. It wove around the base of the trees, muffling everything, and she felt surrounded by ghosts.

"Nora, where are you?"

Owen's low call pulled a startled "here" from her throat. Turning in the direction she'd heard his voice, she pushed through a bush the height of a maple tree and tripped over a thick vine crawling around its trunk, catching herself on her hands. A centipede scuttled over her knuckles. She forced herself to stay still so it didn't pierce her skin with its forcipules and watched, enthralled, as its hundred tiny legs roved over her fingers, tickling her.

She smiled when it toppled to the ground, and she stood and brushed at the leaves and clumps of dirt clinging to her damp skirt. She needed to find the rest of the team. Dusk bathed the magenta-flowering rhododendron ahead of her in silver. A moth, larger than her palm, landed on one of the flowers. She approached it with soft steps. Its pale green wings shimmered against the bright flowers.

How lovely.

She held her finger to the flower and, when the moth stepped onto it, brought it to eye level. Two fern-like antennae framed its furry face. She smiled when it lifted its pink legs and traveled the length of her hand.

She pinched the wings between her fingers and turned it over. Its underdeveloped mouth worked as she squeezed either side of the moth's thorax, careful not to crush it. When it became immobilized, she pulled a jar from her sack and slid the moth inside.

Paralyzed, the moth didn't beat its wings against the jar and damage itself, and Nora watched as its wiggling legs grew still.

She held up the jar, allowing the shadowed light to filter through it, and admired her new specimen. Through the glass she saw past the moth and into the canopy of a cluster of trees. She lowered the jar and squinted at an odd, pieced-together globe hanging from a branch.

She tucked the kill jar back into her rucksack and approached the tree. Brittle brown leaves looked to have been sewn together to make the globe, and a few orange ants crawled from a crevice and marched around its perimeter.

She gasped. *Oecophylla smaragdina*. Weaver ants!

Tramping feet alerted Nora to someone's approach, and Mr. Alford and Owen appeared from between the leafy foliage of the rhododendrons.

"Anything?" Mr. Alford asked. His lank hair hung over his eyes, and he pushed it back with a fine-boned hand.

"Not the butterfly you wanted, but look." Nora pointed up at the weaver ant nest, and Mr. Alford cast a dismissive glance its way.

"We may as well head back." He looked at the sky. "It's going to pour any minute. What a waste."

"I'm going to look at it," Nora said, grabbing a low branch and pulling herself up onto it. Her skirts twisted around her legs, and she grabbed a fistful of the material and bunched it in her palm. With a gentle bounce, she tested the branch's strength. Satisfied it would hold, she pulled herself up to the next one and wrapped her legs around it.

"Nora, we aren't here to study ants. Come down." Mr. Alford's curt words just barely cut through her mission.

"Just a few moments. I've been fascinated by weaver ants since Professor Comstock first told us about them. Don't you remember, Owen? It was last year during his discussion on the world's most painful insect bites. Light the lamp for me and hold it up. It's getting too dark."

Owen chanced a glance at Mr. Alford but lit his lamp and held his arm aloft. "Give her a second. There really is no dissuading her."

As Owen and Mr. Alford argued, she inched toward the nest. The weaver ant was aggressive. After biting, it would rub its abdomen against the skin, infusing the fresh wound with a smear of formic acid. Nora's hands shook with anticipation. How marvelous.

She sat so close to the nest now that she could see a steady march of ants exiting it. They walked downward over each other, clinging to one another to form a chain that swung over the ground. Nora laughed at their behavior. She'd never seen anything like it.

They must have felt the vibrations from her movement against the branch, because the chain dissolved, the ants scattering over the branch. One moved toward her, and not willing to vacate her perch, she flicked it from the tree.

"Nora! Come down now. The other men have gathered."

Her head shot up at Mr. Alford's call, and she wrinkled her nose. "Just one more moment. I want to see inside it." She pulled a twig from the branch above her and slid closer to the nest. Just as she poked at it with the stick, another call came.

"Maybe you should come down," Owen said. "Haven't you learned your lesson climbing trees?"

She sighed. "Owen Epps, what type of entomologist is so afraid of falling from a tree that they'd abandon their study of such a fascinating creature?" She used the stick to separate two of the glued-together leaves and pushed one to the side. She peered inside the nest and grinned. Over a hundred ants scurried around, dancing to music only they could hear. "They're incredible."

A few of the ants scuttled from the nest, and Nora removed her twig when they began to walk along it. She banged it against the branch, knocking the ants free, then stuck the twig back into the nest. This time she leaned over, only inches from the opening, and saw the larvae glowing white against the leaf wall. She poked at the nest with her finger. How had they made it so sturdy? Amazing.

The tree trembled beneath Nora, and Owen grunted. "How did you get up here? That wasn't easy." He popped his head above the branch where she sat.

"I'm good at climbing trees."

"You're also good at falling out of them."

"I won't fall this time." She lifted the nest with the stick, intent on seeing how they had attached it to the tree. "Look at this. They use the silk from the larvae to glue together their nests."

She bit her lower lip. Steady. She propped the twig beneath the nest, and . . . it popped from the tree and tumbled through the air.

Mr. Alford screamed. Nora and Owen looked at each other with wide eyes, and Nora chanced a glance below, where their team leader smacked at his head with his hands, the weaver ants swarming his hair, face, and neck.

"Oh no . . ." She pushed at Owen and scrambled off the branch.

Owen jumped from the tree, and after she sat on the bottom branch, he gripped her waist and lowered her to the ground. She hurried to Mr. Alford and joined the other men in brushing the ants from him.

Razors sliced at her palms as the ants used their strong mandibles to bite through her skin. Her admiration at their cunningness fled as fire spread across her hands. She stomped and crushed every little devil she saw.

Finally, their frenzy ended. Mr. Alford pressed his hands against the raw, reddened skin along his temples, jaw, and neck. His fingers spanned his face, and through the gaps between them, he glared at Nora, tears pooling in his eyes.

"You—" The word came out as an accusation, and in it Nora heard all manner of insults.

"I'm so sorry. I didn't mean for this to happen." Her palms

throbbed, and she spread her fingers so that the air circulated around them.

"You stupid girl." Mr. Alford spun and pushed through the weeds and brush. Mr. Steed smirked at her, then followed.

Mr. Taylor pushed his hat up and scratched his head. "Well, this will probably set you back in your quest to prove yourself to him."

"It was an accident. It could have happened to anyone," William said in a mournful voice. "But it's bad luck it happened to you."

When they turned and left, Owen came alongside her and gripped her hand in his. She gasped at the pain but allowed the comfort of his touch to soothe her heart.

"It'll be okay," he said.

"Your optimism in me is undeserved."

She shook off his hand and followed the men back to the road, an easy feat given the loud string of curses trailing behind Mr. Alford.

Chapter
Eleven

Nora watched William and Mr. Alford pull the table from the cabin. Mr. Taylor followed with a couple of cardboard boxes, which she knew contained the butterflies the men had found over the previous two days.

"Oh, honestly." She stomped over to Owen's tent. "I must talk with you."

He pushed aside the flap, and she stepped back at his sudden closeness.

"You need to talk to Mr. Alford," she said. "He still has me working only on illustrations, and he hasn't spared me a word since the . . . incident."

Owen bent over her, and she caught the scent of his lovely cologne. It had to be imported, though how he managed to smell so good when the other men stank of body odor and garlic was beyond her. When he spoke, his breath sent the tendrils that had escaped her chignon dancing, and they tickled her ear. "You should do something to endear yourself to him."

It took a moment for his words to register, but when they

did, she frowned. "I'm not going to manipulate him in order to further my career."

"Making yourself useful isn't manipulation. Try being . . . pleasant."

Nora's mouth dropped. "Aren't I always?"

His eyebrows leapt as though they pulled a laugh from his throat and held on while it danced across his face. She watched with fascination. She'd never seen a man so expressive.

So handsome.

She inhaled sharply. Where had *that* thought come from?

"It might be hard for Mr. Alford to see pleasantness," Owen said, "beneath all of your other idiosyncrasies."

He sauntered toward the cabin, where the rest of the men huddled.

Idiosyncrasies? That sounded like an insult.

She stalked after him, catching up before he reached the cabin, and poked him in the back. When he turned, she said, "Fine. You're right. I haven't properly apologized. But I'm not admitting to any *idiosyncrasies*."

Nora took a few steps toward Mr. Alford, whose face was mottled by angry red marks. He drew his thin brows—so different from Owen's—together, and his mustache drooped, giving him the look of a sad hound.

Something twinged beneath her ribs. He looked terrible. And, as much as she wanted to blame him for standing under the tree, Owen was right—it was her fault. She'd been bullheaded in her determination to study the ants despite Mr. Alford's probably appropriate objections.

She stopped in front of him. "I'm truly sorry you were hurt, Mr. Alford. It wasn't my intention, and I never dreamed that thing would go flying through the air."

Mr. Alford ran a finger over the welts covering his jawline. He narrowed his eyes but said nothing.

"I'd like to go out with you today. I give you my word that I'll do only what you ask of me, even if I see something interesting.

I'd be a help to your team. My knowledge and experience in tracking butterflies would be an asset."

His pale skin between the ant bites turned vermillion, and Nora couldn't tell the marks from his flush. "No."

Her shoulders sank, and she could almost feel herself shrinking. She tried to resist the despair. Tried to throw back her chin and look him in the eye and *demand* he respect her abilities. But she knew he was no longer denying her because of her gender. He didn't want her around because he didn't trust her. And she had only herself to blame for that.

A deep sigh shuddered her chest, and she pressed her lips together, knowing she had to overcome an even steeper mountain of effort to win his favor. "Okay. I understand. I might, though, when my work is done, do a little exploring on my own."

"There are tigers and leopards in the shola and grasslands. You may go if you wish to be eaten. It is safer in a group." He shrugged.

"Mr. Taylor goes out alone all the time searching for his elusive land leeches. Do tigers not like the taste of British men?"

Mr. Taylor, who stood beside the fire, drinking a cup of tea, leveled a stare at her. "Few things like the taste of British men."

Owen snorted and leaned close. "Something you have in common with them, Peculiar?"

She nudged him with her shoulder and didn't break eye contact with Mr. Alford. "You leave Pallavi and me alone every day in camp. Is that unsafe?"

"Tigers won't attack a human if they have an abundant food supply. However, if you chance upon one outside of camp, they just might grow annoyed enough to bare their claws and teeth." Mr. Alford stared at her, unblinking, until his eye twitched. He whirled and waved his hand above his head. "Come on, men, let's get things packed up." Then he stomped toward his tent and disappeared inside.

Owen laid his large hand on her shoulder. "You tried."

Warmth traveled down her arms at his touch, right to her fingertips. "It didn't seem to help."

He turned her toward him and gripped her hands. "A soft answer turns away wrath. Don't worry. He'll come around."

"I didn't realize you were a philosopher."

His teeth flashed in a boyish grin. "That's from the Bible. Proverbs. Do you want me to finish it?"

His blue eyes fixed on her. Nora thought it incredible that the same theory observed by Hooke and Newton—structural coloration—could affect both insect wings and Owen's eyes. She tipped her head toward him, trying to get a closer look.

"All right, tell me," she said, hoping to distract him a moment longer.

His mouth tipped to one side as though he knew her motive. "A soft answer turns away wrath, but a harsh word stirs up anger." He blinked, his fair lashes sweeping over his eyes, cutting them from her observation, and she focused on what he was saying. "I admire your strength and drive, but sometimes those things need to be tempered with grace. Words, especially, can bring healing or pain."

"Have I ever spoken to you in a way that brought you pain?" she asked, not sure she really wanted to know. They'd gone to school together long enough that she was certain she must have.

He rubbed his thumbs over her knuckles, and Nora, having forgotten he still held her hands, drew a deep breath. His eyes grew soft, almost as though someone had filled the pigment with pastel chalk.

"It doesn't matter. Your words don't intimidate me."

"Do you think that's what I mean to do?" She dropped her voice and stepped closer so that only the whisper of a dragonfly's flight separated them. What had gotten into her? Her hands began to sweat, and she didn't know if it was the sticky humidity, Owen's clasp, or her own forward behavior.

There was something about India. . . .

Owen's lips settled into the laugh lines running down the sides of his face. She wanted to run her finger over those creases. She tugged one hand from his and kept it there, hovering between them like a fly caught in a spider's web. Trapped between the wanting and the knowing. She felt the languid pace of her new home seep into her pores and thicken her blood so that it traveled through her veins as unhurried as the Indian people who lived life without any clocks.

Nora lifted her hand, her trembling fingers only a hairsbreadth from his jaw. And for once, Owen's brows stilled. They rested over eyes so filled with wonder and hope that her breath hitched, and she made a small noise in her throat.

And then something sounding very much like an elephant stampeded into camp and shook Nora from her hazy dream as it shrieked and stomped and wailed.

Nora whirled. Pallavi wrestled a little girl—about eleven—in an embrace that seemed more intent on harm than affection. She could hardly keep her grip on the child, though, who hollered and struggled.

Owen rushed toward them. "Pallavi, what are you doing to that poor child? Let her go."

Pallavi loosened her grip but gave her head a harsh shake. "No. She can't be here." She smacked the girl on the side of the head, sending her eyes skyward.

When Owen pried Pallavi's hand free, the cook let loose a stream of Tamil and shook her finger in the girl's face. The child remained stoic, standing just outside Pallavi's reach, but a single tear dripped down her dirt-streaked cheek.

A thread of empathy twisted around Nora's heart, and she hurried over. "What's going on?"

Pallavi stuck out her lower lip and crossed her arms. The child looked up at Nora with brown eyes so wide and deep that Nora felt unable to keep from sinking beneath the despair she recognized in them.

"I am Sita." The girl spoke perfect English.

Owen crouched. "You seem to have made an enemy of our cook."

Sita sent a scornful glance at Pallavi. "She is my aunt. My father's sister."

Nora's eyes widened. "Why would your aunt treat you so abominably?"

Sita lifted a slim shoulder and scratched at her scalp.

Nora pursed her lips and looked at Pallavi, whose fingers reached for Sita's bare arm. "Pallavi?"

"She needs to stay away!" Pallavi punctuated her words with a ringing clap. "She's very bad. Stubborn."

Sita's chin trembled and her nose wrinkled, turning her expressive mouth into a sneer—a look of defiance Nora well knew covered a broken heart.

Nora pulled the girl to her side and rested her hand against Sita's shoulder. "It sounds like we have much in common."

Sita turned her face upward. "I only wanted to see the foreign lady scientist everyone speaks of, *Akka*."

"That doesn't sound like it deserves punishment, Pallavi." Owen touched the small of Nora's back. She shivered, which seemed an odd response to the heat pouring through her shirt-waist.

She forced herself to ignore the pressure of Owen's touch and put her attention back on their cook just as Pallavi grabbed Sita's arm, her bony fingers biting into the girl's soft flesh.

"I won't let her come. I said no. I will lose my work and have no money!"

Sita wriggled from Pallavi's grip, and Nora imitated her mother, using as soothing a voice as possible. "Pallavi, you're not going to lose your position because Sita wanted to meet me. I'm quite flattered by her—"

"What is that beastly child doing in my camp?" Mr. Alford's strident voice cut through their conversation. Sita dropped her chin to her chest and began to spin the gold bracelets circling her wrist.

"I told her not to come." Pallavi jerked her arms heavenward, palms out.

When Mr. Alford huffed and approached them, Owen stepped to the right, blocking him from reaching Sita. Nora stared at his broad back, his shoulders pulling at his shirt's seams when he held up his arms. Why had she never noticed how *good* Owen was?

"What's the problem with her visiting?" Owen asked. "She's just a child."

Mr. Alford tried to sidestep Owen, but Sita slithered around Nora's legs, wrapped her arms around Nora's midsection, and buried her head into the small of her back.

"That *child* managed to undo a week of work the last time she was here. Emptied all of our insect boxes and used their parts to create a portrait of one of their idols."

"I didn't!" Sita's arms tightened, crushing Nora's hips.

She extricated herself. "You didn't destroy the insects?"

Sita's eyes filled before she blinked away the tears, and her lips flattened. So stubborn. And rebellious. This child, this girl with the silver stud in her nose and the mischievous glint in her eyes, captivated Nora.

She bent and whispered in Sita's ear, "Tell me what happened."

The little girl's jaw tightened and worked. Her eyes skittered between Owen, Pallavi, and Mr. Alford before landing on Nora, lighting up when they paused on her brooch. Sita touched it with a fingertip. "It's beautiful." She tipped her head. "It's a *cilvantu.*" She squeezed her eyes shut and wrinkled her brow. "A cicada?"

A smile tugged at Nora's lips. "It is. What a smart girl you are."

Mr. Alford sighed. "Just get her out of camp as soon as you can." As he walked past, he shook a long finger at Sita. "And don't get into anything."

Pallavi muttered beneath her breath and shoved at the always-burning fire with a stick. It sent sparks through the air, and Nora pulled Sita farther from the flames toward the grouping of camp chairs.

"Come and sit with me." She shook her head at Owen when he started to follow them and shooed him away. Some things were better left to feminine pursuit.

"Look," she said after they'd sat down. She removed her gold and jade brooch and nestled it in Sita's palm.

Sita stroked the scarab-embossed stones studding the cicada.

"My father gave it to me," Nora said. "It's very special."

Sita smiled and gave it back to Nora. "Thank you for letting me hold it. It's beautiful. I'd like to draw it sometime."

"Do you like art?"

Sita nodded. She glanced at the cabin Mr. Alford had disappeared into, and her shoulders slumped. "I did take apart the insects. They were so nice, and I saw what they could be if I put them all together."

"Why did you say you didn't?"

She leaned close, a wide grin flashing and swallowing her face for a moment. "I meant I didn't make a picture of an idol."

"What did you make a picture of?"

Sita's eyes shuttered.

Nora could see her pulling away. Closing a door. "Please tell me. I will keep it secret, if you want." She didn't know why she wanted to know this little girl. Why did she want to understand her? Hear her story?

Sita nodded once, and her nostrils flared with a quick intake of breath. "They showed us a picture of him at school, but I wanted him to look like me, so I used the black wings for his hair and beard. It took three white and tan butterflies to give me enough tan for his skin, but I pieced it together. And there was one butterfly with soft brown wings that I shaped into his eyes."

She didn't look guilty for having destroyed so many specimens. Nora thought she looked . . . radiant.

"Who were you making?"

The girl peered around Nora, then put her mouth to Nora's ear. "Jesus."

Nora pulled back. "Why is that a secret?"

Sita slumped against her chair and hugged her legs to her chest, the embroidered edge of her tunic fanning out around her square feet. "I am dedicated to Yellamma." She sat upright and grasped Nora's hands, squeezing them until they tingled. "You cannot tell my aunt that I am a Christian. What would my father say? A servant of the goddess who has placed all of her trust in a foreign god."

She released Nora's hands and stroked them, her calloused fingertips rubbing small circles over Nora's smooth knuckles. She bowed her head, and Nora felt an urge to hug the child. She ignored it and spoke logic instead.

"Why does that bother you? You don't have to believe what your father tells you to."

Sita raised her face, despair written in the premature lines between her softly arched brows. "Because after I bleed, I will be sent to the temple to work. I cannot serve Yellamma, and if I don't, my father will turn me out."

Chapter Twelve

Nora sat hunched over the detested table that held her work. Elbow resting on the splintered wood, chin in her palm, she tapped her fingers against her cheek and watched as Mr. Alford prepared to leave camp without her yet again.

She'd hardly done anything but paint pretty watercolors and sketch diagrammed butterflies since arriving in India a month earlier. The monotony was broken only by Sita's almost daily visits. After the men left in the morning, she'd come into camp, avoiding her aunt's pinching fingers and glares, and watch Nora work. Then they would run into the shola, Nora's rucksack bouncing against her hip.

Nora had never been so grateful for a friend, even though that friend was much younger than she was. She'd always appreciated time spent alone, but here, loneliness stalked her, peering from the fringe of forest and waiting until her defenses were down to overtake her at the strangest moments. Even when surrounded by the others, she couldn't shake the sense of not belonging. Mr. Alford had made no secret of the fact that she didn't.

But with Sita, Nora had found purpose that extended past the need to produce illustrations of other people's discoveries. With Sita, Nora found relief from the loneliness and isolation.

Sita had told Nora the day before that she wouldn't be visiting today, and Nora found herself missing the young girl. It had taken nearly half a year to develop the kind of friendship with Bitsy and Rose that most women seemed to take for granted, but when Sita stumbled into her life, she'd bypassed all of that and found Nora's heart. The thought set Nora on edge, making her wonder if they'd become too close, too quickly. Good relationships took time, and this one seemed to have exploded into being.

Thankfully, Mr. Taylor and William were staying in camp today, distracting her from uncomfortable thoughts. Mr. Taylor because he wanted to dedicate a little time to his own project—studying the habits of leeches—and William because he'd been banished from Mr. Alford's presence after accidently shattering a collection jar and losing a specimen.

Because of that mishap, Nora had nothing at all to keep her busy today. She'd taken some time before anyone awoke to write to her mother and Anna. She tidied up her tent, gathering the items Pallavi would wash later that day and folding her lightweight blanket into a perfect rectangle. She trimmed her nails with a small pair of scissors.

William had brought the table outside for no reason other than it had become his habit, and she now sat at it for the same reason. There were no boxes of butterflies or tray of paints on the table. Only a paper fan she'd bought the last time she'd been to town.

Pallavi slid a plate of papaya slices onto the table, and Nora sighed. She loved the fruit, but eating it without a fork was a messy process. "I'm going to get a napkin."

When Nora returned to the table, a handkerchief tucked into her sleeve, the plate was gone. Her jaw stiffened when she saw Mr. Steed holding the empty plate, a sticky grin the only evidence of his crime.

"That was mine." She crossed her arms and tapped her foot. She'd grown up never once wishing for a sibling, and now that she felt as though she lived with a troop of brothers, she knew she'd been right.

He shrugged. "You weren't there."

"That doesn't mean I wasn't going to eat it."

He burst into one of his interminable operettas, his eyes flashing with mischief that wouldn't have looked out of place on the face of a child. Her fingers itched with the urge to slap him. Instead she yanked the fan from the table and flapped it at her face. The heat made her impatient and waspish.

"Enough, Jeffrey," Mr. Alford interrupted, and for once Nora was glad for his shrill voice. "Let's get going. Owen, you take the supply bag William usually carries."

With that, the three men set off, Owen sending Nora a small smile that held no joy, only contrition and guilt.

Mr. Taylor dumped the remaining bit of his tea into the grass and handed the cup to Pallavi. He disappeared into his tent, and Nora watched the flap with interest. A moment later, he reappeared wearing cotton duck gaiters above his boots and carrying a stuffed rucksack over his shoulder.

"Where are you going?" she asked.

"Collecting leeches. There's a swamp I believe will yield a bounty about half a mile from here."

She sat up straight and worked to keep the eagerness from her voice. "Can I join you?"

"No."

She slumped back down, and he patted her shoulder.

"I prefer to work alone, Miss Shipley, and I rarely get the chance to enjoy my own company. If you have no work, you might consider doing the same."

"Mr. Alford said there are tigers in the area."

"There are, but not this close to camp. You'll be fine as long as you don't go too far into the forest." He checked his jacket pockets and the clasp on his rucksack, then jerked his chin at something behind Nora. "Why don't you go with William there? He's near useless most of the time, but he'll make a good distraction if you're confronted by a big cat." With a small smile breaking his stoic expression, he left.

"I heard that," William called after him. He turned to Nora and grinned. "Do you want to do some exploring? Don't worry about Frederic's warning about tigers. I've been here for months, and I've not seen evidence of even one. The scariest animal about this area is the gaur, but they tend to run the opposite direction if they hear you coming. Oh, and the snakes. There are elephants too, and they aren't afraid of anything, so you have to steer clear of them. And—" He pasted a bright smile on his face. "You know what, let's just go. Everything will be fine."

Nora's eyes had widened during this speech, and her stomach clenched. When she'd been left in Kodaikanal by herself and walked back to camp, she hadn't known the forest had been full of deadly animals. She'd thrilled in her lonely exploration, happy in her oblivion. She had no wish to be trampled by an elephant or bitten by a snake. But she also had no wish to return home having made no discoveries or done anything of importance.

She eyed William's lanky frame. He was tall but not broad. And likely not able to protect her from anything with teeth or claws. But she had no choice. She stiffened her spine and willed her heart and stomach to settle. She'd stay to the perimeter of the forest, near the wide grasslands that quilted the hilly landscape. Hopefully she wouldn't need to rely on William's questionable bravery and strength to stay alive.

They gathered their supplies, each of them stuffing a rucksack with kill jars, field examination kits, and tweezers. Nora pulled a water-filled canteen over her head, then secured her broad-brimmed hat with pins.

Laden down, she nodded at William, who wore an eager grin and his own hat, a monstrous one that promised to shade a small village. "Ready?"

Setting off, their feet crushing the overgrowth, Nora felt a loosening in her chest. The thick, moist air that had clotted her lungs released, and she drew a deep, purging breath. Sometimes she felt she could hardly breathe in India. She didn't know if it was the weather or the stifling atmosphere Mr. Alford created, but here, stepping beneath the canopy where ferns as tall as trees closed them off from the open grassland and shaded them from the sun, her body relaxed.

"What are we looking for?" William asked, already covered in a fine sheen of sweat.

"Anything."

"It'd be easier to find it if you narrowed your prospects. *Lepidoptera*? *Hemiptera*? *Araneae*? *Odonata*?" He slapped away an overhanging branch. "Or are you more interested in insect ecology? The relationship between insects and diseases? If that's it, you'd be better served going to one of the bigger cities like Calcutta or Madras."

Nora trailed him through the brush and brambles. She stared at his narrow shoulders swimming in an oversized linen jacket. "I didn't realize you knew anything about entomology."

He threw a glance at her. "Then why do you think I'm here?"

She tilted her head. "I don't know. Mr. Steed said you're only here because your father knows people. I just assumed you wanted an adventure."

"I was born and raised in India. This isn't an adventure for me." He held out his arm and welcomed her beside him when the path widened. "I want to go to school in England and work in the field. My mother hasn't been able to release me, though. My brother died last year, and she's holding the rest of us closely. My father thought this would be a good way to ease both of us into the separation."

"And your parents are missionaries?"

"Yes. In Bangalore." He pointed out a bee-eater fluffing its vibrant yellow and green feathers in a nearby tree. "I don't think the birds in England come in those colors."

"From what I've heard, the only thing in England that isn't gray are the ladies' gowns." She shrugged. "Those are black."

He laughed, and they pushed forward until the trees thinned, the ground grew steep, and their breathing labored, and they crossed into open grassland. Ahead of them, something brown flashed, and a powerfully built deer galloped toward the woods.

"It's really beautiful here. There's so much diversity in the topography, flora, and fauna. I don't think I've ever seen so many species of insects in one place." Nora looked out over the tapestry of stitched-together land. Sholas and grasses and hills and, in the distance, the Western Ghats disappearing beneath a mantle of mist.

"You should see the rest of India. Kodaikanal is beautiful, but it's not really representative of India. You'll find more British and Americans here than Indians, and the culture is decidedly European. If you're able, you should travel to Kerala and see the backwaters, or Jodhpur, the blue city, or Hampi, which is littered with ancient temples. India is an amazing country. It would be a shame to only see this little corner of it."

Nora shook her head and smiled at the idea. "No. I'm just here for this one trip. Traveling isn't really for me."

"Really?" He cocked his head. "You seem exactly the type to enjoy traveling."

She laughed. "Everyone keeps saying that. I'm beginning to think I don't know myself as well as I thought I did."

Something buzzed past her ear, and her hand shot toward it. The large beetle escaped her grasp, bumbling toward the forest line just ahead. She lifted her skirts and tore after it, her heart beating to the tempo of discovery.

William's steps pounded after her.

Nora lost sight of the insect but continued running, hiking her skirts even higher and exulting in the freedom. In cutting through the wet air and sucking in deep breaths. In knowing nothing would stop her in this quest—as futile as it was.

The beetle was long gone. And still she ran.

When she reached the forest, sliding over damp earth and decomposing leaves, she slowed to a walk. William kept pace with her, pinching his side and grinning in his enthusiastic way. "What was the hurry?"

"I saw something interesting and gave chase." She stopped in front of a spindly tree and bent to brush the silky purple petals of the orchid growing at its base. "This entire place is full of interesting things to see. I've spent too much time in camp. I'm glad I came out today."

William knelt and snapped the orchid halfway down its stem, then stood and tucked it behind her ear, his face as red as the berries hanging from the tree's branches. "That's exactly what someone who enjoys travel would say."

Nora laughed as Sita surged ahead and broke through the tree line into the grassland where camp had been set. After painting an especially beautiful crimson tip, Nora had grown bored and decided to step into the forest.

She hadn't forgotten William's words from two weeks earlier. *"That's exactly what someone who enjoys travel would say."* She'd taken every opportunity to explore, discovering beautiful flora and fauna, sketching everything, rebuilding her collection with the specimens she found beneath logs sprouting with mushrooms or collecting nectar from showy flowers. She didn't want to take this opportunity for granted. When the trip was over, she might never leave New York again.

"Do you want to come explore with me?" Nora had asked Sita when the girl crept into camp, sidling past her aunt, who was taking a nap near the cabin, her arm thrown over her eyes. Of course Sita had agreed.

They studied the ponderous movements of a green beetle and watched a brilliant blue flycatcher eat a dragonfly and tripped over moss-covered rocks that made stepping-stones across transparent creeks.

Being with Sita and enjoying the diversity of this foreign wood felt familiar and comfortable. But soon the sun had begun to fall from its peak, and Nora knew she needed to return.

She hiked up her skirts and trailed after Sita, who was poking her head into each of the tents.

"What are you doing? Come sit with me and help me finish my work."

Nora pulled out the little stool at the table and ushered Sita to it. Dragging a camp chair up next to her, Nora sat and pulled one of the boxes forward. She removed the lid and pulled the canvas she'd been working on toward her. This particular butterfly had been giving her problems. She couldn't quite replicate its iridescent blue hind wings that faded to black.

"Why is she here again? I thought I told you weeks ago to send her away."

Nora lifted her eyes and looked at Mr. Alford, who stood only paces away, staring down his aristocratic British nose at Sita.

Sita wiggled in her seat and kicked her foot against the table leg. Nora had spent enough time with the child—had listened to her chatter on about school and family and friends—to know she became restless when confronted. But she'd also realized that Sita's quick defenses and ill-mannered expressions, her squirms and impulsivity, hid a girl with a sensitive heart.

Nora reached across the divide between their chairs and rested her hand on Sita's. She wouldn't deny the satisfaction she experienced when her touch settled Sita. Set her at ease.

"Sita visits nearly every day, and she is quite helpful while I work."

Mr. Taylor and William stumbled into camp, clutching their stomachs, and made beelines for their tents. Owen and Mr. Steed followed at a slower pace, stopping when they reached Nora's table.

"What are you doing back this early?" she asked.

Mr. Alford crossed his arms, and his long fingers tapped out a tempo against his sleeves. "Leonard and William are unwell.

Owen, Jeffrey, and I will head back out. Please tend to our patients."

Nora stared at him. "You don't expect me to . . ."

His expression pinched, and he ran his hands through macassar-oiled hair. "What is your purpose here if you can't help where I need it?"

Mr. Steed coughed and slunk away, but Owen mouthed the word *pleasant*.

Nora pushed back her chair and stood. She flicked away stray shavings of pencil from her bodice and tucked an errant curl behind her ear. All the while she looked at Mr. Alford, took his measure, forced her pulse to stop galloping beneath the thin skin at her wrists and temple. His brow furrowed. He looked around at the tents, Pallavi stirring lentils over the fire, and the shrubs circling everything, as though they offered refuge from Nora's steady gaze.

"I came," she said in her best *pleasant* schoolmarm voice, "to work with a team of dedicated scientists on a book for the Crown. My expertise lies in entomological research, not nursing."

His eyes narrowed, and he looked past her. A sardonic smile curled his lips. "Evidently you also have little expertise when it comes to children." He jerked his chin toward the table.

Nora whirled and saw the back of Sita's head, bent low over Nora's canvas. Sita's arm slid back and forth over the table as she rubbed something over Nora's painting, her tongue poking from between her lips, oblivious to Nora and Mr. Alford's attention. She sat back and studied her work a moment. Picking through the pastels, she chose one and ran it over Nora's mediocre rendering.

Mr. Alford chuckled behind her, and Nora nearly lost her grasp on the calm demeanor she'd forced her expression into. Because of him, not the child. It wouldn't take long to replicate her work—she'd not gotten to the challenging part—but Mr. Alford, with his hubris and self-satisfaction, made her vision narrow.

She touched Sita's back. "What are you doing?"

Sita turned and flashed a dimple. She lifted the canvas, holding it aloft with all the pride a child of eleven could muster. "Do you like it, *Akka*?"

Nora gasped, then snatched the picture from Sita. "Oh my."

She'd expected scribbles. Inappropriate colors. An immature likeness.

But this . . . Sita had perfectly replicated the butterfly's magnificent color. Somehow she'd managed what Nora had struggled to do—the blue looked dusted on, blending seamlessly with the black. Thin black markings, highlighted with white, shot through the wings as though painted on by a fairy's pen.

"How . . . ?" Nora turned to Mr. Alford and blinked up at him.

He smirked. "That bad?"

She shook her head, too flabbergasted to take his delight at her possible downfall personally. She turned the canvas around. "It's perfect."

Owen whistled, and Mr. Alford plucked at a piece of dry skin on his lips, his glance skittering from Nora to Sita. "You did that, Sita?"

Sita gave a slow nod. "I thought I could help." She scrunched up her nose. "I'm sorry."

Nora set the picture on the table and touched Sita's shoulder. "It's a wonderful thing. How did you do it?" She brushed a fingertip over the blue wing.

"The watercolor was the right color, but not the right . . . I'm not sure how to say it, but the butterfly wing glowed."

"Saturation." Nora nodded. Sita was right. The blue watercolor was the perfect hue but didn't display the wing's dimension.

Sita continued. "I thought, if I used the blue and white pastel over the blue watercolor, it would look more like it."

"Clever." Nora bit her lip, then smiled. "It's perfect, and I love it."

Sita glowed beneath Nora's praise.

"Mr. Alford," Nora said, "I want to apprentice Sita."

"What?" He laughed. "Why would I allow that?"

She turned, careful to arrange her expression into one of neutrality. "The child is interested in entomology and displays a rare artistic talent. I insist."

He sputtered. "You can't insist on anything."

"Really? Because as far as I can tell, you have no other illustrator. Do you really want to wait another month or two for one to arrive? I've allowed you to dismiss my education and experience, to underestimate and devalue my work. Despite Professor Comstock's belief that I would be a useful part of this team, I've been asked to illustrate and shop and nurse. I will train Sita, or I can go home."

Owen crossed his arms and winked at Nora. "If Nora leaves, I'll have to escort her back to the States." He moved to her side and slung his arm around her shoulders, giving her a squeeze. "We're a team, she and I."

Warmth spread from Nora's belly to the tips of her fingers and toes. She touched her fingers to his, as light as a hummingbird, and then fisted the side of her skirt to keep from slipping her hand into his. It seemed she had to travel halfway across the globe to learn the depth of a man she'd spent three years dismissing.

Mr. Alford tossed his head. "Fine. What do I care? Just keep her away from my work. We leave in ten minutes, Owen. Be ready."

As Mr. Alford sauntered away, heading toward Pallavi and haranguing her over yet another meal of lentils and rice, Owen dropped to the stool beside Sita. "You're talented." Sita grinned and turned her attention back to her work. Owen looked up at Nora. "She's really been here every day while we've been working?"

Nora shrugged. "I've been bored. You're all gone all day, exploring and discovering. I needed to do something other than draw, or I'd go crazy." Pallavi and Mr. Alford's arguing grew louder. "Anyway, if you hadn't returned early, he'd never have found out. She's always gone before you come back."

"We had just discovered a strange symbiosis between an ant species and some sort of *lycaenid* when William began . . ." Owen's face went a bit green. "Leonard soon joined him, and they were so weak, we needed to see them back. Frederic wants to get back to the site as soon as possible so we can continue our observation."

Nora bumped Sita to the corner of the stool and perched on its edge. She clasped her hands and leaned toward Owen. "Tell me what you found."

He shook his head, and his brow wrinkled. "A caterpillar was resting on a leaf, and ants were swarming it. We expected them to carry it away, or at least kill it, but after a while, it appeared they were protecting it."

She blinked and leaned against Sita's shoulder. "Why?"

"I'm not sure. But when a hornet tried to attack the caterpillar, the ants chased it off."

Nora reached for a piece of cast-off paper and a pencil. She pushed them over to Owen and said, "Draw the larva. While you're gone, I'll look through the books and see if I can find any mention of it."

He took the pencil and bent his head low. His hand made quick, broad strokes, leaving a basic rendering of a brown caterpillar sporting haphazard setae. He gave her a wry smile. "It's not as good as yours or Sita's would be, but it'll do."

She took the paper. "It's fine. I'll find it if there is anything in the literature about it." She traced the drawing's bold lines with her finger.

Owen reached out and touched her hand, startling her. "I wish you could come with us. This is the kind of thing you most love."

The sadness in his voice touched her. She'd never thought it possible, but she'd come to think of him as a friend. And especially in the absence of Rose and Bitsy, she appreciated that. Needed it.

He gave a surreptitious glance around and squeezed her hand while leaning closer. "When everyone is asleep, let's sneak out. I'll show you where we found the caterpillar. It's not far, and I don't think it's going anywhere, at least not until its next instar."

"I'd love that," Nora said, not knowing if she was more excited about studying an interesting species or spending time with Owen.

Oh, heavens.

Chapter Thirteen

Soon after the healthy men left, disgusting sounds came from Mr. Taylor's and William's tents. The contents of Nora's stomach threatened to spill into her throat. She was grateful that in all the years she'd tended her mother, vomit had rarely appeared.

"So," Nora said to Sita, switching to Owen's vacant chair and forcing cheer into her voice, "where did you learn to draw like that?"

Sita tipped her head. "Learn? I learned English and maths at the mission school. My father is a clerk for a British family. They sent me to school. But this"—she waved her hand toward the canvas—"I just see in my head and draw it. It's easy."

Nora wouldn't call art easy. It took her intense concentration to flesh out what she saw before her. God had given the child a gift, of that Nora was certain. What a shame to waste it. "How would you like me to teach you about insects and methods for illustrating them?"

Sita nodded, the little gold bells dangling from her earlobes tinkling as they struck her jaw. "I want to learn to write better too. My spelling of English words is poor."

"Good. You can transcribe my notes. That will help with your spelling and handwriting, and you'll learn about insects in the process. Do you have school?"

Sita's lips and eyes drooped. "No. I finished last year. There isn't any point in continuing when I'm destined to die."

"Die? Surely you're being dramatic."

Sita picked up a blue pastel and mushed it against the table. Pushing her finger through the powder, she drew whirls and curls. She scratched her chin, leaving a chalky smudge, and heaved a sigh too great for one so young. "When my father brings me to the temple to begin my duties, I will refuse. He might not let me live if I humiliate him. If I don't honor his promise to Yellamma."

Nora had no concept of what it would be like to serve in a Hindu temple. No idea, even, what Hindus believed except that they had a thousand gods and most of them lived in the lavishly decorated shrines that peppered the countryside. "Do you want me to talk to your father?"

Sita laughed. Hard laughter that sent tears rolling down her cheeks. Laughter that turned to sobs before Nora could even react to the unexpected mirth. Sita leaned toward her, forcing Nora to wrap the little girl in her arms. To rub her hand down Sita's thick braid and whisper comforting sounds against her temple.

When Sita's tears turned to hiccups, Nora pulled away and gazed at her. "Now, tell me what's wrong." She rested her elbows on her knees and perched her chin against her fists.

Sita gave her a sad smile, and in the girl's eyes, Nora thought she saw an understanding—knowledge—of something Nora couldn't fathom. Something Sita tried to hide from her when her lids fell and her lashes brushed against the youthful swell of her cheek.

But that was ridiculous, because Nora had benefited from a Western education, and Sita had only spent a few years in a mission school.

Sita patted Nora's cheek, her dusty fingers trailing Nora's jaw. "You are very different from Indians. You don't understand our customs."

"I want to understand."

"One of my duties, should I obey my father, will be servicing men who come to worship."

"Servicing?" Nora shook her head.

Sita remained silent. She only watched, waiting for understanding to dawn, and when it did, Nora's chest tightened as though the weight of the world rested on her lungs. The same weight Sita must carry upon her small shoulders.

"Your father has consigned you to prostitution?" Nora tried to keep the horror from coloring her words, tried to speak in a calm and modulated tone so judgment didn't sharpen her voice and shut down Sita's trust in her.

She didn't know if she succeeded, but Sita lifted wet eyes toward her, and her chin trembled. "It is considered a great honor. Especially since the girls are usually from poor families. But we are not poor. Not in money, at least. We were only poor in boys. And Indian families *need* boys. My father had four daughters, and he promised Yellamma one of them if she gave him a boy. My brother was born after me."

"And in that dedication, you must . . . service men?" Nora couldn't keep the squeak from her voice. How horrifying. How unfair that a child would be sacrificed on the altar of misogyny. She would spend the rest of her life a slave to the depraved appetite of grown men.

Nora knew Sita's fate was far worse than anything she would ever experience. Even if she never attained her career goals, even if every man she worked with treated her like Mr. Alford did, it wouldn't compare.

"I will become a sacred prostitute." Sita, looking so tiny curled up beside her, shrank even smaller. She lifted her feet to the chair and rested her head against her knees. "You see my plight? I cannot serve that way and honor my faith. I cannot tell my father I'm a Christian and refuse because he will send me away, alone. Maybe even kill me. Especially after the dishonor of my—" Her eyes darted around before landing on her lap. "What should I do?"

The air between them grew thick with Sita's expectation and hope. No one except for her mother had ever relied on Nora. No one *needed* her. Certainly no one had ever thought Nora could save them from a terrible fate.

Dryness filled her mouth, and her heart—which had spent the previous six years sheltered beneath a barely-there veneer of phlegmatic constraint—twisted so violently, she thought the pain must rival being stung by a thousand fire ants.

For a moment, she couldn't tear her gaze from Sita's imploring one. The child held her captive. How could Nora have fallen in love with her so quickly, so completely, that Sita had reached a place she'd kept sealed from touch since her father's death?

A hacking, retching noise slid from Mr. Taylor's tent, and his desperate plea drew their attention. "Help me."

Nora allowed the call to distract her from Sita's small, tear-stained face. She pushed away the choking sense of almost-certain failure. How could she bear that? Failing Sita would be far worse than most any other failure. And Nora was only one person, standing in the gap for a child who shouldered a burden heavier than she'd ever faced.

Nora turned to Sita. "I'm being summoned."

As Sita left the camp with silent steps, swaying her hips and arms in a dance to music only she could hear, Nora realized that even though she sometimes had as little control over her own choices as Sita, the end result didn't look at all the same. Society would relegate Nora to parlors and quilting parties. Sita, though, would end up warming the bed of men twice her age.

Nora blinked at the sudden prick of unwanted tears and stood with resolution. She couldn't help the situation, so she wouldn't think about it. She forced her thoughts to nursing, something she had a good deal of experience in. It meant little in light of

Sita's plight, but the work would distract her from the strange emotions churning in her belly.

She strode toward the pot of watery yogurt that fermented in the shade of an acacia tree. She filled a tin bowl, wrinkling her nose at the tangy scent. She'd not yet developed a taste for it, but Pallavi had insisted it would help settle the ill men's stomachs. She carried it into Mr. Taylor's tent and set it on the metal table beside his cot. Whey sloshed out, and he turned bleary eyes toward her.

"I'm so very sorry." His normally placid expression was twisted into one of misery. Sweat beaded his hairline, and his skin had taken on the pallor of someone who had released all body fluids in a short amount of time.

The poor man. He was the bedrock of their team. Reliable and unflappable. Always willing to share his findings with her and listen to the bits of things she'd gleaned on her lonely excursions into the shola. He raised a trembling hand for his cup, and Nora easily fell into her much-practiced role as nursemaid.

She slipped her arm behind him and tipped the bowl against his lips. When yogurt dribbled down his chin, she wiped it with the handkerchief tucked into her waistband. She snugged his blanket around him, made sure the bowl was within reach, and left him with the handkerchief, then stepped back into the sunshine.

Pallavi sat on her heels near the ever-lit fire, pounding a rainbow of spices together against a smooth rock. Her limp braid gently swung against her back as she dumped a small pot of coriander seeds atop the already ground cumin and pepper. Nora's mouth watered. Pallavi prepared some of the most flavorful food she'd ever tasted.

And she was Sita's aunt.

Nora strode toward her, kicking up dust in her haste to ferret out the truth. To understand the motive.

Pallavi glanced up at her approach, continuing to grind the pestle as she stared at Nora, censure in her expression. "You should not let Sita come."

Nora ignored the comment and knelt beside her. "That smells

lovely. You are a wonderful cook. Much better than our house-maid at home." Certainly a little flattery wouldn't hurt.

Pallavi narrowed her eyes. "Sita is to stay away."

Nora drew in a slow, steadying breath. Then she smiled. She'd been told on a few occasions that she had a nice smile—straight white teeth and pretty lips. She'd never attempted to use her smile, or any other part of her person, to get what she wanted, but she knew most women did. Rose did so without pretense or thought. Bitsy, with her languid stretches and sideways glances, knew exactly what she was about.

By the tight line of Pallavi's mouth and the way she rolled her shoulders inward, Nora could tell her attempts had fallen flat.

She was being ridiculous. And completely uncharacteristic. Directness had never failed anyone. "Is it true that Sita was dedicated to a goddess and will be prostituted?"

Pallavi stopped pounding the spices. Her fingers twitched against the smooth acacia pestle, and the line of her shoulders went rigid. "It is the custom."

"She is a child."

"She won't work until she bleeds, so she will be a woman."

"But it will still be against her will."

Pallavi's head snapped up, and her eyes flashed. "How many things are in our will? We are women. We do nothing we want." Her sneer dripped with disdain. "*You* do nothing you want, even though you are a foreign woman. You are white, but you have breasts." She shrugged as though she'd just diagnosed all the world's injustice. "And if Yellamma smiles on Sita, a rich man will make her his own."

"He will marry her?"

"No, but he will take care of her, and it will honor her family." Pallavi turned back to her spices and began singing in her high, warbling voice. Nora didn't know any Tamil, but she knew a love song when she heard one. In any language, they sounded of yearning and desire.

And helplessness.

Chapter Fourteen

All that afternoon and into early evening when the rest of the men returned, Nora scuttled back and forth between William's tent and Mr. Taylor's. She tipped cups of cool water toward their mouths and wiped their brows. She told Mr. Taylor everything she knew about North American leeches and watched over William as he rested.

She sat there now, beside his bed, waving a sheaf of papers at her face to disrupt the still air.

"What is it about Sita that has you pouring so much into her?" William's voice didn't show an inkling of his typical exuberance.

She dropped the papers into her lap, and her eyes fell to the writing—William's notes on a beetle he'd observed just before falling ill. She wondered how to answer. How much to share.

He reached for her hand, and his skin burned as hot as his eyes. The fever battered his body, and she didn't know if he'd even remember anything of their conversation. Plus, she needed to talk about it. To work things out with someone who might understand. Or at least explain.

"My father died when I was fifteen. In front of me."

William made a murmur of sympathy. He struggled to push himself up, and sweat beaded along his temple.

"No, don't get up. I'm not telling you this for any reason other than to say that I identify with Sita. She's stubborn and hardened, but really she's just scared. Lonely."

"Has her father died too?"

"No, but he's abandoned her just the same." She tilted her head and worried her lip. Maybe she could ask him. It would be improper to speak with him about such things. Not done. But maybe he could explain it.

"Sita is to be sent into prostitution."

His eyes slid closed. "Temple prostitution or British?"

She shook her head. "What's the difference? It's awful either way."

"It is, but it's a little less awful for Sita if she becomes a temple prostitute. At least then she'll be provided for and respected. She won't be abused, and any children she has will be considered legitimate. She'll be able to own property. If she is sent to stay in a British *chakla*, her life will be one of dehumanizing drudgery." He opened his eyes, and even in their fevered state, she saw compassion.

Her head whirled with the information. "It's temple prostitution. Her father dedicated her to a deity called Yellamma."

"She's not worshiped here in Tamil Nadu, but I'm familiar with the practice. There's a temple not far from Hubli, where my parents have worked, that many devotees pilgrimage to."

"Sita's family is from Trinomalee originally. Her father promised the goddess a daughter if he was given a son."

"And he got a son?"

Nora nodded. "And after they moved here, Sita attended the mission school and became a Christian. She can't be dedicated to a Hindu goddess."

"That is a problem."

"Yes." She lifted his cup from the crude little table near his cot. She held it to his lips, letting him take a small sip before she set it down. "I'm determined to help her."

"That might be a bigger problem."

Nora lifted one shoulder in a shrug. "Being a problem comes easily to me."

~~~~~

Later that night, when the moon, as round and gleaming as the silver ball studding Sita's nostril, rose above Kodaikanal, Nora joined Owen near the trees fringing the camp. The air smelled as spicy as the eggplant she'd eaten for dinner.

Owen held up two kerosene lanterns, and Nora reached for one. She lifted it to shoulder height, and the flame caught the cadmium eyes of a spotted owl peering at her from its hollow in a tree.

"Let's go," Owen whispered.

The lamps gave off enough light to surround them in a glow, and she followed Owen as he led her to the location of the caterpillar. They didn't walk far before they ducked beneath branches heavy with ripe mangos, and she moved her lamp in a wide arc.

A small creek traversed the spot. Scattered boulders covered in lichen appeared to have been dropped by a giant. The trees arched over them, the canopy making a living roof, and everything was hushed. Only the sound of moving water interrupted the peace. On the other side of the creek, the land rose, spindly trees clinging to its gentle slope. They were cut off. Alone.

"Is this safe?" she asked.

He lifted his lamp, and the light cast eerie shadows over his face, painting half of it in a dark mask. "Are you afraid of the wild animals or me?"

She rolled her eyes. "Hardly you. I don't think you're capable of hurting anyone."

"I wrestled all four years of college."

"Not sure that will help us if a tiger decides we'll make a good midnight snack."

His laugh was a Christmas fire. It was the quilt her mother had tucked around her every night as a child. It was her father's hands, warm and comforting, on her shoulders.

Owen was a man worth knowing. A decent man.

A man who would never harm a woman, much less a child.

Ensconced in their private bower, Nora released the air that had been stuck between her breasts and ribs since her conversation with Sita, and it whooshed from her lungs, catching a sob as it escaped. She pinned the next cry between pinched lips, shuddering against the strength of her grief.

Owen lowered his lamp and peered into her face. "Are you all right, Peculiar? It sounds like you're about to cry."

She pulled away from the lamp. "Don't be ridiculous. I'm fine. Where's this caterpillar you were talking about?"

He stared at her and scratched at his jaw, his nails scraping against the prickly hairs on his chin. But he didn't push her. He took measured steps toward a bushy shrub. "Frederic said this is a jujube."

Nora followed him, picking her way across the uneven ground. Taking time to collect herself. To pull all thoughts of Sita back in. When she reached the bush, she followed Owen's example and held her lamp aloft.

"There it is," he said, pointing to a leafy branch.

At the base of a large leaf, just where it met the stem, three large red ants crawled over a caterpillar. Nora brought her lamp closer.

"It looks like they're eating, doesn't it?" Owen asked.

"I think they are. When you went back out this afternoon, I found a mention in one of the books of the *Cigaritis lohita*. Mr. Alford has the adult in his collection—it's the butterfly that has false antennae on its hind wings. The pupa releases a sweet secretion that the ants 'milk.' In turn, the ants provide protection from birds and carnivorous insects."

"It's a symbiotic relationship. Fascinating. This one looks about to molt. There were a couple others on the plant, but Frederic took them back to camp."

Nora frowned and lifted her lamp to see his face. "Why didn't you tell me that? We could have just looked at those instead of tromping out here."

He gave her a sheepish smile. "I wanted to spend some time with you alone."

"Owen!" She laughed. "I'm taking a risk, coming out here with you alone. It's the kind of thing that could ruin my reputation."

"No one will know. I just want more time with you. Frederic hasn't made that easy, forcing you to stay at camp while we work."

"I wish he'd let me go with you." Her smile turned sardonic. "And for more reason than just to be with you. There's so much to see and discover here. I'm afraid I'm going to return home with nothing to show for it. It feels unfair to be judged incompetent because of my sex. And I don't even have it as bad as some. I don't have it as bad as Sita."

"What's happening with Sita?" His forehead furrowed, and Nora wanted to run her thumbs over his uncivilized brows, the wrinkles between them, the hard edges of his cheekbones, the soft peaks and valleys of his lips. . . .

Her cheeks warmed. She tore her gaze from him and stared up at the arthritic-looking branches above them, inhaling deeply and counting to ten. When her heart once again rested between beats and the heat left her body, she returned her attention to him, this time careful not to focus too intently on his face.

"She has been given over to a goddess, where she'll become a . . ." This was harder to discuss with Owen than it had been with William, and Nora didn't want to explore why.

"Become a what?" he asked. "Dancer? I've seen girls dancing in front of the idols we pass on the way to town."

She shook her head and forced herself to meet his eyes. "She will be prostituted to the men who come to worship Yellamma."

His eyes darkened, and the color in his face, deepened already by time spent beneath the burning sun, drained. "What . . . how is that . . . why would they?"

His halting words, spoken in a soft whisper, spilled healing into her bruised heart. She took his free hand into hers and worried her lower lip. "I need your assistance."

"Anything."

"Will you help me talk with Mr. Alford? Maybe he can do something. Intervene."

He dropped his eyes to their hands, and she saw a tremor run over his shoulders. When he looked up at her, his jaw had grown slack. He swallowed hard and nodded.

But Nora knew, even before then, that he would help. Because the expression in his eyes told her that Owen Epps might be willing to do just about anything for her.

Unfortunately, Mr. Alford didn't seem as enraptured by Nora as Owen was.

"We stay out of local matters." He shifted in his camp chair beside the fire the following evening. He raised a cup to his lips and grimaced. "I abhor this stuff. Why ruin a perfectly good cup of tea with all manner of spices that don't belong in it?" He dumped the remains of his drink onto the ground.

"But Sita is only a child. Surely the local missionaries can help." Nora pressed her hands together, hoping to soften him with a supplicant demeanor.

"I forbid you," he said. "You will only hurt our work, which, need I remind you, is to collect, catalogue, study, and illustrate local butterflies."

He forbade her? Nora dropped her hands and clenched them at her sides. She took a step toward him, preparing a speech that would leave him entirely befuddled.

Owen stopped her with a light touch on her arm. "Frederic, Sita has become something of a camp pet. She's here all the time—"

"Of which I disapprove, as you both well know." He leveled a glare in Nora's direction.

Owen sighed. "But it has happened. She is a talented child who needs protection. Surely it is our Christian duty to offer it?"

Mr. Alford stood and tossed his empty cup into the bucket four feet away. "We are not here at the bequest of the Church, but the Crown. And the Crown wants us to study butterflies, not spend our time rescuing Indian children from Indian customs."

Nora bit back the words clawing at her throat. The words that made the whole situation worse but probably wouldn't change Mr. Alford's mind.

Sita is a Christian. She can't serve an Indian god.

She didn't trust Mr. Alford to keep that information private, though. He might tell Pallavi, and Sita would be put in danger. But Nora didn't have to follow Mr. Alford's directive either. Maybe he held sway over her in the camp, but when she stepped onto the road just beyond, she could make her own decisions.

Chapter
Fifteen

Within a week of arriving in India, Owen had set up a nursery, having collected larvae and meticulously arranged them each in a glass jar topped with netting. Lining a two-tier shelf, shielded from the elements by a sheet of canvas held aloft by poles, the containers housed caterpillars and pupae. Beside the shelf, Owen had driven stakes into the ground and draped it with the stitched-together bags of half a dozen nets, creating a makeshift enclosure for butterflies. He'd amassed quite a collection over the last couple months.

Nora had managed to build a nice collection of her own from the insects she found on her walks with Sita. After sketching each one into her journal, she dictated notes to Sita, then mounted it into one of the paste boxes she'd fitted with paper-wrapped cork. But her project took much less time and attention than Owen's, mostly because his insects were alive, while hers were killed right away for illustration purposes.

She hadn't realized how diligent a scientist he was until she witnessed him, a week after her conversation about Sita's unhappy plight, gently brushing frass—caterpillar excrement— from the jars, one at a time, with a small paintbrush. At school, he'd seemed dismissive of work. Easily outscoring their class- mates, he never appreciated the effort the rest of them had to put into their studies. But here, across the world, Owen had come into himself, throwing every bit of energy into his work.

As the sun rose and burnt off the morning dew, she approached him, two cups of tea in hand, and waited while he slid a caterpillar back into a jar and selected a few twigs of jujube from the ground near his feet. He arranged the branches, placed the slip of net over the jar's mouth, and secured it with a rubber band.

Before he could begin his ministrations on the next jar, Nora cleared her throat and held out one of the cups. Through the drink's rising steam, she saw him straighten and smile at her.

"Good morning." He took the cup and raised it to his lips, his eyes closing at the first taste. He groaned with pleasure. "I don't understand Frederic's distaste of this. It's delicious. I'll be spoiled off regular tea forever." He winked at her. "I'll have our cook running all over New York, looking for the proper spices. I wonder if you can get cardamom at home."

"You can take some back with you."

"Good idea. I'll travel home loaded down like a spice mer- chant."

He turned to examine his insect crèche, and Nora's gaze roamed the expanse of his linen-clad back. No jacket or cravat, he stood with his hands on his narrow hips and his head bent in study, his shirt stretched across his shoulders. The sun had browned his neck, and Nora thought she felt the heat of it on her own neck. It grew hotter the longer she looked at him. She forced her eyes off him and onto the unattractive larva.

With leathery green skin and an oblong body that flattened toward the anal segment, it looked like an enlarged form of the pill bugs she'd played with as a child. She hoped the adult form wouldn't disappoint Owen. She knew some of the most beautiful butterflies came from the plainest caterpillars.

"What are you hoping for?" she asked.

Owen lifted the jar and held it aloft. The larva had attached itself to a leaf and was steadily chomping its way through it, storing up energy for its coming transformation. "I haven't any idea." He set it down and picked up another jar, where another ugly caterpillar lived. "I have two of them left, one in a cocoon. My previous three have already hatched *Tachinidae*."

Nora's lips twitched at the disgust lacing his words. It was common enough, waiting a week or two for a butterfly to hatch, the anticipation jangling nerves and setting the pulse racing with curiosity, and then watching as a parasitic fly emerged. Owen's voice held real insult, though, as if the wasps had purposely ruined his great moment.

"Hopefully at least one will result in a butterfly." She lifted her cup and sipped, the tea making a warm trail down her throat and into her belly, sending sparks through her limbs. Or maybe that was the result of Owen's smile, warmer than the tea.

"*Kalai! Kalai!*" Pallavi's shrill call roused the rest of the men from their tents.

Mr. Alford stumbled through the flap of his, poking his fingers into his ears like a little boy. "English, Pallavi. How many times must I tell you?"

Pallavi whirled and banged her wooden spoon against the pot, filling their little settlement with its cacophonous summons. "*Kalai!*"

"Breakfast!" He charged forward, stopping feet from Pallavi. "The word is *breakfast*."

Pallavi jerked her spoon toward Mr. Alford's face, sending a spray of potatoes across his cheek. She grinned. "Breakfast."

Mr. Alford slapped his hand across his face and rubbed the food on the leg of his trousers. He slumped into a chair and buried his head in his lap.

"What's wrong with him?" Owen asked.

"I don't know, but I hope he's not in an even worse temper than usual," Nora said.

They approached the circle of chairs, Nora making a wide berth around Mr. Alford, and took their seats while Pallavi dished up yet another stew over yet another mound of rice.

Nora took the tin plate and smiled her thanks, but as soon as Pallavi turned back toward her pot, Nora grimaced. She lifted a bite of potato to her lips and chewed. Mustard seed, chili, cumin. She pushed the rest around with her fingers, making saffron-colored trails across the plate.

"Do you not like it?" Owen whispered.

"It's delicious. Just . . ." She glanced at Mr. Alford, who stared miserably at his plate, and understood what he felt. "Sometimes I want toast and jam for breakfast." Pallavi walked past and dropped a banana in her lap, and Nora smiled, certain their cook was softening toward her. She peeled the fruit. "It's early, isn't it, to eat such heavy, spicy fare?"

Owen, his cheeks stuffed with food, nodded. His eyes said *I commiserate with you,* but the way he shoveled the potatoes and rice into his mouth said *I have no idea what you're talking about.*

He finished swallowing and took a swig of tea. "Are you homesick?"

Nora's initial desire was to refute it. She wasn't a fragile maiden, in need of coddling and familiarity.

But Owen shrugged and said, "Because I'm a little homesick. I miss the smell of roasting meat—surely not everyone in India is a vegetarian, right?—the sound of Cascadilla Falls, the morning chill, and turning leaves."

"Maybe." She wrinkled her nose. "I miss Bitsy and Rose, the laboratory at Cornell, and baths."

"I'd love some bacon and eggs with that toast and jam." He scooped another large lump of breakfast into his mouth. "But this isn't so bad if you don't compare it."

"I'd love that banana," Mr. Steed, sitting beside Nora, said. Before she could take a bite of her fruit, he grabbed it with his thick fingers and ate it in three bites.

Nora stared at him, mouth open. "Why do you keep doing

that? Get your own fruit." She waved at the mound of bananas near the rest of the food Pallavi had purchased for the day's meals.

He chuckled and licked his lips, but his mirth twisted into disgust at the sound of retching. Mr. Alford purged his previous night's dinner onto Mr. Steed's shoes, who cursed and leapt from his chair so quickly, it fell over with a clatter.

Another one had fallen to whatever tropical illness was sweeping through the camp. Nora bit down a smile. Justice served.

Mr. Alford turned the color of a mantis and darted into the trees.

"It's not my *kalai.*" All heads turned toward Pallavi, who stirred the potatoes in the pot.

"No one thinks that," Owen said. "I'm sure he has what made Leonard and William ill. I hope no one else comes down with it." He cast a glance at Nora, concern shading his eyes.

She stuck her thumb in her mouth, removing the mustard-seed-studded sauce with her tongue, and rejected the impulse to smooth the worry wrinkles from his forehead. She pulled her thumb free. "I'll be fine."

He reached toward her and rubbed the pad of *his* thumb over the corner of her lips, making Nora wish she hadn't resisted her desire to touch him. He licked his finger clean and grinned at her, as though knowing a shudder sighed its way across her body.

Leonard—he'd told her to call him by his given name after she nursed him during his illness—tossed his dirty plate into the metal bucket near the fire, then clapped his hands against his knees. "Well, looks like we're on our own today." In typical Leonard fashion, he pressed his lips together into a firm line, gave a terse nod, and strode with purpose toward his tent. He remerged a moment later in his gaiters and carrying a net.

Owen grabbed Nora's arm. "Spend the day with me."

Kodaikanal bustled with activity. They walked down Bazaar Road, Nora holding on to Owen's elbow, and sidestepped a huddle of boys in white *dhotis* dashing past. Owen secured her more firmly to him with a hand on hers when one of the boys bumped into her and flashed a brilliant smile.

Moss-covered trees overhung the crooked little shops that lined the dirt street, absorbing the calls of hawkers and the steady pounding and squeaks of ox-pulled carts. Nora's skirt swished around her legs, stirring up dust. She eyed Owen's breezy, lightweight pants with a frown before lifting her gaze to the Palani Hills rising above the town. They were swathed in hazy blue clouds, looking like something out of a fairy tale. She sighed, wondering what interesting things those hills contained, then looked down the street hemmed in by tightly packed shops.

"What are we doing here?" she asked. Outside of the trips she'd made with Pallavi to the market, Nora hadn't had much opportunity to explore the town.

He glanced at her and teased the inside of her wrist with his fingers. "Do we need to be doing anything? Let's just enjoy being halfway around the world for a while." At her frown, he rolled his eyes. "I have a plan too. In a bit. *After* we walk around with no agenda."

"No agenda? How will I survive the day?" She bumped him with her elbow, a self-deprecating smile making her words sound playful. Flirtatious, even.

"I have no idea, but I mean to find out. Let's start there." He pointed across the street at a building that seemed better kept than the rest, with curved glass windows and scrubbed, whitewashed bricks. The sign hanging above the door proclaimed *Butani Jewels*.

They paused to allow a man pulling a blue-painted cart to pass in front of them, and when Owen tugged her forward, Nora asked, "Why are we going into a jewelry shop?"

"To look at jewelry."

She huffed. "But why?"

"Because it's interesting to see what the artisans produce. Don't you want to bring home something no one else has? Something you can't order from the Bloomingdale's catalogue?"

Nora had never in her life ordered jewelry from the Bloomingdale's catalogue. In fact, the only time she'd even looked through one was when her mother asked if she'd rather have a Thomson's ventilating or Ball's Health Preserving corset. Not that she intended to tell Owen that.

He pulled open the shop door and ushered her inside. Nora turned in a small circle, taking in the hand-printed calico covering the walls, the dark wood cabinets showcasing brilliant gems—necklaces, rings, bracelets—and the lush carpets beneath their feet. The street sounds didn't come through the thick door or closed windows, and Nora imagined herself in a little jewel box come alive.

A man behind a low cabinet put his hands together in greeting. "Welcome."

Nora smiled and wandered toward him. Beneath the glass of the display case, rubies, diamonds, and sapphires glinted in settings of gold and silver. "They're beautiful."

The merchant smiled. "What can I help you find? A necklace, perhaps?" He turned and pulled out one of the drawers from the towering cabinet behind him. Lifting a heavy piece dripping with rubies, he brought it to her. "With your dark hair and fair skin, this is the perfect piece for you."

Before she could pull away, he draped it over her bodice. She held her hand up to it, capturing it against her collarbone, the cool metal biting into her skin. "It's a little ornate for me."

"Something simpler?" Owen said.

The man nodded, his eyes dimming. But he took the necklace away.

Nora turned to Owen, and her hand went to her cicada pin. "I don't wear jewelry, except for this."

"Why?"

"It's too fussy for me."

"Not all jewelry is fussy."

Her eyes swept the room full of pieces that demanded attention, exhibited wealth.

Owen laughed. "Well, maybe most of it is fussy, but let's see what he has."

The merchant returned with a velvet-lined box open to display several styles of earrings. Nestled amid the flamboyant gem-encrusted hoops and drops and studs, she saw a pair almost bare in their simplicity.

She lifted one of them. A teardrop of filigreed gold cradling a brilliant diamond.

"Do you have your ears pierced?" Owen asked.

She nodded. Her one concession to Mother's demands when she turned fifteen and showed no interest in traditionally feminine pursuits. Nora had resisted the intricate hairstyles and ridiculous bustles, but her mother had been mollified when she agreed to pierce her ears and wear her grandmother's diamond studs. She'd removed them permanently two years later, but the holes remained.

Owen took the earring from her and held it against her ear. It brushed her cheek, along with his fingers, and she flushed. "They suit you."

"I don't wear jewelry," she whispered.

"You also don't travel, and yet here you are." He leaned close and brushed a curl from her face. "Your mask is slipping."

Her throat went dry, and she swallowed. Owen saw through her exoskeleton and recognized the vulnerable, soft parts of her she'd never wanted exposed. And yet she'd never felt so safe.

She looked at the merchant. "All right."

Before she could stop him—and not sure she would have anyway—Owen slipped the hook into her piercing, then did the same with the second one still sitting in the box. She turned her head, enjoying the foreign pressure of jewelry brushing her skin. Enjoying the expression on the face of the man she was coming to admire.

She paid for her purchase and left the shop, lighter of step and coin.

They wandered another hour, stopping to look at baskets and daggers and little brass cups. Imported Chinese silk and pashmina shawls and bags embroidered with beetle wings. They peeked inside tiny shops, their owners sitting cross-legged on low counters, that sold brilliantly painted statues of gods and goddesses. Everyone greeted them warmly, encouraging them to purchase wares they had no use for. Nora touched her earrings and smiled. She wanted nothing else, but she bought a few small gifts for Mother, Rose, Bitsy, and Anna.

A peacock carved from soapstone. A tangle of beaded necklaces. A tiny painting of a woman greeting a man on an elephant. A gold perfume ewer.

They passed a man standing over a pot of oil that sizzled as he swirled batter into it. With wooden tongs, he turned the fried dough, revealing a golden brown underbelly. Then he flipped it into a bowl to soak it in whatever deliciousness he'd concocted. When he finished his task, he smiled at her and said, "*Jalebi.*"

Nora didn't need any more encouragement. She held up two fingers and paid his price.

"Does this make up for breakfast?" Owen took one of the spiral-shaped treats and made an appreciative sound as he bit into it.

"It's delicious. I actually enjoy the food here. I think I could get used to eating it every day eventually. Everything about India is so much more . . . well, *more.* More colorful and vibrant and flavorful. It feels very different from what I should enjoy, but very much like where I belong." She finished her *jalebi* and eyed Owen's remaining portion.

"Here." He handed it over and, lacking a towel, licked his fingers.

Nora had just finished off her treat when a small child darted from a doorway across the street and grabbed her hand, tugging her forward. "Hello, *Akka.*"

"Where are we going?" Nora laughed.

The girl giggled and continued to pull them along until they reached a small stone structure fronted by a low-slung verandah. An adult version of the child, with a wide smile and swath of shiny hair pulled back into a braid, motioned them inside. She was draped in a red and gold sari, and its thick flower-embroidered hem spilled around her feet, swishing with the movement of her hips as she walked through the carved teak door.

Owen pressed his hand against the small of Nora's back as they followed, reassuring her. Providing a bit of comfort to the unexpected adventure.

The interior of the room took Nora's breath away. Lining each of the three complete walls were floor-to-ceiling shelves, creaking and sagging beneath the weight of a thousand saris. Nora had never seen so much color in one place. Silks, gossamer-thin and thick with brocade, begged for a wandering hand. Every hue of the rainbow and all those in between, folded in neat piles.

The woman motioned for Nora and Owen to sit on the plush carpet. Nora tucked her legs to the side and traced her fingers over the blue branches and birds and flowers. The wool tickled her fingers the way Owen's breath tickled her ear.

"Do they think you're going to wear Indian clothing?" he asked.

She shrugged and, for a reason she didn't understand, hoped he wouldn't want to leave. There was something about the shop, the street sounds muffled by fabric, that cosseted her. Made her feel as though she sat in a magical bower, safe from past sins and angry stepfathers and every failure that mocked her. She wanted to run her fingers over the edges of the saris, pull one out and drape it over herself. The urge surprised her, because Nora had never cared for fashion. Had always gone for simplicity and sensible skirts and bodices. She'd certainly never wished for the gold that dripped from the shopkeeper's ears, ringed her wrists, and made a swoop from the jewel in her nose.

The child, who had disappeared, reemerged from a door in the corner of the room, carrying a large silver tea tray. She set it before Nora and poured two cups of tea from the ornate pot. The woman said something in Tamil, and the girl crouched before Nora. "*Amma* says the tea is grown here, in the Ghats. It is special."

Nora lifted the steaming cup, and her first sip told her the child didn't lie. Dark and aromatic, the tea tasted crisp after the heavily spiced masala tea of that morning, and it left lingering flavors of rose and blackberry.

The way the woman and her daughter watched them drink told Nora it wasn't an everyday tea. When they finished and set their cups down, the girl whisked the tray away, and her mother stood and turned in a slow circle, her eyes bouncing from Nora to the saris to Nora again.

Then, in a whirlwind of peacock colors, Nora found herself curtained in half a dozen lengths of silk. Red, cerulean, green dotted with prancing elephants, a cobalt paisley—all shot through with gold and silver thread.

Nora pushed aside the ornate hem of a particularly vivid sari. "I'm so sorry, but I can't wear one."

The woman cocked her head, then whirled back toward the shelves as though not understanding. Which Nora knew was probably true. Where was the child? Nora didn't want to offend their hostess while trying to disentangle herself from the fabric and the situation.

Owen's deep laugh drew her attention. He leaned back on his elbows, looking comfortable and unencumbered by an ambitious shop owner's ill-placed hopes.

"She has to know an American can't wear one of these, right?" Nora asked. "I doubt she's sold any to the missionaries or the British."

He crossed his legs at the ankles. "I don't know. But I think I'd like to see you in one."

"Owen!" Nora watched the shopkeeper as she reached for a

shelf above her head, the curve of her back visible through the sheer fabric of the sari spilling over her shoulder.

The woman turned and sauntered back toward them, moving with a languid sort of grace that reminded her of Bitsy.

Nora looked at Owen, expecting him to be watching the shopkeeper—she was beautiful—but instead he watched *her* from beneath hooded eyes. Her eyes widened. Was he imagining her dressed in a sari? *Oh, heavens . . .*

"This is the one, *Akka*." The girl stood above Nora again, and she grinned with approval when her mother took one edge of the sari in her fingers and let the length of it unfurl and puddle into Nora's lap.

It fell in a shimmering river the color of purple thistle. Gold embroidered tigers and elephants cavorted around trailing branches. Nora lifted the silk in her hands. It was cool and smooth, and just touching it made her feel more sensuous.

"It's beautiful . . . but I can't wear this."

"Why not?" asked the girl.

"Yeah, Nora," Owen said, "why not?"

She flicked her finger against his chin. "Because it's unseemly."

"Since when have you been worried about that?"

She opened her mouth but could find no words to refute him. It was true. She'd spent her entire life flouting convention. Why stop now? And, oh, she wanted to know what it felt like to be draped in silk. No corsets, petticoats, or layers and layers between her and the fabric.

She stood and nodded. "Okay."

Owen sat up straight. "Really? You're really going to try it on?"

"Yes. And maybe, when I'm done, you'll try on a *dhoti*." She flounced to the door the child and woman had disappeared behind, motioning her to follow, then said, "I'd love to see you in one, Owen."

She shut the door behind her, blocking out the sound of his choking laughter.

The room behind the shop was small, the walls covered in

rugs. A large mirror dominated the back, a small stool set beside it. Lamps in the corners of the room cast shadows across the polished wood floor. The shopkeeper handed the child the sari and began unbuttoning Nora's bodice as she made clucking noises and muttered beneath her breath.

"What is she saying?" Nora asked.

The girl shrugged. "That English women wear too many clothes. It's unnatural and doesn't allow your skin to breathe."

"I'm American," Nora said. Her skirt was unhooked and fell to her feet. She still wore her corset, chemise, petticoat, and stockings, but she felt lighter already.

With each layer removed, she inhaled more deeply. And then she stood naked, free of constraints. She pushed her arms through the short sleeves of a blouse that didn't reach her navel. She stepped into a white linen skirt. Then she allowed herself to be wrapped in silk like an Egyptian mummy.

Finally, the shopkeeper stepped out of the way, and Nora saw her reflection.

Only . . . it wasn't really her. It was a specter—a beautiful woman from another place. She approached the mirror, the sliding of silk against the exposed strip of her back and torso raising the hairs on her arms. It was almost more sensual than being unclothed. But it looked *right* on her. This garment was close in shade to her ridiculous graduation dinner dress, but it sheathed her body in elegant lines instead of consuming her in froth and froufrou. It made her look taller, somehow. Gracefully exquisite. She ran her hand down her torso, feeling the dip of her waist and shallow of her belly button. She wondered if this other *she* had been inside her all the time. Had she been waiting to be released? Waiting for an opportunity to show her face?

Waiting to feel alive. Here, in India.

Living a life she'd never dreamed of. A life that split the chrysalis—of Ithaca, the journal, and Cornell—freeing her to be what she was always meant to be. After all this, could she return to her life, sitting behind a desk and writing about insects instead of studying them?

Nora pulled out the pin attaching the pleats of the sari to the underskirt. She unwrapped the silk from around and around her waist and tugged it off, allowing herself one moment to enjoy the feel of it slipping over her shoulder. She stepped out of the petticoat and unhooked the snaps traveling up the blouse.

She reached for her clothing piled atop the table behind her. "Thank you for letting me try your beautiful clothes, but I can't possibly purchase them. I would like some scarves, though."

She wouldn't indulge in this silly experiment. It wouldn't lead to discovery or knowledge. It only made her question her priorities.

She needed to focus on what truly mattered, and that was securing the scholarship and control of the journal. She owed it to her father to keep his memory alive through the publication he'd loved.

India was a means to an end. She'd wrapped herself in a silk chrysalis, but instead of a butterfly, she found herself facing a parasite—the realization that once she shed all tethers to home, she no longer missed it. No longer cared for toast and jam at breakfast. No longer wanted to return to school or tie herself to a floundering scientific journal.

No, she wanted to stay in India and drink tea grown in the hills, wear silk, and watch butterflies grow with Owen.

And she couldn't have that. Not when she had obligations to fulfill and guilt tethering her to a memory she'd rather forget.

~⁓⁓

Nora purchased five fringed scarves made of fine wool. They didn't sing a siren's song, calling her to forsake her plans. They didn't tumble over her body and pull her toward desires best left concealed. But they were beautiful and would make lovely gifts for the women in her life.

She carefully folded them into squares and placed them in her rucksack. Slinging the bag over her shoulder, she left the store without a glance at the bewildered shopkeeper, her daughter with the all-too-wise eyes, or Owen.

"Where are we headed next?" she asked when he caught up with her.

"It's a surprise. I heard about it last week, and I think you'll love it."

He waved down a *mattu vandi*, and the driver forced his oxen to a stop. The wiry man, wearing white knee-length breeches, a long shirt, and a wide belt at his waist, haggled for a moment with Owen.

A shout drew Nora's attention. Turning, she saw the child from the sari shop running toward her, wide feet beating against the dusty ground. "*Akka!* I have this for you." She thrust a paper-wrapped parcel into Nora's hands. "I know the customs are different. I learned that at school. But you loved it."

Nora unwrapped the bundle while the child looked on, eagerness making her eyes sparkle. Inside lay a ribbon made from the purple sari, just a two-inch-wide strip with an embroidered elephant chasing after a tiger.

It was a small enough part that it didn't threaten Nora's ambitions, but large enough to remind her of the moment she first discovered the woman hiding beneath all her layers and walls. "Thank you," she whispered.

She removed her hat, pulled the three large pins from her proper knot at the crown of her head, and drew the curtain of hair around the front of her shoulder. With nimble fingers, she braided the length of it and tied the ribbon at the end, letting the large loops and drooping tails rest against her waist.

"Are you ready?" Owen asked.

With a gentle touch, Nora stroked the girl's cheek and accepted a smile. Then she turned and took Owen's hand as he helped her into the rickety curtained box.

As the oxen took off in a lumbering walk, she could feel Owen's eyes on her. She stroked the loops of the sari bow.

"Your hair looks pretty like that." He took the bow from her and held it against her cheek. "It's a good color on you." Dropping it, he leaned against the seat back and closed his eyes. "I still want to see you in it."

The tension in Nora's chest released, and her shoulders relaxed. She pushed away all thoughts of desires and dreams and journals. "That's never going to happen, Owen Epps."

He laughed, and Nora spent the remainder of the ride to their secret destination peeking out through the curtains while Owen sat with his elbow propped against the side of the cart, chin in hand, as he snoozed.

They took Bazaar Road past the star-shaped Berijam Lake to Ghat Road, where their driver took them up and down hills covered in dense vegetation. The cart bounced, and Owen sat up, blinking sleep from his eyes.

Nora heard the thunder before seeing anything. Its familiar roar drew her halfway off her seat, and shoving the curtain aside, she gasped, delighted that Owen knew enough about her to know she'd love this. She grabbed his hand and waited, tapping her feet against the cart's floor until they stopped.

Before Owen could climb down and offer his assistance, Nora leapt to the ground and darted toward the sound. She pushed through brush and bushes, startling a macaque, who chided her with shrieks and trills.

And then, finally, she stood before a waterfall ten times as high as Cascadilla Falls. She'd been to Niagara Falls before her father's death, and she thought this might even be higher than that great wonder.

The pebbles beneath her feet shifted as she approached the falls. By the time Owen slipped into view, she'd hopped from one large stone to another across the shallow pool and stood facing the tumbling water. She smiled into the fine mist it sprayed across her face. It wasn't a heavy fall, though she imagined it would be during the monsoon, but the water glowed silver, and

Nora closed her eyes, becoming reacquainted with this cousin to her beloved Ithaca waterfall.

When she opened them again, Owen sat at the edge of the grass surrounding the water, watching her with a satisfied smile. "Happy?"

She ducked her head and bit her lip, feeling unaccountably shy.

"Come sit by me," he said.

Grabbing fistfuls of her skirt, she stepped back over the rocks and sat beside him. "Thank you for this."

He smiled and handed over her rucksack, which she'd left in the cart in her haste to see the waterfall. She set it aside, and her stomach growled. "It feels like hours since we ate the *jalebi*."

"I'm prepared for hunger." He lifted the strap of his bag over his head and pushed aside the flap. He pulled out a paper-wrapped parcel and, peeling back the layers, revealed a triangular pastry. "Pallavi calls them *samosa* and said they're perfect picnic food. And I paid the *karar* for the day, so we can stay as long as we like. I've heard there is some great insect biodiversity here."

They grew quiet as they munched on the spicy potato-stuffed lunch. A macaque inched toward them, and Nora threw it a handful of crumbs. It grabbed for the food with dexterous fingers, then bared its teeth at her and bounded away. Ungrateful animal.

A butterfly flew in lazy circles above them before landing on a nearby rock about six feet away. Its oddly colored wings drew Nora to her feet. She narrowed her eyes, straining to see it.

"What is it?" Owen asked.

"That butterfly . . ." She took a few steps toward it, and it left its perch. She followed it toward the tree line, making sure not to lose it.

"It's only a cruiser. We have specimens of every subspecies already."

"Yes, but something about this one is different." She glanced at him, and he must have seen something in her expression, because his eyes widened, and he jumped to his feet.

"An undiscovered species?"

"I don't think so."

The butterfly rested on the trunk of a flowering crape myrtle. Nora took another step toward it, careful not to make any noise. The butterfly lifted off the trunk, dropping its forewings, and she gasped. She lunged forward, pinching the insect's wings between her fingers, quickly immobilized it, and hurried back to Owen.

"Look," she said, falling to her knees. He crouched behind her and peered over her shoulder. She opened her fingers, revealing the butterfly in her cupped palm. "Do you remember Professor Comstock's lecture on sexual dimorphism?"

Owen grunted and leaned even farther over her, his ear brushing her cheek. She heard his even breathing and matched her own exhalations to his.

She pressed her pointer finger to the middle of the butterfly's fuzzy thorax. "He mentioned an anomaly called gynandromorphism. Do you recall?"

"That class was months ago. How do you remember anything he said?"

"It was interesting. Look at it, Owen. It's incredible. I never thought I'd get to see one."

She tilted her hand so they could peer at its hind end. Owen's eyes widened. "It only has one clasper. On the male side."

She grinned and admired its bilateral asymmetry. The *Vindula erota*'s dimorphic coloring made it easy to catch the deviation. One wing featured the male's orange wings and black markings, the other the subtle green, blue, and browns of a female. It was a random aberration that produced a highly collectable, and uncommon, specimen.

If she didn't discover a new species, she could use the gynandromorph as the basis of her lecture. "Give me the kill jar from my rucksack."

When Owen headed toward her dropped bag, Nora pulled

a thin handkerchief from where she'd tucked it into her sleeve that morning. Using her teeth, she tore it in half and dipped it in the tepid water of the stream. He returned as she was squeezing it out.

"Here. I'm glad you thought to bring your bag with you." He held the jar toward her.

"I bring my bag everywhere. Just in case." She smiled and dropped the damp handkerchief into the jar. She didn't want to risk the butterfly growing brittle and breaking before she had the chance to mount it. Then she slipped the insect into the jar and waited for the cyanide to do its work.

"It's kind of sad, isn't it?" Owen asked. "It doesn't know what it is or how to behave. It's trapped between two different worlds, just as paralyzed as it was a moment ago."

A dull ache took hold of Nora's throat, and tears made her nose burn. What a strange thing, commiserating with an insect over a shared experience.

Chapter Sixteen

When they walked back into camp that evening, William and Leonard were huddled around Owen's shelf of specimens. Their murmured conversation carried across the yard.

"Such a shame," Leonard said. "He's had no luck getting this butterfly to hatch."

Beside Nora, Owen groaned. "Another tachinid. I gathered half a dozen caterpillars, and now I only have one left. I was hoping at least one would make it to maturation." He rubbed the back of his neck and shook his head. "Do you want to draw the pupa, chrysalis, and parasite? If the other hatches a butterfly, you'll have a great life cycle illustration."

She smiled. "Like Maria Merian?" The seventeenth-century naturalist had been the first scientist to draw butterflies on their food source along with the egg, larva, and chrysalis, proving insects didn't grow from the mud. Nora followed her example whenever given the opportunity. Maybe one day people would credit her with a new scientific process, or even a discovery.

Owen blinked, giving her a blank stare, and Nora shook her head. Even Maria hadn't made enough of an impact to be recalled by modern entomology students.

She trotted to her tent and located an empty mounting board. With practiced efficiency, she mounted her mixed-up butterfly and slid it into a box. Then she grabbed her art supplies and went back outside.

Owen held the jar containing the spent chrysalis up to the sun. He squinted at it, his brows making a shaggy, untidy seam above his eyes. William and Leonard disappeared into their tents, but Mr. Steed sat on a chair near the fire, peeling a langsat. Nora's mouth watered. She hadn't eaten enough at lunch, and the sweet-sour fruit had become a favorite.

As she passed Mr. Steed, she swiped the last langsat from his lap and tucked it into her palm. He sputtered, but his mouth was too full of fruit to articulate any words, and Nora pretended to not hear him as she approached Owen. Served him right for all the times he'd stolen *her* fruit.

"What is it?" Nora set her paint box and sketchbook on the shelf beside the jar containing the remaining cocoon and stretched onto her toes. She poked her thumbnail into the langsat's thin skin and peeled it off in one complete piece.

"I have no idea. It's rather small, isn't it?"

She broke off a segment of fruit and took it between her teeth, tugging the flesh from around the bitter pit. She motioned for the jar, settling back flat on her feet when Owen handed it over. Inside, a small *hymenoptera* buzzed around the jar, bumping against the side in a desperate bid for freedom. The metallic greenish-blue wasp was smaller than any parasitic fly she'd ever seen, but the hole in the side of the chrysalis proved its origin.

She set the jar on the shelf and tossed another piece of fruit into her mouth. Her teeth met slight resistance before popping through the langsat and spraying the back of her throat with its citrusy juice. She chewed slowly, thinking, then wiped her sticky fingers against her skirt and pulled the cheesecloth from the top of the jar, covering it with her hand so the wasp wouldn't escape.

"What are you doing?" Owen asked.

"I've never seen such a small parasite emerge from a chrysalis. I wonder . . ." She plunged her hand into the jar and pulled it out. She swiftly bound the fabric back atop the jar, trapping the wasp again, then held up her hand, the chrysalis nestled in her palm. "Let's see what's inside."

Still lounging in the chair, Mr. Steed snorted. "Waste of time."

"We have nothing better to do, so we may as well study," Nora said. "And if my hunch is right, it will be an exciting thing to see."

Mr. Steed chewed on the corner of his lip before shrugging and pushing himself up from his chair. "All right. I'm in."

Nora thought she heard a note of respect mingling with the curiosity in his voice. Maybe she was finally proving herself to him.

She lifted her chin and led the two men to the table set up outside the cabin. There, a lidded box held all the necessary entomological tools. She laid the chrysalis down and chose a sharp knife. With a gentle touch, she sliced through the hardened chitin. Using the knife and her free fingers to press open the chrysalis, she saw the small brown fly puparium nestled into a knob of decaying tissue. The puparium was a little larger than an apple seed and sported an exit hole in its side. She laid the knife down and tipped the chrysalis into her hand, freeing the puparium.

"My father once told me he'd discovered a hyperparasitoid wasp—that is, a wasp that has oviposited inside another parasitic wasp or fly." She placed the puparium into Mr. Steed's hand and rolled it to better show off the hole. "The tachinid fly killed the butterfly pupa, and in turn, the hyperparasitic wasp killed the fly, emerging from the chrysalis. There's not much literature on the phenomenon, but it's often seen in field research. You have to be looking for it, though." She pressed her hands to her sternum and sighed, an unrestrained smile twitching her lips.

"I've never heard of it," Mr. Steed said, "but this is my first time doing field research. My specialty is ecological entomology."

He didn't seem impressed with Nora's discovery, which she couldn't understand. He spent his career studying and teaching on how to subdue pests yet found hyperparasites dull? She shook her head and plucked the puparium from him and gave it to Owen, whose focused gaze and prodding fingers offered a more suitable response to their exciting find.

With one final cursory glance at the chrysalis on the table, Mr. Steed ambled away. "I'm having trouble breathing this heavy air." He ducked into his tent.

"He'll be singing in a few minutes," Owen said with a laugh. "I don't think hyperparasites can compare with his bottle of opium tincture."

Nora huffed. "He isn't easily impressed, is he?" She shone a bright smile at Owen. "He's probably never seen anything like this before. Have you?"

Owen slipped the puparium back into the jar and shook his head. "Never. I think it's fascinating. But how you remembered a childhood conversation you had with your father is even more fascinating. You have a mind like a snare."

He met her eyes, unblinking, taking her measure. She didn't know if what he saw pleased him. Occasionally, when she looked in the mirror, she thought she might be pretty, but she'd never spent too much time thinking about it. Her mother was beautiful—or at least she had been, before illness and grief had turned her into a shadow. And Nora had been told she looked like Mother.

Did Owen like what he saw? The way his tongue darted out and wet his lips said so. As did the even breaths he took and the almost imperceptible way he leaned toward her. She'd never have noticed except that she was staring at him.

She blinked and looked away. Her hands fumbled on the jar as she lifted it and set it back down. "Why are you looking at me like that?"

He cleared his throat, and when she glanced back up at him,

a grin curled his lips into something resembling the old Owen from college—the irritating one who constantly tried to best her in class. Her heart slowed its frantic beating, and the heat left her face.

"Have you ever considered doing fieldwork permanently?" he asked. "You obviously love it."

She crossed her arms. "I want to resurrect my father's journal. I can't do that from India."

"But you love the discovery. It nettles you that Frederic hasn't allowed you to join us since the ant fiasco. Not that you're missing much. It's a whole lot of wading through muck and staring at tree limbs. Though, if you came along, you'd see something with your eagle eye that the rest of us missed."

A mosquito buzzed near Nora's ear, and she smacked at it. Pulling her hand away, she saw it smashed against her fingers, her own blood staining her skin. The awful things were sucking the life from her. *Like your duty to something you don't want to do for the rest of your life?*

She flicked the dead insect away and rubbed her thumb against her forefinger to remove all traces of the mosquito's lunch. She closed her eyes. She wanted to run the journal. Her father had loved it. She loved it.

Owen laid his hand over hers. When she opened her eyes, she saw he'd drawn so close to her that only the wind could fit between them. Still holding her hand in his, he drew it close to his chest. "I think maybe God's path for you is bigger than anything you've ever considered. You could be the next Maria Merian—yes, I heard you, and yes, I know who she is—but not if you're stuck in Ithaca, toiling away on a periodical. Maria went to Suriname. Maybe you're supposed to travel around the world and make your own mark on science."

Nora shook her head. "It's a lovely idea, but fanciful. Life isn't an adventure novel, Owen. I have commitments and responsibilities in Ithaca."

"I understand. Really. I've spent my entire life being told

what I should do and be. But I think I'm done with all that. It only ever led to disappointment—for me and everyone else."

She looked past him, into the trees that teemed with so much life that most of it hadn't been discovered or named or labeled or catalogued. And yes, she wanted to be a part of that. Wanted to live in this dreamy, misty world nestled between mountains. Wanted to be like Maria Merian. But Maria hadn't had an ill mother. Or a father's expectations.

"I can't ignore everything in Ithaca. That's real life. This . . . this is a dream."

Owen's mouth tipped into a half smile. "There are stranger things than dreams coming true, Percipient."

Nora tossed on her hard narrow cot, Owen's words ricocheting around her mind. They fought for precedence with the night sounds—the insects and birds calling to one another. Then a guttural growl echoed around the hills, quieting the other wildlife. Even quieting her thoughts.

Nora sat up straight and shifted beneath the blanket twisting around her legs. Mr. Alford had warned them not to walk in the forest at night alone. The nocturnal Bengal tiger hunted after sunset. This was the first time she'd heard its presence. Her heart tripped despite the knowledge that she was safe in camp with the others and a roaring fire.

Another sound, this one choking and softened by whimpers, drew her toward the end of the cot where she'd draped her wrapper. She shoved her arms into it and quickly buttoned it as she approached the tent flap. When she pushed it aside, she saw Owen pacing outside Mr. Alford's tent. She stepped into the open, and Owen crept toward her.

"He's been vomiting for ten minutes. I don't know if he wants help or to be left alone. He hasn't called for anyone."

The moon, hanging heavy above them, shone silver light over Owen's white nightshirt. He shuffled, drawing Nora's attention to his bare feet and calves poking below the hem. A fuzz of fine blond hair covered his legs, and Nora felt as though she'd bitten into an unripe persimmon. Her tongue stuck to the roof of her mouth. At least her nightgown fell to her feet. There was no chance of Owen seeing her legs. But she'd never have thought the sight of a man's legs could so affect her.

"Well? What do you think?" he asked. "Should we see if he needs help?"

Her stomach rose as the sounds coming from Mr. Alford's tent intensified. She pressed her knuckles against her mouth and swallowed a belch. Finally, after it seemed Mr. Alford had emptied every bit of sustenance he'd consumed in the past week, the sounds of insects reigned again.

Owen and Nora looked at each other, eyes wide. She knew from tending Leonard and William that Mr. Alford must be in the middle of the worst of it. Leonard had been nearly senseless, unable to reach his own water or clean himself up.

She groaned. Another patient. "I guess I'll tend to him. It seems to be my lot here."

She ducked into her tent and quickly shed her wrap before donning her skirt and shirtwaist over her nightclothes. It would have to do. She stumbled past Owen, her bare feet scraping against the sharp edges of a stone.

He stopped her with a hand on her shoulder. "I'll clean up if you sit with him and help him get some fluids into his body." He motioned her toward the covered pot of water, and she nodded.

By the time she'd located a tin cup, filled it, and slipped into Mr. Alford's tent, Owen had already mopped up the floor beside the bed with a linen sheet. The closed room smelled of vomit and sweat. She pushed the flap open, securing it with the tie, then lit the lamp sitting on the small, cross-legged table and took in the dim interior.

Mr. Alford was meticulous. Neatly stacked books lined the

far wall, and a trunk in the corner sported tools arranged in a precise row. No pictures, mementos, or personal effects. He lay supine on the cot, his arm thrown over his eyes. With his other hand, he clutched a blanket to his chin, and Nora saw his form trembling beneath it. Sweat trickled down his cheeks, and dark circles hollowed his face. He groaned, and Nora almost felt compassion toward him.

Pragmatism took over. "If you're done cleaning that up, Owen, will you get me a clean towel and a bowl of water?"

Owen nodded and left the tent, arms full of malodorous laundry. She dragged a camp chair from near the trunk across the tent and set it beside Mr. Alford's cot.

He tilted his elbow up and peered at her. "What are you doing?" His words sounded scratchy, and a slick of vomit moistened the corner of his mouth.

"Seeing as I've already nursed two men through this illness, I think it's only right I offer you the same."

"You didn't offer to help the men. I forced you. But I don't want—"

She held the cup to his lips, stopping his words. She tipped it slightly, dribbling the water into his mouth. When he turned his head, she pulled it away. "You did force me to nurse them. Just like you forced me to stay in camp, so now I have little work to do and might as well see that you get better."

Owen returned, carrying a bowl of water. A folded bit of toweling was draped over his forearm. He set the bowl on the table. "The water is tepid. I wish we had access to a cool spring or ice. I'm not sure this will help bring down his fever." He took the cup from her and handed her the towel.

"It'll have to do." Nora dipped the corner of the towel in the water and wiped Mr. Alford's mouth before dampening the entire thing and laying it over his forehead.

Mr. Alford tossed his head, and the towel slipped to his pillow. "Leave me."

"Stop being a child. You're ill, and you need someone nearby."

She picked up the fabric and rearranged it, her hand boiling when it brushed his skin. She glanced at Owen, who looked as worried as she felt. "His fever is high."

"I'll sit with you." He left, returning a moment later with another chair, which he set beside her. "I hope you don't come down with anything."

She nodded. How awful. She'd hate for Owen to see her like this. Mr. Alford thrashed weakly and exhaled a series of rapid breaths before growing still. His hand fell from his head, and his chest rose and fell with a steady rhythm.

"He's asleep," Owen said. "If you want to return to bed, I'll stay with him."

"I won't be able to sleep. You can leave."

"I don't want you to be here alone all night."

So they sat, sharing the same fetid air, and watched over Mr. Alford, until Owen slumped into his chair and fell asleep, his soft snores keeping Nora company.

Less than half an hour later, their patient bolted upright and covered his mouth. Nora slid a bowl onto his lap. When he'd finished, she carried it outside and dumped it beside the tent, the tiger's scream still fresh in her mind. She wasn't about to approach the forest alone. Mr. Alford was wiping his mouth with his sleeve when she returned.

She pressed her hand against his forehead, satisfied the fever didn't burn hotter, and resettled into the chair. She smiled at Owen, whose head was tipped back, his mouth open. He'd sprawled out. His legs stretched in front of him, and his arms hung limply at his sides. No pretense clung to him. Even in sleep, he embodied frank confidence.

The cot creaked as Mr. Alford lay back down. "Have you known him long?"

"Since I started college. Three years."

"Do you have an understanding?"

"An understanding of what?"

He motioned a trembling hand between her and Owen. Nora's

face burned. Did he think . . . ? "We don't have an understanding. We're friends. Colleagues."

He snorted. "Colleagues aren't friends. They can't be trusted."

"You worked with Mr. Steed at Oxford and thought enough of him to ask him to join you here."

"I don't *trust* Jeffrey, I only know what to expect from him. And that's a more reassuring trait to have in a colleague anyway. My family learned firsthand that colleagues aren't people you can refer to as *friends*."

Owen jerked and sank even deeper into his seat. Nora reached to adjust his head, which hung at an uncomfortable angle, but snapped her hand back and forced her eyes away from him. Instead, she straightened the blanket at the foot of the cot and smoothed out the wrinkles.

"What happened with your family?" she asked.

Mr. Alford gasped and clutched his stomach. Nora held up the bowl, but he waved it away and closed his eyes. For several long minutes, he lay there, face gray and glistening with sweat, as he emitted a lengthy, miserable groan. He grew silent, and Nora thought he'd fallen asleep, but then his eyelids fluttered open, and he focused on her.

"Wretched business, this malady." He folded his hands atop his chest and sighed. "My father was a botanist and worked with Joseph Hooker here in India about ten years ago."

"I've heard of him."

"Everyone has heard of him. But no one had heard of my father, despite his pioneering work on Indian carnivorous plants. Until he ran for president of the Royal Society when Hooker stepped down. It was almost a certainty."

His voice had dropped to a whisper, and Nora leaned closer, resting her elbows on her knees. She hadn't realized his father was so esteemed a scientist. The elder Alford had even worked with the world's most celebrated botanist.

"Everything went well until my father identified a rare pitcher plant in northern India. His research assistant, the youngest son of a baron but also close friend to a duke, took credit for the discovery, even going so far as to steal my father's notes and present the findings to the British Royal Society. The papers loved him, and he soon stole the society's vote, becoming president."

Nora exhaled, realizing she'd been holding her breath. How awful. "Where is your father now? Is he still in India?"

Mr. Alford shook his head. "After losing credit for his labor and the honor of leading the society, he lost all desire to work. He died a few years ago. I hope my research here reestablishes my family in the scientific community and I'm able to redeem my father's place. Nothing means more to me. I can't even imagine returning home having failed."

He rolled onto his side and presented his back to her. In only a second, his breathing took on the even cadence of sleep, as though the telling of his story had stolen the last of his energy.

Nora knew the need to make good a blot on family history. She knew how exhausting the endeavor to salvage a father's legacy. And as she watched Mr. Alford sleep and listened to Owen's reassuring snuffles, she wondered if it was worth it. Did all the sacrifice and striving and bitterness really bring honor, or was it all vanity?

⁓

Mr. Alford's situation wedged its way into Nora's heart. The desperation he felt, so similar to her own, wouldn't release her. All the next day, as she mopped his brow with a damp towel and spooned sour-smelling yogurt between his lips, she watched the thawing of her heart with a wary eye. He was a challenging, unlikable man and had done nothing to deserve her respect, let alone her compassion. Yet with each of his heaving spells and ill-natured complaints, her thoughts turned toward kindness.

After lunch, when she went to her tent to wash and change, she saw the gynandromorphic *Vindula erota* mounted on its board. It was the type of butterfly that could make a collection exceed satisfactory. The type of butterfly that could catch the eye of a scientific society.

She shook her head, walked across the tent to the bowl set on the table beside her cot, and splashed water over her face. The humidity, a precursor to the heavy rains that made the clouds look swollen, left a layer of sticky sweat over her entire body. It sucked the thin, sheer fabric of her chemise against her torso, becoming a second skin. She wished for nightfall and its cooler temperatures.

Mr. Alford must be miserable, with his high fever holding steady. Her eyes strayed once more to the butterfly. She scrubbed her neck with the cloth, relishing the trickle of water dripping beneath her collar. Setting the cloth aside, she undid the buttons of her bodice, pulled out her arms, and let it hang from her waist.

With slow steps, she approached the box still atop her makeshift desk. She lifted the box and sat on the edge of her cot. Her eyes took in the butterfly's lopsided wings and uneven coloring. "You're mine."

A memory surfaced of another butterfly. One she'd loved from the moment she saw it in her father's case, wings spread. They were clear like windows, rimmed in brown, and they'd captured her imagination. *Greta oto*, the glasswing.

"*Why do you have to give it away? It's ours.*" *Nora couldn't bear to part with the brush-footed butterfly.*

"*I'm sending it to a friend for his exhibit in Paris. He'll take good care of it.*"

"*But I want it!*"

"*But he needs it, Bumble Bea.*" *Papa pinched her chin and smiled.* "*Sometimes we have to give up things we want to fill someone else's need.*"

She closed her eyes. Her father's words tore at her conscience.

"Okay," she whispered. She set down the box, finished dressing, and attempted to brush through the tangled knots in her hair. Giving up, she twisted it back into a bun at the nape of her neck and secured it with a few pins.

With a deep sigh, she collected the butterfly and stepped outside. A rustling came from the trees, and Owen emerged from between a cluster of flowering shrubs. Water droplets clung to the hair falling over his eyes—he needed a haircut—and his shirt stuck to his chest, moisture making the fabric translucent.

His eyes sparkled with a full night's sleep and a proper cleaning. "There's a great little spring a quarter mile into the shola. It's close enough that you can go by yourself." He noticed the open mounting box in her hand. "Are you going to paint your butterfly?"

Nora shook her head, the words lodging somewhere between her heart and throat. "I'm not keeping it."

He gave a swift shake of his head, sending a spray of fern-scented water across her face. "What? Why? It's amazing."

"I feel . . ." She choked on the foreign word. When did she ever do anything based on feeling? But this was right. She couldn't explain it, but she knew it. "I feel like I should give it to Mr. Alford."

Owen held the back of his hand against her forehead.

She swatted at it. "I'm not ill, Owen."

His hand fell to her cheek, and he caressed her earlobe. "All right. Just making sure."

"I think it's the right thing to do. Last night, Mr. Alford told me he was trying to honor his father. Maybe I can do something to help."

The hard lines of Owen's jaw softened as a gentle smile caressed his lips. "Just when I think I have you all figured out." He dropped his hand and hooked his thumbs into his waistband. "You could submit an article to a paper. Receive some recognition. Do you want to illustrate it first, at least?"

Oh, she did. More than anything. "No. I want Mr. Alford to receive the credit for this." Honor had been stolen from his family, and she had the chance to offer him an undeserved gift. She didn't think she'd ever done that before. It didn't make any sense. It wasn't practical or logical or—

Her fingers tightened around the box, and she ground her teeth together. Before she could change her mind, she spun and marched into Mr. Alford's tent.

"I have something for you," she said. She walked to the side of the cot and stood, stiff and straight.

He groaned and turned his head toward her. "What are you doing? Shut the flap. The sun is giving me a headache."

Dark circles made half-moons below his eyes. The room smelled of illness and the myrrh Pallavi had insisted they burn in a brass censer, and the air was a heavy blanket wrapped around them. He looked miserable.

"I need to give you this." She would do the right thing, but there was no way she could make her voice sound anything but harsh. Obedience would have to be enough for now.

He sighed and pried open one eye. "What do you want?"

Nora resisted the urge to hide the box behind her back. She knew it unlikely he'd show appreciation, but after the way he'd opened up to her last night, she'd thought he'd be kinder.

Nora placed the box in his lap and watched as he brought it up to his face. He narrowed his eyes. "What is this? A deformity?" He blinked and wiped at his eyes.

"It's a gynandromorphic *Vindula erota*."

"Gynandromorphic?" His eyes narrowed as he studied it. "You mean . . . ?"

"The butterfly is half male and half female—its body, its brain."

Mr. Alford's eyes widened. "I've never come across something like this in all my years of study."

"I understand it's uncommon. I'd never seen a specimen until my outing with Owen yesterday."

"Have you studied it?"

"A little."

A shudder jerked his shoulders, and he shoved the box back into her hands. He clutched his belly and moaned, tears squeezing from the corners of his eyes. When the episode ended, he said, "Put it on the trunk, and you can tell me about its habits later. Then you can illustrate it for the book. It'll be a showpiece."

Before Nora could do as he asked, his breathing slowed and deepened as he fell back to sleep. She pressed a kiss to her fingertips and held them against the side of the box, then set it down and escaped the sickroom.

Sita sat at the table outside the cabin, making broad strokes on a sheet of paper with a green pastel. She bit her lower lip, revealing the deep dimples in her cheeks. Her silky braids were caught up into two rings tied with wide indigo ribbons. She sat back and studied her artwork for a moment before reaching for the pile of fennel seeds mounded beside her paper. Pinching some, she tossed them into her mouth and crunched on them.

The taste of vomit whispered against Nora's throat, so when she reached Sita, she scooped a teaspoon of the seeds into her palm and pressed her tongue against them. The licorice flavor reminded her of the box of breath fresheners her mother kept in the drawer of her bedside table. Maybe Nora would pack some into an envelope and send them with her next letter home.

She chewed the seeds as she studied Sita's picture. It was unlike anything she'd ever seen before, as were most of Sita's original pieces when she wasn't practicing the illustrations Nora assigned her. In this one, green swirls of palm fronds outlined abstract maroon and yellow flowers. The green shot off toward the edges of the paper, twisting into the heads of caterpillars.

Owen, now dry and fully dressed, joined Nora, and they watched as Sita picked up her pastel and made a few final flourishes. She turned a smile on them. "What do you think?"

"It's incredible," Owen said. "Amazing that you've had no formal training."

"You're a rare talent, Sita." Nora lifted the paper and held it up. The sun shone through the vibrant colors, making it look like a stained-glass window. "Maybe one day people from all over the world will travel here and buy your art."

Sita's face fell, and she looked at the table. With nimble fingers, she replaced the pastels in their wooden case and clicked it shut. Then she rested her open mouth against the edge of the table and swept the rest of the fennel seeds into it. Sitting up straight, she rolled the seeds around her mouth and swallowed. "Do Christians believe in bad luck?"

"No," Nora said. "Christians believe God is omnipotent and omniscient. That means God knows everything and has unlimited power." She laid the paper on the table. "Luck is also untenable. Nature proves there is order." Except for her gynandromorph. There were always aberrations.

Sita rested her elbow on the table and her cheek in her hand. She gave a lusty, impressive sigh. "Bad things always seem to happen to my family, and my father thinks we are cursed."

Nora wanted to dismiss Sita's concerns—they were ridiculous, of course—but she looked so forlorn. So miserable. Nora knelt beside her and cupped Sita's face in her hands. "God has a plan for you. A plan to prosper and not harm you."

"Then why is He letting my father do this terrible thing to me?"

"It hasn't happened yet. And I promise I will somehow free you from it."

Owen coughed, and Nora looked at him, her eyes widening when he shook his head. Did he not want her to help Sita? A deep line appeared between his brows, and she saw worry in the tight way he pulled his lips together. Maybe he was only worried she wouldn't be able to keep her promise. He didn't know her well if he thought she was prone to failure.

He sighed. "I'll stay and watch over Frederic if you and Sita want to go for a walk."

Sita looked up at Nora and nodded, her eyes darting to the woods. Maybe she needed a distraction. Nora knew she did.

"That sounds lovely." She shouldered her rucksack. "Just in case," she told Sita with a wink. "You never know what you'll discover when you're roaming around."

Those words, spoken a decade earlier, stirred a memory of her father. *"Keep your eyes open, Bumble Bea. You never know what you'll find if you're looking."*

So often, Nora focused on one narrow thing—an idea, a hope, a specimen, a dream—that she missed everything happening around her.

She took Sita's hand, and the little girl dimpled. "Let's go find something."

They tramped through the grass and tripped over ferns and logs and lichen-covered stones that lined winding streams. Nora kept her eyes on Sita, watching the child laugh and poke around and mimic the bugs and birds she saw. *I'll keep my eyes open. I might find some way to save her from this fate if I'm looking.*

Chapter Seventeen

Two days later, when Mr. Alford was well enough to sit unassisted and bark commands at anyone unlucky enough to enter his line of sight, Nora rapped on the front door of a two-story house made of pale brick. Nearly overtaken by purple clematis, it housed the Greater British Missionary Alliance, and she was eager to meet with Christians who had dedicated themselves to the welfare of the native people. Mr. Alford's conscience might have been consumed by thoughts of the mating rituals and life cycles of tropical butterflies, but surely the missionaries would be more sympathetic to Sita's plight.

A servant wearing a full beard and turban opened the door and led Nora to a light-filled office just off the hall. A moment later, a well-fed man sporting a heavy mustache that flowed into lacy gray muttonchops entered the room. His eyes wrinkled in the corners, and a relaxed smile pushed up his round cheeks. Nora felt certain he would help her. He had an air of joviality and kindness.

"Please, have a seat." He waved Nora into a spindly upholstered chair opposite an imposing desk covered in all manner of paper.

Nora settled herself.

He undid the bottom button of his vest and sat behind the desk, with cracking joints and a satisfied sigh. "I am Mr. Jacob Welling, director of missions for southern India. What can I do for you?"

Nora relaxed her face into what she hoped was a pleasant expression and introduced herself. "I'm looking for help for a young friend. Her father has dedicated her to worship at the temple of Yellamma and all that that entails."

Mr. Welling had lived in India for years. Hopefully he wouldn't expect Nora to expand on Sita's fate.

A knowing light entered his watery eyes, and his jowls settled into an expression that reminded Nora of a bloodhound, all drooping skin and sad expression. "Terrible business," he said. "But there isn't a lot we can do."

Nora blinked. "But you're head of the mission here."

"And this is a local matter. It isn't illegal in India to give children into such practice."

She swallowed against the sourness filling her mouth. It slid down her throat and burned a trail to her stomach. "But you're here on a calling from God. It's your duty to help the disenfranchised."

Mr. Welling sat back in his chair and rested his folded hands over his belly. "You are a softhearted woman, Miss Shipley. It's a credit to your sex and—"

She held up her hand, palm toward him. "Please don't patronize me. I'm neither softhearted nor like most women. I merely see a need and want this child helped."

"Unfortunately, I'm not in any position to help. I am here to support the needs of the local missionaries."

"I thought you were here to reach the Indians with the news of Christ. To reduce yourself so that He might shine through you."

Mr. Welling smiled, small, even teeth peeking from behind his mustache. "Have you ever considered entering ministry, my dear?" When she sighed and rubbed at her temple, he coughed. "No, of course not. But, you see, if we interfere in this, then the Hindus will grow angry, and we wouldn't be welcome any longer. Kodaikanal is a place of respite for our ill and weary workers. In order to continue meeting the needs of our Christian brothers and sisters in India, we must not start a revolt among the locals."

"This girl is a Christian, converted at one of your mission schools. Do you set the captive free only to leave them in the very cages they thought they'd escaped?" Nora's heart pounded against her rib cage. She didn't know what she'd do if Mr. Welling was unwilling to help.

He sighed. "That is unfortunate."

"Quite the understatement, Mr. Welling."

A soft cough sounded from the doorway, and Mr. Welling's eyes rolled toward the ceiling as though he were praising God for the interruption. "Mr. Davies! I'm so glad you've come." He stood and offered Nora a placid smile. "I'm sorry, Miss Shipley, that I can't be of more service. I'll keep your little friend in my prayers and hope God preserves her."

Nora stood. "I'm certain God will find your sacrifice pleasing." She ignored the wounded expression in his eyes and turned away.

Swathi Davies and her husband stood in the doorway, Swathi's pinched face cradling a soft smile. Charan frowned at Nora and gave a slight shake of his head.

"I will see Miss Shipley out." Swathi patted Charan's hand and reached for Nora's.

Approaching her, Nora nodded to Charan, and behind his brittle façade, she saw fear. For his wife or position, she didn't know, but she sent him a smile. He had lost his child, and although his wife still stood beside him in body, her soul and mind were broken and not altogether present.

Swathi curled her fine-boned hand around Nora's arm and led her from the house. They stopped on the marble step outside the door, and Swathi's grip turned desperate. Hard.

"Please don't think ill of me for eavesdropping, but I overheard your conversation with Mr. Welling, and I might be able to help." Her eyes darkened, and she glanced behind them. She released Nora's arm and slid the door closed. "Come."

Nora followed Swathi down the step and up the pebbled lane to the gate. Hope, in the guise of a swarm of butterflies, fluttered in her belly. She reached for the iron balustrade to steady herself. "Please, tell me."

Swathi's tongue darted out and wet her lips. "If anyone finds out I told you this, it could ruin my husband's career. Mr. Welling, as kind as he is, doesn't brook noncompliance among his missionaries. My husband is in a precarious position, as he's not fully British. The Eurasians are looked down on by both father and mother." When Nora shook her head in confusion, Swathi continued, "The British don't fully embrace their children, but neither do the Indians. They are both but neither. My parents—" Tears welled, and she sniffed, pulling them back. "My parents weren't happy I married Charan, even though my family has been Christian for a hundred years. Even though they sent me to the English school. And Charan's father went back to England after he secured him this position. We have no one and nothing. So please, you must not tell anyone I spoke with you about this." Her chin trembled, and she blinked.

"I give you my word."

Swathi leaned in, and her whispered words brushed Nora's ear. "There is a woman outside Madurai. She runs a home for children who have been rescued from your friend's fate. Some worked for a few years, but many escape before they're given over."

Nora pulled back and pressed her hand against her heart. God had made a way.

The front door creaked open, and Nora squeezed Swathi's

arm. "I'll come to you when the information is needed. Thank you."

Swathi bit her trembling lower lip. "Will you . . . will you come for lunch tomorrow? I know I don't know you well, but I've no one here, and my husband is so busy."

Nora looked at the house and saw Mr. Welling standing on the step, shading his eyes with a hand and staring after her. She smiled brightly and waved at him, then looked at Swathi. "I'd love to come."

Then she slid through the gate and turned toward camp, the gentle stirrings of restored faith spurring her forward.

Lunch with Swathi proved interesting. Educated and articulate, she had Bitsy's quick wit and Rose's sweet spirit. Mr. Davies came home to dine with them, and their conversation continued with his thoughtful responses.

Their cook—a man who had worked for them in Madurai—prepared the best meal Nora had eaten in India thus far, though she wouldn't tell Pallavi. *Dosai* stuffed with mutton, fish cooked in a well-spiced broth, *sambar*, the ever-present rice, plus an array of dishes Nora had no name for and knew she'd never be able to describe.

When they finished eating, Mr. Davies took Nora's hand. "Thank you for visiting with us." She saw more in his eyes than his words expressed. The look he gave his wife was tender. "We've been lonely since leaving our home."

Swathi had been lonely, he meant. He'd been kept busy. She stayed in a house, empty save for her cook and a man who cleaned and worked in the garden. No child to fill her days. Her movements exhibited a sluggishness that spoke of deep grief, her eyes wandered when their talk slowed, her skin wore a gray cast, and she only picked at her food.

When Mr. Davies left, Nora glanced at Swathi, who clasped and unclasped the fork sitting beside her plate. Nora had rejoiced when she first saw the utensil, knowing she'd be able to eat her fill, but now the item seemed to have absorbed all of Swathi's sadness, and Nora wanted nothing more than to ease it.

Over the course of a single lunch, she'd developed a deep regard for Swathi. Maybe because she missed her friends and the easy conversation that sparked between them, or maybe because the tension she'd carried in her back since meeting Mr. Alford and failing, repeatedly, to impress him had dissolved the moment she stepped into Swathi's cozy bungalow. Either way, they'd fallen into an instant and deep friendship.

"I lost my father," Nora said.

Swathi's eyes filled. "I'm sorry. It's a terrible pain."

"It never really goes away. But it does become bearable. Eventually."

"My family has been lucky. Until Lukose, none of the children died young. We are a robust people, and I became complacent, trusting that he would be safe. Because of that, and because God loves us. Isn't that silly? It's terrible theology, Charan would say. I haven't told him how angry I am that God didn't protect my son. Does that shock you?"

"No. I understand it."

She looked at Nora for a moment, then nodded. "It's hard to talk about such things with others. They *don't* understand. Even my family . . . my mother believes marrying Charan caused a weakness in our child. The British often don't fare well in India. They contract every disease, die so quickly. Most of them send their children away to England before they turn six, knowing they'll be more likely to survive. Do you think my son's British blood made him susceptible to typhoid? Did it make him too weak to survive it?"

Nora shook her head. "Fully British people survive typhoid. And fully Indian people die of it. I think it was just a terrible thing that happened, and none of it had anything to do with your husband's heritage."

Swathi shuddered and sank against her seat. "Thank you,"

she whispered. "Sometimes my faith becomes so twisted up in fear and emotions, I forget we live in a natural world."

A small laugh escaped Nora's throat. "Sometimes my thoughts become so consumed by the natural world, I forget about faith. I should remember it more often."

She thought of Sita and her situation, realizing she might have to rely more on God than her own understanding. An uncomfortable position for someone who had spent years cultivating a sharp mind and explanations backed by science.

⁓

Three days later, Nora stood at the table in the rickety cabin and peered at the stack of books brought from England. Her fingers ran down the spines.

"*Illustrations of New Species of Exotic Butterflies, Lepidoptera: Indigenous and Exotic, The Cabinet of Oriental Entomology* . . . there. That'll work."

She pulled the book from the middle of the stack and flipped open to the spread illustrating *Meloidae*.

The day before, after Nora had finished her work, she and Sita had taken their jars and set out to find something interesting. And they had. A large blister beetle Nora warned Sita not to touch. They'd studied its ponderous movements for a quarter of an hour, then carefully slid it into a kill jar. Sita loved its bright orange stripes and ability to burn the skin with a poisonous secretion, and she wanted to mount it—the beginning of her own insect collection. She was less interested in butterflies than the many insects that could sting, bite, or spray.

"*Mylabris pustulata*. Orange blister beetle." She bent to smile at the jar that contained Sita's discovery. "Well, now you have a name, and we must get you pinned."

She replaced the book and took the jar with her into the glaring sunlight.

"What have you got there?" Mr. Alford asked, his question

showing interest but the sneer on his face saying something else entirely.

She wondered if he couldn't help his sour expressions. "Just a beetle Sita found yesterday while we were on a walk."

His eyes narrowed a little, but then he shook his head and said, "You're coming with us today."

"With you where?"

"We're traveling more afield than normal and will be spending the night in the shola." He rubbed hard against his face and glowered. "Despite being here over a year, I've yet to gather enough illustrations and information to fill my book because of the constant illness my team has suffered. I can't give any more excuses and plan to leave when you and Owen return home in a few months."

"Have you forgiven me for dropping a hundred ants on your head?"

He rolled his eyes, but a small smile tugged the corners of his lips. "No, but your gift of the gynandromorphic butterfly was generous and a boon for my project." He cleared his throat, and his next words came out sounding harsh. "Pallavi will come with us to chaperone, and I told her to bring her monstrous niece, since she seems adept at finding things the rest of this team misses."

Nora grinned. "Mr. Alford, I think you might be warming to us. Sita will be so happy to be included."

His mouth fell into its usual frown. "See that she doesn't get in the way. And call me Frederic."

She smiled at his retreating back.

An hour later, with Sita tripping at their heels and Pallavi carrying a large copper kettle on her head, they plunged into the forest. Two porters followed close behind, their shoulders weighted with skins of water and boxes of supplies.

Nora patted her bag, which bounced against her hip as she trotted along the leaf-strewn path. Her heart danced along with her steps, and she couldn't help but admire the vibrancy of the land around them. The green leaves and showy blooms and brambly floor. The earth welcomed her freedom and sang with joy along with her. She trod lightly over the soft ground, her chest clenching with anticipation, and wondered at the interesting things they'd see.

A small hand slid into Nora's palm, and she looked down into Sita's serious face. "I am happy to come with you." She flashed a grin and tugged until Nora lowered her head. "I know where the special butterflies go. Frederic hasn't found them yet, and I heard him talking with Owen about it. They are uncommon in this part of India. Maybe we will see them." Then she bounced toward Pallavi and tried to talk the cook into relinquishing one of the *jalebi* tucked into the sack hanging from her arm. Nora's mouth watered. She'd been thrilled to see Pallavi had brought a box of them back to camp along with the requisite mangos, rice, and lentils.

Owen glanced back at her, then paused until she came alongside him.

"I'm glad you've come with us," he said, as though she'd been the one resisting joining them. "You have a knack for discovery, and you're sure to help us."

Nora dropped her eyes to the trail. She'd thought he might want her along for her own sake, because he enjoyed her company. She'd never considered herself a silly woman, but her disappointment in his answer contradicted that.

"And," Owen continued, "I like being with you. I like you."

She jerked her head up. His lips curled in a boyish grin, but she couldn't tell if he was teasing her or meant his words. He did have a reputation on campus for being a flirt . . . but he had been so attentive.

She swallowed the pleasure tickling her throat and chose pragmatism. "Flattery doesn't work on me."

"What do you think I want from you?"

She shrugged, then heard her mother's rebuke—*"don't shrug, darling, it isn't feminine"*—and lowered her shoulder. "I don't know, but you must want something, or you wouldn't say such things."

Owen bit his lower lip. "You can't believe I have a sincere interest in you?"

"I don't see why you would. You are the smart, charming son of a successful New York City businessman."

"And who are you?"

Absolutely no one. Nora shifted her bag, easing its pressure on her hip. She winced when a sharp pain shot across her lower back. They'd been walking for hours, and she wasn't used to trekking such distances.

Owen slipped the strap from her shoulder and lifted it over her head. He tucked her rucksack into the larger bag he carried. "I'll tell you who you are. You are Nora Shipley, daughter of the most interesting man I've ever met."

She slid a glance toward him.

"It's true, and it amazes me that you think I'm charming when you were raised by such a man. He made a favorable impression on everyone who met him."

Her estimation of Owen, already having risen so high since they'd arrived in India, grew. She chanced a light touch on his arm, which drew a smile from him. And his smile warmed her.

The path before them dipped, and Owen held his arm out for her. "Here, don't slip. I'd hate to have to carry you all the way to camp." His gaze swept her face, and his lids grew heavy. "Actually, I might rather like carrying you all the way to camp." He wrapped his arm around her back, his hand resting just below her rib cage.

Her heart hammered against her chest. And when the rest of the team disappeared around a bend in the footpath, it pounded a fierce tempo. But still Owen didn't release her.

He drew her closer.

And tucked a curl behind her ear.

And bit his lip, which drew her attention to his well-formed face. To the beard prickling his chin and cheeks and the slight tug of his lips as he held back another smile.

His fingers trailed her jaw. "I'll tell you who else you are. You are a woman of uncommon intelligence and beauty. A woman above all other women. A woman I could happily spend the rest of my life learning about."

Nora's eyes widened, only to slip closed as Owen tilted her head and lowered his mouth.

She'd never been kissed. Never wanted to be kissed. But now . . . here, with him . . .

A slapping of steps came from somewhere down the path, and Sita's voice yanked Nora's eyes open and Owen's hand away.

"*Akka*, they're setting up camp. Come, I will show you the spot I mentioned."

Sita ignored Owen's muttered argument, grabbed Nora's hand, and pulled her off the trail and through a copse of densely packed trees.

~⁓

By the time Sita led Nora to a muddy stream twisting and curving between and around evergreen trees, Nora's stomach growled from hunger. She stopped when mud slurped at her boots, and shook a collection of twigs and burrs from her skirt.

"I hope this butterfly you want to show me is worth the hike."

Sita flashed a smile and pointed at a spongy slick not eight feet from them. Nora squinted at the flock of dusty blue and black butterflies flitting about. She crept nearer, careful not to disturb them, and sifted through her mental catalogue of *Lepidoptera*.

"I believe it's a *Chliaria othona*. They are rare this far south." Nora knew Frederic was looking for species uncommon to southern India. He'd been in a dither a few days previous because he'd heard William had spotted an orchid tit, but when they returned to the spot, the elusive butterfly hadn't been there.

And here . . . here Nora had a dozen at least.

"We need to go back to camp and tell Frederic about this. He'll want to watch and record their behavior."

Sita crossed her arms and stuck out her lip. "You should watch and draw them. Don't tell Frederic. Then he will have the honor of finding them."

"I'm part of a team, and Frederic leads it. He's going to get credit anyway."

"I showed *you*. I want you to study it and show me how to draw it. Why don't you print your own book?"

Nora cupped the back of Sita's head. "It's not as easy as wanting to. I committed myself to Frederic's team. Anyway, even though it's a lovely butterfly, it will benefit Frederic more than me."

Sita jerked away and pushed Nora. "I won't let him see them. I'll send them away!"

She whirled, and Nora grabbed her arm before she could rush at the butterflies and scatter them. She pulled Sita into her arms and wrapped her in an embrace.

"Sita, whatever is wrong? Do you hate him so much?"

Sita burrowed her head against Nora's waist, trembling. "It is nothing. I don't want him to have my butterflies. I want *you* to have them."

The stirring of something ugly and outrageous flirted with Nora's thoughts. Something she'd never have considered before learning Sita's fate. But no. She couldn't think . . .

"Okay. I won't show him your spot, but may I take one back to camp?"

Sita frowned. Then she nodded and stepped back.

Nora reached for her rucksack but realized Owen still carried it. "How far is camp from here?"

Sita sniffed. "Half a kilometer. Not far."

"Run and get Owen. Tell him to bring my bag and net." She bent, pressed a kiss to Sita's temple, and whispered, "But don't tell Frederic. It'll be our secret. We'll just show him proof of our discovery, not where to find the entire treasure."

A grin split Sita's face, large enough to force Nora's suspicions back into the oblivion where they belonged, and she darted away on nearly silent feet. Nora settled nearby, willing to throw herself over the entire lot of orchid tits if they made an escape.

A *Delias eucharis*, its brilliant stained-glass wings flittering, landed three feet away at the very end of the mud flat. Nora didn't think she'd seen one in Frederic's collection when she was working on the illustrations. The Common Jezebel was common, for sure. Swarms of them flew over India. Maybe it didn't suit Frederic to have such an ordinary butterfly in his book, but it was certainly lovely, and she imagined most British people would enjoy seeing one illustrated. If it was still around when Sita returned, she'd collect it along with the rarer orchid tit.

Nora leaned against a tree and filled her eyes, mind, and soul with the beauty around her, wanting to escape the vile scum that muddied her thoughts.

~

That night they slept on scratchy blankets with only the ground for pillows. Nora, sandwiched between Pallavi and Sita, lay beneath their tent. Pallavi, the drape of her sari wrapped around her like a blanket, took up as little space in sleep as she did awake. Which was good, because Sita tossed and turned with nightmares.

Despite spending the better part of the afternoon and evening walking through the forest, the team had discovered nothing. Except for the secret orchid tit, which Nora had put in a jar with a wet cloth and drop of antiseptic and stuffed into the bottom of her sack—and the Common Jezebel she'd snagged along with it—the trip had been a complete waste of time.

Of course, there had been that moment with Owen. . . .

And the orchid tit, which held more significance.

Nora turned onto her stomach and tucked her hands beneath her head. Sita snuggled against her, triggering warm affection and a desire to protect. And on the heels of that maternal emotion came the hiss of bees, an ever-growing buzz in her throat.

Anger, raw and hot and stinging, clawed at her lips until she felt helpless to resist it. She squeezed her eyes closed and wished for the oblivion of sleep. She didn't want to think about it.

But she knew Sita's response earlier might signify something heartbreaking.

Something wrong.

Something that could unleash all the anger Nora had ever suppressed.

She reached through the darkness and laid her hand on Sita's soft head. *Lord, please . . . What she prayed for, she didn't know. Please save her. Please help me help her. Please stop this—whatever this is. Please let me be wrong. Please. Please. Please.*

"Nora."

Nora rolled onto her back and strained to see through the crack where the canvas flaps didn't quite meet. "Yes?"

"I need to talk to you."

Owen.

Did he want to talk about their almost-kiss? She didn't think she could do that right now, with her emotions so ragged and raw.

She got to her feet, careful not to disturb the other two, and reached for her shawl, which she'd been using as a makeshift pillow. Draping it over her shoulders, she made sure her bodice and skirts were straight, then crept from the tent.

Owen stood a few feet away and motioned her toward a cluster fig tree across the clearing. As soon as they ducked beneath its overhanging branches, he said, "I've been thinking about that orchid tit. I don't feel right keeping it from Frederic. We're part of his team, and you discovered it while working for him. Maybe if you had found it on your own time . . ."

Nora nodded. "I'll show him the one I captured, but I can't let him see their gathering place. I promised Sita, and she feels strongly about it."

"She's an odd one, isn't she?"

The high moon spilled light through the tree branches and dappled Owen's face. The kindness in his expression softened his insult, and Nora thought she'd never seen anyone as hand-some. Or as thoughtful and trustworthy and smart.

"You remind me of my father." The words slipped from her mouth before she'd even formulated them in her thoughts.

Owen's lips tilted, just a little at the corners. "Thank you."

She had known only two men she trusted—her father and Professor Comstock. But Owen had somehow managed to join them. She didn't know when it had happened. Maybe as they traveled thousands of miles across the ocean. Or maybe it was because he'd worked so hard to convince Frederic of her worth. But whatever the reason, Nora allowed herself to be enveloped by the comforting knowledge that she could rely on him.

And she knew she couldn't keep her suspicions to herself. "Can I tell you something . . . unpleasant?"

Owen stiffened and ran his hand through his hair before nodding. He leaned against the tree trunk, and his eyes shuttered as his lips grew thin. He looked for all the world as though she was about to break his heart. Her breath caught, and she wondered at the heat rushing through her. Not that she wanted to break his heart, but the knowledge that the possibility would affect him that way made her feel, for the first time in her life, as though she held a certain amount of power.

How proud you are.

She stepped toward him so only a few inches of tropical air, heavy with the promise of monsoon, separated them. "It's about Sita. And Frederic."

He tugged at his ear. She'd never noticed how well-formed his ears were. She shook her head. *Focus, Nora.*

"I believe something might have happened between them. Something . . . improper." She swallowed against the lump in her throat.

He grabbed her hands. "What are you saying, Nora? Please be clear so I don't speculate."

"I believe Frederic may have behaved unseemly toward her. In a physical manner." She saw Owen's face redden and knew her own matched his. Whether from anger or embarrassment, she didn't know.

He tugged her hands toward him and whispered, "What do you want me to do?"

"I don't know. I just needed to tell someone. I'm going to get her out of Kodaikanal anyway."

"You're going to get yourself in trouble."

Nora shook her hands free and crossed her arms. "No one else is willing to, though. Owen, she needs me. If I don't do something, I'll always wonder if I could have saved her from a terrible fate, and I'll never forgive myself."

He gave a quick nod. "All right. We can't very well accuse him of something so heinous without proof, but between the two of us, I'm sure we can make sure he isn't left alone with her. Let's keep an eye on things."

All of the tension that had tightened her muscles and joints since Sita's outburst loosened. She was no longer alone with her terrible suspicions. Owen would support her in this.

He sought her eyes, and she wondered if, amid her determination and love for Sita, he also recognized her growing regard for him. But then a deep cough caught his attention, and he looked toward the campsite. Nora turned and saw one of the porters stumbling away from the knot of tents and into the brush. He reappeared a moment later, tying his *dhoti*. He dropped back through his tent opening without even a glance in their direction.

"You should get back before anyone notices us out here." Owen straightened and reached toward her but dropped his hands before his fingers touched her skin.

She turned back to him and stepped forward. Maybe if she could capture his gaze again, he would see how she felt. She wouldn't have to speak the words, because everything would be laid bare in her eyes. She blinked up at him and clasped his upper arms. Sliding her hands down, she stopped at his wrists, and his pulse thrummed against her fingertips. She could almost hear his heartbeat, a percussion against the melody of India's night sounds.

"Owen."

His breathing deepened, and when she dropped his wrists, he pulled her close, his hands spanning her back. "Nora, I—"

His brows mashed together over the bridge of his nose, and he released her so quickly, she stumbled back. He slapped at his head, and two cockroaches, their ends joined together, hurtled from his hair toward her. With a screech she ducked, but they landed on her, scuttling apart and skittering around her neck and scalp. Their setae grasped at the strands of her unbound hair, and her voice rose, edged in panic and heavy with her worst memory.

"Papa, I want that butterfly for my collection."

"Bumble Bea, it's too far away. The tree isn't sturdy enough. We'll have to find another one."

Nora looked at the pretty blue insect that rested on a spindly limb of the willow oak extending over Cascadilla Falls.

Her father started away, leaving Nora to wonder if she could scramble up and snatch it before he noticed. She was fast.

But he had still noticed.

Chapter Eighteen

G et them off!" Nora's scream bounced off the thick trees and reverberated around the camp.

"Calm down, Nora. It's okay." Owen cupped her jaw with one hand, and when she stilled, he used the other to run his fingers through her hair, picking the roaches out one at a time and tossing them into the weeds.

Violent tremors shook her body, and she sank to the ground. She grasped fistfuls of velvety-soft grass and pulled. Over and over, until the patch around her became barren. Owen knelt near her, close enough that she knew he was there, but not so close that he interfered in her doomed attempt to forget.

She never forgot, though, and the roaches tormented her with guilt and regret.

Heavy footsteps drew her attention. Frederic stood over them, glaring down his nose and scratching at his head, which signified another pest altogether. "What is going on?"

Nora just shook her head.

"It's nothing," Owen said, standing. "She was startled by some rather large cockroaches."

Frederic's thin lips twisted. "Cockroaches? You were fright-ened by some roaches? Of all the ridiculous things."

His words cleared her fog, and she got to her feet and clapped the dust from her hands. "I apologize. It won't happen again."

"I should hope not. I thought Comstock sending you here showed a lack of common sense, but now I know he's com-pletely off his crumpet. An entomologist frightened by roaches, indeed!" He spun and stomped back to his tent and the still-sleeping porters.

Nora chanced a glance at Owen and saw curiosity and con-cern in his knotted brows. "I think I should return to my tent," she said.

"I think you should tell me what just happened. It wasn't the first time. You had the same response in class when the cockroach—"

"Yes, I remember." She shuddered, still able to feel its wiry legs prickling her calf through her stockings. She rubbed at her head, trying to erase the ghost of the mating pair's touch.

"I've never known you to be fearful, especially of an insect. What's going on?" Owen asked.

She wondered if confessing her sin would absolve her of it. Maybe she'd spent too long holding it within her own mind, and if she gave it wings, it would fly away, and she'd be left with peace.

She knew her feelings were irrational. Knew it wasn't *really* her fault. She'd been impulsive and headstrong, yes, but Father had made his own decision. The image, though, was seared on her soul.

"The day my father died, he took me collecting. He'd given me a drawer in his cabinet and told me I could fill it with whatever struck my fancy." She drew Owen deeper beneath the tree's can-opy, hoping the dense branches muffled her words. She inhaled, drawing strength from the rush of oxygen, and plunged into her story. "We spotted a beautiful blue butterfly I hadn't seen in my father's collection, and I wanted it—more than anything

I'd ever coveted. It rested on a tree branch, and my father told me to leave it. The branch hung over Cascadilla Falls."

Even in the thin moonlight, she could see the pallor curtaining Owen's face. He knew, of course. Everyone knew how Professor Shipley had died. But they didn't know *why*. And now she was about to tell the one person who'd come to mean more to her than almost anyone else.

She grabbed the ends of her shawl and knotted it at her chest. Then she untied it and tugged at the fringe, fiddling until Owen covered her hands with his. The warmth of his touch was a balm.

"You may have learned I'm willful," she said.

He smiled. "You wouldn't have accomplished all you have if you weren't."

She flexed her fingers inside his, and when he released her, she grasped his hand. She needed that connection. Needed to be grounded by his touch.

"When my father turned to go, I attempted to climb the tree. Looking back, I can see how idiotic it was. The falls were swollen from rain, and they tumbled below in a frenzy that should have warned me. But I wanted the butterfly."

She hadn't cried when her father died. Nor at his funeral. Nor afterward when her mother isolated herself in her room and sobbed for months. She didn't cry at holidays or his birthday. It was as though her part in his death forever forbade her from showing how deeply losing him affected her. As though she was too unworthy to share in the grief.

But now, as the words slipped from her mouth like the millstones they were, tears trickled down her cheek. She disentangled her fingers from Owen's and swiped at them. "My father saw me and pulled me down before I got too high. He laughed and called me his resolved little Bumble Bea—that was his pet name for me because my middle name is Beatrice—and then he said something that sent my heart soaring. He would get it for me."

Owen drew her toward him. He wrapped his arm around her

back, and she pressed her head against his chest, the *thump-thump* of his heart beneath her ear. He didn't make her finish the story but spoke it for her, and she loved him for it.

"He fell while trying to capture that butterfly, didn't he?"

She nodded. She had watched him tumble into the falls. Heard his shout and then a sickening splash. And she saw the butterfly lift from the branch and fly away after his spirit.

"It took me so long to get to the creek bed that when I arrived, his body had already washed up onto the grass. I pulled him out, but I couldn't leave him, and so I screamed for help. But no one came. For hours, I just sat with him. A cockroach crawled on top of him. It moved over his face, into his mouth, down his shirt. I was too scared to do anything but watch. They torment me. When I see one, I feel as though I'm watching him die all over again."

Owen cupped the back of her head, and her tears wet his shirt. He didn't say anything. He only stood with her as she remembered, the reassuring sound of his heartbeat joining with the chorus of cicadas, serenading her in its healing hymn.

Two days after they had returned from their exploration, Nora stood with Frederic at the fire, sipping a cup of tea. He grimaced but swallowed anyway. Nora imagined he felt the same way about her as he did about the spiced tea—tolerating both of them because there were no other options.

Frederic coughed. "I'm taking the men out today since we're done cataloguing everything. You will stay here, of course."

He had no butterflies for her to illustrate. But she didn't blame him for refusing to allow her to join them. She'd made a fool of herself. Again. And she was too tired to fight it.

She set down her cup and went back to her tent in search of a peace offering. She reemerged a moment later and carried the orchid tit to Frederic. "I stumbled upon this while we were gone." She shoved the jar into his hands. "It's been relaxing for a couple days and is probably ready to be mounted today. I'll illustrate it, as well."

His mouth dropped. "Is this a *Chliaria othona*?"

She nodded. "I managed to study it for over an hour. I've already had Sita transcribe my notes for you."

"I've been looking for one of these for a month. Where did you find it?"

Nora waved her hand. "Just saw it mud-puddling while we were hiking about. Along with a *Delias eucharis*. I have that, if you'd like to see it."

Frederic stared into the jar, only darting a quick glance at her, and said, "I'm sure you're mistaken. The Jezebel doesn't puddle."

"I'm certain of what I saw. But I'll add it to my own collection if you don't want it."

He tossed the contents of his cup into the fire, shrugged, and said, "It's yours. Even if it is a *Delias eucharis*, those are too common to be worth space." He held up the *Chliaria othona*. "But this one is going in the book. See that you do it justice."

When he had gathered the men and they'd all left for the shola, Nora called to Sita, who had been arranging sticks in geometric patterns near the fire. "Take this back to my tent. I'll show you how to mount it later."

Sita beamed, took the jar from Nora's hand, and rushed it to her tent. Nora's fondest memories were of her father leaning over her while he guided her in mounting insects. She'd offer that to Sita, so that when Nora left, there would be a string of memories connecting them across the ocean.

Nora's scalp prickled. What would Sita do when she left? She had to find her a safe place before then. She'd been in India for less than three months of her six-month stay, though. She had time.

Pallavi moved from tent to tent, gathering dirty laundry from each one into a basket resting atop her head. She disappeared around a thicket of trees as she headed for the stream. Nora wished she could rely on Sita's aunt for help, but she knew Pallavi wouldn't risk angering her god to free Sita from her father's vow.

Sita peeked out from the tent flap. "Can we draw it first, *Akka*? Now?"

They had nothing else to fill their time. Sita had spent hours the day before reprinting Nora's notes in tiny, uniform letters. No flourishes, no embellishments. Just lines of neat print and perfectly rendered copies of her observances. First for the *Chliaria othona*, and then for the *Delias eucharis*. She deserved a more engaging task.

"All right."

Nora laid fresh canvases on the table and pulled her boxes of watercolors from their place in the stacked crates.

Sita stepped from the tent, carefully cupping two jars. When she reached Nora, she pressed the jar containing the *Chliaria othona* to her nose and peered at the butterfly waiting for them to immortalize it in watercolor.

"Do you want to illustrate the other one too?" Nora pointed a paintbrush at the jar in Sita's other hand.

Sita shrugged. "It was on the table. I see these all the time, though. It's not as special, is it?"

Nora smiled and took the jar. She unscrewed the lid and, using a pair of narrow forceps, removed the butterfly and placed it on her canvas. "Just because something is common doesn't mean it's not special." She carefully spread its wings so that they fully displayed their brilliant colors. Maybe not as brilliant as she recalled, though. This one's wings were a little faded. "Look how pretty it is. The Common Jezebel has lovely orange points." She turned it over and pointed toward the markings. "See how they're arrow-shaped . . ."

She blinked. That wasn't right.

Sita giggled. "They don't look like arrows."

Nora's heart lurched, and she spread the hind wing so that it separated from the forewing. She gasped. *This isn't a Common Jezebel.*

Sita shook Nora's arm. "*Akka*, what is it?"

"I haven't any idea."

What is it? Nora didn't know of a butterfly that mimicked *Delias eucharis*. Her father had had one in his collection, sent to him by a friend in Asia. Its hind wing was much wider than this one, and it most certainly had arrow-shaped orange spots along the edge of its wing. She'd spent years of her life poring through her father's treasury of insect publications. She'd never seen this butterfly.

"Sita, come with me."

With nimble fingers Nora plucked the butterfly from the table and cupped it gently in her palm. Motioning for Sita to follow, she loped toward the cabin.

Inside she gently set the butterfly on the table and rustled through the stack of books until she found *A Catalogue of Asian Insects*. Rupert Mills had never failed her before. In fact, it was this book that had provided the name of the caterpillar Owen had shown her.

Flipping to the right page, she sat on a wobbly chair, settling the book in her lap and the butterfly on the book. Right there, halfway down a paragraph about the Common Jezebel, was a picture of it. And though her butterfly resembled it, there were obvious differences.

Nora covered her mouth with her hands, capturing the shriek that slipped past her lips.

Sita, peering over Nora's shoulder and sighing over the beautiful illustrations, jerked. "*Akka*?"

"Oh, this is wonderful!"

"What is?"

Using two fingers to scoop up the butterfly, she nudged it into the palm of her hand and held it up for Sita to see. This was going to make all the difference. It would win her the scholarship, and Lucius would have to turn the journal over to her.

"Sita," she said, her voice shaking with the promise of a granted dream, "we've discovered a new species."

Chapter Nineteen

I feel like dancing, Sita."

After they illustrated the surprise butterfly—they both decided that would be more interesting than the other—they ate a lunch of leftover flatbreads and papaya so juicy it left sticky trails dribbling down their chins. Satisfied and dozy, they lay on a thick carpet of grass. Nora crossed her arms behind her head and stared up at the brilliant sky marred only by misty gray clouds gathered above the Western Ghats in the distance. The sun, not yet clothed in the filmy veil, shone a beatific face over them, bathing everything in its smile.

"Then dance."

Wouldn't that be lovely? Dancing when one felt like dancing instead of only when one ought to. Nora imagined what her stepfather would say if she flouted expectation and did a jig just because the joy rushing through her blood made her want to move.

Toss it all. "I think I will."

Nora clambered to her feet, Sita following suit, and lifted her skirts to her knees. Counting the beat in her head, she turned a quick circle.

Sita laughed and clapped her hands.

Nora whirled, the tents, trees, crackling fire, and cabin swirling together as though she'd run a wet paintbrush through her palette. When her breath gave out, she grabbed her knees and panted.

Sita continued to clap. "Sing, *Athai*," she called to Pallavi, who laid clothing out to dry in the sun.

Pallavi squinted at them but shrugged and warbled a high-pitched melody.

Sita swung her arms over her head, and with jerky little movements, her hands, arms, chest, hips, and legs kept time with the song. Her bare feet stomped the ground. Her white teeth flashed, along with her dimples, and with every wiggle and flick of her fingers, she tossed joy toward Nora.

"Dance with me." Sita sway-stepped around Nora and put her hands beneath Nora's elbows. With only a bit of guidance, Nora's stance resembled Sita's, and she thought she might look like one of the female reliefs she'd seen carved into the stone walls lining the harbor when their ship docked in Madras Port.

Nora pretended she wore a belly-baring top and a brilliant emerald sari—how shocking!—and she undulated her arms so that they brought to mind the movements of a caterpillar. So fluid and natural. *Maybe God created us to move this way. Not in the precise, stiff patterns of a waltz*. She knew she should have been horrified at her unconventional thought, let alone at the way she moved her body. But she only wished she could dispense with her corset and stifling layers. Feel the sun hot on her arms and the breeze weave its way across her torso.

The excitement of the morning's discovery buzzed through her, twitching her fingers and wrists, her feet and knees. Bouncing her shoulders and fluttering her lashes like Sita, Nora gave in to her emotion, perhaps for the first time in her life, and enjoyed the brief moment of being.

With her eyes closed, Nora found herself borne away on Pallavi's song, which had somehow tangled itself in her very movements. She heard neither the wind brushing the leaves on the trees nor Sita's light-as-air steps tapping out a telegraph. She felt nothing but the sheer freedom of being alive where she was at the moment, glorying in God's blessing.

Until Sita giggled and tugged on her arm, and Nora opened her eyes to see Owen watching her from across the campsite.

He stared at her, slack-jawed and covered in a sheen of perspiration.

Nora froze, her arms akimbo and her hip jutting at an awkward angle. "What are you doing back here so early?"

"I don't feel well." He took a few steps toward her and raised his hand. "You're incredible."

Then he crumpled to the ground.

~~~~~~~

The candle flickered, sending a long shadow against the tent's wall. Owen, feverish and restless, groaned and rubbed his head against his small flat pillow. Nora dipped a cloth into a bowl of cool water. She squeezed it, the droplets the only sound breaking the silence, and laid it against his forehead.

She shifted on the tiny camp stool and undid her shirt's top button. Swiping her fingers beneath her clavicle, she turned an ear toward the tent's roof. Rain, released from the clouds in a sudden river, pounded the canvas. Maybe it would bring relief from the heat. The inside of Owen's tent ventured toward hellfire. She'd thought fresh air might serve Owen more than being closed up, but Frederic refused to allow him near anyone else, lest the illness spread. If William's and Leonard's lengths of incapacitation were any indication, Owen would be unable to work for at least a week.

Nora watched the shallow rise and fall of Owen's chest beneath the light blanket and wanted to rest her hand against his heart. Feel the strength of it beneath her touch.

She dipped her fingers into the bowl and touched her forehead, allowing the water to dribble down her nose and onto her lap.

"I'm sorry." Owen's voice held no strength.

She set the bowl aside and took his clammy hand. "What for?"

"For becoming ill just when you most needed me." His eyes had taken on a feverish glint, and she didn't know if his sickness or his feelings for her had caused it.

"I'll still be here when you're better."

He smiled, and then his eyes dipped closed, and she resumed her vigil.

The lush scent of rain swept into the tent, and Nora looked over her shoulder. Swathi stood in the doorway. "May I come in?"

Nora motioned toward Owen. "He's sick. I'm not sure what it is—malaria or an infection of some kind."

Swathi's thin shoulders rose. "It doesn't matter. I've survived worse."

Nora crossed the tent and dragged another chair to the bedside. "Sit here beside me. Did you travel in the rain?"

"I got here the moment it began. It'll stop in a couple of hours." Swathi settled into her seat. "I heard about the illness that's visited your camp, and I wanted to make sure you hadn't become ill."

Nora shook her head. "No, I'm well. First it was Leonard and William, then Frederic, and now Owen."

Swathi's shoulders relaxed, and the tightness in her jaw eased. She released a heavy breath. "I'm so glad. I was worried. India is hard on Europeans."

Nora glanced at Owen, who had tossed his arms and legs akimbo, restless and uncomfortable. "Hopefully he'll recover quickly. He's strong."

"What are the symptoms?"

"Vomiting, lethargy, dizziness. They've all complained of aches and pain."

Swathi's face drained, and she stood. With nimble fingers, she undid the buttons of Owen's shirt and tugged down the collar. She sighed and sank back down into her seat. "There is no rash."

"No. None of them have had a rash."

"I'm glad. It was one of the first symptoms Lukose and I had with typhoid." She shook her head, clearing the shadows that had curtained her eyes. "How is your little friend?"

Nora cupped the back of her neck and twirled the stray curls escaping her knot. Owen had fallen ill two days prior, and she'd told Pallavi to let Sita know not to come until he was better. She didn't want Sita exposed to whatever had felled three grown men. She didn't want Sita around Frederic without her protection.

"She is in the same situation as before." Nora shook her head. "Actually, I believe she may have drawn the attention of someone who means her no good."

An agonized expression flitted across Swathi's face. "I cannot bear the thought. Have you considered finding her a safe place to live until she is ready to go to Madurai?"

"I haven't thought about it. Where would she go?"

Swathi glanced around, though no one but Owen was present, and he slept as deeply as a pupating moth. "I've talked to my husband about her, and we are willing to offer her a home for as long as necessary."

There was a desperation in Swathi's hurried words and grim expression. And a small flicker of hope, as well. Her eyes flamed with something Nora understood well—the need to be useful. Appreciated. Needed.

How much more difficult was it for a mother without a child?

She took Swathi's hand. "Thank you, my friend. I will keep that in mind. It sets my heart at ease that, if necessary, Sita will have a safe place to live for a time."

Swathi opened her mouth but quickly snapped it closed again, her teeth clicking against each other.

"Is there something you wish to tell me?" Nora asked.

Her friend's eyes glittered with unshed tears. "I only want you to know that I will see to her needs—physical and emotional. I have so much love to give, and no one to lavish it on."

Swathi's eyes strayed toward Owen, and she clasped her hands in her lap. Nora wondered if Swathi and her husband were exactly who Sita needed.

It was already obvious that Sita was exactly who Swathi needed.

Chapter Twenty

Nora, her arms wrapped around a cotton terry towel, tiptoed from camp, the stars her only witness. For four days and nights, she'd sat near Owen, wiping his face and offering him tepid cups of water. She'd felt his brow a thousand times and reassured him she didn't mind a thousand more. Then, yesterday, he'd felt well enough to sit up on his own and read through some of the books Frederic had brought from England.

Sure that Owen was on the mend, and having had enough of hasty sponge baths and the prickly feeling of unwashed skin, Nora had decided to find the spring Owen had told her about.

She crept down a small slope and found the stream hidden behind a huddle of myrtle and mahogany trees. Dawn's pale peach light pierced the fog-enshrouded hills rising around her and offered Nora a sense of solitude. No one would bother her except the singing cicadas and ancient shola, which grew thicker the deeper she plunged into it.

Less than a quarter of a mile from camp—too close to society for tigers to prowl, but far enough away that she was promised privacy—she came to a tangle of stunted trees, stepped through a thicket, and entered a fairyland.

Sunlight streamed through the canopy and dappled the pool, which was fed by a small waterfall not much taller than she was. Foamy water spilled over rocks made smooth by years of current. The sound of it was gentle, nothing like the great crash of Cascadilla Falls. Vines crawled up the trees, heavy with a flock of amber birds, and sent their roots into the moss-covered ground, providing a carpet that begged the traveler to nap.

Nora imagined herself shut off from the rest of the world. She wouldn't be surprised if she met a yaksha, wide-hipped and languid, lying on a bed of Persian violets.

Of course, Nora didn't believe in such spirits, and she only met a cloud of *Mycalesis oculus*, which flew a hairsbreadth from her face when she startled them.

She made quick work of her clothing and then slipped a sliver of rose-scented soap from the folds of her towel. She dipped her foot into the water, which came only to her knees, before sitting.

Nora rubbed the soap over her arms, chest, and belly, then splashed herself, ridding her body of a week of stench and itch. Bubbles coated the water streaming around her, carrying the scent of illness away.

She stood, lifting the curtain of hair off her back, and turned in a slow circle, surveying her sanctuary. She would return here. In the still hours before the sun rose above the hills, before the men woke and Pallavi began her rhythmic pounding of spices and laundry, before she saw Owen and spent the day splitting her thoughts between him and the butterflies she continued to draw, she'd creep back to this spot. It was a nicer way to get clean than rubbing her skin with a damp flannel cloth.

A smacking sound drew her attention to the branches above her head, and not six feet away, a bonnet macaque flipped its lips and watched her holy moment with heavy-lidded eyes.

Nora resisted the urge to cover herself—it was only a monkey, of course—and tucked the memory away. Her morning date in a secluded fairy pool with a monkey whose wrinkled brow put her in mind of a scholar.

The crashing sound of something stumbling toward her bathing spot spurred Nora from the water. She grabbed her towel and wrapped it around herself, the wise little monkey forgotten.

"*Akka*! *Akka*, where are you? I need you."

"Sita?" Nora called.

Sita burst through the trees, and her pale, tearstained cheeks sent alarm through Nora. Sita ran toward her, arms outstretched, and buried her head into the softness of Nora's towel.

"Darling, what's wrong?"

On the tail end of a hiccup, Sita said, "My bleeding has started, and I'm to begin my work next week." She looked up at Nora, her plump cheeks drawn inward. "And I know a man who wants me."

Something churned within Nora's belly. "Not Frederic."

Sita's brows pinched. "No, Frederic hates me. Why would he—"

"You were so angry about the butterflies we found, I thought he must have done something terrible to warrant such a reaction."

"He has done something terrible. He got my older sister Madhavi pregnant. Madhavi thought he would marry her, but he wouldn't. The baby was born a month before you came." Sadness, which went deeper than Sita's own future, filled her eyes, and tears clung to her lashes. "I brought the baby to him, but he turned his face. My father left her to die in the forest. She was so beautiful, *Akka*. Her skin golden and so many black curls on her head."

When Nora's father fell into the falls, her entire body had frozen, causing momentary paralysis. She couldn't move. Couldn't think. That was how she felt now.

Frederic had allowed his child to be killed.

And poor Sita had tried to stop it.

Nora pulled her in again, wrapping her arms around Sita's shuddering form and resting her chin on her head. "I'm so sorry. So sorry."

They wept, Nora forgetting that she rarely cried. Something about India drew every suppressed sadness, every long-buried heartbreak, from her and yanked it out until she was forced to face it.

To experience it.

And for once she wanted to embrace her sorrow. She wanted to grieve the injustice of a world where loving fathers died in front of their children, neglectful fathers failed to save their babies, and desperate fathers offered their daughters up to gods who turned them over to depraved men.

And with the sorrow came the bees. Buzzing and swarming so that she thought they might consume her.

~~~~

When Nora and Sita returned to camp, the sun was just tipping into the horizon. Snores still broke the silence, and Pallavi hadn't arrived yet. Nora pinned up her hair as she approached Owen's tent to check on him.

He sat in bed, his Bible in his lap and color in his face.

"You're up." Nora bustled toward him and pressed her hand to his cheek. "And you're better."

Owen captured her hand against his face. "Thanks to you. I may have been delirious most of the time, but I knew enough that someone was with me."

She blushed and pulled away, but he pressed his lips to her palm, and she shuddered. She licked her lips, and his eyes fell on them.

He couldn't kiss her now! Not when she needed to get Sita out of camp before the men awoke and Pallavi trained her eagle eye on Sita's movements. Nora sat on the edge of his bed. She needed an ally.

"Did Sita find you?" he asked. "She was looking for you earlier and told her I'd heard you sneak out of camp not too long ago."

"Yes." She swallowed hard. "When Frederic awakens, will

you keep him occupied until he leaves? Don't let him know I'm not here."

Owen's forehead wrinkled. "Where will you be?"

"It doesn't matter. Just not here. But I don't want him to know."

"I won't lie for you, Nora, as much as I—" his eyes darted away, and he swallowed—"care for you."

Contentment, heavy and pleasant, enveloped her. He cared for her, maybe even loved her—had he been about to say that?—and she wanted to sit beside him and bask in it.

But no. Not right now.

She stood. "Don't lie. Just keep him distracted long enough that he doesn't call for me. He won't go to my tent."

"I wish you'd tell me what you're up to. Maybe Frederic can help you."

She snorted, an action that would have horrified her mother. "Frederic is the last person I'd go to for help." She leaned over Owen and tucked the blanket more tightly around his waist. "He didn't do what I thought he might have." She ignored his sigh of relief. "He did something else just as bad."

She let her fingers linger against Owen's chest and then hurried from the tent, eager to get Sita to safety before Yellamma made her claim.

~⁓~

When Nora and Sita arrived in Kodaikanal half an hour later, the town was just stirring from its slumber. Fruit sellers, with papayas and bananas piled onto rickety wagons, lumbered down the roads, calling their wares. Wiry men pulling two-wheeled carts hurried toward their destinations, and a pack of stray dogs yipped and snapped at passersby.

At the end of the clamor, just off a quiet crape-myrtle-lined street, Nora found Swathi's quaint house. Sita shivered beside her and pulled the end of her *davani* from her shoulders, draping it over her head.

"It'll be okay," Nora said. "You'll like Swathi. She's very kind."

But Swathi didn't answer the door. Mr. Davies did. His eyes slipped from Nora to Sita, and something like dismay passed over his face. "This must be the child Swathi told me about."

Nora nodded, hoping she hadn't put Sita in an untenable situation. Mr. Davies didn't look as though he shared Swathi's desire to help.

He sighed and held the door open. "Come in."

Nora followed him, and Sita followed her. He led them into a small sitting room across from the parlor, furnished with a fine gold and red rug and wicker sofas.

Swathi jumped up from where she sat in an alcove tucked beneath a corner window and approached them. Nora introduced Sita, who shyly peered up at Swathi from beneath the fabric draped over her head.

"Sita needs a safe place until we can get her to Madurai," Nora said.

Swathi held her hands out toward Sita, who took them, and bent to search her face. "*Vanga vanga, ulla vanga.*"

At Swathi's Tamil welcome, Sita's face blossomed, and a string of words spilled from her lips.

Swathi looked up at Nora. "She can stay as long as necessary."

"You'll contact your acquaintance? I fear she will be found."

"Yes, when the time comes."

Nora frowned, quite certain the time was now. Swathi led Sita by the hand to a sofa, and they settled onto its cushions. With their heads bent toward each other and Swathi whispering words of comfort, Nora thought they looked as though they'd spent a lifetime together, forging a relationship. Her stomach twisted, and she worried her lower lip.

Mr. Davies came beside her. "We will see she is well cared for." He watched his wife for a moment, and a cautious, thoughtful expression entered his eyes. "I'll contact the woman who runs Malarkal Vitu—it means house of flowers—and let you know when Sita can be sent."

Across the room, Swathi held Sita's hand and spoke of her

garden back home where she'd grown orchids and flowering vines. She tugged a few jasmine blooms spilling from a vase on the table nearby and wove them into a crown. Sita tilted her face up toward Swathi, who placed it on her head.

"Lukose was, and will always be, our only child." Mr. Davies's voice held a heaviness Nora hoped never to experience. "Having him nearly killed Swathi."

"It was the same with my mother."

Charan looked at her. "It must be difficult for her, you being across the world."

"She has her husband."

He shook his head and exhaled. "It's not at all the same."

Chapter
Twenty-One

I *do wish you'd come home, darling. I miss you.*

Nora reread the elegant, loopy words traveling across the lilac-scented paper. Her mother must have written it not long after Nora left. What would she be feeling now, almost three months later?

Were Mr. Davies's words true? Did her mother miss her as much as Swathi missed poor Lukose? Nora could return, though, and her mother knew that. Maybe that was consolation.

She folded the letter in thirds and slipped it back into the envelope. She'd respond later. She planned to visit Sita and Swathi this morning after the men left and then spend the afternoon searching for the mimicking butterfly she'd discovered. She needed to study them before presenting her find. Before naming it. And she *would* name it, because she was certain no one had yet discovered it.

The harsh sound of masculine shouting came from outside, and Nora dropped the letter and rushed from her tent. Pallavi gripped a man's arm and spoke with whispered urgency. He pushed her off and yelled back, his hands making jerky circles, and the other men poured from their tents. Leonard and William flanked her, but Mr. Steed stayed back, puffing on his pipe.

"Where's Owen?" Nora asked Leonard, keeping an eye on the stranger.

He shrugged. "What's going on?"

"I've no idea."

Frederic tossed aside the flap to his tent. He was dressed as relaxed as Nora had ever seen him, in a khaki shirt rolled to the elbows, but he blanched upon seeing the man. He swallowed, his prominent Adam's apple bobbing. "Muruga."

The man turned, and his face went red. "You've already ruined one daughter. Must you ruin my entire family?"

Pallavi choked out a sob and began to screech and moan.

Frederic sliced his arm through the air. "Silence, woman."

Pallavi crumpled to the ground, buried her face in her hands, and rocked back and forth. William went to her, knelt down, and patted her back. Nora was about to join him when she saw Owen slipping from his tent, his fingers making clumsy work of his shirt buttons. He stepped over the tent stakes, keeping his eyes on the stranger as he made his way toward Nora.

"Do you know who that is?" he asked.

She shook her head as she studied the man—his heavy brows, wide nose, and handsome bone structure—and awareness caused her to gasp. He looked like an older, angrier version of Sita.

"What is it?" Owen asked.

"I believe he's Sita's father."

Frederic's voice rose. "I have no idea what you're referring to."

"Sita. She has been gone since Thursday morning, before anyone awoke." Muruga stepped toward Frederic, and although he stood half a foot shorter, he was stocky and his glower threatening.

"I have no idea where she is. I had nothing to do with her, except for having her join us on that one foray into the shola, which Pallavi said she gained permission for." Frederic turned, his eyes searching until he found Nora. "Have you seen her?"

Nora went hot then cold, and her hands grew clammy.

Muruga stalked toward her. "Where is my daughter?"

Nora pushed back her shoulders and raised her chin, but still she trembled. She searched Muruga's eyes, hoping to see remorse, love, pain—anything to convince her she could tell him where Sita was—but all she saw was anger and fear warring for ascendancy. "I haven't seen her since Thursday morning."

Muruga's neck corded, and his face flushed. A thin line of sweat beaded at his temples. "She was seen walking into Kodaikanal with a foreign woman Thursday morning. Where is she?"

Nora's heart dropped to her stomach, and she crossed her arms, gripping her elbows, to stop her shaking. She said again, in a whisper, "I haven't seen her since Thursday morning."

Muruga let out a guttural shout and grabbed her forearm. He yanked her toward him, and pain snapped across her neck. "Where is she?"

Owen shouted and lurched toward Muruga. "Release her at once!" His hands shot out, and he grabbed Muruga's elbow and wrist, twisting them so forcefully that Muruga yelled and let go of Nora.

She stumbled backward, Leonard's arm making a safe cradle behind her back, and stared at the violent red mark marring her skin. The bees buzzed, bumping against her teeth and forcing her to reckon with them. She turned narrowed eyes toward Muruga, who Owen had trapped between his arms. The bees escaped, each one forming a hard, assertive word. "No. I will not tell you, and she won't be dedicated to Yellamma."

Owen's head snapped up, and his eyes widened.

Frederic groaned. "Nora, what have you done?"

Leonard's arm tightened around her, an imperceptible support that made her straighten her spine and lift her chin.

Owen spoke, his words slow and threatening. "Don't ever come back here."

He pushed Muruga toward Pallavi and, with a jerk of his head, motioned for Nora to follow him. The rest trailed them, and Pallavi wailed her dirge as they all stepped into the cabin.

Nora walked to the far corner, where sunlight spilled through beams of warped, unfinished wood. She pressed her head against the wall, not turning until the shuffling footsteps stopped and quiet fell. Only Mr. Steed's rhythmic smoking broke the silence. She looked at him first, because she cared least what he thought. He only tilted his pipe toward her and puffed a ring of smoke.

William took a few steps toward her. "Are you all right? Your arm."

She circled her thumb and forefinger around the fading mark. "I'm fine."

But looking around, she knew the word held little truth. A memory, so dusty she could hardly see it beneath the layer of years and memories, surfaced. Her father taking their old spaniel to the backyard, wrapped in a blanket and trembling beneath the weight of pain.

"I have to, Bumble Bea. The tumor is too large. Sometimes we have to make hard choices for someone else's good, even if it hurts us."

"I'm sorry if you disapprove of my decision," she said, preempting whatever words Frederic was planning to shout at her.

But he didn't shout. In fact, it might have been less intimidating had he done so. Instead, he spoke so quietly, she had to lean forward to hear him. "You have no idea what you've done."

His words tickled at something on the edge of her consciousness. Those same words, spoken by another person. And as they came into clarity, Nora remembered Lucius's simmering anger after the dinner party. Her accusations and insults. His furious response. The fire. But this time she'd had no choice. This time she was thinking of someone other than herself. This time she'd done the hard thing, not for her own pride, but to save an innocent child.

Fredric looked angry, but Nora saw something else in his

tight jaw and the set of his shoulders. Fear. Why? Surely not of Muruga. Sita's father was brutish, but Nora didn't think he'd actually harm a man working for the Crown. She glanced at Owen, who raked his hands through his hair and wouldn't meet her eyes.

She stepped toward Frederic and pressed her hands together. Knowing Sita was safe at Swathi's, Nora could reveal the secret that had bound the child in fear. "I couldn't allow him to dedicate Sita to Yellamma. She's a Christian. It would be a sin against God. Even if it hurts our work . . . I'm sorry, Frederic, but she's worth it."

William crept nearer, whether to show his support of Nora's decision or to protect her against the arrows of accusation being spit her way, she didn't know.

Frederic groaned. "I sympathize with the girl, but we're not here to interfere in matters of culture. We aren't missionaries, beholden to help the needy."

Heat rose to her face, and a sour taste filled her mouth. "It's acceptable to interfere enough to impregnate someone, but not acceptable to save a child from harm?"

Frederic recoiled as though struck. "Of which child do you speak?"

She ignored his pale face and the way he brought his cigarette to his mouth with trembling fingers. "Sita. And yours."

Owen came beside her and touched her shoulder. "Nora." His voice held a warning she was in too deep to heed.

Frederic's eyes turned cold. "We'll ignore your obtuse comments about *my* child and instead discuss what your stunt may have cost us." He looked down his narrow nose at her. "We are here at the request of my queen. My entire career rests on how well I do my job." His Adam's apple bobbed. "You *know* what this means to my family."

"I don't see how helping Sita will harm your work." She twisted away from Owen, who had grasped her arm.

He leaned down and whispered against her ear, "Listen to him, Nora."

Frederic tossed his cigarette onto the floor, leaned his back against the table, and crossed his arms. "What do you think will happen to our work if the locals decide we are no longer welcome here? You virtually kidnapped one of their children, undermining their faith and way of life. Do you think Muruga is the only one who will find your actions reprehensible?"

Nora chewed her bottom lip. She'd done the right thing. She'd seen a child in need and helped the only way she knew how. "I'm sorry this places your work in a difficult position, but I saw no other choice. I didn't think about anything except getting Sita to safety."

Frederic pushed up from the table. "You've shown yourself unable to listen to authority, follow directions, or handle field research without hysterics. In truth, you've neither exceeded my expectations nor surprised me. But I am disappointed. For a moment, one brief moment, I thought having a woman in camp wouldn't end in disaster. I was wrong."

Nora's eyes darted to Owen, hoping to find an ally, but instead he looked at her with a pained expression, conflicted and distressed. William hung his head, and Leonard leaned against the wall, his feet crossed and eyes closed.

Only Mr. Steed, with his steady gaze and quick nod, offered her the compassion and understanding she'd been searching for. And she didn't understand it coming from him.

Frederic tilted his head, and a deep wrinkle appeared between his eyes. "No one would blame me for sending you home today."

Nora reached across the space between herself and Frederic, holding her hands up in supplication. "Having me here is not a mistake. I can prove my value. I've discovered a new species of butterfly. I found it mud-puddling. I'm certain, if we find a swarm and can study them, it will set your book apart."

She hadn't intended to offer her discovery to him. She'd wanted it for herself, in order to secure the scholarship, but if Frederic cast her out and sent her home, she could give up every hope of obtaining it. No one would take her seriously, and she couldn't bear the thought of disappointing Professor Comstock. Of giving Lucius another reason to send her to Long Island. She needed to redeem herself, and the butterfly could do that.

"Please," she said.

Frederic cast narrow eyes toward her hands. "If you're talking about the *Delias eucharis* you found, I'm not interested. It was discovered over a hundred years ago and has been studied by every entomologist in Asia."

"It's a different butterfly. One that looks like the Jezebel."

He let out a disgusted huff. "Enough, Nora. You can stay, but on probation. I don't want you going into town without my permission. You'll be illustrating only, and—"

"I think that's a little—"

"You will do as I say, or you will go home. I will risk losing Owen, although he would be stupid to give up his career for you. You will stay in camp and draw. And if you adhere to my rules, I might not tell Professor Comstock what a mess you've made of things." He stared at her for a moment, his eyes dark and flashing. "I thought you had more sense."

He strode toward the door and paused, not looking back at her. "One more thing. You will tell Muruga where Sita is. Fix this." He nodded at the men, who followed him out. All but Owen.

When the cabin door slammed shut, Owen touched her arm. "Are you okay?"

Nora shook him off and swept outside. She ducked into her tent to grab her rucksack and a butterfly net and, on her way into the forest, paused in front of Frederic, who was speaking with Mr. Steed. "May I go for a walk?"

Frederic waved his hand. "I don't think you can cause too much trouble searching for your mythical butterfly. But don't get lost. I won't come looking for you."

As Nora made her way toward the shola, she inhaled the heavy air, thick with the smell of decay and possibility of rain, and allowed it to clear out her lingering anger. She plunged deeper into the Palani Hills, using the net's handle to push back creeping vines and bushy-leafed branches.

There was no use in anger. Frederic had responded the only way he knew how—following convention and not stirring things up. Though Nora thought it highly hypocritical of him after how he'd treated Sita's sister and niece.

Pounding footsteps alerted her to company.

"Nora, wait."

She sighed. She'd spent so much time with Owen over the last few months that she'd thought he would realize she liked to be alone after confrontation and arguments. She didn't slow down. If he wanted to talk to her, he'd have to find her first.

She veered off the trail and wove through some trees, her boots sinking into the heavy layer of decomposing leaves and brush. The nose-tickling scent of water drew her forward, and she reached a small pond, glistening like the jasper stone on her mother's favorite brooch.

Nora skirted the sludge rimming the shore and settled against a spindly tree. She stretched out her legs and rested the net over her knees.

One of the first things her father had taught her, a small child chasing his long strides through the forests of home, was how to sit still. Quiet and patient. No matter what she watched for, if she waited long enough, she would almost always see it.

Familiar with the habits of the Common Jezebel, Nora hoped she would notice the new butterfly. It might take a while if it was a good mimic, but since she couldn't visit Sita and Swathi now, she had time to wait.

She heard the parting of vegetation, and a moment later, Owen sank down beside her, huffing and puffing. "I know you heard me calling your name."

She ignored the accusation in his voice and trained her eyes on the shallow end of the pond directly in front of them. She dug the heel of her boot into the mire and searched for the brilliance of butterfly wings.

From the corner of her eye, she saw Owen rest his crossed arms on his knees. "Are you going to ignore me?"

"I'm not ignoring you. I'm working."

"I wish you hadn't spirited Sita away."

"I wish you'd defended me. You told me you'd help us!"

"I didn't realize you were going to sneak her out. You've put us all in a difficult predicament."

"They were going to dedicate her to the temple of a goddess. One who requires unconscionable sacrifice. Why am I the only one who sees how deplorable that is?"

Owen sighed and shifted his body toward her. She met his gaze. She had nothing to be ashamed of.

"It is awful. I don't disagree with you. I wish there were some way to help her without putting our team and work at risk." He rubbed the back of his neck. "You probably made the right choice. Of course Sita is more important than some insects. Of course she is."

Nora watched emotions flit across his face and knew he agreed with her. Naturally he was torn—he hadn't had the time she had to think through the issue. But she trusted him. *Knew* him. And the moment his eyes slid shut, she knew he accepted her actions.

His hand reached for hers. "I just want you to succeed here. To go home and get that scholarship. Have you forgotten your goal?"

If her actions hurt their work here in India, the news would follow her home. No one would care that she had done it in order to save a child. They would only feel justified in their beliefs that women had no place in science. In a field dominated by men, it would be the end of her career.

"I haven't forgotten, Owen, but what else can I do? I have a feeling my father would rather I saved a child than his magazine."

After silence had filled the space between them for a few minutes, Nora asked, "Don't you want the scholarship for yourself? I thought your father wouldn't pay for you to continue your education."

"He won't."

"Are you no longer interested in pursuing entomology?"

He shrugged.

His responses needled her, and she squeezed his hand. "Well, why do you want them to offer the scholarship to *me*, then? It seems illogical."

The tips of his ears reddened, and he coughed. "I want you to succeed."

"At the expense of your own success?" Everyone always spoke about how mystifying women were, but no one had ever confounded her as much as Owen did.

He gaped at her, then shook his head and smiled. "What are we watching for?" He stretched his legs in front of him, crossing his ankles, and wove his fingers between hers.

Nora blinked at the sudden change in both his conversation and expression. "I'm sure the butterfly I collected at the mudflat is a new discovery. It's a good mimic of the Common Jezebel, but it's not the Jezebel."

"How do you know?"

"My father had one in his collection. They have distinctive arrow-shaped orange spots on the bottoms of their wings. This one doesn't. Its spots are blunt."

"Couldn't it just be a variation or mutation?"

"I don't think so. The wing shape is also much wider. Anyway, I'm going to find it and watch its habits. I'm familiar with those of the *Delias eucharis*. They were a particular favorite of my father's, and we read everything we could on them."

"Can I stay with you?"

"Aren't you going out with Frederic?"

"Not today."

Something crossed his face, an expression Nora couldn't quite make out, but she felt certain fear flickered in his eyes.

Was he afraid for her?

She remembered Muruga's angry words and the vein throbbing in his neck. He had been furious. Furious enough to hurt her, though? Nora glanced behind them as dread snaked its way down her back.

Ridiculous.

A tangle of butterflies lifted from a rock across the pond, their yellow-and-orange wings marking them as either a Common Jezebel or her butterfly. Releasing Owen's hand, she stood and walked to the edge of the pond, narrowing her eyes and gazing out over it. She lifted onto her toes and strained to see, but they were too far away. "We have to go around to the other side."

She grabbed her bag and net and set off in a trot. Owen kept pace with her, and she shoved her bag at him when pain threaded through her rib cage.

By the time they rounded the pond, the butterflies had escaped their resting spot and were only a rainbow of spots dancing against the clouds. Nora, her breath caught between her chest and corset, leaned against her knees and heaved as the air slowly wended its way back into her lungs.

She tilted her head and watched the butterflies—her future—drift away. Standing, she waved her net toward them. "Come back."

Owen snickered. "I'm quite sure that's not how it works."

Nora blew at the tendrils of hair that frizzed around her forehead and grinned. "How does one use a butterfly net? I'm not sure I'm capable of keeping that information in my little brain."

He stepped behind her and wrapped his arms around her, placing one hand over hers. Together they lifted the net and swung it so that the bag caught the air and fluttered. His other hand crept over her hip, and she thought he might have caught her heart, if not a butterfly.

"It's easy." His breath tickled her ear, and he pressed his cheek against hers. "You must first find a butterfly. Then you swing."

"And then it's caught?"

"It's as easy as catching anything, I suppose."

She turned in his embrace. "I've never caught anything but insects."

A smile played on his lips, and he chucked her beneath the chin. "I wouldn't be so sure of that."

When he looked at her like that—as though he'd rather watch and study her than a new species—her heart twisted so violently, she wasn't sure if it was with pain or pleasure. He leaned toward her, and his beard brushed her chin. She tipped her head toward him, and nothing but an act of God could keep her from accepting his kiss.

Or the flash of brilliant wings.

Nora pushed out of his arms and started for the tree not ten feet away. Its knobby roots clung to the edge of a muddy ledge and sank into the boggy water.

"Nora!" Owen laughed and dashed after her.

She glanced over her shoulder at him and pressed her finger to her lips. Stopping a foot from the tree, she watched the butterfly's delicate wings beat a slow tempo as it flew languid circles above their heads.

"Is that it?" Owen whispered as he drew near.

"Maybe."

As though possessed by Hermes, another butterfly shot past Nora's head, made a few erratic loops, and ran into the first butterfly, which fell in a graceful arc to a low-hanging rhododendron branch.

"What in the world?" Nora rushed toward the rhododendron, but before she could reach it, she saw the second butterfly land and begin to stroke her butterfly's antennae with its own.

She gasped.

"What?" Owen rested his hand on her shoulder and leaned over her.

"They're in copula." She bit her lower lip, then grinned.

"So?"

She flipped open her rucksack and dug through it for a kill jar. "Common Jezebels *do not* fly like that. They're slow, methodical, steady. Even while mating." She turned back and scooped the butterflies into the jar.

Owen pressed close, and she held up the jar so he could see them, still connected, as they breathed in the poison. She faced him again, his hand still on her shoulder, and their eyes met through the glass.

"Owen, this is an undiscovered species. I'm certain of it."

He pressed his lips to her cheek in a brief kiss. "I think you'll be receiving that scholarship after all."

Chapter
Twenty-Two

Nora knelt inside her tent and dug through the chest at the foot of her cot. She plunged her hands between neatly folded skirts and shirtwaists, undergarments and stockings. A silk scarf twisted itself around her fingers, and she swept it away before pushing her arm deeper. When she touched the bottom of the trunk, she sat back and buried her head in her hands.

Where is it? She dropped her hands to her lap and looked around her tent. She knew she'd left the butterfly—the original one she'd discovered mud-puddling—mounted and nestled in a box behind a stack of books on her makeshift desk.

Nora got to her feet and crossed to the desk. She shifted the books—for the fifth time—and peered beneath the stool. It was gone. She'd scoured the entire tent, and it was gone. Her hand crept to the cicada brooch pinned at her collar. The cool metal reassured her. She tapped her fingers against the desktop before whirling. The other two butterflies, mounted in their own box, sat on the upturned basket beside her cot.

She grabbed the box, closed the lid, and shoved it deep into her rucksack.

"Nora?" Frederic called. "I need to speak with you."

She dropped the bag to the floor and slid it beneath her cot. For good measure, she bent and pushed it in even farther. Then she slipped from the tent and raised her hands to shield her eyes from the glare of the midmorning sun.

"You're going to a dinner party tonight," Frederic said.

"Pardon me?"

"Jacob Welling is hosting a dinner for many of the local missionaries and Europeans. You'll be joining them. Owen will accompany you."

Nora grinned. "What, Frederic, you don't want to go?"

He arched a brow. "Thank you. No."

"I'm neither a missionary nor European. Why am I to attend?" She hated the idea of a dinner party. She'd never been partial to them—finding the superficial conversation stilted—but now, after the disastrous party at home, she was even less inclined to go.

"The Greater British Missionary Alliance is a powerful presence in Kodaikanal. As representatives for the Crown, it is expected we forge connections."

"Why can't you go? Surely you would find it more comfortable and familiar, being British."

"I have work to do."

Nora cast a longing gaze behind her and could just see her microscope through the slit between the flap and the tent. She'd planned to spend the evening studying and illustrating her new butterflies. Frederic may not think her own work valid or important, but Nora would rather spend a hundred hours peering into her microscope than attend a dinner party with strangers.

Frederic crossed his arms, and his lips pinched. "You're in no position to argue with me."

He had her trapped, and he knew it. He'd use her to see to all the things he needed to get done but didn't want to do. If both she and Frederic would rather work than attend a soiree, Frederic would get to stay at camp. And if she argued, she'd find herself on the first ship bound for England.

Then again, if Mr. Welling was hosting the event, there was a possibility Swathi and Mr. Davies would be present. Nora could get word on Sita.

"Fine. I'll go."

~~~~~

Hours later, Nora found herself questioning her quick capitulation when she'd endured a two-hour dinner sitting between an eighty-year-old career missionary and the pimpled sixteen-year-old son of a retired military captain.

The only bright spot was seeing Swathi slip into the large parlor as the dinner party finished their meal and made their way out of the dining room. Nora had pushed to the front of the crowd, hoping to capture Swathi's attention, but her friend had sat at a piano and begun to play—quite expertly—an interminable ballad.

Nora stood in the corner of the room, arms crossed and foot tapping, waiting for Swathi to finish her display of musical genius. Mr. Davies caught her eye from across the room and nodded, concern on his handsome face.

"What is wrong with you? You're behaving abominably." Owen took Nora's elbow, forcing her to relax her arms.

"I dislike dinner parties. Intensely."

"Yes, we can all see that."

She glared at him. If he only knew . . . but she wouldn't tell him why she hated the beastly things. How mortifying. Her eyes swept his figure. He did look fine. He'd worn a dress coat on their ride to Mr. Welling's house—Frederic had a *jatka* pick them up, and the horse-drawn carriage was an improvement over the lumbering *mattu vandi*—and they'd been separated as soon as they'd entered the door, so she hadn't realized what a figure he cut in his starched shirt and swallowtail coat.

He tipped his head toward her, and she realized she'd been caught staring. She coughed into her hand and looked away. "You look nice. Quite dashing. I wouldn't have thought you'd pack something so frivolous."

Owen laughed. "Why must you always follow a compliment with an insult?"

She blushed. Did she do that? "I . . . I don't know."

He didn't respond, and she forced herself to look at him, afraid she'd hurt his feelings, but a soft smile played on his lips. His gaze took in her figure, and she supposed he dragged the moment out in retaliation for either her own unabashed study of him or the insult that had so casually dropped from her lips.

She rubbed her hands down the skirt of her dusky rose silk gown. She wished she'd followed her mother's advice and packed an evening gown. Nora had insisted she'd have no use for one and, in a compromise, offered to bring this dress, which she'd had made for her graduation ceremony. "I'm not properly dressed."

"You look stunning. We're among missionaries. I'd say I'm overdressed."

She looked around the crowded room and realized he was right. Most of the women wore what she would consider Sunday best, and the men—

Nora's thoughts froze. "Did you say I look stunning?"

"I did."

"Why?"

"Because it's true."

She raised her hand to her head and patted the chignon she'd spent ten minutes shoving pins into as she'd rushed around her tent, looking for her gloves. "No one has ever—"

"It's true."

Nora had always been too busy to spend more than a moment thinking about her looks. Occasionally she'd catch her reflection as she placed a hat on her head near the foyer mirror or as she fished her hand in the water below the falls, looking for water bugs, and she'd see that she had her mother's eyes or her father's ears. Beyond her heritage, though, she didn't care overmuch about her appearance.

But the conviction in Owen's voice sent waves of pleasure through her, reaching all the way to her toes. Maybe she cared just a little, at least where he was concerned.

"I always thought my lips were too full to be considered attractive," she said.

"You don't have to insult yourself after someone offers you a compliment." Owen lowered his voice. "And I quite like your lips."

From the corner of her eye, Nora saw Swathi slip from the piano and cross the room. In the opposite direction.

"Excuse me, Owen. I need to see to something." As fast as she could without drawing attention, Nora hurried after Swathi.

When she finally reached her, she grasped Swathi's arm and marched her to a quiet corner near a set of ornately carved wooden doors.

"Are you avoiding me?" Nora asked.

"Of course not." Swathi lifted her face. Her mouth tightened, and something flashed in her eyes—anger? Nora raised her brows, and Swathi's face crumpled. "Yes."

"Why?"

"I knew you would ask about moving Sita, but I'm just not ready."

"I don't understand. You know it's unsafe for her here."

Swathi's eyes filled, and her chin trembled. "I miss having a child around."

Oh, dear. "I sympathize, but her father came to our camp. He knows I had something to do with it, and he won't stop looking for her. The longer she stays with you, the more likely it is he'll find her."

Something like courage steeled across Swathi's face, and Nora couldn't help but admire her. Swathi offered Nora a brave nod. "I'll get everything ready."

Relief lifted from Nora's shoulders. Soon Sita would be safe, and Nora could face whatever repercussions Frederic meted out. "Are you hungry? You didn't join us for dinner."

Swathi sniffed. "You're so consumed with your insects that you've learned little about how things are done in British India. Do you think *they* would eat with us? How little these Christians know of God." She clapped her hands over her mouth, and her gaze darted around. Then Nora heard a nervous giggle squeeze past Swathi's fingers.

Nora blinked, her focus sharpening on Swathi's large dark eyes and high cheekbones. There was no hiding her friend's ancestry. Even Mr. Davies, who had an English father, would never be fully accepted by those who ruled this maddening, complex, astonishing country. Nora suddenly became aware of the danger she'd put them in. They could lose everything. They were risking everything for a child they didn't know.

God, forgive me my arrogance. For weeks, Nora had assigned herself the role of Sita's hero. Her savior. Without her, how could Sita be safe? Without her, how could Sita escape? Only she could sacrifice big enough to lead her friend to freedom. But with Swathi's chastisement, Nora recognized her pride for what it was. Nora, too, knew little of God. He was bigger than she was. Bigger than Sita's predicament. And much more able to arrange for one girl than she was. And her sacrifice was small in the face of what Swathi and Charan risked.

Nora grasped Swathi's hand and gave it a squeeze. "Thank you."

Then she left, not wanting anyone to connect them.

She hadn't taken three steps when Mr. Welling intercepted her. "I'm glad you were able to attend our dinner, Miss Shipley."

Nora inclined her head, hoping her cool smile would dissuade him from further conversation, but he seemed oblivious to the hint and chattered for a few moments about the superb meal his French-trained chef had prepared and the splendid music, and could she believe a native played so well?

Nora resisted rolling her eyes and scanned the room for Owen. She saw him conversing with a man who sported a long beard and a twirly mustache, and her heart leapt.

Goodness, he was attractive. And, she'd come to realize, quite kind. Maybe the kindest man—after her father—she'd ever known. She also knew that, despite his flippant attitude toward work and education, he was intelligent.

". . . he's not your greatest admirer right now, Miss Shipley, but that can be changed, don't you agree?"

Oh, I think he admires me a great deal. Her lips twitched.

"I don't see the humor in this situation." Mr. Welling's words, couched in joviality, drew Nora's attention. "And I suggest you rectify it immediately."

Nora frowned. "Who are you speaking about, Mr. Welling?"

His jowls jiggled as he sputtered. "Frederic Alford, of course."

"Of course." She blinked. "Why are we discussing Frederic?"

"Frederic is concerned about your interference in the life of a local child. Sita, I believe her name is. I agree with him, of course. You must return her to her father."

She rubbed her forehead and sighed. Now she understood Frederic's real reason for sending her. Had he and Mr. Welling conspired to coerce her compliance? They didn't know her well, if so. "Mr. Welling, with respect, I cannot—I will not—reveal her whereabouts."

"You must."

"Why must I?"

"If you don't, it will cause the Indians to become unsettled. She attended the mission school our board runs. If parents find out a student was taken from her family, they will not continue to send their own children to be educated. What would happen then?"

"They would have to learn to read in their own language, perhaps."

Mr. Welling's nose reddened, but he kept his lips pulled into a taut smile, and Nora couldn't help but be impressed. Her *rebellion*, as Lucius called it, had brought many weaker men to passionate ire. "You do not understand the seriousness of the issue, which is expected, as you are neither a missionary nor an Indian."

"I do understand the seriousness. A child—brought to faith in Christ at your school—was to be forced into a life she neither wanted nor could endure. And no one but an American scientist was willing to help her. That is serious."

Mr. Welling's smile dropped, and his watery eyes held a warning. "It was not your place." His rich voice rose, and the nearby guests grew silent, a silence that rippled through the room until only a few straggling whispers lifted from the corners.

A commotion stirred from Owen's direction, and Nora looked up to see him elbowing his way toward her. When he reached her side, she saw censure in his eyes, but directed toward her or Mr. Welling, she didn't know.

Nora sighed. Must she be at the center of every ruined dinner party? "Mr. Welling, I'm quite aware it wasn't my place to save Sita from her fate. She attended your school and was introduced to Christ by your teachers. Therefore, it was *your* place to see to her safety."

Mr. Welling sputtered, and those within hearing gasped.

Owen took her arm. "I believe we will take our leave. Thank you for your hospitality, Mr. Welling."

He pulled Nora from the room, his fingers gripping her upper arm. When they reached the front garden full of roses spilling over low stone walls, he gentled his grasp and chuckled.

She pulled away from him and set off for the road, her shoes clicking against the marble walk leading away from Mr. Welling's house.

Owen hurried after her. "Don't be so angry."

She paused at the gate and sighed. "I'm not. All I want to do is study insects, and I can't seem to keep myself out of trouble." Why couldn't life be simple? Why did she always manage to get herself into one scrape or another? "At least

I'm keeping someone from harm this time, not leading them into it."

Owen placed his arms on either side of her, hands resting against the iron filigree bars topping the gate. "Except for yourself."

He chewed on his bottom lip and crushed his brows together, the wiry hairs pointing in every direction. Nora had wanted to smooth those brows for months, and now she wanted to smooth the worry from his expression, smooth the fear from his heart.

She lifted her hands within the circle of his arms and followed the rounded arch of his eyebrows with the pads of her thumbs. They were coarse and rebellious, not giving in beneath her touch. His eyes and lips relaxed.

He bent his head toward her, his breath hot against her mouth. "I want to protect you. Even from yourself."

"I don't need protection."

Owen tugged a lock of hair from her chignon and twisted it around his finger. He rested his forehead against hers, and his lips brushed hers as he said, "Let me. There's never been anything I've wanted as much."

Nora nodded. And when their lips met—was it him or her who closed the distance?—her heart crashed against her rib cage, and she thought she just might want Owen Epps more than the scholarship.

A cow lumbered by, shaking its massive head, and the bells tipping its horns tinkled. Shoving its wet nose through the bars of the gate, it nudged Nora's back, and she pulled away from Owen so she could push her palm against its bumpy head.

For a moment she considered letting it into the garden. Imagined Mr. Welling in the morning surveying his devoured roses. But the daydream was enough, and in the end she took Owen's hand and set off down the road, firmly latching the gate behind her.

Owen nodded toward a path that veered from the main road and disappeared beneath a canopy of trees. "That's Coaker's

Walk. Do you want to see it? I'm not ready to head back to camp."

The trail wended up Mount Nebo, and soon they stood overlooking the mist-enshrouded trees surrounding Kodaikanal. The waxing moon, pregnant with the desire for completion, poured its ghostly light over the houses trailing down the hill.

As Owen wove his fingers between hers, the cicadas began to sing. Nora wondered if they were God's own choir, sent to serenade them into each other's affections. She tilted her head back, trying to see into the thick canopy, but the insects were elusive, lost to the darkness.

Together they edged from the rocky path and toward the ridge, fringed in knee-high grasses. Below them, the valley lay in fog. On clear days, Nora had heard one could see all the way to Madurai, but tonight they could only see the outlines of the hills.

Owen looked at her, his eyes glinting with something that caused her mouth to go dry. "Whatever happens," he said, "I'm glad I came to India with you."

"I'm—"

A scuffling sound caught Nora's attention, and the hairs on the back of her neck prickled.

She twisted to look back at the path. "Who's there?"

Owen released her hand, leaving her feeling exposed. "Stay here."

He crept toward the path, and Nora watched, her chest growing tight and her breathing shallow.

Muruga stepped from behind a tree and crossed his arms over his chest. "Where is my daughter?"

All her life, people had asked Nora, *"Why are you so willful and stubborn?"* and *"Why can't you be a normal girl?"* She had never been able to answer then, but now she knew. God had made her that way for this moment. When faced with danger and society's reproach, she wouldn't back down.

"I won't tell you that," she said.

"I made a vow to Yellamma I plan to keep," Muruga snarled. "I will not allow a foreign woman to be the scourge of my family."

"I don't want to hurt your family. I only want to protect Sita."

Muruga gave a sharp shake of his head. "That will hurt my family. You cannot break a vow to the goddess. My son will suffer."

For weeks, Nora had harbored anger toward this man. How could he value having a son over the well-being of his daughter? How could he deliver her into the hands of those who would abuse her? But now she saw that he didn't deserve her anger, but her compassion. He was trapped serving hundreds of gods who would never be appeased. Gods who demanded he give up what he should treasure.

"Muruga, I don't believe that to be true, but I know you do, and I'm sorry for it. Sita asked for my help. I didn't force her away against her will. I won't tell you where she is."

He snapped a short command, and a man in a *dhoti*, his wiry body attesting to a life of hard physical labor, stepped out from behind a tree. He approached them, and Nora pressed her face against Owen's back. He loomed over the man, and Nora was glad college wrestling had made him strong.

"Step back, Nora," Owen said over his shoulder.

She flew to a jackfruit tree, heavy with fruit and clinging to the side of the slope, and gripped the smooth trunk.

Owen held his arms wide and crouched. "We don't want any trouble."

The man circling him grinned, revealing a patchy smile.

Muruga shook his head. "She invited trouble when she took my daughter. I will make her return Sita so I can fulfill my vow."

Because Owen still faced off with the first Indian man, he didn't see Muruga motioning toward the tree line. Another man, this one larger than the first, darted toward Owen's back, hands lifted.

"Owen, watch out!" Nora's shout came too late.

The other man wrapped his arms around Owen and took him to the ground. Together they wrestled for a moment, Owen quickly gaining dominance, until Muruga snapped something at the first man, bringing him forward to slam a fist into Owen's head.

Owen groaned, and his eyes rolled as his head snapped backward. He slipped from his place atop the second man and slumped to the ground.

Nora shrieked, and her heart jumped to her throat. "Stop! Don't hurt him." She fisted her hands, and her nails bit into the tender flesh of her palms.

The two men continued to pound at Owen as Muruga stalked toward her, his jaw clenched. She rounded the tree and wrapped her hands around a bumpy jackfruit the size of a small dog. Pulling and twisting, she yanked it from the trunk and hefted it to her chest.

When Muruga stood before her, she lifted it above her head. "Don't come any closer. I will hurt you."

He held up his hands. "I'm not an unreasonable man. I only want my daughter back. If you tell me where she is, *I* won't hurt *you*."

The fruit weighed heavy in Nora's hands, which had grown slick with nervous sweat. She saw no way out of her situation. Always, there had been a way out.

Except once. She could never escape her father's death.

The sick sound of fists against flesh stopped, and then there was nothing but the sound of chorusing cicadas, oblivious to the violence being committed in their chapel. Nora waited to hear Owen's shout, but she only heard their attackers' heavy breathing. A smile twisted Muruga's mouth. She whimpered, knowing she was again responsible for the injury of a man she cared for.

"Owen," she choked out.

She heard him struggle against his captors. "Let me go. Nora!" *Thank you, God.* Relief, cold and welcome, forced her attention back to Muruga. She rotated the fruit in her hands and hurled it at him. He ducked, but not in time to avoid its impact against his face.

Nora twisted another fruit from the tree. "I won't tell you where Sita is."

Muruga brought his hand to his cheek and said something that sounded like a curse, then ran toward her. She tossed the second fruit at him, but he lowered his head and rammed into her stomach.

All the air in Nora's lungs whooshed from her lips, and she fell to her back, wheezing and staring at the stars sprayed across the sky like diamonds.

Muruga stood over her. "Where is my daughter?"

She closed her eyes and rolled onto her stomach. Rising to her knees, she coughed. *All I wanted to do was study insects.*

His kick came fast and hard, and pain exploded across Nora's rib cage. Too shocked to scream, she fell to the grass and curled into a ball.

Muruga crouched beside her and, fisting her chignon, yanked her head back. "Where is my daughter?"

"I can't let you give her to Yellamma."

"Why? This isn't your concern. You are a foreigner. A Christian."

He sounded so reasonable. His words sensible. And what she'd done—hiding an Indian girl from her family and probably ruining her own career in the process—wasn't sensible. It was irrational.

But she knew God had her in India for this moment. For this reason. She was called to honor Him in her decisions.

And so was Sita. She was His. She didn't belong to Muruga any more than Nora belonged to Lucius. And because Nora wouldn't allow Lucius to dictate her life, she couldn't allow Muruga to dictate Sita's.

"So is Sita," Nora said.

Muruga shook her head, and Nora's throat burned. "What?"

"Sita is a Christian. She does not want to be given to another god."

Fire leapt into Muruga's eyes, and they glittered like obsidian. Malevolence, thick with fury, shadowed his face. He released his hold on her hair and growled. "You will regret this, and I will find her."

With a shout, he left her, and Nora listened to the men trample back through the trees, the soft grass cradling her bruised face and broken heart.

Owen!

She forced herself to stand, wincing and clutching her side. Picking her way across the grass, she fell to her knees near Owen's crumpled form. She took his wrist, and his pulse beat an already familiar song against her fingertips.

"Owen?"

He groaned. The moon slipped from behind a cloud, illuminating his battered face. A tear slipped an unwelcome trail down her cheek, and she impatiently brushed it away. Of all the times to cry.

"I'm so sorry," she said.

He opened his eyes. "I'm fine." He lifted a finger to her cheek and caught a tear, bringing it to his split lip. "I've had worse at wrestling meets."

Owen struggled to sit up, and Nora supported his back, crying out when his weight proved too much for her bruised rib.

He turned alarmed eyes on her. "What's wrong? Did he hurt you?"

Nora's throat grew thick with the tears she refused to allow, and she coughed. Inhaling sharply, she pressed her hand against her side.

His jaw tightened. "I'm going to find him and—"

Her hands went clammy, and her legs began to shake. "I'm okay. Please don't follow him. He's already hurt you enough for my sake." She buried her head in her hands and yanked her hair free from what remained of the chignon. "I always do this."

"You're always attacked by vigilante bands of Indian boxers?"

She sniffed and leaned her head against his shoulder. "I always get myself into situations that end up hurting someone I love."

Nora's breath stopped, and she bit her lip.

"You love me?" Owen repeated. "You love me."

She heard the wonder in his words. And the joy, which seemed so incongruous with their broken bodies and wounded spirits. She whispered, "I do love you."

He laughed, a rumble that began in his chest and shook her head off his shoulder. "Oh, ow. That hurts." Then he laughed again. And kissed her. "I've loved you since that cockroach crawled up your skirt and I saw your humanity."

Nora's heart leapt. "That was years ago."

He kissed her again.

And the cicadas sang.

Chapter Twenty-Three

The mile-long walk back down the hill took them an hour. They limped along the trail, yelping and groaning and holding back coughs.

But they talked. And they held hands. They listened to the muffled thump of their feet against the leaf-scattered road and pressed their shoulders together when pain sliced through their ribs.

When they reached the *jatka*, the *vandi karar* stared at them and said something in Tamil that sounded concerned. Owen convinced him to help Nora climb in and take them back to camp.

The driver set a plodding pace, and Nora laid her head against Owen's shoulder and allowed her eyes to close, the cool night air kissing the abrasions on her face.

After they passed through the shola, Owen stiffened, and Nora sat up straight. In the bright moonlight, she saw him leaning out the window. "What's wrong?"

"Something isn't right. Do you smell that?"

She sniffed, catching the tickle of something familiar. Shouts, angry and persistent, drew their attention. Nora leaned out the other window, hitching a breath against the sharp pain searing her side. They were nearly to camp. So close she could see the fire leaping.

She blinked, trying to make sense of the sight. The fire was large. Much too grand for their camp. It leapt and grew, ravenous. And against the backdrop of that orange blaze, three men darted away from camp and dashed toward the trees.

A sudden flash of flames and insect wings and a man gone mad spiraled through Nora's mind and sent a snake of dread into her belly. "My work."

The *vandi karar* shouted something, and the cart drew to a halt. "Fire!" he said and yanked open Nora's door.

She ignored his hand and tore away on nearly numb legs, crashing through the brush and thigh-high grass, Owen at her heels. Pain, sharp and demanding, crushed her torso, but she forced her breaths to continue and pushed forward. Thorned branches snagged her gown, pulling her back and hindering her progress, and the uneven ground seemed to roil beneath her feet, as though India sought to punish her for stealing one of Yellamma's daughters.

The smoke affected her before the fire did, and she covered her mouth and nose with her arm. But as soon as she reached the camp's perimeter, the heat from the scattered fires smashed against her. She made for her tent, the biggest inferno by far.

"Nora, don't," Owen called, not far behind her. "It's not safe."

Frederic and the other men rushed around the cabin and their tents in nightshirts, tugging crates, jars, and papers into the open. Their shouts were nearly drowned out by the crackling of flames and popping of wood. Leonard whipped past her, his arms around two clacking water jugs.

Nora hunched over and clenched her knees as she coughed the smoke from her lungs.

Owen grabbed her arm and pulled her back. "Get out of here. I'll try to save your work."

But she jerked herself free and dove toward her tent. She cried out at the pain that slashed her side and heard Owen curse behind her.

"Help us in the cabin, Owen," Frederic called. "Nora, get out of camp before you're hurt."

She didn't wait to see what Owen did. Burning sheets of canvas flapped around the tent entrance. She waited a few counts, until a blast of air pushed the material away, puffing steaming smoke into her face, and she ducked beneath the cross beam.

Stinging tears seared her eyes, and she captured her breath. A roar pummeled her ears. She couldn't see or hear or feel.

Get to the trunk. Get your butterfly and notebook.

Blistering pain seared the back of her neck, and she strangled on a scream as she fell to her knees. And then it wasn't about insects or validation or the scholarship, but about life. Trapped in a furnace intent on devouring her, Nora inhaled the final gasps of clean air near the ground. *Please . . .*

Strong arms grabbed and lifted, and then she was lying on her back, the decomposing leaves beneath her tearing at burned skin. She blinked away the curtain fogging her vision and stared at the spangled sky as the men fought to save their year of work and research.

Leonard knelt beside her. "Nora? Nora, are you all right?"

She managed a nod and a shuddering sigh.

"Just lie here. I don't want to have to worry about you, so *stay put.*" His words were harsh. Desperate. But the hand that touched her forehead was as gentle as a butterfly's kiss.

Everything was lost. All her work. Her only chance at redemption.

But life . . .

She forced herself to her feet, rubbed away the smoke itching her eyes, and stepped toward the men. Which way? What was most important? They had doused the flames licking at the cabin and had moved on to their tents. Only hers had been consumed.

"What can I do?" she shouted.

Leonard whirled, his face streaked with soot and deep lines of worry. "Stay put!"

The force of his command shoved her back to her spot of safety. She would only get in the way. Cause worry. Mangle everything.

She lay back on the ground and curled onto her side to ease the pressure against her burns. Wrapping her arms around her head, she blocked out the sound and sight of destruction and drifted into a hazy place of charred dreams and fractured possibilities.

When an early morning shower cleared away the drifting smoke, Nora came fully to and clenched fistfuls of earth. The drizzle did nothing to ease the waves of pain crawling across her neck in cyclical attacks. It did nothing to clear the poison from her chest or ash from her hair. It did nothing to ease the despair choking her.

But it did bring her Owen, exhausted from his battle, limping and clutching his ribs. He curled on the ground around her, wrapping his arms around her waist, and pressed a kiss above her burn.

"My love."

His whisper did for her what the rain couldn't. It soothed all the parched, scorched places and showered her in healing.

~⁓

Only Nora's tent was fully destroyed. Leaping flames had done their work on the cabin, leaving the structure unusable, but the men had managed to pull its contents to safety before they were damaged. The attack had been purposeful and targeted.

Soft petals of pink light unfurled above the hills, promising an end to night and fire and devastation. But Nora stared blankly at the men picking through the crates, assessing the loss and damage, and submitted to Pallavi's archaic ministrations. She sucked a breath through her teeth when Pallavi squeezed a tea bag over her burn.

"It is good and will steal the heat from you." Pallavi tsked. "*Muttaa ponnu*. What made you go into your tent?"

"Everything important was in there. What did you just say to me?"

Owen walked by, a dazed expression slackening his features. He still wore his suit from the party, though it was now torn in places and crusted in blood and soot. He paused, swiveled, and strode toward where he'd set up his butterfly collection. She didn't know how they'd fared. Had all of his work been destroyed? Had all the waiting and watching been for nothing? She sighed and tore her gaze from him, not wanting to see dejection slump his shoulders.

"Stupid girl, everything important is out here," Pallavi said, squeezing Nora's chin between her gnarled fingers and forcing her head in Owen's direction.

Nora watched as he lifted one of the jars and clutched it to his chest. Her throat closed and she nodded, but her heart still weighed heavy in her chest. Yes, Owen was more important than her research, and he was more important than any discovery, but she couldn't help the devastation that squeezed the energy and fight from her.

Pallavi pushed Nora's hair over her shoulder and swiped a thick layer of honey over the burn. When Pallavi finished, Nora trudged across the scarred earth and stood over the men clustered around a basket of jarred and mounted specimens.

"Have you lost much?" she asked.

Leonard shook his head. "No, thank heavens. Most of the devastation was your tent. We managed to hear the flames before they destroyed the work cabin."

"Were my illustrations spared?"

"Yes." He patted the stack beside him.

That was a blessing, at least. She couldn't imagine doing all that work again.

Frederic stood, his face as pale as the few white spots peeking through the smears of ash on his nightshirt. His chest rose and fell with rapid breaths, and he dragged a hand through his hair, mussing it further. "I knew something like this would happen when you refused to give up the girl's whereabouts. I told you to stay out of cultural issues. You have no understanding of them."

The other three men exchanged nervous glances.

"I'm sorry," she said.

Frederic blinked—whether at her apology or because she didn't give an argument, she didn't know. She'd rarely offered the one, and too quickly offered the other. But weariness had consumed her, and she had no strength left to debate. She shrugged, even that slight movement sending waves of pain and exhaustion through her.

"We are only allowed to be here by the goodwill of the people. You've ruined that for us." Frederic rubbed his upper arms. "Will you please return Sita to her father?"

Nora dropped her head and toed the dirt. He couldn't ask that of her. Especially after Muruga's brutal attack. "He assaulted us—Owen and me." She looked at Frederic. "How can I send her back to him? What would he do to her?"

Frederic's eyes roved her face, and he stilled. Nora knew that beneath the grime, she wore bruises and abrasions. His shoulders fell, and his hands dangled at his sides. He closed his eyes.

Owen drew up beside her, his hand a reassuring pressure on the small of her back. He leaned down and whispered, "One of them hatched. It's a *Castalius rosimon*."

A smile split Nora's cracked lips, pushing painfully against a small burn above her mouth. She took the jar Owen held toward her and lifted it. A small white butterfly, black spots scattered across its wings, dangled from a twig, shriveled and shaking as it dried its wings after its transformation. Despite the attack, the fire, and the devastation, it had survived.

When Frederic cleared his throat, Nora handed the jar back to Owen.

"I promised Muruga," Frederic said on the tendrils of a deep breath, "that I would stay away from his family after the . . . compromising position I put his eldest daughter in."

"Madhavi." Nora swallowed the acidic bile spilling into her mouth.

"Muruga insisted I marry her when her pregnancy became obvious. Either that or he'd abandon the baby to the elements."

"Why didn't you?" Owen asked. Anger simmered beneath the surface of his innocuous question, and he tucked the jar beneath his arm.

"My wife wouldn't have cared for competition. Besides, if I returned to England with an Indian wife and child, my family would disown me. It would cause a scandal. I'm trying to restore my family's honor, not destroy it even further."

"Then you should have acted honorably. How could you let him kill your child?" Disbelief so shadowed Owen's voice that it dipped into a whisper.

Frederic grabbed fistfuls of his hair and groaned. "I had no choice. But you . . ." He looked at Nora. "Why didn't you listen to me? You've put all of our work—our lives—at risk."

She pressed her hand against her bruised rib. "I didn't have a choice either. I love Sita."

Frederic shook his head. "This is why women have no place in science. Ruled by emotion instead of logic." He shook himself and stood tall. "You'll have to leave if you won't comply. We won't be allowed to stay if you don't. As it is, I'm not sure we can stay anyway."

Nora nodded. There was no longer any reason to stay. All of her work was destroyed. Every bit of tenacity drained out of her. She felt herself shrinking, caving in on herself beneath the weight of her failure. But then Owen pressed his hand against the middle of her back, supporting her. Shielding her from her own accusations.

He lifted the jar and stared hard at the common Pierrot inside, before snapping away the rubber band and pulling the cloth from the top. Slipping his fingers inside, he scooped up the butterfly and held it up to the sky. With a small smile, he watched it fly away.

"Owen." Frederic's voice was hard. "You have a decision to make. Your future or Nora."

"The way I see it," Owen said, handing Frederic the empty jar, "they're the same thing."

Chapter
Twenty-Four

As Nora and Owen trudged up the Davies' front steps, the sky exploded with color, the sun gilding the trees in gold. India's sunrises were much like every other aspect of the country—startling in their intensity and allure. Owen motioned for the driver to stay with his trunk in the cart William had hired for them. Nora had lost everything—all of her clothing, the gifts she'd bought for her friends and family, and worst of all, the insects she'd caught and had hoped to use in the rebuilding of her decimated collection. The earrings she'd bought at the jewelry shop with Owen dangled from her lobes, and she touched one with the lips of her fingers. She'd put them, along with her brooch, on before the dinner. They'd been saved because of a party she hadn't wanted to go to.

Had that been less than twenty-four hours earlier? Her shoulders sank beneath the weight of grief and failure.

Swathi opened the door at their knock and gasped. "What happened?"

She drew them inside, and Owen explained their departure from the party, Muruga's attack, and the fire.

Swathi hugged Nora and called for her servant to make some tea. "I'm so glad you're safe. You'll stay here as long as you need to."

Nora pulled back and shook her head. "We need to get Sita out of Kodaikanal. Otherwise Muruga will find out we're here and realize she is too."

Swathi shook her head. "I was expecting more time with her."

"She doesn't have more time." Nora's words came out harsher than she intended. Louder. And they drew Mr. Davies and Sita from a room down the hall.

"*Akka!*" Sita ran toward them and flung her arms around Nora. Nora sucked air in through her teeth at the stabbing pain from her bruises and burns, but she pasted a grim smile on her lips and ignored Sita's questioning look.

"Hello, darling. You must go pack your things. It's time for you to leave Kodaikanal. Your father isn't happy, and he'll soon find out where you are."

Fear flashed in Sita's eyes. "I will."

"No, I'm not ready." Swathi pulled Sita to her.

Mr. Davies gently loosened his wife's fingers from Sita's shoulders. "She's not safe here, Swathi. You know that. And we must stay. At least until you are well."

Swathi's stricken cry tore at Nora's heart, and she caught Owen's eye, wishing she could fix this for her friend.

Sita took Swathi's hand and pressed her lips to it. "Why do you cry?"

Swathi smiled down at her through her tears. "I'm a mother without children."

Sita opened her mouth to say something, but a knock at the door startled everyone.

"Who is that?" Swathi said.

"Sita, go hide." Nora pushed her toward the hall, and Sita darted away.

The servant glided past them with silent steps. He set a tea tray on a bamboo table beneath a mirror, gave them all a hard stare, then answered the door.

Pallavi stepped inside.

"What are you doing here?" Nora asked, censure and accusation in her voice.

Looking even more hunched than normal, her squinting eyes lost in the folds of her face, Pallavi hurried toward Nora. "Where is the child?" When Nora didn't answer, Pallavi gripped her hand in a claw-like grasp and shook it. "I know she is here. You have no other friends in Kodaikanal and had no time to get her anywhere else. I told Muruga so this morning when he returned. Even now, he is gathering men to come and take her away. Where is she?"

Nora pushed her words past the lump in her throat. "Why should I tell you?"

"She needs to leave. Now. Muruga told me Sita has become a Christian, and I know he will kill her. Do you have a place to send her?"

Swathi pushed past her husband and stood in front of Pallavi. "Yes, I know a place."

Nora pulled her throbbing hand from Pallavi's grip. "Why? Why help her now?"

Pallavi wrung her hands, and a shadow of hopelessness crossed her face. "Our family has already lost one daughter. I won't lose another." She hung her head. "After her father left the baby to die, Madhavi ended her disgrace and torment. She hanged herself from a tree." She pierced Nora with her gaze. "I will save Sita now. I will make it right."

Her ragged words spurred everyone to action

"I'll gather her things," Swathi said, clattering down the hall.

Nora shouted, her voice thin and shuddering, "Sita, come now."

Minutes later, after a frenzy of good-byes and hugs, Sita, Owen, and Nora sat in the back of the covered cart, the driver smacking the leather reins against the horse's back. In four hours they would reach the Kodai Road train station, and soon after, they would be on their way to Madurai and the woman who would care for Sita.

Nora shifted closer to Sita, the rough wood planks of the seat digging through her skirt and into her legs. Sita looked up at her, a strange gleam in her eyes. "Why didn't you tell me your sister had died?" Nora asked.

Sita played with the worn strap of the bag Swathi had given her. "She lives on still." Nora didn't have a chance to question her before Sita lifted her chin and said, "*Akka*, we need to stop somewhere first."

Startled, Nora glanced at Owen before shaking her head. "Where do you need to stop? It's not safe."

"We must stop." Sita pushed up the leather flap sealing them into the muggy, dusty cart and said something in Tamil to the driver. He shouted at the horse, and they turned down a street crowded with cows snoozing in the road. The cart stopped and started, taking too long to pass by the animals.

"I hope this is important, Sita," Owen said, "because you're risking your own safety. Nora's, as well."

Sita's face glowed with certainty. Nora wished she could bottle it up and take it home with her. When had she ever experienced such tranquility? Her whole life had felt like a battle to be fought against convention and limitations. But here sat a child whose life had been auctioned off, who was about to set off on a multiday journey toward an unknown future, and she watched Nora with wise eyes that knew peace.

A peace that surpassed understanding.

Finally, the last cow lumbered away, insulted by the driver's shouts, and they pressed forward to the end of the road. When they stopped, Sita hopped from the cart. "Come, *Akka*."

Nora and Owen followed her into a squat little house. Though not much more than a hovel, it was clean, and the smell of spiced lentils permeated the dirt floor and mud walls.

An old woman sat cross-legged on a bed of lumpy mats and

blankets. She held a baby in her arms and tipped the long spout of a pot into its mouth. The baby gurgled and kicked its skinny legs.

"Why are we here?" Owen asked.

Nora's stomach clenched. "Sita, we don't have much time."

Sita approached the woman and said something to her. The woman nuzzled the baby's cheek, handed it to Sita, and placed her hands over both their heads. She said something like a prayer, and Sita scurried past Nora and Owen and back into the sunlight.

Nora hurried after her and frowned when Sita climbed into the cart, the baby snug in her arms. When Nora and Owen climbed in, the cart set off again.

"What is going on?" Nora asked, casting a glance at the baby.

Sita settled it in her lap and counted the baby's fingers and toes. She turned shining eyes up at them. "I stole a watch from Frederic's tent and sold it to give money to the Bible-lady. She needed the money because her husband died, and she had no family. Will God forgive me?"

Nora didn't want to diminish Sita's sin, but Frederic had been guilty of far worse, and she thought a stolen watch the least of his problems. "I'm sure He will, if you repent."

Sita wrinkled her nose. "I don't regret it, though. Because it paid for the Bible-lady to take care of the baby." She forced the infant into Nora's arms, and Nora held the child in an awkward embrace. "I followed my father to the forest and brought her to safety."

Nora's eyes slipped to the baby's narrow face, serious and capped by a thatch of dark hair. The infant gummed her fist and stared back. "You saved your sister's baby?"

Sita nodded and gently rubbed a whirl against the baby's scalp. "I couldn't let her die, even if helping got me in trouble."

Owen touched Nora's hand. "Sounds like something someone else said this morning."

When they got back to the Davies' home, a huddle of men stood on the front steps, Muruga at the front, clenching his fists in Mr. Davies's face. Owen hissed a command through the little window that allowed them to speak to the driver, and he passed by, drawing not even a glance from their attackers.

Nora's breath released in a whoosh. The baby kicked her legs, brushing Nora's arm with a narrow foot. She lightly pinched the baby's toe, as small and red as a ladybird beetle, and smiled.

"I knew as soon as I met Swathi and Charan that they were supposed to be the baby's parents." Sita brushed her hand over the child's wispy hair. "I wanted to wait until I was sure my father wouldn't find me to bring her to them."

They drove to the lake, and Nora pushed back the curtain so they could see the sun glinting off the water. Sita pushed her face toward it, gently squishing the baby so she could lean over Nora's body and take in the scene, perhaps for the last time. Owen took the baby. Over Sita's narrow back, Nora watched as he snuggled her to his chest and put his nose to her neck. His eyes met hers, and in them she saw something that made her breath catch in her throat. Something that spoke of more than stolen kisses.

Their driver took them through Kodaikanal's streets, circling the market and zigzagging through narrow alleys. Nora dropped the curtain as they drew closer to Swathi's house twenty minutes after they first passed.

She peeked through the window. "Muruga's gone."

Owen had the driver pull around the back of the bungalow, and they crept toward the back door, Owen and Nora flanking Sita and the baby. Not bothering to knock, Owen pushed the door open and ushered the rest of them into the parlor. Swathi and her husband, sitting together on the cane settee, bolted to their feet when they entered the room. Mr. Davies kept his arm around Swathi, whose red-rimmed eyes and quaking shoulders bore testament to her heartache.

Sita, holding the baby in her arms, pulled away from Nora. She smiled up at Swathi and Mr. Davies. "This is my sister's baby. She has no parents. She has no mother."

Swathi gasped and fell to her knees. She pulled Sita to her chest, one hand on her back, the other resting on the baby's head. Mr. Davies knelt beside her and enfolded them in his own embrace. The baby began to cry, a thin wail that separated their cluster. Swathi stared at the child still nestled in Sita's arms, and her own twitched.

Sita pressed a kiss to her niece's head, her eyes sliding closed for a moment. Then she gently shifted the baby to Swathi. "Good-bye."

Swathi held the baby to her heart, and a suppressed sob made her body shudder. She tilted her head back, eyes on the ceiling, and her lips moved in a silent prayer. Then her gaze fell on Sita, whose small face shone. "I wish you could stay with us. I would love you too."

"I know, *Athai*, but it's enough that you love her."

Owen took Nora's hand and squeezed it. She leaned her head against his arm, and beneath the layers of grime and torn silk and the frantic beating of her heart, something whispered to her. A cool cup of water soothing her parched throat. A breeze in the middle of India's scorching summer. A dance beneath monsoon rains.

This is right. This is good. This is worth it.

She turned her face into Owen's chest, inhaling the scent of ash and sweat, smelling only his strength and goodness. She didn't hold back her tears. Didn't deny them. Didn't feel the need to dash them away.

"Peculiar," Owen whispered, his lips brushing her ear, "you're crying."

She nodded. He wrapped his arms around her, and together they swayed to music that sounded like joy and sorrow all bound together.

In Madurai, they rested at the home of a woman named Aneeta. She lived in a compound an hour from the city, surrounded by tamarind trees and laughing children.

She'd taken in over a hundred girls and a few boys over the

years, most rescued from British *chaklas*, child marriages, and temples where they were prostituted. Some were the children of women who had already lost hope of escaping. They chattered in a dozen languages, darting around the huts and palms, flashing like peacocks in their brilliant saris and bangles.

On the first day, Nora had slept, her body wrapped around Sita's, on a soft mat beneath an open window. They woke and ate *idli* and listened to the parrots trilling in the banana trees outside. Then they slept some more.

After two days, Nora joined Owen on a trip into Madurai, where she replaced some of her clothing. Aneeta had offered them the use of a cart and driver, and now they rode back to Malarkal Vitu as dusk descended, bracing their hands against the splintered board that served as a seat and gasping from their injuries every time they were jostled against one another.

"Your face is finally showing color again," Owen said.

She patted her cheeks. "I've had time to rest and think. And I'm so relieved Sita is safe."

"She's already made friends. And Aneeta is a warm woman. I'm sure Sita will thrive here."

"I wish she could have stayed with Swathi and the baby. Maybe when they return to Madurai?"

"Maybe."

They turned onto the palm-lined path that led to Aneeta's home, and Nora rearranged the skirt of her new dress. Not a style she normally wore, the cream linen was sprigged with pink and blue flowers and the bodice featured a frill of lace and pearl buttons. Her mother would love it.

Nora had gone to the dressmaker's that morning as soon as they arrived in the city, and was promised something simple before she left. When she went back to pick it up and change out of the silk gown that was long past needing to be shed, she groaned at the sight of it.

"It's too much," she told the little Welsh woman who dressed all the fashionable Europeans in Madurai.

"It will look wonderful on you!"

"I only want to look clean and presentable."

The dressmaker glanced toward the door that shut out the rest of the shop and Owen. "He'll like it."

"*I* don't like it." But Nora had sighed and stripped out of her clothing, kicking the dress into the corner. "Fine. I need something to wear. Just make sure all the rest of the items I've ordered are unadorned. Simple." She took the skirt and wrinkled her nose at the pleats and ribbons trailing down the back. "I guess I'll have to purchase a bustle today as well." She could already hear Owen laughing at her.

But he hadn't laughed. Even now, he sent admiring glances at her that warmed her insides.

"Stop looking at me like that."

"Why? You look beautiful."

"I look exactly the same as I do in my regular attire." She crossed her arms and stared forward, over the head of the driver.

Owen poked her side. "Percipient, your prickles are showing."

She bit down a grin. He *liked* her prickles. And even if he thought she looked nice in lace and ribbons, he liked her still in plain wool.

"Look," he said, pointing toward the sky.

Above them, a butterfly flapped. It dipped and landed in Nora's lap. There it spread its brilliant wings, showing dusky blue and black as soft as the fabric of Nora's skirt, and round orange "eyes."

"It's a blue pansy, I think," Owen said. "*Junonia orithya*."

Nora held her hand over it, ready to cup her fingers and trap it beneath them. Ready to catch one final keepsake. One that wouldn't disappear in flames.

Her hand wavered. The butterfly fluttered its wings.

"Do you want it?" Owen asked.

"Yes." But she couldn't bring herself to pinch its thorax. To see its life seep away and watch it become still. "I think . . . I think I'd like to remember it just like this." She slid her finger toward its legs, then lifted it between them, shifting so that she faced Owen. Her eyes met his over the blue pansy. "Some things are better left to memories." They couldn't always be caught and mounted, a token of things that had been.

The butterfly lifted from her finger just as they pulled onto the expanse of dirt that circled the main house. A half dozen children, Sita among them, spilled from the door.

"*Akka!*" Sita darted toward the cart. The weariness stooping her shoulders had lifted in the days since they'd arrived. Her bright smile and dimples flashed without reserve now, and she ran and played and danced without concern.

Owen hopped from the cart and came around to help Nora down. With his hands spanning her waist, he set her on the ground, and a gaggle of children surrounded them. Sita's warm hand slipped into Nora's, and she tugged her forward, chattering about a caterpillar she'd discovered. A mosaic she'd made out of beads. A friend she'd made.

Nora smiled down at her, feeling more than seeing the soft edges of memories hemming Sita's thick braid and shining brown eyes. A dream floating away. One that wouldn't be caught and pinned down.

With her free hand, she reached for Owen's, and he rubbed his thumb over her skin. As though knowing her thoughts—the crushing sense of loss—he leaned toward her. "Just enjoy this moment, Nora."

Beside her, Sita hung on to Nora's hand and hopped down the path after her new friends. She was all vibrant color and un-restrained joy. A butterfly who had escaped. A drifting dream.

Three days later, Nora's clothing was ready. She wished she'd ordered more than two simple skirts and three bodices. More than two sets of underclothes and a nightgown. Because then she'd have more time in this place of rescue and peace. More time with Sita.

Sita walked beside her now, down the palm-lined path. They'd finished breakfast, and Aneeta had shooed them from the house, telling them to say good-bye in private, away from dozens of prying eyes.

"Must you leave? Can't you stay?" Sita clasped Nora's hand.

"Our ship leaves from Madras next week, and we must get the next train from Madurai if we're to make it in time."

"What if you just stayed? There are so many insects in this area. Beautiful *Lepidoptera*. I could continue assisting you."

A macaque scampered in front of them and launched himself up the trunk of a palm. Settling atop a tight bunch of coconuts, he screamed down at them. Nora tugged Sita farther along the path. "I wish I could, but it's time for me to go home."

"I will remember you always."

"And I you."

Nora was well-acquainted with grief. She recognized the symptoms—the heaviness in her limbs and thickened throat. The leaden way she walked beside Sita, as though she couldn't take another step. The way her heart—an organ she was certain had little to do with her actual feelings—tightened and then seemed to shatter within her chest.

She recognized them and was helpless to resist.

She stopped in the middle of the dusty road and drew Sita to her. She rested her chin on the child's head and sniffed to stem the tears. "You have changed everything. For me. For your sister's baby. For yourself. You are brave, and I'm so proud to know you."

Sita tilted her head, peering up at Nora from eyes that had seen too much. "Let's not cry today."

Nora dashed away the tears that had slipped down her cheek and smiled. "All right. What shall we do?"

A mischievous grin appeared on Sita's face, and she splayed her hands above her head. "Let's dance, *Akka*."

Nora laughed and matched Sita's pose. Sita began to sing a beautiful song in a language as different from English as India was from Nora's own country. A song that told a story in words Nora couldn't understand, about joy and beauty and life.

A song of friendship and love.

A song that pierced Nora's spirit and made her forget her grief.

They danced beneath the shade of palm trees, Sita's sweet voice punctuated by an irate monkey's shrieks. They moved—Sita gracefully, Nora less so—in tandem.

And as they swiveled their hips and waved their arms, Nora impressed Sita's smile onto her heart and into her mind. She never wanted to forget its brilliance. Never wanted to doubt, for even a moment, the value of what she had learned and discovered in this faraway place.

Nora stood at the ship's railing as it slipped from the Madras harbor and began its three-week journey to England. They'd stay with Owen's widowed aunt in London for a week before boarding another ship to New York. She'd be home soon.

She had sent a letter to her mother from Madurai, telling her she was headed home, but not explaining why so soon. Hoping she wouldn't ask.

Small fishing boats slid past them, the rowers balanced on flat feet and pushing shirtless bodies against the long oars. The city disappeared into the smoggy horizon, and Nora, blinking eyes gritty from lack of sleep, turned away from India.

"Are you okay?" Owen touched her arm. The skin beneath his eyes sank into dark circles, and worry lines pulled his mouth taut.

She nodded. Then shook her head. "In truth, I don't know. I can't help but feel I'm leaving too soon. I want more time to work. More time with Sita and Swathi. I want to stay more than I want to go home. Everything feels a little undone."

Owen chewed on his lower lip, then turned back to look toward the city. When she joined him at the rail, eyes trained on the city of Madras fading on the horizon, he asked, "What do you see?"

"Water. And just past that, a mind-bogglingly complex country full of paradox. Colorful insects that capture the imagination. Children who capture hearts. A place that has captured me fully."

"You should be a poet."

Her quiet laugh danced around the edges of her mouth. "I think I'll stick with science."

"You accomplished so much here. I see a land where you learned your worth as an entomologist."

She tilted her head. "You see that?"

"You discovered a new butterfly species in this place. You learned to let go and dance." He glanced at her, and his eyes softened with the memory.

Nora flushed, remembering the way she'd moved beneath the heavy sky to music that pulsed just below her skin. Even now, she swayed just a bit, as though she could hear Sita's song in the sea breeze.

Owen cupped her cheek, his thumb rubbing the planes and angles of her jawline. "I see a place where you made a stand and realized some things are more important than your career. A place where you learned to let your guard down and allow something more than science and work and insects—and yes, even that journal—fill your heart."

Warmth filled her belly and swept through her. She leaned into Owen's hand, then turned and pressed her lips to his palm, breathing in the earthy scent of India's land and air.

He bent to whisper in her ear. "India is the place you loved me first, and for that, it's my favorite place of all."

She wished for a lonely shola forest. She wished for a waterfall that sprayed her face with cooling mist. She wished for a few more moments alone with Owen in a bouncing *mattu vandi* before life went back to normal.

As she leaned as close to Owen as she dared in so public a setting, her heart soared upward, a small piece breaking away and staying behind in this land of unfinished work and intoxicating dreams.

Part Three

ITHACA, NEW YORK

October 1885

Chapter
Twenty-Five

Nora returned home in the middle of autumn, when a muted palette of yellows and reds colored the mountains and hills of upstate New York. Ithaca was flush with students still excited about the new school year, and their hurried pace and chatter pierced Nora with longing for that simplicity. She wished she could join the people walking past her house and through the cemetery on their way to comparative literature and biology classes. But she couldn't. Not only because she'd expected to be away until February and had no commitments, but because India had changed her.

"Tell us again how everything with Owen happened." Rose leaned forward in the iron chair set beneath their garden arbor, her round eyes sparkling with the thrill of romance.

Nora wanted to tell her and Bitsy about Frederic and Sita and Swathi. About Muruga and Pallavi. About the hypocrisies of the mission board and her love for an Indian child. But she couldn't. Those stories were sacred, and she didn't want to minimize their impact by sharing moments, piece by piece. It was a story that needed to be told in its entirety, so until Nora's mind didn't race with worry every time she said Sita's name, and until she could speak about Muruga's attack without her teeth chattering, she would only tell them about Owen.

She didn't think she'd ever tell them about her butterfly and the precious few days she'd thought she would make her mark as a scientist.

Nora crossed her ankles, luxuriating in the waft of lilac that caressed her nose every time her skirts rustled and released the scent of the sachet they'd been folded away with. India had wended its way through her very marrow, and she missed the languid days, the scent of spiced tea waking her up every morning, and monkeys calling to one another. But she didn't miss the smell of four unwashed men. "I've told you this story already."

Bitsy leaned her elbow on the small round table and flicked her wrist, her fingers resting in an elegant pose. "You know Rose lives for romance stories. She reads through those sentimental novels faster than she can eat a chocolate bar. And she's always stringing together fairy tales, as though life works like that."

Nora indulged Rose with a smile. "Thankfully, neither Owen nor I struggled with seasickness. We were able to stand at the railing and listen to the ocean break against the ship. I should have hired a companion, because we spent too much time together. There may be scandalized Englishwomen still clucking their tongues over the forward Americans."

Rose leaned farther toward her, and even Bitsy showed a gleam of interest.

"When we arrived in London, we stayed with Owen's aunt again. On the way to India, we only had two days, and Owen spent much of that time with family. But this time we had a week, and his family might as well not have existed. I didn't have the proper attire to go out and do the usual things, but we rode through Hyde Park and spent hours talking over books in his uncle's library, and stole kisses in the garden." Nora blushed as she remembered those kisses. "He told me he loved me."

Rose clasped her hands together and pressed her fingers to her lips. "Is that why you came home early? To be married?"

Nora blinked. "What? No. We haven't discussed that at all."

Rose showed no signs of having heard Nora's response. She swayed in her chair, looking for all the world as though she were about to swoon, and a featherlight smile spread her lips. "It's so romantic. Just like a fairy tale. You fell in love in an exotic location, far from home, while walking on a jasmine-scented cloud."

"Oh, for goodness' sake." Bitsy laughed. "I'm sure it was nothing at all like that. Nora is entirely too practical to walk on jasmine-scented clouds."

Nora smiled when Bitsy winked at her, but it had kind of felt like that. India, and everything that happened there, spoke to her in whispers that caressed her memories, wrapping everything in exotic perfume and sultry, cicada-song nights.

She ran her fingers over her lips, remembering the press of Owen's. She hadn't seen him since they'd parted ways at Grand Central Station—he to spend time with his family in Manhattan before returning to Cornell, and she to continue the journey home—and she wondered if he'd truly been a part of that hazy dream.

She'd abandoned her sensibility on the shores of New York when she'd left four months ago, and now that she'd returned home and stepped into that coat again, it felt snug and ill-fitting. Maybe India had changed her. Or maybe it just revealed to her that she'd been wearing a costume for years.

"What is he doing?" Bitsy asked. She studied the back of Nora's house, a speculative gleam in her eyes.

Nora turned but saw nothing amiss about her home's gray clapboard siding. "Who?"

"Lucius." Bitsy jerked her chin upward. "He just peeked out your bedroom window, then drew the curtains. It's suspicious."

A flame, set by Lucius's bonfire, flickered in Nora's stomach, burning off all thoughts of dreams and Owen. "I'll be back in a moment."

When Bitsy and Rose stood, she waved them back to their seats, then strode across the garden and into the house. As she marched up the back stairs, she formed all kinds of arguments in her head. Most started with *I have no insects for you to destroy*, but when she opened her bedroom door, her rehearsed lectures hadn't prepared her for what she saw.

Lucius stood before her dresser, picking through her jewelry box. He held up an emerald ring that had belonged to her great-aunt, turning it this way and that before slipping it into his pocket. When he lifted her cicada brooch, Nora's entire body went rigid. That brooch, given to her by her father and adored by Sita, didn't belong in Lucius's rough fingers.

She marched across the room. "What are you doing?"

Lucius jumped, and the brooch fell to the floor. When she bent to retrieve it, he beat a hasty retreat to the door.

She snapped upright. "Stop. I want answers. Why are you rifling through my jewelry? Why have you stolen my ring?"

He turned and faced her, then rolled his eyes toward the ceiling and heaved a great sigh. "I need money."

Money? Her mother's inheritance should have taken care of them for years. The house had no mortgage, and they didn't lead an excessive lifestyle. "Why do you need money?"

"Do you not remember that I lost my position? I haven't been able to contribute anything in months."

Nora's heart sank to her stomach. "And my mother's money?"

Lucius's lips flattened. "That is none of your concern."

"You're stealing my jewelry. I think it is my concern."

"You seem to have forgotten that everything in this house belongs to me, but here, take it." He dug into his pocket and pulled out the ring.

Nora held out her hand, making him cross the room. When he laid it in her palm, she said, "You may own the house, but this jewelry belongs to me."

He lifted a shaking hand and scrubbed his face with it. When he dropped his arm, his eyes were on the ceiling and a twitch quivered his jowls. "I'm not going to beg you, Nora, but my only other option is asking your mother to sell off some of her jewels. I wanted to spare her that stress. You know she isn't strong."

Nora, in the process of taking inventory of her jewelry, froze. Her mother, though no longer bedridden, had only left the house twice since Nora's return. She retired early and slept late, didn't eat much, and constantly complained of headaches. Stress, any stress, triggered dizzy spells that put her in bed for the rest of the day. Nora didn't think her mother would respond well to Lucius's request for her jewels.

"Is Mother aware of your financial straits?"

"Of course not. I didn't want to lay that burden on her. Had you been receptive to courting Mr. Primrose, this would have been resolved with a wedding."

"I was never going to marry someone who thought so little of my work and sex." Especially after experiencing Owen's support and encouragement.

Nora sifted through her box, testing the weight of the pearl necklaces, gemstone rings, and gold bracelets. She never wore them. Couldn't stand jewelry, really. Her tastes ran toward simplicity—neutral shirtwaists and skirts, simple hats, sensible shoes. The only piece she wore regularly was her Lalique brooch. She lifted her hand to her ears, where the earrings she'd bought in India with Owen dangled. And these. Now she also wore these.

She refocused on the jewels in the box. Her father had left her mother in Nora's care, and even though Lucius had turned up to take over that role a year later, Nora believed it still to be her responsibility. She'd failed so many people. She couldn't bear the thought of failing again.

She plucked the brooch from the box and flipped the lid closed. "Take whatever you need from there to pay your bills." The brooch was a reassuring weight in her palm. She held it up. "Except for this and my earrings. Don't ever touch those."

Nora tucked the blanket over her mother's lap, then joined her on the swing on the front porch. The day had wound down, and people passed the house on their way home from jobs and classes, waving at them as they gently swung.

"I missed this," Nora said.

Contentment shadowed her mother's smile. "I missed you. I do hope you got that out of your system and you'll stay home from now on."

Nora didn't tell her about Lucius's ultimatum—that she was to live with his sister if she wasn't awarded the scholarship. The board wasn't hosting the scholarship contestants' lectures until February, when she and Owen were initially expected home. Her mother didn't need to fret and worry until they made their choice and Nora knew if she was to stay or go.

"I met a woman in India who'd lost her son. Her husband seemed to think my absence caused you great distress." Nora kept her eyes focused on the progress of a boy jogging down the street after his nurse, a toddler hanging on to his hand.

"He was correct." Her mother grasped Nora's hand.

A young man, wearing the pin of a newly initiated Delta Upsilon member, crossed the street before them and took the porch steps two at a time. He doffed his hat and held a letter toward Nora. "From President White."

Nora took it, and the student leapt from the stairs and ran back toward campus. She slid her finger beneath the flap, and her heart leapt to her throat. What if Frederic had contacted them? She pulled out a thick piece of stationery embossed with Cornell University's seal. Skimming it, she saw that President White wanted only to inform her that the board, despite not knowing the reason behind their early return, wanted to take advantage of it and move up the lecture series so that they could award the scholarship in time for the winter term.

Nora inhaled deeply. They were to present in a week.

She should tell the board what had happened. Professor Comstock had asked, of course, wondering why they'd cut their trip short by three months. Nora and Owen had agreed to tell him only that their work was finished and they were no longer needed. But where things stood, she and Owen had equal opportunity to receive the scholarship. If she told them what happened, there would be no chance for her.

She pushed away the conviction and guilt, instead focusing on the most important benefit of the board's decision—Owen would be returning soon. She wrapped her arms around herself and laid her head against the back of the swing. Soon she'd be in Owen's embrace, and this would all be over.

~

Nora knocked on the door of a White Hall apartment. Owen had returned to Ithaca from Manhattan only the day before and planned to stay with his friend until after the scholarship was awarded. He'd stay for another two years if they selected him. Nora didn't know if he'd stay if she won it.

She smoothed her hands down her burgundy wool skirt and fiddled with the bow at her throat. Would he still feel the same about her? Had returning home changed things? She imagined a man with his wealth and family connections would be sought after by all of New York's single society ladies. Who was she but a small-town entomologist with nothing but a jeweled cicada brooch to her name?

The door swung open, and Nora found herself swept into Owen's arms. Her heart stuttered when he pressed his face into her hair. He was clean-shaven, and she was surprised to find she missed his beard.

"I knew I'd miss you, but that was too great an affliction," he said.

She pulled back and tipped her head, exposing her throat, which Owen stared at. His lips twitched, and she wondered if he wanted to press his mouth to the pulse beating an erratic cadence just beneath her skin.

She swallowed, and he raised his eyes. "I missed you too."

He trailed his finger around her hairline, tugging out a curl. Then he gently touched his lips to hers.

Too gently. They'd been apart for such a long time.

She pressed into the kiss, her heart leaping to her throat when he groaned her name.

She pulled back and smiled. "How was your visit home?"

He blinked. "I . . . it was . . ."

"Cat got your tongue, Owen Epps?"

His slow grin appeared. "Someone else entirely."

She laughed and pressed her hand against his chest, forcing some space between them. "Really, how is your family?"

With obvious effort, he answered her question. "My brothers couldn't be bothered to take time off work, so I didn't see them. Mother fussed and said I had lost too much weight. It was comfortable and clean, and Cook made sure to feed me well. The only person who asked me about my work or experience was my grandmother. She enjoyed hearing about everything."

"Everything?"

His smile sparked, and a flame lit beneath her breast. "Everything."

"What did you tell her about your work and experience and . . . everything?"

"I showed her the specimens I had collected. She particularly liked the red-disc bushbrown butterfly. I told her about William's obsession with sun protection and Jeffrey's 'asthma' and Leonard's love of leeches. I didn't tell her too much about Frederic, but she's an astute woman, and I'm sure she gathered enough from what I didn't say to make a fair impression of him. I told her about the spicy food and awful illness and Sita— though I didn't tell her everything about Sita. My grandmother is wonderful, but the shock of that story might be too much for even her. I told her about Pallavi and your friend Swathi and the monkeys and cows."

She swallowed and gave a slow nod. Then Owen laughed

and tilted toward her, pressing his forehead against her own, his hands clutching her shoulders. They breathed the same air, inhaling and exhaling each other's presence.

"And I told her about you, Peculiar. All about you."

"What did you say?"

"I said you are the smartest, loveliest, most infuriatingly stubborn woman I've ever met." He pulled back, and his shoulders drooped. "Then my father walked in and asked about my plans for law school." He released Nora and raked his hand through his hair. "The few moments he spent with me, he used to demand I choose a school. I'm surprised he hasn't threatened to disown me if I don't comply."

"You'd be a terrible lawyer."

Owen smiled. "You know me better than my father does."

She leaned against the doorjamb and sighed. "There's no winning this. If I'm awarded the scholarship—which is doubtful, but you never know—then you have to leave. If you win the scholarship, I'll have to leave."

"Long Island isn't so far, and it will only take a couple years to finish my degree."

She straightened with a sudden thought. "You told me in India that you hoped I won the scholarship. If you no longer compete for it, I'll have a greater chance. Then I can stay here in Ithaca, and Lucius will turn the journal over to me."

Owen's mouth dropped. "Nora, I can't do that now. My father will force me into law school if I don't get it. Plus, it seems unlikely you'll be offered it now. Maybe if you still had your notes and specimens . . ."

"If I don't get that scholarship, I'll lose any chance to fix everything." She hated the tears clogging her throat and swallowed, hoping he didn't notice the warble in her voice. Knowing he had to hear her desperation. "I'll have failed my father and what he wanted for his work."

"If I don't get it, I'll have to follow my father's directives. Would you rather have the journal or me?"

The question settled over Nora like a weight. "That's an unfair question."

"How so?"

"That journal has been a part of my life for years. You're a new addition."

"Nora, you don't really want that journal." Owen held up his hand when she opened her mouth to protest. "I watched you come alive in India. Despite the limitations placed on you, you bloomed doing field research. Why would you chain yourself to something you don't love?"

Heat boiled through her veins. "It's all I have left of my father. And he wanted me to have it. I know he did."

"But not if it meant giving up what you really love to do. He loved you more than his publication."

"He made the ultimate sacrifice for me. Saving it is worth any sacrifice I have to make in order to honor him."

"Even losing me? I'd like to know what you'd choose."

"I'm not answering."

Owen rested his elbows against the door on either side of her and pressed a light kiss to her temple. "Does a publication make you feel the way I do?"

Nora ducked and slipped away from his trap. "It makes me feel useful. It makes me feel a connection to my father."

He pushed back his cowlick with a snap of his wrist, then crossed his arms. "It isn't a person, Nora. It's not your father. It's just a magazine. Just words and paper."

Her mouth fell open. Just a magazine? How could she have spent so much time with him and he not know it was everything? "You know what it meant to my father. You know it's all I've ever wanted."

He winced. "I thought maybe you'd found something else you wanted a bit more."

Behind Owen, his roommate shuffled around the small, cluttered parlor, pretending to be tidying up but with his ear toward the open door. Nora lowered her voice, and her words came out clothed in a hiss. "Are you hoping I'll give up the scholarship? Does loving you mean sacrificing my dreams for yours? Do you really care for me, or are you manipulating me?"

With every word, Owen's jaw grew tighter and his gaze more distant. She saw the effect of her speech and tried to stop, but her fears bubbled beneath the surface, demanding release. Demanding answers.

Owen stepped into the apartment, his hand clutching the edge of the door. "I'm starting to think India and everything that happened there was a wonderful dream that ended the moment we crossed the Atlantic. How could you think, after everything, I'd expect you to give up your ambitions? But your dream isn't that magazine." He huffed a laugh. "I know you better than you know yourself. But it seems you don't know me after all."

She watched as the door shut, finality in the click of the lock. What had just happened? She held her head, which had begun to pound with regret, and whispered, "I'm sorry."

But she couldn't say it to him. Because when it came down to it, she wouldn't give up the journal for anyone or anything. Not for her own desires, and not for Owen Epps of Manhattan. No matter what he thought he knew.

Chapter Twenty-Six

Professor Comstock tapped his pen against the letter on his desk, and the rat-a-tat set Nora's nerves on edge. He'd sent for her that morning, and when she entered his office, he'd waved a piece of paper at her. She saw Frederic's restrained signature at the bottom and knew he'd told the professor everything.

Professor Comstock pinched the bridge of his nose beneath his wire-rimmed glasses and peered at her over his fingers. "You understand that sending you to India put my reputation at risk. Science is a difficult place for women, and I wanted you to have every benefit before you launched into your career. Your actions have called into question my professional opinion and work."

She watched him from beneath lowered lashes, hoping he would misconstrue her anxiety for contrition. But he'd spent his entire life studying the smallest life-forms beneath microscopes. He wasn't fooled.

He dropped the glasses back into place and rested his hands on the desk. "You don't seem remorseful."

"Everyone is telling me I should feel bad about what I did," she said, "but I just can't. I helped a child in need. Isn't that what Christians are supposed to do?"

"But you weren't there representing the Church. You were there representing Cornell. Me!"

Professor Comstock had been like an uncle to her, especially since her father had died. She hated that she'd inadvertently caused harm to his reputation or career. "What else could I have done? Ignore that a child was being sold into prostitution? What would you have done?"

Nora hated the desperation in her voice. Hated the way her hands fluttered around her waist, like a pair of butterflies fighting for territory. She hated even more that she'd had to choose between Sita's good and her beloved teacher's.

He rested his elbows on the desk. "Maybe sending you there was a bad idea. You are so sheltered. You have no experience with the world. Something like this was bound to happen."

She shook her head. "I'm glad you sent me. Another student would have ignored Sita's plight. Maybe, in the end, that's why you sent me. Maybe there was a bigger reason than just advancing my career."

He picked up the letter and scanned it. "Frederic says you were instrumental in helping him find a few species that will make the book stand out, and he's grateful, but he suggests I never again recommend you to work with a team in the field. He also says you claim to have discovered a new species, but he's sure you can't be trusted in that area. However, despite your impulsivity, you've always been of sound mind. Will you tell me about it?"

Nora launched into an explanation of her butterfly, the habits and mimicry she had observed, the similarities but also differences between it and the *Delias eucharis*. "I have no doubt that it's an undiscovered butterfly."

The professor's eyes had taken on a gleam that grew the longer Nora spoke. He rubbed his hands together and nearly bounced in his seat. "Well, where is it?"

"I lost the first one I collected. Sita's father destroyed my others, along with all of my notes and illustrations, in a fire." Nora's eyes slid shut, and she once again smelled the smoke wafting through the air, heard the crackle and snap of the flames, saw her dreams disintegrate.

"That was rather unreasonable of him. I'm glad you suffered no harm. But a shame about the loss of your discovery."

"Will you tell the scholarship board about Sita? I believe they would look upon my actions unfavorably."

His fingers stilled. Professor Comstock was a good man. A fair one. But he also valued truth and responsibility. If he believed her actions wrong, he would not keep her behavior to himself. Her breath caught when he spoke.

"I will not bring it up—"

She reached across the table and grasped his hand.

"But," he said, warning in his words, "if they hear anything about it and question me, I will have to tell them the entire story."

"How would they hear anything? Frederic isn't aware of the scholarship, and Owen won't say a word. . . ." Nora's mouth slackened and she blinked. He wouldn't. No, of course not. But she recalled his despondency when he told her about his father's plans to send him to law school. He'd hate law school. The only thing he seemed to enjoy was studying insects. Field research. Travel.

Her.

He wanted her to choose between him and the journal, though. And when she couldn't, he'd shut the door in her face. If he knew he could jeopardize things for her and secure the scholarship for himself, he just might. Because Nora doubted he saw a future with her anymore.

And he couldn't see a future in law.

~～

Nora sat in the middle of Library Hall behind a woman wearing a high-crowned hat bedecked with silk flowers, ribbons, and a stuffed hummingbird. Nora could hardly see over it to the podium where one of her classmates had just finished speaking. Owen made his way up the stairs and looked out over the crowd. Nora ducked. Surely he couldn't see her.

She'd considered not attending his lecture, positive he'd find her presence obnoxious after their argument three days prior, but in the end, she couldn't stay away. She wanted to see him, to support him . . . to appraise the competition.

She'd already sat through two presentations—both men she'd attended school with and who had done field research with Professor Comstock in Illinois over the summer break. Next week she'd present with the other two students vying for the scholarship. Six people, but only she and Owen had a real chance. Both top of their class and having studied overseas.

She wouldn't present on her butterfly, of course. Without proof of its existence, without notes and field reports, no one would take her seriously. So she'd discuss gynandromorphism in the *Vindula erota*. It wasn't as exciting as the discovery of a new species, but it would do.

Owen crossed the stage and took his place behind the podium. He cleared his throat, rustled through some papers, and began his speech.

He spoke about the symbiotic relationship between the ants and the *Cigaritis lohita*. He spoke well. His confidence and excitement for the subject projected, and with charm, he drew the audience in. He peppered his entomological research with personal stories that drew laughter from the crowd. She had no chance.

From the corner of her eye, she saw Lucius walk into the hall. She frowned. She hadn't seen him at Cornell since his embarrassing "resignation."

The audience erupted with clapping, and Nora looked at Owen, who had gathered his papers and was stepping off the stage. When she looked back toward Lucius, he was gone. The lady with the hat stood and stepped aside, revealing Owen talking with President White near the front of the room.

Lucius joined them.

Nora tugged on her earring. She should find out what they were talking about. Clutching her reticule, she stood, but then President White motioned Professor Comstock over, and two of the men on the scholarship board joined the circle.

"Nora!" Rose skipped toward her, Bitsy following at a more sedate pace. "We thought you weren't coming. You could have sat with us. We had seats in the front row. Owen did magnificently, didn't he? I'd be surprised if he didn't get the scholarship." Bitsy elbowed Rose, drawing a sharp gasp. "Why'd you— oh. Well, you know what I mean, don't you, Nora? Of course you're brilliant and they'll give *you* the scholarship. I don't think for—"

"Stop prattling." Bitsy rolled her eyes heavenward.

Nora waved her hand to quiet them both, and they followed her gaze to the tight huddle at the front of the room. Lucius gestured with his hands, prodding at the sky and shaking his head like an excited ornithologist.

"What do you think they're discussing?" Nora asked.

"Maybe how well Owen did." Rose yelped, and Nora assumed Bitsy had jabbed her again.

"But why is Lucius here?" Nora wiped a slick of sweat from her upper lip. Professor Comstock glanced at her, his expression sad, and nausea unfurled in her stomach, sending grasping talons into her chest and throat and head. *No.*

President White searched the hall, his eyes coming to rest on her. In his stiff frown and narrowed eyes, she saw censure.

The scholarship vanished, and she groaned. "I'm moving to Long Island."

She tried to make words out of Owen's moving lips. She caught her name, maybe the word *save*, but nothing else. Lucius clapped him on the back, and Nora's fists curled. She dug her nails into the tender flesh of her palms. Lucius turned and caught her eye, and her legs went numb. She sank onto the chair behind her and pressed her lips together.

"He wants to ruin my life." Nora had always known Lucius disliked her. But this . . . this was more than a personality conflict. Lucius had a personal vendetta against her. She didn't know why. Couldn't fathom what would cause someone to destroy their stepdaughter's every happiness. But when he sauntered toward the door with light steps, Nora knew he'd somehow found out what had happened in India and realized it would influence their decision. And he wanted her gone.

Rose glanced down at her with a worried expression. "You don't know that. Don't borrow trouble."

Bitsy grabbed Nora's arm and hauled her up. "You need to find out what happened."

Nora craned her neck to see Owen shaking President White's hand, then the donors'. He swiveled his head, eyes raking the crowd, then stepped out of the circle, traced Lucius's steps, and pushed his way through the throng.

Bitsy gave Nora a gentle shove. "Go figure this out."

Nora took off after him. When she rounded the sand-colored brick walls of the hall, she saw Owen jogging to catch up with Lucius. They met beneath the clock tower, and their conversation was full of gesturing and interruption.

Nora started forward, but then Lucius laughed, and Nora halted and smashed her teeth together so hard, pain shot through her cheeks. She couldn't see Owen's face because he stood with his back to her, but she saw from his wide stance and the way he rocked back on his heels that he felt comfortable with Lucius.

Her throat closed, and she gasped, her breath coming in quick, shallow puffs. He couldn't betray her like this. Her heart, which she'd kept protected behind a curtain of study and aloofness until Owen freed it, contracted, and she thought it might shatter into a million pieces.

And she knew, if Owen asked her again what was more important, him or the journal, she'd answer in a completely different way.

Nora walked away, her heels clicking against the stone pavers. Absorbed in her thoughts and heartbreak, she didn't notice Anna until her mentor's hand shot out and grasped Nora's wrist.

"You're in a hurry," Anna said with a laugh. Happy lines wrinkled the corners of her eyes, and her cheeks rounded. She tugged Nora down beside her on an iron bench.

Nora sighed. "Everything I do ends in disaster." She squinted up at the sky, tracking the clouds' progress and seeing in them fanciful insects.

"Are you speaking about what happened in India?"

Nora looked at her and drew her lower lip between her teeth.

Anna smiled. "There's very little Mr. Comstock keeps from me."

"What happened in India, what happened with my father, what happened at the dinner party, what happened"—Nora's voice cracked—"with Owen."

Anna didn't question her. She didn't pry. She answered in her matter-of-fact way, cutting right to the core of the issue. "Sometimes the consequence is entirely too harsh for the action. In your case"—she winked at Nora—"I'd say most of the time."

Nora groaned. She was cursed.

"I think you made the right decision regarding your Indian friend. An unpopular choice, for sure, but really, it was the only one you could have made. You knew she was worth the consequence, and in the end, knowing that child is safe makes almost anything worth it."

Nora smiled. "She *was* worth it. I love her like a sister."

Anna touched Nora's arm, and her happy wrinkles disappeared. "And I love you like a sister, so I'm going to tell you something that will hurt you. But I want you to be prepared."

Nora didn't think anything could be worse than knowing the man she loved had colluded with the man she disliked most in the world to keep her from realizing her dreams, but she still considered bolting. Hiding in the cavern of Library

Hall or beneath a nearby shrub. She didn't want to hear more bad news.

"There has been talk about Lucius. About his financial situation."

Nora lifted a shoulder. "I know about that. He's already sold my jewelry. He said he's had trouble paying bills since he lost his job."

Anna shook her head, and a sad smile crept across her lips. "It's more than that. He's been seen gambling. A lot. It's the reason Cornell fired him. He has significant debts, and he's borrowed money from nearly every employee of the university."

Nora stared at her. "My father left my mother comfortably provided for."

"It's gone, Nora. All of it. He's mortgaged the house."

Nora pressed the heels of her hands against her eyes. He couldn't have. What would they do?

Footsteps approached. "Nora, I have some dreadful news," Professor Comstock said.

Nora removed her hands and blinked up at him. "What, more?" A bitter laugh fringed her question.

He carefully touched her arm, as though she might break. "Somehow, Lucius has heard enough about what happened in India that he was able to convince the board you are unfit for the scholarship. They've determined they don't want a rabble-rouser benefiting from their largesse."

"I figured as much." Nora choked on the bile spilling into her mouth. She swallowed it, and it burned a path down her throat and into her chest.

Everything was gone.

They had nothing. She had nothing. No hope for continuing her education. No job prospects. No collection to remind her of her father. No new exotic butterfly to propel her to prominence. No Owen to love her.

Nothing.

Chapter Twenty-Seven

Nora stumbled over a branch covered in decaying leaves. She kicked it out of the path and forged ahead toward the only place she knew that would offer solitude and comfort.

Cascadilla Falls in autumn smelled of age and wisdom. The water, rushing over ancient sandstone, smoothed everything in its path. Nora hoped it would smooth away her worries.

She'd held out hope that the board would reconsider their decision to cut her from the line of students vying for the scholarship, but the next lecture series came and went, and Nora sat in the chair beside her bedroom window, twisting the fringed edge of a pillow between her fingers.

Today, when she'd sat down to toast and boiled eggs for breakfast, she saw Lucius with his nose buried in the morning paper. Emblazoned across the front page was a headline that declared Owen had been awarded the scholarship.

She would have been thrilled for him had it not meant the end of her own dreams. Had he not betrayed her to get it.

A breeze carrying the scent of winter rustled the remaining leaves clinging to the trees. She wrapped her arms around herself. Only wanting to get away from the dining room where she had to read about Owen's success and witness Lucius's gloating, she'd forgotten her shawl.

Instead of veering left toward the creek bank, feet from where the water plunged down a giant staircase of stones, Nora hiked up the overgrown incline. She reached the top of the falls, huffing and pinching the stitch in her side.

She stood next to the tree. Its limbs still hung over the falls, but its branches were no longer spindly. Now they looked as though they could hold the weight of a man. Its heavy trunk sank into the ground, a stalwart reminder of Nora's poor choices.

When she ran her hand over its brittle bark, chunks fell into her hand, revealing tunnels and holes in the wood. She flicked at some sawdust-like frass, and a few brittle pupal skins tumbled to the ground.

It seemed a borer would be the end of the tree that had been the end of her father.

She leaned her forehead against the trunk and wished for a different outcome. *If only I had obeyed. If only he hadn't followed. If only, if only, if only.*

Nora pushed herself away from the tree, knowing the falls would bring her no peace today. Her mind and heart were too bruised and wretched to receive any balm. Tripping her way down the incline, she raised her arms above her head and let a scream tear from her throat. It bounced around the gorge before being drowned by the pounding water. Again and again, she released all her pent-up frustration and anger and brokenness in short, forceful shouts. Her feet propelled her down, and by the time she reached the bottom, she had nothing left to offer the sky, trees, and water. She'd sacrificed her dignity and composure, finding blessed release in letting go.

The moment she stepped onto the narrow path leading back to Cornell, though, she found herself wound tight again.

"I thought you'd be here," Owen said, standing at the foot of the path. Dark circles made crescent moons beneath his eyes, and she thought he looked tired. Guilt, maybe?

She pulled a brittle leaf from the sloppy knot she'd wound her hair into that morning. It had rained the night before, and the air was heavy with residual moisture, making the curls around her face frizz. Nora imagined she looked a fright.

But not quite as bad as Owen.

"Are you going to say anything?" he asked.

Nora quirked her brows, the only movement she allowed to break her stoicism. Her chest tightened, forcing her heart into a canter that sent blood rushing to all parts of her body. But Owen didn't have to know that beneath her flat expression and nonchalance, everything squirmed in turmoil.

"I shouldn't have put you in the position of choosing between me and the journal," Owen said. "I haven't declared myself to you, and it wasn't fair. But, in my defense, I'd hoped we'd reached a point in our relationship where you valued me over a magazine."

"Is that why you colluded with my stepfather to convince the board to exclude me from the scholarship?"

Owen shook his head, and a deep wrinkle appeared between his eyes. "I don't know what you're talking about."

"Someone told Lucius what happened in India, and he told President White. Only four people here knew about it. You, me, Professor Comstock, and Anna. I hadn't even told Bitsy and Rose. Because of my indiscretions, the board decided I was no longer a candidate."

"Why would I speak to Lucius about it?"

Nora stared at him.

"Okay. I can see why you'd think that. But I didn't. I have no idea who told him."

He seemed so earnest, and she knew he valued honesty. But if he hadn't, who? "I saw you follow him after your lecture. You spoke with him."

"I did talk with him, but it wasn't about India or the scholarship." Owen dropped his head and toed the dirt path, worn thin by years of trampling undergrads. "I only asked how you were. Told him to tell you hello. He asked if I was going to release him from the burden of managing you. I said you didn't need managing. Then he laughed and walked away."

Her face burned, and she was a panicked student batting away roaches all over again. Exposed. Vulnerable. "You said nothing at all to Lucius—to anyone—about what happened?"

"Lucius did tell the board, and they questioned me." His shoulders drooped, and he shoved his hands into his pockets. "I couldn't lie, Nora. I confirmed the story."

Her hope flashed like a *lampyrid*, one moment bright and the next snuffed out. She swallowed hard and dropped her eyes to the ground. He had large feet, and they almost touched the hem of her gown. She stepped back, her skirts swishing, then settling a hairsbreadth farther away. So much more than that, really.

The space wasn't enough to keep him from grasping her shoulders. She jerked her head up, surprised by his pained stare.

"What choice did I have? Professor Comstock himself answered affirmatively. Would you hold me to a different standard than him?"

She pulled away, surprised when the urge to pound against his chest lifted her arms. She clenched her fists and forced them down by her sides. What had loving Owen done to her? Her composure was gone, and her flaring temper made her want to cause him pain. It was too much.

"I shouldn't have expected anything at all from you." She tried to step past him, but he blocked her way.

"That's unfair. You were told, repeatedly, to stay out of cultural matters. You didn't listen. Just did what you wanted, the consequences be—"

"I wouldn't have been able to live with myself had I ignored Sita's plight. What choice did I have?"

"You're allowed to make that argument, but I'm not? When

forced to choose between two difficult options, you chose the moral one. So did I!"

"How is divulging a story you knew would disqualify me from the scholarship the moral choice?" She stomped her foot, regretting her childishness the moment she did so. Taking a deep breath, Nora smoothed her fingers over her hair, pushing the errant curls around her temple beneath her hat. She pressed her lips together and silently counted to five. *Hold it together. Nothing is worth behaving unhinged.* "I know the scholarship was your way to escape your father's plans for you. To get out of having to go to law school." Her throat thickened with tears. "But you have so many choices open to you, and it was my *only* one. The only thing standing between me and saving my father's legacy was that scholarship."

"You can do anything you want, Nora. It's just a magazine, after all."

The tightness around her eyes sent sharp pain shooting through her temples. She sighed. "There are other options when you're an educated man with family connections. It's not so hard for you to do what you want. But what about me? I'm a woman trying to forge a path through a man's world. I'm not wanted, Owen. Lucius would have given me the journal if I'd gotten that scholarship. With a master's degree, I could have taught like my father. I could have made a difference. As it is, I doubt I'll be able to find a position in science. Be able to support myself."

Owen took her by the waist and pulled her toward him. "Why do you have to support yourself? Let me do so." The tips of his ears turned red. "Marry me, Nora. I can take care of you."

She took a few steps away from him on shaky legs and stretched out her arm, hand up, when he attempted to follow her.

"Let me help you." His voice cracked.

Nora shook her head. "How can I trust that you'll help me when you believe your dreams are more important than mine?"

"That's not fair."

"Not much about life is."

Nora sat on the French walnut chair in the parlor, a book on American spiders open on her lap, and watched the flames in the fireplace dance up the chimney. She tried to return her attention to the illustration of *Lactrodectus geometricus*, but her eyes wandered.

Lucius sat on the nearby settee, swirling amber cognac in a snifter. Her mother had left for bed only minutes earlier, unable to pry from Nora the reason for her discontent.

Nora uncrossed her feet and shut her book. Before she stood, though, Lucius cleared his throat.

He sipped from his glass, then settled against the back of the settee, crossing one leg over a knee. "You've never liked me."

It wasn't phrased as a question because there had never been any question. Nora hadn't liked Lucius since the day he stopped by their house when she was heading out the door with her father to hunt beetles. He'd asked her father why he wasted time teaching a girl the things he taught men at the university. She had been eight, and she'd known then, just as she knew now, that Lucius didn't compare favorably to Alexander Shipley.

She looked at the fire, holding her hands toward it. The almost-winter wind shook the windowpanes, and a chill seeped into the room despite the leaping flames.

"You don't have to answer, but I know it's true." There was no sadness in Lucius's voice. No desire to be accepted or loved.

"You are nothing like my father."

He gave a short laugh. "Not many men are." He shifted his bulk and sighed. "Your father was the best of men, and life was good to him."

Nora turned disbelieving eyes toward him. "He died too young."

"But until then, his life was good. He had the heart of your mother, a promising career, and the devotion of a child. It seems unfair that one person should receive so much."

The floorboards creaked above them as her mother readied

for bed, and Nora wondered, for the first time, if she ever compared her second husband to her first. "My father worked hard and was honest. He gave to people—his time, education, and friendship. Life didn't just hand him respect and love. He earned it."

Lucius studied her as he ran his thumb over the rim of his glass. Nora didn't turn from him, knowing he was testing her mettle. Finally, his lips turned up in a crooked smile. "I've always been weak. Your mother could have had another man—a decent one. I'm not sure why she chose me."

Nora knew she'd never have a loving relationship with her stepfather. Most of the time she managed to be polite, if distant, and that was enough. But tonight, her heart fractured and her spirit bleeding, she thought she might as well submit to the recklessness that so often tore from her mouth. "Probably because you took advantage of her grief while other men allowed her time to mourn."

Lucius didn't look surprised or angry. In fact, no emotion at all colored his expression. "You may be right. I've never thought I was worthy of her, but I have tried to make her happy. My only goal has been to shield her from anything that might weaken or hurt her. Your mother isn't like you, Nora. She is fragile and easily overwhelmed."

Nora glanced away, unsure what to do with his almost-compliment.

The glass clinked as Lucius set it on the table beside him, and he clasped his hands together, resting them against his stomach. "You know, I loved your mother long before your father met her. I introduced them, in fact."

Nora frowned. She hadn't known that. And something about it didn't sit right with her. She pinched the bridge of her nose and looked into the fire.

"I told him," Lucius said, "that I had every intention of pursuing her. But she fell in love with your father instead." He laughed without humor. Everything he did seemed backward somehow.

His laugh, his love, his goals. It was as though he fought through life, not realizing no one else joined in his battle.

A jolt of recognition shot through her middle. Maybe she and Lucius had something in common, after all.

Nora stood. "It seems as though, in the end, you got what you wanted."

"Thanks to you."

Ice doused her. She rubbed her throat, needing to force open the airways that had closed so suddenly. "What?"

He couldn't know. No one had been at the falls that day. The only witness was God.

Lucius gave her a quizzical look. "If she hadn't had a child, your mother would never have remarried. She adored Alex and knew he couldn't be replaced, but she also didn't want you growing up without a father."

Nora sucked in a breath and sank back into her chair. She clutched the heavy book with white fingers and rolled her dry lips inward, moistening them. "You were a poor substitute."

He lifted his glass in agreement. "I won't argue that. All I wanted was to see to Lydia's happiness, and for some reason she believes you are instrumental to keeping her happy." He picked up the decanter of cognac and poured another glass. "It seems I'll be the one who most disappoints her, though."

His hand shook as he brought the glass to his lips, and Nora wondered if he'd been drinking away their money as well as gambling. She shook her head, not understanding how her mother had thought this sorry man could fill her father's place.

She stood again, wanting nothing more than to shed the pins pricking her scalp and the day's heartache. To climb into bed. Hopefully her dreams would give her a measure of escape.

Lucius held up a finger, indicating his desire that she stay. She sighed and waited.

"She will soon know how I've hurt her. Everyone will know. I've done something I promised her I wouldn't, and there is no way of hiding it from her anymore." He swirled his glass, the alcohol capturing his attention. His words came from very far away, as though he'd disassociated himself from them. "Do you know Mr. Primrose is headed to Long Island? He's part of my sister's social circle. There still might be a chance you can recover what you lost. What I lost." His eyes snapped up from the glass and caught her gaze.

"I've lost my chance at everything I've ever wanted professionally. I'm not willing to lose my personal life so you can escape the consequences of your poor decisions. I know you've gambled, Lucius, and lost our house." Rancor filled Nora's mouth with bitterness. This was her home. Her parents' home. Lucius had only been a guest—an unwelcome one—and he'd managed to steal it from them. She wasn't going to let him steal anything else that belonged to her, and her choice of a husband might very well be all she had left.

Lucius frowned but didn't question how she'd come into that knowledge. His eyes held only resignation. He took another sip of cognac. "If only that were it, Nora, but there are some things worth more than a house. And I've managed to lose it all."

~~~

Nora had only met Martha Farnesworth, Lucius's sister, once—at Mother's wedding. Soon after that, Martha's husband, a prominent Long Island doctor, fell ill, and Martha spent all her time caring for him.

Which was why Nora stood confused, hand on the front door, blinking at the imposing woman who smiled at her from beneath the brim of a wide hat.

Martha pulled Nora into her ample bosom. "It's so nice to see you again! My, you've grown."

"Aunt, you've come," Nora said blankly. She pulled back and glanced behind Martha at the carriage but saw no one but the driver standing beside a large trunk. "Where is your husband?"

Martha's smile slipped, but just a little. "Poor Frank. He died two weeks ago."

Nora stared. "We had no word."

Martha waved a hand as if to say *not to worry* and lifted two small cases from the porch. She bustled inside past Nora. "I sat down to write after the funeral but then thought, Why not just visit? I haven't seen you since the wedding, and I had a letter from your mother"—Martha turned, and her voice dropped to a whisper—"which led me to believe all is not well."

Nora held the door open for the driver, who had hoisted the trunk onto his shoulders. He stomped his feet before entering the house, then followed Martha into the hall. "Where should I take this, ma'am?"

Martha looked at her in expectation, and Nora inhaled, trying to center herself in the whirlwind of her aunt's arrival. "The guest room is at the top of the stairs, third on the right."

The driver followed her directions, and Martha removed her hat. "Well, where is my brother?"

"He and Mother are in the back garden."

Nora led Martha through the house and out the back door. Lucius walked the gravel paths of the rose garden, Mother's hand in the crook of his arm. Nora had encouraged her mother to go outside, the weather today being much milder than mid-November normally produced. It couldn't be healthy, staying inside all day, inactive and closed off from the world.

Martha marched across the lawn, her stiff skirts flapping with every step. Nora followed her.

Lucius halted, his eyes growing wide when he saw Martha. "Sister?"

"I have come to set things right." Martha planted a kiss on his forehead, then patted his cheek as one might a child.

"Set things right?" Lucius plucked at Mother's sleeve, sending her a hesitant smile that didn't reach his eyes.

Martha planted her hands on her hips and rooted herself to the spot. An immovable boulder standing in the face of poor management and disorder.

Nora quite liked her.

"I am under the impression," Martha said, "that there are some concerning problems afoot. You didn't tell me you'd lost your position."

Lucius's eyes shot to Nora, and he pulled his lips back, revealing a grimace of large, straight teeth. "Why must you involve yourself in things that don't concern you?"

Nora held up her hands. "I had nothing to do with this."

She had never heard anyone speak to Lucius the way Martha did—a no-nonsense tone that caused Lucius's mouth to snap closed. "Leave that poor girl alone. She did nothing wrong. Lydia wrote to me and hinted at trouble."

Lucius looked at Mother with a wounded expression. She dropped her eyes to the ground, and her chin quivered.

"Where is your husband?" Lucius asked, turning back to his sister.

"In his grave, and it's about time." Martha huffed. "That stubborn man refused to die when the good Lord called for him."

Lucius sputtered. "Martha!"

The corners of his sister's lips turned up for just a moment, as though she knew her words were shocking and she reveled in her ability to ruffle Lucius's sense of decorum.

Goodness, Nora *really* liked her.

"Lucius," Martha continued, "the man was ill in bed for five years. Five years of fetching things for him, reading to him from his dreary medical books, listening to him complain and whine. He was a terrible husband when he was well. Unbearable when he was ill. The only consolation was that he couldn't raise his hand against me for weakness."

An unnatural quiet descended on the garden. Of course, spousal abuse wasn't rare, but no one talked about it. For Martha to divulge the ugliness of it in the light of day, so unvarnished, seemed ill-bred. Why, though, Nora didn't know. Why shouldn't people discuss it? Maybe abuse happened because the secrecy allowed it to flourish.

Nora touched Martha's arm. She didn't offer pity because

her aunt didn't seem like the type of woman to take kindly to that, but she hoped her touch offered understanding. Solidarity.

"I didn't know," Lucius said, his words abnormally gentle and soft.

Martha patted Nora's hand. "It is done. Now, why don't you have tea made for me, Lucius? I'm quite famished."

She turned toward the house, and that was when Nora saw it. The green-and-yellow ribbon pinned to the lapel of Martha's fine woolen cape. "You're a suffragette!"

Lucius coughed and choked, his face draining of color. "Please tell me you're not." He looked so horrified, Nora didn't know whether to gloat or pity him.

Martha fingered the ribbon and said with a self-satisfied smile, "Of course I am. I joined the day after Frank died. It is my new mission to fight for women's rights—both civic and personal. If there is one thing Frank taught me, it's that women need to rise up and stand against injustice."

"I've learned," Nora said, "that when women do that, we suffer tremendously."

Martha threw back her shoulders and raised her head. Nora couldn't help but compare her to her mother, who seemed drawn into herself, probably still worried that she'd overstepped in writing to Martha about their problems. Martha—vibrant, stout, and forthright—wasn't worried about offending.

"The suffering is worth it if we've caused change." Martha eyed Lucius. "Don't you agree?"

Something passed between them—a secret understanding—that caused conflicting emotions to cross Lucius's face. He stiffened beside Mother and wrapped his arm around her—hiding her within the safety of his bulk—as though trying to shield her from whatever he and Martha knew. He turned to her and said, "Darling, I believe you've spent enough time outdoors."

Lydia didn't question him. She pressed a kiss to his hand and hurried toward the house.

"It is a good thing you came," he said after she'd disappeared inside. "I've been meaning to contact you about a situation that has left us unable to remain here in Ithaca."

Not live in Ithaca? Nora knew he'd lost the house, but there were other, smaller houses. Why did they have to leave?

Lucius didn't meet Nora's eyes. He gazed at his sister as though she were a lifeline. "I have heavily mortgaged the house. In order to pay my debts, I've been forced to make difficult decisions. I've done the best I could."

Nora forced her frozen lips open and formed words she didn't want the answer to. "What have you done?"

He ignored her, instead speaking to his sister, as though Nora didn't deserve an explanation for why he'd destroyed the life her father had worked so hard to create. "We will need somewhere to stay until I'm able to secure a new position in a different town. And moving will incur expenses I'm currently unable to support."

"What have you done, Lucius?" Nora's breathing grew shallow, and the cold air, which only a moment ago had felt brisk and refreshing, paralyzed her lips. Unable to form any more words, she wrapped her arms around herself and rocked.

She knew about the house and the money. Knew he'd sabotaged her chances for the scholarship. But he'd said there was something else, something that would break Lydia's heart. And the only thing Nora could think of was his losing the one thing she wanted most in the world.

"I have significant debts, outside of the house, which must be paid."

"From gambling!" Nora's accusation hung between them, full of vitriol and years of contempt. "You gambled my father's money and house. You've ruined everything."

Martha sighed, and it contained more than just disappointment over her brother's actions. "I expected more from you, after everything I sacrificed to give you a better life. I thought you'd learned from Father's example. What have you done?"

Lucius pressed his white lips together, and his jaw went rigid.

He turned on Nora, and his words, spilling over with accusation, hit their mark. "This is your fault. You ruined our chance when you insulted Primrose. If you had kept your mouth shut, I wouldn't have had to sell the journal."

Her limbs stiffened, and she repeated his words, not sure she believed she'd heard correctly. "You sold it?"

"It isn't final, but it's practically done. There's no going back on it."

Nora threw her head back and stared at the sky, her gaze tracking a formation of geese flying south. She swallowed hard, wishing she could sprout wings and join them. Escape the terrible knowledge that she'd never have the chance to save her father's journal. That she'd never have the chance to prove she was worth his belief in her. To make up for her part in his death.

"Your impulsive words destroyed my chance to keep it going." Lucius's words this time held less confidence. They were devastating in their blow, but the effect was minimized by his shaking voice.

Martha drew Nora close, the weight of her arm offering comfort. "Do not accuse the child. This is your fault, just as surely as our predicament when Father died was his."

Lucius ignored her chastisement. "Whoever's fault it is, the journal is as good as gone. And I can't say I'm upset. The only reason I kept it going as long as I did was because I promised Lydia I'd hold on to it until Nora was old enough to take over. It generated little income and used too much of my time."

"But you didn't honor that," Nora said. "You broke your word. The journal was mine." Why had her mother never told her it was meant for her the whole time? "Why didn't you turn it over to me when I asked you months ago? You knew I wanted it."

"I needed to pay off my debts. Threats were being made. I hoped turning it into a commission publication would make money, but it was too late. I needed to sell. At least I turned a small profit on it."

"You said I could have it if I proved myself and finished my education."

"And you met my expectations. I wouldn't have made you that offer if I believed you capable of attaining it. I mainly wanted you out of my house."

"Father's house, you mean. The journal was self-supporting until you ruined it. I could have helped you turn a profit."

"Like I said, I had debts that needed to be paid. After I lost my teaching position, that was the only money coming in. I tried extending credit with the printer, but you know how that went."

"There are other printers!"

Lucius turned his back on them and walked away, showing as much care for her grief as he'd shown to the promise he'd made her mother.

Nora looked at Martha, gleaning a measure of comfort from her stalwart presence. "There are other printers in town."

Martha shook her head. "Not for someone known to be a gambler. I doubt any of them would have offered him credit."

Nora's eyes watered, and she blinked to clear them. It had all been for nothing. Going to India, trying for the scholarship, choosing the journal over Owen and refusing his proposal.

"It wasn't his to lose."

Chapter Twenty-Eight

Martha guided Nora toward the house. The stiff brown grass crunched beneath their boots. "Do show poor Lucius some grace."

Nora pressed her lips together. "He has made a series of terrible choices that have indebted my family and destroyed my father's legacy. My mother isn't well. What do you suppose this will do to her?"

Martha tucked Nora's hand into the crook of her elbow as they entered the parlor. Nora usually loved this room, with its jasper-colored anthemion paper, floor-to-ceiling windows, and ornate moldings, but a shadow had been cast over her home. It no longer belonged to them.

After Martha had settled Nora into a chair, she sat opposite her. "You had the benefit of a wonderful father during your formative years. Lucius wasn't so lucky."

Lucius never spoke of his family—except for Martha—and Nora knew nothing about his parents, except that they had died years ago. She realized she'd never thought to ask him about his childhood.

Her aunt twisted the lace at her wrists and sighed so deeply, her generous bosom rose. "Our father, too, gave in to the scourge of gambling. He was a lawyer by trade, the son of a lawyer, and had never experienced need or want. When he married my mother, who was beneath him in class and education, his parents disinherited him. He died when Lucius was sixteen and I was eighteen. We were left penniless."

Compassion pricked Nora's heart, an emotion that, when directed toward Lucius, felt wholly unfamiliar. She shifted in her seat, and the beginnings of empathy soured her stomach.

"What could my mother—the daughter of a blacksmith—do? She'd always been beautiful—I take after my father." Martha chuckled. "Men . . . wanted her. So she did what she had to do in order to take care of her children."

An ache burned the back of Nora's throat, and she saw Sita's beautiful face. Such different stories, but they could have had the same outcome. How terrible for Lucius, watching his mother debase herself.

She looked down at her lap. A year ago, she might have judged his mother harshly, but she'd learned that life could be very hard. "She must have loved you very much."

"She did," Martha said, her words soft and ripe with untold stories.

Heavy steps brought Lucius into the room. "She may have loved us, but she made us a target for derision and acrimony. It would have been better had we starved."

Nora frowned. "You can't possibly mean that."

He stood in front of her, his barrel chest and crossed arms meant to intimidate. "I do mean it. Women, when given a chance, will always stumble toward sin and depravity. My mother could have found a different way, but she did what was easy. Expedient."

Martha huffed and drew herself up so that she matched Lucius's stance. "Much like you, it seems. Gambling instead of taking better care of your finances. Expedient, indeed."

He grunted as though Martha had hit him in the middle. "You've changed since your husband died. Every woman needs a man to keep her on a straight path so that her emotions don't consume her good sense."

"Nonsense. I married a terrible man so you might have a future." Martha turned flashing eyes toward Nora. "For all my husband's cruelty, he did send Lucius to school, and I'll never regret my choice for that reason alone. But I will not marry again." She tipped her chin at Nora. "Lucius, you have a bright, sensible young woman sitting in the middle of your parlor."

He didn't even glance in Nora's direction. "She is the epitome of unsexed behavior and an overreliance on emotion. Her conduct in India showed an extreme lack of logic."

"How do you know what happened in India?" Nora demanded.

Lucius did look at her then—though she imagined he didn't *see* her—and a proud smile pulled his mouth into a caricature. "You received a letter from someone named Jeffrey Steed. I knew you were hiding something, so I took it upon myself to read it. He mentioned how foolish it was that you interfered in local matters and went on to recount your responsibility in having the camp burned down. After you left, the rest of the team was run out of India. They did have enough work to keep their commitment, though. Does that make you feel better about your stupidity?"

Gooseflesh rose along her arms and legs. "Why do you hate me so much?"

"I don't hate you. You've been indulged, and a woman indulged is a dangerous thing. I've already lost one family to poor decisions made by an irrational and unfeminine woman. I won't allow you to destroy this one."

"Give me the letter."

He gave her a hard look, then turned and left the room.

Nora stared after him. "He is unbelievable. He thought nothing of ruining my future."

Martha clucked her tongue. "You can come live with me."
She dropped her voice. "Lucius must, too, though he doesn't yet
realize it. I certainly won't be giving him the money he wants,
given his history. Between the two of us—I'm sorry, Nora, but
your mother will be no use to us in this matter—we will ensure
Lucius grows in his understanding of women. We'll make him
a proponent for suffrage."

With a groan, Nora sank into the settee and pulled a pillow
over her face. "Aunt," she said, her voice muffled by the velvet
cushion, "I don't want to change the world one man at a time.
I only want to study insects."

And, Nora realized with a sinking stomach, now she wouldn't
even be able to escape Lucius if she moved to Long Island.

~~~

Dear Miss Shipley,

*I'm taking the liberty of contacting you to tell you what
happened in India after you and Mr. Epps left. Frederic
has given me permission and sends his (not quite warm)
regards.*

*When you involved yourself in local affairs, I thought you
stupid and enthusiastically waited for the consequences to
fall. I will admit, I didn't expect them to rain fire down on
our camp.*

*You already know we lost none of our work, for which
Frederic is grateful. I wouldn't have minded spending another
half year away from England, but he felt it was time to return home. The local people weren't happy with our presence
thanks to your interference.*

*So home I went. I was invited back into my house by my
wife and nine daughters.*

Yes, nine.

*As they hugged me with enough exuberance to send me back
across the Channel, I remembered your foolishness and admit-
ted you might have also shown a measure of bravery I lack.*

My daughters will never know anything but comfort and privilege. And, except for as many forays away from them as I can muster, I've never thought they deserved anything else. But I certainly wouldn't have sacrificed my work and career to ensure someone else had those things.

So, Miss Shipley, your actions may have resulted in a burned camp, a shortened stay, and ejection from Kodaikanal and the surrounding areas, but you showed a strength of character I will never forget.

Don't feel the need to respond to this letter.

Mr. Jeffrey Steed

When the moon dipped below the horizon, Nora climbed the stairs, clutching Mr. Steed's letter, which she had read half a dozen times. She wished Lucius hadn't gotten a hold of it, but she didn't wish Mr. Steed had not written it. He'd meant well. And, coming from someone who hadn't really liked her, his words offered more validation than from another, more pleasant person.

As Nora neared her mother's open door, she paused. Lucius hadn't had to tell her to keep their conversation from her mother. Over the last few years, they'd both conspired to keep Lydia from becoming aware of distasteful news. It was this environment of secrecy that had led Lucius to sell the journal without consulting Lydia first.

Nora understood his reasoning. That sort of news was likely to send her mother into a relapse and cause her already weak condition to deteriorate. But Nora thought maybe Martha's behavior—her honesty and transparency—offered something better. A chance to share one another's burdens. The exposure of poor choices. Nora was sure she'd heard a Bible verse relating to that very thing. Fools walked in darkness, and she'd been a fool, allowing Lucius to convince her that Mother needed to stay in darkness.

If Mother had been aware of her husband's gambling, would she have allowed him to retain control of the journal?

Nora cleared her throat and knocked on the doorjamb. When she peeked into the room, her mother motioned for her to enter from her place on the bed. "Darling, I'm so glad you're here. Will you read to me for a while?"

"Of course." Nora settled into the chair beside the bed, lifting the book into her lap. *A Little Tour in France.* Nora rarely read anything but scientific texts and papers. Her mother, though, adored every new book that was released. She particularly loved books that took place in other countries, maybe because they took her far from the four walls of her house.

Nora flipped through the pages of Henry James's newest. She'd like to publish a book one day.

She froze, startled by the thought. She'd spent so many years dreaming about running the journal, she'd never considered another route to publication. But, really, why not? If Frederic could find the backing to publish his field research, surely she could too.

Nora shook her head, clearing it of the farfetched fancy. Her mother watched her with guileless eyes. Which came first, her mother's naiveté or Lucius's desire to keep her in the dark?

"Mother, are you aware we need to move?" Nora asked.

Lydia's smile tightened. "Read the book, darling. I'm curious to hear about his travels."

"Lucius has lost our house. I will move in with Martha, if Lucius holds to our agreement, and you will have to leave Ithaca, as well."

The blanket covering Lydia's legs wrinkled beneath her grasping hands. She balled it into her fists. "Every other book on France centers on Paris. This one should prove entertaining and enlightening."

Nora sighed. She flipped the book to the first page. Maybe her mother knew her own limitations. Knew she couldn't cope with the truth. But how unfair that Nora alone was burdened with it. Lucius wasn't her choice, after all. Her mother should bear some of the brunt of her own husband's character flaws and failings.

"When did you plan on giving me Father's publication?" she asked.

Lydia's smile turned genuine. She released her hold on the blanket and smoothed her fingers over the puckered cotton. "I told Lucius before you returned from India that he should begin the process as soon as you got home. I thought it would give the two of you a chance to work together. Has he spoken to you about it?"

Nora tipped her head and tapped her fingers against the book. How could her mother be married to someone for five years and know so little about him? "He has. He sold it."

Lydia's expression fell, and she leaned against the bedframe, tugging the blanket up toward her chin. "I'm tired, darling. I don't think I want to be read to after all."

It's not my place to tell her. It's Lucius's. But Lucius wouldn't tell her, and Nora had grown tired of pretending all was well to save her mother from the distressing reality of the man she'd chosen to wed.

"Of course, but first you must know that Lucius has gambled away your money. All of it. He's lost the house and journal. He's been selling my jewels."

Lydia's pale lashes lay against her even paler cheeks. A shudder ran through her body, and then she grew still.

"Mother! Everything is gone."

Nothing so much as fluttered in recognition of Nora's exclamation. Her mother's words were slow and thin. "I'm sure Lucius will take care of everything, darling. Don't worry."

By the time Nora had set the book aside and stood, Lydia's chest rose and fell with the steady breaths of sleep.

Chapter Twenty-Nine

Nora peered past the fringed drapery and out onto the street. Leaves scattered the front yard, tripping and flipping in liberty, and the glass was cool beneath her hand. She might go to Cascadilla Falls. She could use some fresh air. Lucius had kept a fire burning in the parlor, saying her mother wasn't well and had woken in the night with chills and shivers.

Nora slipped her finger beneath her collar, swiping at the sweat slicking her clavicle. She turned from the window in time to see Lucius enter the room carrying a box straining beneath the weight of a hundred stamps.

"You've got a package." He dropped it on the small table beside the settee.

Nora hurried toward it. "It's from India," she said after studying the markings. She carefully untied the string and removed the brown paper wrapping. Lifting the lid, she saw a thick envelope and a cardboard box.

"What is it?" Lucius asked.

"I have no idea." She flipped open the envelope and pulled

out a stack of papers. As she shuffled through them, her heart stuttered. Page after page of wobbly script, transcribed from her notes on her butterfly—the habits she managed to observe the two times she studied it alive, the mimicry it managed so well, the differences between it and the *Delias eucharis*. And, on the final page, a perfectly illustrated image of the butterfly, so lifelike that Nora thought that if she touched the paper, the wings would flutter and the insect lift off the page.

"It's my butterfly," she whispered, her nose beginning to burn. She lifted the small cardboard box and read the note attached to the top.

Akka,

Before you left for Madras, Owen told me all of your work had been destroyed. I'm sending you the copies I made. I hope it helps you. I must confess, I stole the first butterfly you found. I thought it might remind me of you, but I think you need it more. My aunt sent me my things, care of Swathi, and I've only now received them. I hope it's not too late.

I love you.
Sita

"Oh, Sita." With shaking hands, Nora removed the box's lid, and on a bed of cotton sat her beautiful stained-glass butterfly. A tear dripped from her nose and splashed against the box.

She looked up at Lucius, who still stood over her. "A butterfly from India?" he asked.

She nodded.

"What is it?"

Nora dropped her eyes to the insect again, but all she saw was Sita. Her wide smile and flashing eyes and dimples that winked so often. Sita, who had placed on Nora the burden of sacrificial love.

"It's a *Prioneris sita*." The name felt right. Greek for "sawtooth," which described the markings on the wings, and Sita for the friend who had shown her that some things were more important than success.

~~~~~

Nora raced up the stairs of White Hall, clutching Sita's box to her chest. When she reached the second floor, she paused and sucked in a deep breath to calm her racing pulse. Then she burst through the open door of Professor Comstock's office.

His snores filled the room—a small feat, given how little space was left from the books stacked in precarious piles on the floor and boxes of various sizes covering every available surface.

Nora picked her way across the room and sat in the chair beside his. She watched his dear, familiar face for a moment and smiled. His wheezy exhales fluttered his mustache, and the gold, wire-rimmed spectacles sat askew on his nose. This man had impacted her nearly as much as her own father, and she wanted to make him proud. Maybe she still could.

"Professor Comstock."

He sputtered and blinked. Sitting up straight, he immediately grasped the pen that had spilled ink over the paper on his desk and began writing. "When the *Corydalus* hatches—"

Nora laughed. "Professor Comstock."

He jerked his head toward her. "Nora! How long have you been there?"

"Not long. I have something I need to show you."

He sat back, and she gently laid the box in front of him. He pushed his glasses up the bridge of his nose and lifted the lid. When he pulled Sita's illustration from the stack, he looked at her with round eyes and released a short puff of air. "Is this what I think it is?"

She nodded. "I named it *Prioneris sita*."

"An appropriate name, I think." He looked at her, and his face glowed with approval. Of the find, the name, or her, Nora didn't know. She hoped it was the latter.

As he looked through Sita's transcribed notes, grunting his interest, Nora sat with bated breath. His thoughts meant everything.

He set the notes and illustrations aside and opened the sample box. "You have made quite a discovery. No wonder no one has noticed it before now. It's an excellent mimic of the *Delias eucharis*. A lesser scientist wouldn't have seen the differences."

"I realized after Frederic told me that the *eucharis* doesn't mud-puddle that I needed to study it further." She pointed to the hind wings. "And see how the orange spots on the underside of the wings are blunted? The *eucharis* has pointed spots. When I observed them mating, the *sita* flew rapidly and with great passion, quite unlike the Jezebel."

Professor Comstock laughed. "The best males of all species are passionate, are they not?"

Nora's only experience with the males of her species had proved her inadequacy in judging whether or not passion proved superior. She'd rejected Owen's passion and felt certain he'd never demonstrate it again. At least not toward her.

She ignored the knot tying up her insides and focused on the hope that had flown back into her heart with the arrival of the package. "Uncle John?"

He looked at her with a soft smile. "You haven't called me that since your freshman year."

"I felt it more respectful to address you as Professor when you became my teacher, but I'm done with school now, and I've missed you as my uncle. I'm asking you now, as my uncle, do you think I still have a chance to make a career in entomology?"

Uncle John shook his head, and the corners of his eyes crinkled. "You've always had a chance, Nora."

"I know I've lost any opportunity for the scholarship. And I won't get my master's. The journal is gone." Her words grew thick. "But maybe I can publish my findings in a different journal and still pursue what I love."

She knew not everyone had the opportunity to do what they

loved. She doubted Pallavi wanted to cook and clean for scientists, and Swathi wasn't happy working with British missionaries—though hopefully the baby would bring her joy—but Nora hoped she might still have a chance to be a woman who forged a path in science.

"I'm certain you've made a discovery that any publication would be thrilled to accept. Just because you offended a few men on the school board doesn't mean your career is over. You might still be able to get your master's, so don't give that up just yet."

"I can't afford it. And Lucius is moving us to Long Island."

He patted her hand. "There are other ways, Nora. I worked on campus in exchange for tuition and board, though I don't think that option is open to women yet."

"I'm not sure it would be a good idea. As much as I don't want to move, there is someone here who might not want to see me for another two years even more." She dropped her head and whispered, "I hurt Owen."

Uncle John leaned toward her and tipped up her chin. His eyes, full of warmth and love, reminded her of her father's, and Nora had never missed him so much as in this moment. "Don't forget your male butterfly, my dear. Passion is a beautiful thing to behold, and it isn't discouraged, or dismissed, so easily."

Nora pulled him into an impulsive hug, then began gathering her things together in an effort to hide her blush. As she passed through the doorway, a familiar scent caused her eyes to slide shut. She tightened her hold on her box, its splintered edges biting into her forearms. She felt Owen's presence before he spoke, and when he touched her cheek, she exhaled a shuddering breath.

She didn't open her eyes. Didn't speak. She held her regret as tightly as she held her future, tucked into a box shipped halfway around the world.

His breath caressed her face. "Professor Comstock is right."

After his lips brushed her cheek, the door clicked shut, and Nora stood alone in the hallway, nursing the hope his touch and words had sparked.

Chapter Thirty

A light drizzle had started as soon as Nora left White Hall. It cooled her burning skin—the place where Owen's lips had just barely grazed—and frizzed her hair. By the time she'd crested the hill and tramped up the drive to the house, her hair had escaped its knot and fallen in matted clumps across her shoulders. As soon as she entered the house, she darted up the stairs toward her room, hoping she could convince Alice to draw a bath. A long soak in rose-scented water would go far in cleaning the stickiness from her skin and easing her troubled mind.

She slid into her room, stopping inside the door when she noticed Alice riffling through the armoire. A trunk lay open beside her on the floor.

"What are you doing?" Nora asked. She made quick work of removing her boots and scooted back so that she lay flat on her bed. She closed her eyes, enjoying the cushioned comfort of her mattress.

"Lucius told me to begin packing your things."

Nora bolted upright. Alice continued to hum, pulling jackets from their hangers and folding them into neat packets to tuck into the trunk. She turned and held up an old work dress, its tan-and-moss-sprigged pattern faded and so ugly that even Nora refused to wear it. "Do you still want this?"

Nora shook her head. "It'll be good for rags. Why did Lucius tell you to pack my things?"

Alice shrugged. "He said you were leaving next week with Ms. Martha for Long Island."

The room grew stuffy, and Nora's vision swam. Blinking, she fisted the duvet and tried to make sense of Alice's words.

Her agreement with Lucius. No complaints.

But that was before Professor Comstock had brought up other possibilities. Before she'd discovered the *Prioneris sita* and realized she could launch her career even without the scholarship. Before she'd decided she wanted more time with Owen.

Now she knew that losing the journal hurt less than losing Owen. And maybe that was her father's greatest legacy—not a scientific periodical, but the capacity to love unreservedly.

And a willingness to sacrifice what was most important for *who* was most important.

Hair and bath forgotten, Nora leapt from the bed and tore down the stairs. She found Lucius in his office, prodding the fire with a poker, Martha working on embroidery in a nearby chair.

Nora paused in the doorway and forced herself to pace her breathing. After twenty seconds, her heart stopped crashing against her rib cage, and she thought she might be able to speak without sounding like a madwoman.

She rapped on the door. "Lucius?"

He waved her in but continued to eye the Lilliputian fire. Nora crossed the room and waited for his attention.

"How are you this morning, dear?" Martha asked. She jabbed the needle through the linen with more force than necessary, and the thread tangled.

"Fine."

Lucius set the poker against the hearth and faced them. "What is it, Nora?"

Martha tugged at her thread, drawing it into a hopeless knot. She grunted and bit it off. "I don't know why I continue to attempt these pointless triflings." She set the fabric aside and turned a shining face up toward Nora. "I'm so looking forward to your company. There is a lovely suffragette group in Queens County. Oyster Bay is a wonderful place to live. You'll have plenty to keep you occupied."

Nora smiled at her aunt. "It sounds very nice, and I do enjoy your company, Aunt Martha, but I want to stay here and continue my education at Cornell."

Lucius frowned. "I thought they offered the scholarship to someone else."

"They did," Nora said, her voice wavering, "but I'd like the chance to stay in Ithaca and see if I can find work."

He crossed his arms. "We had a plan. You'll move in with Martha. I will seek employment elsewhere, and your mother and I will settle somewhere . . . not on Long Island." He sent Martha a tight smile. "With your help, of course, sister."

Martha sent Nora a secretive look, then cleared her throat. "I thought you'd like to be a part of the movement, Nora. We could use an intelligent, passionate woman like you. With your help, women could have the vote in the next few years! Just think, we might help the next president be elected."

Nora dropped her eyes. She hated to disappoint her aunt, who had been encouraging and kind to her, but she didn't want marches and ribbons and jail. "It's not what I want to do, Aunt." She looked back up. "I'm sorry to disappoint you."

Martha's face fell, but she nodded. "What do you want to do?"

"Whatever you want to do," Lucius said, "do it on Long Island."

Martha shot him a withering look and smiled at Nora, encouraging her to answer.

Nora inhaled, steadying herself. "I want to get my master's, publish my findings in a journal, and . . . get married." She bit down on her lower lip so hard, she winced.

Martha raised her brows. "I would advise against the last bit."

A soft smile teased Nora's mouth, blooming when Owen's face drifted into focus. "The man I want to marry is marvelous. Not at all cruel."

"Marry him on Long Island," Lucius muttered.

"I'm not sure why you intend to hold me to our agreement, Lucius. You won't be here anymore, so why do you care where I live?"

He shot her a withering glare. "I have your best interest at heart."

She blinked, and a laugh brimming with disbelief bubbled up. "You're joking."

"I'm not. Continuing your education will put even more fool-hardy ideas into your head, and you will cause your mother no end of grief. As much as I enjoyed living without you, your time in India devastated her. I will try to find a position first in New York City. That way you can visit her when she needs you. Ithaca is too far for her peace of mind."

"Stop being so dramatic, Lucius," Martha said. She looked at Nora and picked up her embroidery again. Squinting, she tried to slip the thread through the needle. "I hope you won't be sacrificing your career for your young man."

"I've realized there's more than one path to seeing a dream fulfilled." She'd pinned all her hopes on the scholarship and the journal, but Uncle John had shown her another possibility. And, undistracted by the only thing she'd thought about since before she left for India, she could remember Owen more clearly. Who he was. How he'd encouraged her every step of the way. His support.

He'd been right. The journal had been a weight around her neck, forcing her to ignore the things she really wanted in favor of misplaced obligation. She hated losing it because it felt like she'd lost her father all over again. But she hadn't. Her father wasn't that journal, just like her dreams weren't wrapped up in it.

Owen wouldn't expect her to sit by the fire and produce mediocre embroidery while *he* researched and discovered. He'd never once indicated that was what he wanted. She'd been too obstinate, clinging to someone else's dream, to see that.

Lucius lifted the poker again and shoved it into the cracking, popping flames. "It doesn't matter what he wants or what you want, Nora. You gave me your word. You're going to Long Island."

Nora sat on the end of her bed and stared at the trunk occupying the space where her father's insect cabinet used to stand. Mother had it removed after Lucius had burned all of the drawers.

Now Lucius had made another decision that changed things. Except Nora couldn't escape this one. Professor Comstock hadn't approached her with another Asian research project, and she was to leave for Long Island in a few days. And it would be selfish to grieve her mother. Besides, Nora had agreed to Lucius's terms.

But that decision felt like it had been made ages ago by a different person.

Nora sighed and stood. She pulled her coat from the armoire, shrugged it on, and grabbed her fur-lined gloves. Maybe life with Martha would be interesting and fulfilling. Maybe she could transfer all of the passion she had for entomology into a new cause—suffrage. She cared about women and the vote—of course she did—but it didn't thrill her like field research.

Not teaching or writing or illustrating . . . but field research.

She paused in her path to the door and clutched the gloves to her chest. She loved field research. Loved searching and discovering and studying. She didn't want to be a teacher. Didn't want to run a journal, though losing it still stung.

What she wanted, what she dreamed of in those moments she allowed her mind to wander, was a shola forest or a jungle. Humidity so heavy it crawled between the layers of her clothing. Food that burned her tongue and people who seared their way into her heart. Sunsets she couldn't replicate with a thousand pots of paint. Insects the size of her hand and a tent not much larger than a cot.

They had been right. Professor Comstock, who told her she was made for something other than teaching. Owen, who stubbornly clung to his insistence she belonged in the field. Even William, who said she had the heart of an explorer.

A laugh escaped her tight chest, and she absently rubbed the ribbon on her cuff. They'd known her better than she had known herself. They'd seen her and told her. But only losing everything else had shown her the truth of it.

If only she hadn't lost Owen in the process of finding herself.

The clock in the library struck the third hour. She'd be late. Nora slid her dangling Indian earrings into her piercings, set her hat upon her head, and dashed down the stairs.

"Where are you off to?" Martha called from the parlor.

Nora backtracked and stuck her head into the room. "Owen was asked to give a lecture in honor of receiving the scholarship. I'm going to watch and tell him good-bye."

She departed on quick feet, eager to leave thoughts of her future in her packed-up room.

Despite recent rain and the risk of mud, she ran through the cemetery, shaving ten minutes from her trip to Library Hall. By the time she arrived, muck spattered the hem of her skirt and her hat had slipped from her head, whacking against the back of her neck with every step. She stopped inside the building to put the hat back where it belonged and catch her breath before sneaking into the crowded auditorium.

"Nora, I'm glad you've come." Owen's voice traveled over the audience's heads.

She paused in the aisle, aware that every eye had turned

toward her and that her hat had slipped off again and now hung from the bow tied around her neck. She yanked at it until the ribbon came undone, and wiggled her fingers at him in a wave. Then she slammed the hat back onto her head and tied the ribbon into a bow so tight, it wouldn't come loose save with a pair of scissors.

She'd kill Owen for drawing attention to her like this. Surely she wasn't the only one late. She crept toward a row, intent on an empty seat.

"I was lucky to work with Nora Shipley in India. While there, she discovered a species that has never been studied before."

Nora stopped short of sitting and stared at Owen over the heads of a hundred people. A cold sweat broke out along her spine. The *Prioneris sita* was her discovery. She'd planned to reveal its existence in a submission to a scientific journal. She wanted to be the first to share it with people. Hadn't Owen received enough? How could he do this to her?

She clenched her jaw and decided to leave. She couldn't be here while he stole her last chance at redeeming herself.

His voice stopped her. "Nora, will you please join me onstage?"

Whispers filled the room as everyone wondered what Owen meant to do. She shook her head and opened her mouth, but there were no words. Only disjointed questions and the realization that everyone was staring at her, waiting for her to do something. Owen watched her as well, a boyish smile and outstretched arm beckoning her to the stage.

She didn't know his intention, but she wouldn't give in to it. She stepped back into the aisle and turned toward the exit. It would be a public insult, ignoring his invitation, one the student body would talk about long after she left Cornell and Ithaca.

She glanced at Owen once more, taking a moment to store up his image in her mind. He beckoned again and even took a step toward the edge of the stage.

Everything they'd shared filled the blank spaces in her mind, and the words came. So many words. Words she couldn't say because they would reveal her feelings for him in a very indecent, public way. And she wanted to be publicly humiliated even less than she wanted to humiliate him.

She took a deep breath, straightened her posture, and walked up the aisle. After she climbed the short set of stairs to the stage, Owen took her elbow and motioned toward her, eliciting polite applause from the crowd. Nora saw President White sitting in the front row between Professor Comstock, who grinned at her, and the men on the scholarship committee, who looked perplexed.

Owen pushed her forward. "I'd like to give Nora the opportunity to share with you her discovery of an interesting and previously unstudied butterfly."

"What are you doing?" she whispered.

Owen gave her ribbon a solid yank and plucked the hat from her head, setting it on the dais. "Giving you a chance, Phenomenon."

She swiveled to look at him, her earrings swaying. "A chance to publicly fail?"

He put his hand on her shoulder and bent so that his words were only for her. "Fail? You? Unlikely." Then he motioned her to the lectern, winked, and jogged down the steps.

Nora swallowed and slowly crossed the stage. Atop the lectern, she spied a pile of paper. When she lifted the first sheet, in Owen's even, broad print, she saw everything they'd discussed about the *Prioneris sita* while sweating beneath the glaring sun and sipping from metal cups of spiced tea.

His notes had been written from memory—they demonstrated none of the linear, organized approach of her own. But enough information was there to help her with an impromptu speech.

She pressed her lips together, but that didn't stop the slow spread of her smile, and she looked at Owen, who now sat in the front row, grinning back at her the way she loved best.

With a short nod, she riffled through the papers and settled on the focus of her presentation. "The more you're exposed to a thing, the more you accept it. And because of that, we sometimes miss the little details that could reveal something bigger than our expectations allow."

Like Owen, whom she'd always thought to be obnoxious and shallow. She'd missed the depth of his heart. The beauty in his character.

"The *Delias eucharis* is common in India. It's a butterfly known to every entomologist, well-studied and understood. We saw them everywhere and never paid them a moment's attention. Because of that, we almost missed out on what might be the greatest discovery of my career. The Common Jezebel isn't alone with its stained-glass-window wings. It has a mimic, one that has never been noticed by researchers because its differences are so subtle, it takes close inspection to recognize them."

Her heart eased its pace as she pressed into the subject. She chanced a glance at Owen, who sat on the edge of his seat, elbows on his knees and hands loosely folded together. Her breath caught at the expression on his face, and her eyes watered. He was celebrating this moment. Proud of her and what she'd accomplished. Thrilled by her success.

"But when you realize what you've found, you know everything has changed. And that's what happened when I discovered a butterfly with orange spots on its hind wing shaped like squares instead of arrows. When I first saw the differences between the Common Jezebel and my own *Prioneris sita*."

Chapter Thirty-One

Nora snuggled deeper into the settee's cushions the next day and tried to focus on the book in her lap.

She didn't think her speech could have gone any better had she prepared for it. Afterward, while everyone stood and applauded, she had raced down the steps of the stage, having every intention of making a spectacle of herself and Owen, but she'd been thronged by undergrads and professors wanting to know more about this new butterfly. She hadn't been able to resist them, and the discussions swallowed the whole of her attention. When she found herself alone again, Owen had gone, and she was left to walk home by herself, wondering when she'd see him again. Hoping he knew how much she needed to talk to him.

"Nora," her mother said, gliding into the parlor, "I'm hosting an impromptu dinner, a going-away party, if you will, tomorrow evening, and—"

"Oh, Mother, please don't. Have you forgotten what happened at the last one?" Nora's chest caved in at the thought of sitting through another of those awful affairs.

"I'm sure you won't allow that to happen again." Lydia tapped the end of a pen against her teeth. "I wondered if you might like to invite some friends, since you're leaving the day after."

Nora groaned. "Fine. Just Bitsy and Rose. And the Comstocks."

A knock sounded at the door, and they heard Alice cross the house to answer it.

Nora's mother sat beside her. "Now, let's discuss the menu."

Nora closed her book—a fascinating look into spider webs around the world—and set it on the table beside her. Her mother wouldn't leave her alone until they'd organized all the details. Menus and seating plans trumped everything. At least in her mother's world.

"Ma'am," Alice said with a light rap on the parlor door.

Nora's mother rose from the settee. "President White. Gentlemen."

Nora jumped to her feet, not nearly as gracefully as her mother. But then, she rarely accomplished that. She dipped her head in acknowledgment.

The men cleared their throats and looked at each other before Professor Comstock stepped forward. "Nora, Owen has decided not to accept the scholarship after all."

Her mouth dropped, and her mother pinched the back of her arm. Nora snapped her lips closed and fiddled with the cicada brooch pinned to her collar. "I had no idea."

"He told us yesterday after the lecture." Professor Comstock gave her a warm smile, so in contrast to the other men's sober expressions.

Nora's mother stepped closer to her and subtly squeezed her elbow. Nora released the brooch, dropped her arm to her side, and forced her lips into a smile. Behind the folds of their bustled skirts, though, her mother clasped her hand, and Nora's heart pounded against her chest.

"Why would he give it up?" Nora asked. He'd have to return to New York City—which would actually make him closer, since she'd be living on Long Island. But his father might send him to law school. Were there any law schools in New York City?

Professor Comstock shook his head. "He didn't say. He only told me that he'd discovered something he wanted more than the scholarship."

President White cleared his throat. "We were impressed with your presentation yesterday, even more so when Owen told us he hadn't informed you in advance that he was going to call upon you. You were succinct yet thorough in your delivery of the subject, and you demonstrated an admirable understanding of the butterfly's habits. Everyone was enthralled."

Another man stepped past President White and grabbed his lapels as though about to make a decree. Nora recognized him as a member of the school board and the scholarship director. "We believe we may have been too hasty in dismissing you from competing for the scholarship, and after your outstanding work yesterday, we'd like to offer it to you, Nora. We'd be delighted, actually, to have such a scientist continue her education at Cornell."

Nora's hand grew slick in her mother's grip. They both knew what this meant. Nora wouldn't have to leave Ithaca, after all. She could stay and finish her degree. It was too late to save the journal, but her career was another matter altogether.

A week after Nora received news of the scholarship, she sat on her bed, organizing watercolor pots, paper, and brushes. Lifting up a beautifully illustrated book of upstate New York's insects, flora, and fauna, she flipped through the pages. Sita would enjoy it, and it would give her a glimpse into Nora's world. The purple-stemmed asters and bluebirds would seem as exotic to Sita as the birds and flowers of India had been to Nora. She wrapped the book in a handkerchief she had talked her mother into embroidering—a little stained-glass-window butterfly in the corner—and tucked everything into the small crate.

Nora unpinned the cicada brooch from her bodice and turned it over in her hand. She ran her thumb over the jewel-encrusted insect and felt the smooth chill of its rounded thorax before pressing a kiss to it. Then she snuggled it into the crate beside the book. Sita had done more for her than the brooch, and Nora's memories of her father weren't attached to any one thing.

Not a piece of jewelry, nor a magazine.

Once everything was packed up, Nora carried the crate outside, intent on seeing it delivered safely to the post office. She breathed in the scent of decaying leaves and the promise of winter. It smelled nice. Familiar.

But a sense of homesickness pricked her.

Which was odd, because Ithaca was home.

Maybe because she'd just spent hours putting together Sita's package, but Nora found herself hoping to catch a sniff of jasmine. Of spiced tea and sandalwood.

She shifted the crate, easing the pinch of it against her arms, and hiked through the cemetery, skirting her father's grave. But from the corner of her eye, she saw a movement. She stopped and squinted in the direction of the headstone. Someone knelt there, head bowed, and Nora tightened her grip on the package.

She needed to get to the post office, but she shuffled off the paved path and down the dirt one she hadn't walked since the funeral. The man—she could tell from his low voice—murmured words. A prayer, maybe? She couldn't make them out. She inched toward him, craning her neck forward, trying to hear.

But he heard her first and turned.

"Owen?" Nora knit her brows together. "What are you doing?"

He stood and brushed bits of dirt from his knees. Offering her a sheepish smile, he said, "Only visiting."

She shifted the crate in her arms, so many words twisting together in her mind, refusing to leave her mouth. "The trustees . . . I . . ."

His lips twitched before transforming into a smile. "You're welcome."

"Your father will make you go to law school now. Why did you give it up?"

"I like entomology, Nora, but I like you a lot more, and you *love* the science. It's everything to you." He rubbed his hand through his hair, making the cowlick stand straight up. "It didn't seem right that I should take something that so obviously belongs to you. But I will take that box. Are you headed to the post office?"

She nodded. "But to President White's first." She slipped her hand beneath Owen's jacket and into his vest pocket. He inhaled a quick breath as she pulled out his pocket watch. "I have to go," she said, tucking it back where it belonged.

He held her hand over his middle for a moment and leaned his forehead against hers. "You can't just do something like that and then leave."

"But my meeting." She drew her lip between her teeth to keep a smile from breaking free.

He sighed and stepped back, took the box from her, and jerked his chin toward the cemetery gate. "I'll accompany you."

They walked in silence for a few minutes, giving her time to settle her nerves. To get used to walking beside Owen again. "Why were you really at my father's grave?"

His eyes skittered toward her, then away again. "I was just thinking."

"About what?"

They were passing a copse of oak trees, its canopy shading the sidewalk, and he put a hand on her arm. "Wait."

He looked at her. Really looked at her, his eyes, she was sure, seeing everything. Seeing deep into her heart. She dropped her lashes and looked at the buttons on his coat.

He tipped her chin up with his finger. Once he'd recaptured her gaze, he trailed his finger up the ridge of her jaw, all the way to her temple and into the mound of hair above her ear. He tugged, pulling out a curl. "I was wondering if I'd ever be the sort of man you could respect as much as you do your father."

Nora remembered the male *Prioneris sita* and its unfailing bid to win its mate. It danced as most Indians did—with a passion and urgency that embarrassed Western sensibilities.

Owen hadn't given up.

Her knees trembled, and she leaned into him. Owen let go of her hair and cupped her face. He shifted the crate onto his hip so he could pull her closer.

"I know I can't make my father happy, and if I'm being honest, getting my master's won't make me happy. But you, Nora . . . I could make you happy. It's your happiness I want more than anything."

Goose bumps rose over her arms and legs and every inch of her skin. He kissed the tip of her nose, but nothing more, and Nora resented the carriages and carts and people in the street. She wished for the leafy branches of a cluster fig tree and the stillness of a humid night. She wished she didn't have to meet President White and could tell Owen that she'd fallen even more in love with him than she had her career.

This wasn't the place, though. So she settled for something less romantic but more necessary.

"I'm sorry. I'm sorry for getting angry at you without even finding out what had happened. I'm sorry I held you to a higher standard than I'd even hold myself. I'm sorry I've been distant when I've only wanted you near." She chanced pressing a kiss to his mouth. One that was too brief. "You are every bit as wonderful a man as my father, and I couldn't respect you any more than I already do."

She just made her appointment. With Owen shooing her on and promising to meet her afterward with her crate, she held a hand against her hat and ran the rest of the way to President White's rambling home.

She sat in his well-appointed office, gripping the armrests of a carved chair and forcing shallow breaths that fit beneath the corset compressing her lungs. If nothing else, she wanted to return to Asia so she could shrug off the odious thing and run without risk of fainting.

She pulled the creased note from her reticule, smoothing out the wrinkles with her fingertips as she reread the brief message.

Please come see me this afternoon at 2 p.m.

Pres. White

Nothing about why he wanted to meet. No indication of the topic he wanted to discuss. She forced her back straight, off the chair, shoulders low and chin high. If she didn't feel confident, she could still look the part.

President White entered the room with a throat-clearing cough, and she slid the note back into her bag. "Nora, how wonderful you came."

He circled the desk and sat behind it, smoothing his hand over his long, scraggly muttonchops. Nora thought his kind face looked rapturous today. His wide smile settled her jumping pulse. Surely he wouldn't offer her terrible news with a grin.

President White settled his folded hands atop his neat desk. "The university has acquired *The Journal of Eastern Flora and Fauna*."

Nora's ears buzzed, and she gave a slow shake of her head. "I'm sorry?"

His voice floated toward her as though coming through a dense fog. "Your father was a much-beloved member of the Cornell community. When we discovered Lucius was selling the journal, we decided the school would purchase it and turn it into a student-run magazine. Everything was finalized yesterday."

Nora released a silent prayer of gratitude on a soft sigh.

"President White, I generally don't care for surprises, but this is the best type of unexpected news."

His smile softened, and he dipped his chin. "Your father was a great friend and one of the best teachers we've ever had here. We are honored to keep his legacy going. We'd like you to take on the role of chief editor. There is no one who will love it like you, and we know you'll see it is successful."

Nora pressed her hands to her chest, and a smile pushed at her cheeks. Then she laughed, relief spilling from her tense shoulders and wrinkled brow. "I'd be thrilled to accept that position. But I'd like to propose something."

"I'm listening."

"Cornell has a proud history of accepting female students from the very beginning. My father, too, believed in educating women. He instilled in me a passion for science that has grown during my years here as a student. I think we should make his publication the first female-run scientific journal. And I would only run it while pursuing my master's. In fact, I'd like the role of chief editor always to be awarded to a woman pursuing an advanced degree in science. As soon as I graduate, I'll hand it over to whomever you feel would best replace me."

And then she would be free to do what she loved best—explore and discover.

President White folded his hands and pressed his lips to his knuckles. Nora could imagine his thoughts. It had never been done, but Cornell was notorious for doing things that weren't done. Would there be enough women in the science program to run a periodical? Maybe this would draw more to the university. Could the magazine survive a constant revolving management? Of course, who else would pour more effort into it than someone whose career rested on its success? Nora silently countered each of the arguments she projected onto him.

Finally, after she'd exhausted herself in her one-sided debate, he nodded. "I believe your father would approve of that."

"Thank you, President White."

Already flipping through a stack of files, he offered her a distracted smile, and Nora knew his mind was elsewhere. She scampered from the room, her feet tapping out a happy tune against the wooden floor.

Owen waited for her on the front step, the crate nestled beneath his knees. When he heard the door open, he craned his neck to look behind him, then jumped to his feet. "Well?"

He stood two steps below her, and she was able to rest her hands on his shoulders and look straight into his face. "They bought it. The journal. Cornell bought my father's journal, and they asked *me* to run it. I told them I would, but only while I'm at school. Then it'll be time to pass it on to someone else." She patted his cheek, then danced down the steps. "There's so much to do! I'll have to find some women who will help me get it back to where it needs to be. Rose and Bitsy for sure. Then I'll need to contact those scientists who have previously submitted and let them know about the change in ownership. Definitely address the issue of selling commissions. That's going to stop right away." She ticked off her tasks on her fingers.

Behind her, Owen laughed. "One thing at a time. Let's go to the post office first so I can put this down. What's in this thing, anyway?"

"Mostly art supplies for Sita." She still hadn't told anyone about Sita—not even Bitsy or Rose. She didn't know if she ever would. Her memories of India, of Sita and Pallavi and Swathi, were shrouded in an otherworldly haze, as though it had all happened decades ago and not months. She didn't want to tear the veil away and see everything in sharp clarity. It felt right—looking back as though at a dream. But she was glad to talk to Owen about it all. Glad they'd shared it together and he understood.

They crossed the street and walked up the post office steps. *Please let this package bring as much joy to Sita as she brought to me.*

Owen opened the door for her and allowed her to enter before following and setting the crate on the counter.

"Nora," Mrs. Brackett said, her wide smile flashing, "I have a letter for you that just arrived this morning." She turned toward the cubbies lining the back wall and pulled an envelope from one of them. "Here you go."

"Thank you." Nora rubbed her thumb over her father's friend's flowing script and the Filipino postmark. The envelope was too small to contain a specimen. Nora slipped her finger beneath the corner of the flap and edged it open.

Owen took the envelope and studied it with interest as Nora opened the letter.

"It's from Mrs. Martín, Father's old friend. She says her husband—he's a Spanish diplomat—connected her with a university in Spain that wants her to compile a collection of Filipino insects, including observances of their habits." Nora scanned the letter, then gasped and looked at Owen. "She wants me to join her."

His eyes widened. "In the Philippines? Nora, what an excellent opportunity for you."

She drew him out the post office door, away from Mrs. Brackett's curious eyes and ears. They walked for a few moments until they had passed the worst of the town crowds and their steps had taken them to campus. Except for the occasional tardy student hurrying between buildings, they were alone.

Nora looked down at the letter she still held, the invitation seared into her thoughts. *You could go.*

And she'd love it. She knew that. But so much had been given to her here. Everything she'd thought was lost. And the Philippines would be there when she graduated, as would all the insects waiting for discovery.

"I can't go." Her heart ached at the confession. It wasn't so difficult this time around to imagine herself wearing linen and chasing butterflies on foreign soil.

They found a bench beneath a maple tree, its fiery leaves clinging to their last moments of glory like faded debutantes. They sat close to each other, hips and thighs touching, an intimate position that sent heat through her despite the layers of clothing.

"Can you not go because of your mother?" he asked.

"No."

"Because of the journal?"

"No, though I am glad for the chance to turn it into something that will make my father proud."

He moved his leg so that his foot disappeared beneath her skirt and slid against her boot. "Because of the scholarship?"

"Not entirely, but don't think I take your sacrifice for granted."

"I never would." He took her hand, twining his fingers through hers. "You *love* fieldwork, Nora. You thrive on it. Why would you pass up this opportunity?"

"Two reasons. One, it's an opportunity that will be offered again, but I may never have the chance to obtain my degree if I give up the scholarship. And two . . ." She stared straight ahead, her eyes feasting on the line of trees that held a sunset in their branches. If only she had her paints, she could capture the essence before it slipped from her, turning into morning mist and barely remembered dreams.

"And two," he prodded.

She faced him, and his fingers found the tender place behind her neck. They stroked the words from her. "Two is . . . you."

"I'm going home, though." He teased a curl free and pressed his lips to the spot it hung from.

She suppressed a shudder. "I don't think you should. Go home, that is."

"What do you think I should do?"

"Stay here. Get your master's with me. You can work on campus in exchange for tuition. Professor Comstock did it."

"And room and board? My father's made it clear that he won't pay for me to get an advanced degree in anything other than law."

"My room and board are covered through the scholarship."

He thrust his fingers into the hair at the nape of her neck and leaned so close, his warm breath fanned her face. "That's progressive even for you, Peculiar."

"It's not progressive if we're married." She closed the space between them—it didn't take much—and pressed her lips to his. "Marry me," she whispered against them.

"I'm supposed to ask you that."

"It didn't take the first time. And you know I'm unconventional."

He pulled back. "Are you sure?"

She pressed her fingers to her lips and nodded. "More sure than I am about anything else I've decided."

"We'll marry and go to school together, and in two years we'll go back into fieldwork? Either in the Philippines if your friend needs help or elsewhere?"

"Yes. I'd much rather travel with you than alone. I'd rather do anything with you than alone."

Owen grinned. "I think you just need someone to keep you from falling out of trees."

"Is that a yes?"

"Yes, Percipient, I'll marry you. And I'll stay here with you or go there with you. I'll defend you against priggish Brits and mating cockroaches and Asian wrestlers. You," Owen said, cupping her cheek, "are the only thing I've ever wanted with desperate, wholehearted, can't-ignore-it passion. And maybe that's why everything else seemed so dull and uninspiring. You stole every bit of my interest and attention with a frantic dance on a classroom chair."

She leaned forward and kissed him again.

~⁓~

Nora lifted the cardboard box from the top drawer of her dresser. She carefully removed the lid and found the bee she'd been able to save from Lucius's inferno all those months ago. Her last tenuous link to the joys and beauty of her childhood. She tipped the bee into her palm, and its fuzz prickled her skin.

"Little Bumble Bea, look at me."

Nora tore her eyes from the bee she'd just finished mounting and, sticking the end of one braid in her mouth, obeyed him.

He tilted her chin and smiled, his eyes crinkling in the corners. Nora sucked at her hair, tugging strands between her teeth. "Bees are interesting creatures. They work hard and are dutiful. But do you know what's most interesting about them?"

She shook her head.

"Bumblebees will travel miles from their hives in order to do what they need to do. They don't stay close to home." He gave her a sad look Nora didn't understand.

But now she thought she did. "You thought I might leave Ithaca one day, didn't you, Papa?"

"That's not what your mother has told me."

Nora closed her hand around the bee at Lucius's voice. She turned and pressed her back against the dresser.

He stepped into her bedroom. "She said President White has offered you the scholarship after all." He crossed his arms and cleared his throat, the sound rumbling from his chest. "It has all worked out in the end, though, because my sister just informed me that she won't give me the money I need to reestablish myself. Instead she will have us move in with her. She knows the head of a private school for the wealthy. It seems he supports the suffragettes"—Lucius grimaced—"and he is looking for a science teacher."

"That is a step down from your previous position, is it not?"

His face sagged, and he dropped his arms. "I have little choice."

Nora's fingers twitched, and she thought she might touch his arm in a gesture of sympathy. But she didn't. "I *am* considering a position that will take me far from Ithaca, but it won't be until after I finish school." She'd sent a letter to Mrs. Martín, letting her know she'd be able to join her in her work in two years. And if she no longer needed help, well, Nora knew there were lots of places on earth waiting to be explored. So many insects needing to be studied. She and Owen would find them.

"I hope you're not planning to go too far. Your mother is already upset at the thought of us on Long Island and you at school here in Ithaca. She wouldn't like for you to be even farther away."

No, she wouldn't. But could Nora live her life worrying about her mother's desire that she stay nearby? Lydia was, after all, a married woman and should be relying on her husband to meet her needs. "I believe it might be good for Mother—and you—if I kept some distance for a while . . . wherever I end up."

Lucius licked his lips. His eyes darted from her and back again before he nodded. "Yes. That might be a good idea."

Mother had married a man Nora could hardly abide, but maybe, with the gift of privacy, Lucius might become a man she could respect a little. If Nora wasn't available to meet Mother's emotional needs, she would be forced to rely on her husband. And that could make all the difference in a man like Lucius— a man afraid of never measuring up. Nora, with her constant reminders that he was nothing like her father, had done her mother no favors. In the end, Nora's harsh comparisons only further distanced her from the one man who could bring her mother peace.

Lucius took a few steps backward, then paused at the door. "No matter what decision you come to, I believe your father would be proud of you."

He slipped into the hallway, leaving Nora standing with her mouth agape.

She unclenched her hand and looked at the bumblebee. "Sometimes the most foreign things happen in the most familiar places."

Chapter
Thirty-Two

Darling, I think I'd like to see Cascadilla Falls."

Nora paused in her packing and looked up at her mother, who stood in the doorway of her bedroom. She tipped her head and looked for signs of delirium on her mother's face, but couldn't find any. Her mother appeared lucid. In fact, she looked almost robust.

Lydia took a tentative step into Nora's room. "I think, since we are leaving for Long Island soon, I should see it."

Nora folded the shirtwaist in her hands and laid it atop the others already neatly tucked into her trunk. Tomorrow she and Owen would wed in front of her family, his parents—who had agreed to attend, though reluctantly—and a few close friends. Then they'd move into their new home. School started in a few weeks, and Nora wanted to settle into married life before studies and work consumed her time. She had a lot to do.

But her mother was watching her with large, timid eyes and looked ready to bolt at the slightest provocation. It was time she saw the place her husband had died.

The walk to Cascadilla Falls wasn't strenuous and normally took Nora less than fifteen minutes, but she and her mother walked at a more sedate pace, taking frequent breaks to admire icicles hanging from gabled roofs and naked trees.

Lydia took Nora's arm as they passed beneath the tree canopy and plunged into the woods. Silence enveloped them, turning the worn, pitted path they traveled into an aisle and the brush and saplings surrounding them into a nave. The cold had frozen the water, and there was no warning that they had drawn near. No happy gurgling sound. No roar. Lydia gasped as they cleared the trees and the falls loomed before them—an icy sanctuary that required reverence and respect.

"This is where . . ." Lydia looked around, and her chin trembled.

Nora pointed high above them, at the tree standing as a marker beside the falls. "There."

Lydia didn't look. Instead she turned to Nora and grasped her hands. Her eyes filled with tears, but she tipped back her head and blinked until they dried up. She smiled, her lips trembling, and Nora knew her mother had more courage than she gave her credit for.

"Your father told me the day you were born that you were made for wondrous things. You never did conform to my expectations, and I'm so glad now. You're doing what he knew you would."

Warmth curled in Nora's belly even as her breath fogged the frozen air. "Will you be all right? I hate the thought of you leaving Ithaca. I wish Lucius hadn't decided you must leave. I wish he hadn't lost everything."

"Hush, darling. Don't speak of it."

"But it's the truth."

"You are pursuing your happiness. Let me have mine."

"In ignorance?"

Lydia sighed and released Nora's hands. She looked out over the falls, and a tear slipped down her cheek. "You are so like your father, always ferreting out truth and trying to understand. Despite his mistakes, Lucius has always been good to me. He does love me."

Nora looked up at the tree on the edge of the waterfall. Its limbs twisted toward heaven, as though reaching for something that would never be. "I wish Papa had never brought me here. I wish I hadn't climbed that tree."

"Sometimes," her mother whispered, "life makes choices for you. Other times you're the one choosing. But in the end, none of us really has much control. We can only do the best thing—the right thing—with what we've been given. That's what I tried to do when I married Lucius. I wanted you to have a father. I also wanted another chance at what I had with your father." She sniffed, then forced a quivering smile. "I'm proud of the path you've taken, Nora."

Nora gazed out over the falls, taking in the way the rocks stepped down as though a giant stonemason had used the waterfall as his staircase, the lichen and moss clinging to the sides of the crumbly limestone, the trees crowding around them. The willow oak that stood strong and erect above it all, its inside carved out by pests, a hollow reminder of Nora's most regretted choice.

Nothing buzzed or chirped or flew. Winter had sent everything into burrows and hibernation. But Nora could picture Cascadilla Falls in the spring, alive with activity and the busy work of insects and birds. She'd visit with Owen, bringing his ratty blanket and an adventure novel. By that time, they'd have stepped into their life. Would have discovered lovely and heartbreaking and difficult things.

Nora took her mother's arm, and they headed back toward town, down the path that led to Owen, her work, and the promise of every wispy dream tangling together in a mess of past and present, desire and sacrifice, waiting and going.

A strong wind sailed over the water that had spent thousands of years carving shale. It rustled the dry grass and knifed through her clothes. In it, Nora heard her father's voice.

"Little Bumble Bea, don't forget this most important lesson."

She stopped her study of the grasshopper and looked at Father. He'd given her many lessons, but never had he called any of them the most important. "Yes, Papa?"

He pressed her nose with the tip of his finger and smiled. "Just this—do you know what separates us from the insects?"

She shook her head.

"They do what's best because of instinct and habit. We do it because of love."

Nora smiled and squeezed her mother's arm. The most important lesson, indeed. One that took a trip across the world to learn. And coming home to understand.

AUTHOR'S NOTE

Dear Readers,

The idea for *A Mosaic of Wings* was sparked when my then eight-year-old daughter said, "Hey, Mom, why don't you write a book about a girl entomologist?" I'd already decided I was going to switch genres from contemporary romance to historical fiction, and I loved the thought of writing about one of the nineteenth-century female scientists who made an impact on history.

But I hated insects.

While researching, every time I'd search for "cockroach mating habits" or "largest spider in India," I'd cover my eyes and squint at the photos through my fingers. Eventually, though, I began to see God's incredible design and creativity in the subjects I was studying. I've dedicated this book to my daughter, who is now thirteen and still wants to be an entomologist, but also to every person who has loved these amazing creatures.

It's especially for Anna Comstock, who, with her husband, John, worked at Cornell University. I learned about Anna as a homeschooling mom who followed a Charlotte Mason philosophy of education. We Charlotte Mason homeschoolers love nature studies, and Anna's book *Handbook of Nature Study* is often referred to and much loved. Not only did Anna illustrate all of her husband's books, she also wrote and illustrated her own. She was instrumental in the nature study movement and became Cornell University's first female professor.

I did my best to portray Anna and John accurately. Of course, they died long ago, and I had to fill in the gaps as best I could. Any mistakes are completely my own, but I hope I've done justice to this wonderful and interesting couple. If you want to learn more about Anna, please read her nature study book, as well as the biography *The Comstocks of Cornell.*

Unlike my feelings for insects, I've loved India for decades. I had the opportunity to live there after high school, as well as visit more recently with a nonprofit I volunteer with. There is nowhere else in the world like India. It's a complex, layered, vibrant country that captures the imagination. It's a place you don't quickly forget, and you always want to return to. I hope you fall for it as madly as I did.

Writing about a culture you didn't grow up in, especially one as flexing and complicated as nineteenth-century India, is always an intimidating prospect. I did a massive amount of research, but there were times I couldn't find an answer and needed to make the most educated decision. My Indian friends and sensitivity reader were immensely helpful—but there were many conversations that ended with one of them saying, "I don't know, Kim. That was a hundred and fifty years ago." Any mistakes are mine, and I'm sincerely sorry for them.

I pray grace over any inconsistencies or errors.

—Kim

ACKNOWLEDGMENTS

So many people have been instrumental in my journey toward publication. So many have helped me bring *A Mosaic of Wings* to you. And since this is my first published novel, I'm going way back. So, thank you to:

Francine Rivers, who wrote *A Voice in the Wind*. I'd always loved books, but that specific book made me want to write them. Thank you, Mrs. Rivers, for honoring God with your creativity.

Mr. Posner, my eleventh grade creative writing and journalism teacher (we all have that one great teacher, right?). You were the first one to tell me I was talented. The first one to suggest I write a book (based on my autobiographical short story set in Ukraine). Different story, different place, but here it is. Your encouragement set me on this path.

My parents, for buying me a typewriter in high school, listening to my truly awful and melodramatic stories, and never telling me I needed a backup plan.

Joy, Flora, and Priya. Every memory I have of India is tangled with your presence. You made those six months full of relationship and pure joy.

Rachelle Gardner, my amazing agent. I still can't believe you signed me. The day you told me you loved my book was the day I began to think this farfetched dream of mine might be possible.

The amazing team at Bethany House Publishers. There were so many reasons BHP was at the top of my publisher wish list. I've not been disappointed. Your support, expertise, and hard work are appreciated. I could not have done this without you.

Jessica Barnes, my editor. Thank you for seeing what this story could be, for believing in it and bringing it to the table, for pouring so much time and energy into making it beautiful. You are everything an editor should be. God smiled on me when I snagged that Blue Ridge appointment.

Bob Nuhn, my "bug guy" and entomologist. I'm not exaggerating when I say this book would not have happened without you. Your excitement for the science, detail-packed emails, and patient responses to my questions permeate every bit of Nora's story. Thank you.

Madhu Balasubramaniam. God's hand was in our meeting. You have become a wonderful friend. Thank you for reading my book and helping me make it accurate, sensitive, and a reflection of my love for India. You are an answer to prayer and my middle-of-the-night cultural, religious, and geographical questions.

My friends and family who have encouraged, supported, and been excited for me. I can't name all of you, but know that I appreciate and love you.

Kristy Cambron. When you said, "Can you send Nora somewhere interesting? Somewhere overseas?" this book was born, and I'll forever be grateful. You encouraged me to write in the genre I love about the place I love.

Stephanie Gammon, my very first reader and sweet friend. Your support and unwavering belief in my writing are constant sources of validation and encouragement. You know me better than anyone outside my family, and the fact that you still love me makes me question your sanity but also value your friendship. I can't wait for the world to learn what a brilliant writer you are.

My girls—Lindsey Brackett, Leslie Devooght, Hope Welborn, and Kristi Ann Hunter. This journey has been made wonderful because of you. I love our Voxer chats, retreats, and Hangout meetings, and can't imagine doing any of this without you. I have to remind myself to hang out with people who actually live near me because our daily conversations make me forget I'm not actually seeing you.

My children—Ellie, Grainne, Hazel, and August. Everything I do, it's because of you. I want you to see in me the possibility of dreams coming true. Of hard work and diligence and effort and never, ever giving up. Of knowing who you are and what you're meant to do, then doing it.

My husband, Shane. This book is especially possible because of you. I love you for never giving up on my dream, even when I was too discouraged to believe in it. For spending all those evenings after work doing baths and dishes and math. For being generous with your time and our bank account so I could go to conferences and writing retreats and Panera more times than I can count. You are the inspiration for Owen—kind, supportive, adventurous, encouraging, annoyingly extroverted, and always willing to speak the truth in love. The only reason I can write a decent hero is because I've watched you be one for over twenty years. I love you.

Kimberly Duffy is a Long Island native currently living in southwest Ohio. When she's not homeschooling her four kids, she writes historical fiction that takes her readers back in time and across oceans. She loves trips that require a passport, recipe books, and practicing kissing scenes with her husband of twenty years. He doesn't mind. You can find her at www.kimberlyduffy.com.

Sign Up for Kimberly's Newsletter!

Keep up to date with Kimberly's latest news on book releases and events by signing up for her e-mail list at kimberlyduffy.com.

You May Also Like . . .

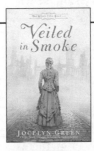

As Chicago's Great Fire destroys their bookshop, Meg and Sylvie Townsend make a harrowing escape from the flames with the help of reporter Nate Pierce. But the trouble doesn't end there—their father is committed to an asylum after being accused of murder, and they must prove his innocence before the asylum truly drives him mad.

Veiled in Smoke by Jocelyn Green, THE WINDY CITY SAGA #1
jocelyngreen.com

BETHANYHOUSE

Stay up to date on your favorite books and authors with our free e-newsletters. Sign up today at bethanyhouse.com.

facebook.com/bethanyhousepublishers   @bethanyhousefiction

Free exclusive resources for your book group at bethanyhouseopenbook.com

More from Bethany House

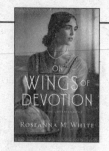

All of England thinks Phillip Camden a monster for the deaths of his squadron. As Nurse Arabelle Denler watches him every day, though, she sees something far different: a hurting man desperate for mercy. But when an old acquaintance shows up and seems set on using him in a plot that has the codebreakers of Room 40 in a frenzy, new affections are put to the test.

On Wings of Devotion by Roseanna M. White
THE CODEBREAKERS #2
roseannamwhite.com

Arabella Lawrence fled on a bride ship wearing the scars of past mistakes. Now in British Columbia, two men vying for her hand disagree on how the natives should be treated during a smallpox outbreak. Intent on helping a girl abandoned by her tribe, will Arabella have the wisdom to make the right decision, or will seeking what's right cost her everything?

The Runaway Bride by Jody Hedlund
THE BRIDE SHIPS #2
jodyhedlund.com

Determined to keep his family together, Quinten travels to Canada to find his siblings and track down his employer's niece, who ran off with a Canadian soldier. When Quinten rescues her from a bad situation, Julia is compelled to repay him by helping him find his sister—but soon after, she receives devastating news that changes everything.

The Brightest of Dreams by Susan Anne Mason
CANADIAN CROSSINGS #3
susanannemason.net